LOST STATION CIRCÉ

LOST STATION CIRCÉ

THE CLUSTER CYCLE

VOLUME TWO

THOMAS WRIGHTSON

DRAGONBRAE

DRAGONBRAE

An Imprint of Roan & Weatherford Publishing Associates, LLC
Bentonville, Arkansas
www.roanweatherford.com

Library of Congress Cataloging-in-Publication Data
Names: Wrightson, Thomas, author.
Title: Lost Station Circé | Cluster Cycle #2
Description: First Edition. | Bentonville: Dragonbrae, 2024.
Identifiers: LCCN: 2024942364 ISBN: 978-1-63373-966-6 (hardcover) |
ISBN: 978-1-63373-967-3 (trade paperback) | ISBN: 978-1-63373-968-0 (eBook)
Subjects: | BISAC: FICTION/Science Fiction/Space Opera |
FICTION/Science Fiction/Action & Adventure
LC record available at: https://lccn.loc.gov/2024942364

Dragonbrae trade paperback edition January, 2025

Cover & Interior Design by Casey W. Cowan
Editing by George "Clay" Mitchell & Don Money

To the spirit of Ursula K. Le Guin

AUTHOR'S NOTE

WHEN THE NOVEL that became *Starborn Vendetta* was accepted for publication in 2019, I was faced with an unsettling challenge. To create a series set in this universe. Rather than continue the story of Mercedes Solari, or any surviving characters touched by her legacy, I decided on a different approach. Tell a more thematic story, a chronology of a society spanning generations.

Following with the theme of old stories retold in sci-fi settings with modern twists, I drew on two classics. Robert Stevenson's *Treasure Island* and Homer's *Odyssey* provided the backbone for a story of self-discovery and restitution set against a quest for riches and fame that turns sour.

Some may read this book and find the ensemble cast odd, unsympathetic, or jarring. That was the point. As Mercedes Solari wasn't a 'heroine', so this story has no true heroes or villains. Only protagonists, antagonists, and points of view. This is a universe with very little in the way of black and white morality. But there is something to be found here in many characters that is more important than ever in the world today; the ability to grow.

ACKNOWLEDGMENTS

TO MY FAMILY, who continue to support me. To the fellow authors and friends who have given me advice, support, and feedback over the years. To my dev editor who highlighted a theme in this book I hadn't even noticed during the writing of it. And again to my inspiring muse, who really needs a day off.

LOST STATION
CIRCÉ

FILE 1

THE JUNK IN THE JUNK

*My poor unhappy man, whither are you going
over this mountain top, alone and without knowing the way?*

—Homer

THE DRIVE CORE for the *Benbow* had been misfiring for the best part of
three days before its spectacular, yet safe, failure. As he slowly clambered up
the starboard coupling to check a few of the feed lines, Faarax felt the support
line cutting into his chest. Taking a hand off the rungs of the maintenance
ladder, he adjusted the support harness and returned to his climb. The hiss
of static through his small earpiece heralded his Ekri partner Sudu. Sudu, the
green-skinned lovable bastard, was speaking from his safe perch on a maintenance catwalk thirty feet below.

"*Hoy, Faarax, what's happening? You stopped. See something?*"

"No, I didn't. Bloody line trying to stifle me."

"*Oh. Well, hurry up. Captain's waiting for a report.*" That informal speech,
so unlike other Ekri even today. "*We've been out of warp for twelve minutes, and
that's twelve minutes too long for him.*"

"All right, keep your scales on."

Faarax increased his speed, almost jumping from rung to rung, his joints
and muscles starting to scream from the effort. Memories pushed through his
tired mind. The demands of Captain Solet for increased anything and everything on this ramshackle piece of junk he called a ship. That one time his harness belt snapped in a key place and wrapped round his neck as he struggled
to hold onto a rusted piece of the drive core shielding, almost throttling him
until Sudu came to the rescue.

It had long ceased to annoy or sting him that he was always chosen for these kinds of repairs. Whether it was crawling through ducts to check on bypass circuitry, descending into the waste processing plant when something went wrong and the canteen food tasted like real waste instead of a good imitation, or warm engine problems like now, it was the same. Captain Solet would make a face like a wrinkled fruit and say, "Send Faarax." No more or less qualified than anyone else on the ship, but he was a human raised from childhood, the lowest in their social structure. All the dirty or dangerous jobs were his to do.

"They send me here, they send me there, they send me every-bloody-where."

Faarax smiled at the unintentional rhythm of his words. He wasn't a natural poet, or singer, or anything like that. He hadn't been given the chance. All his more erudite leanings he had at second or third hand, from passing traders and employers, or the tongue-in-cheek wording of a contract. His adopted mother also spoke to him sometimes in an old-fashioned way, using strange paraphrases and quotations. She'd often said he would know about such things someday, but would he? Did it even matter?

He finally reached the place where the emergency warning beacon had triggered, and saw the problem. A fused secondary plasma conductor. These old Black Engine models were all the same. If even the tiniest auxiliary line failed, the whole engine would shut down. It wasn't fun to drop out of warp with barely ten seconds warning, with momentum taking hold and the gravity field struggling to catch up. He had been coming out of a shower when the ship slowed and he was thrown into the opposite wall.

He spoke into his earpiece. "I'm here, Sudu. I've found the trouble. Switch on the lighting matrix for D-12 coupling section, Starboard Side."

He slipped on his shaded goggles just in time, as the whole area was flooded with a harsh white light. Securing his harness to the surrounding rigging, he searched his satchel and got out the tools he needed. For a simple plasma conductor repair this close to port, all that was needed was a reroute using some of the surrounding spares. It wouldn't stand a sustained trip, but a short warp hop to Cape Cisternaea wouldn't strain it too much.

It took the best part of half an hour to isolate and decouple the ruined conductor. Whatever the nature of its failure, it'd been spectacular, fusing the nearest brackets and power cut-offs. He needed to shuffle along, repositioning his anchor points, and cut off the power at earlier sections either way. Solet would be annoyed at the delay, but he'd just have to lump it. But for all the grumbling, it was curious what might've caused the failure.

"Probably some kind of energy build up." It was a mere mutter as he activated the final cut-off and positioned himself one last time. "Or a knot developing. Or perhaps a few of the plasma streams fused when critical. If they did…." He glanced at the large warp drive. "Good thing it didn't blow itself up."

With the section powered down, he opened the six auxiliary hatchways on either side of the fused coupling and drew out the secondary wires. The warmth of the pulsing plasma wiring hummed through his gloves, and as he connected them was careful about any feedback. Plasma feedback wasn't like the old records of electric shocks on Ancient Earth. One bit of plasma on his wrist would take his hand off and leave him screaming in agony for a week from the poisonous aftershocks.

The secondary conductors were all in place, and after flicking the stand-by switches for each, he reconnected that section. The auxiliary conductors glowed, and the section's electronics hummed and purred in satisfaction. All was well, for the moment. He signaled down to Sudu.

"All fixed. Conductor burned out. We'll need to fix it at Cape Cisternaea."

"Okay, I'll note that."

"Also make sure it's a full half-length. The damage spread out a bit."

"Understood. You'd best come down now. Solet's probably panting to get going again and we don't want to be in here when the warp drive activates."

Faarax repelled down in record time. Both Faarax and Sudu knew the old saying about someone caught in a warp field—seen today in the ship, seen tomorrow on seven different planets. A ship's mass and control mechanism kept the warp bubble in check, but a human body could still be torn apart and thrown out in an unknown location by the warp discharge, whether to a point some distance off or into an adjoining room. They were out and behind the twin doors separating the engineering platform from the warp drive a good ten minutes before the warp field started up again and the ship charted its course.

A voice blared out over the intercom. "Faarax to report to the bridge immediately. I repeat, Faarax to report to the bridge."

Faarax sighed and left Sudu to perform the fine adjustments to the warp controls so the auxiliary connectors would hold out until Cape Cisternaea. Leaning against the wall of the old-fashioned lift as it rose and then shuttled along with the grating of old runners and power feeds, he prepped himself for the usual mixture of thanks and criticism which was Solet's standard greeting.

Stepping onto the bridge, he noted for the thousandth time the worn metalwork, the gungy console interfaces, the pretentious captain's chair in which Solet sat with an upright posture directly mirroring his twisted morals. It looked like a perverted Ancient Earth fantasy. Not surprising, it was built by humans, bought by the captain for a song when it was about to be scrapped as a "useless and outmoded relic," and continually refitted and held together since then.

Solet twisted round, glaring at the human. "Well?"

"The connector burned out. It took the adjoining sections with it. I've rerouted, but we'll need to replace it as soon as we get to Cape Cisternaea."

"At least we have warp now." Solet turned back to his controls. "And we can make it. We'll be arriving in less than fifteen minutes."

"Are you all right?"

A deep-toned female voice came from across the bridge. Faarax turned. A Feles, perhaps twenty years older than himself, tall and graceful with locks of her short mane worked into a dozen dreadlocks. This was his adopted mother.

"I'm fine. I didn't get burned or anything."

"I keep telling the captain we need an official repair officer."

Solet grimaced, his voice irritated. "They don't come cheap. An operation like ours doesn't have much slack for luxuries."

"If you consider essential safety a luxury, I suppose so."

"Officer Lenore, if you don't like it, you and your precious son can get off at Cape Cisternaea and find somewhere else."

Lenore did not respond to this. Faarax and she shared the same thought. She knew that Solet was the only captain who had been willing to take them in after....

Faarax flexed his shoulders, feeling the slightest rip along the seam of his shirt. It was getting too small for his muscular frame. Better find something in the second-hand markets when they docked. Assuming he had the money. Welfare there may have been in the Capitol sector, but here in the Outer sector it was less than useless. Without cash, you either indentured yourself, got a job, or starved. Solet caught his eye and snorted.

"Don't worry. You'll all get your shore pay. But don't think it'll be any extra just because you did a little rerouting."

I'd like to see you rerouting a plasma connector on short notice, was Faarax's thought as he suppressed a glare.

"ATTENTION, ATTENTION." THE ship's Kavki navigator Alkmeney spoke with a mock computer vibration in her voice. *"We are approaching Cape Cisternaea space. All personnel prepare for exit from warp field. Transmitting docking clearance codes."*

Lenore smiled at this little detail even as she watched her "son" leave the bridge. The codes they had were worthless if anyone bothered to look at them. But no one did out here. The junks and tramp ships carrying goodness knew what were allowed to pass on their way. It was the unspoken truth. They kept the Outer Worlds' economies from collapsing under the financial weight of the Capitol Worlds. Even the Synod recognized it, so they kept their eyes shut.

The ancient frame of the *Benbow* shuddered as it dropped out of warp just shy of the buffer zone, passing through the checkpoint unopposed. They heard the slight proximity beep as another ship of Kavki design swooped past them. Solet growled, and Lenore imagined the thoughts drifting through his mind. Damn Kavki, always hogging the space ways. Damn their bloody tech. If there weren't Kavki present, he would have given verbal vent to those feelings, with a few more expletives.

Their captain often neglected to remember that the ship technology which allowed the Cluster's current connection and speed of travel was based on human designs. It had then been refined by Feles and Ekri engineers, and only then adopted by the Kavki over their self-made, but sluggish, hypersleep-reliant subluminal drives. In essence, his people had in part allowed the Kavki commander he cursed their bullish attitude.

Lenore grinned at Solet's anger. She liked seeing him angry. She had little liking for him, though she respected his leadership as a captain. The others felt similar, though they were more in awe of him. He had taken them in when most ship captains would discard them at best and kill them at worst. Lenore had seen a ship execution once, and shuddered slightly at the memory. The prisoner, bound and gagged, thrown into an open plasma conduit. Quick, but horribly painful for the half-second they retained full consciousness. Alkmeney swiveled in her seat.

"Got any plans?"

She was looking at Lenore with narrowed eyes and a jovial smile. The Feles shrugged.

"Not really. Find somewhere to get some food that hasn't been preserved in our freezers or processed into packages. Then find somewhere to sleep that isn't my bunk."

"How low are your ambitious."

"We poor Feles are limited in that regard."

The Kavki laughed. The two often had little sessions of banter like this. It meant nothing. They were just playing on ancient species stereotypes, joking with an old enmity that reached back to the Xeno Conflict. They still had a trace of that, an old instinctual dislike for the other's species, but any conscious animosity was swept aside. All that remained was the dream of all on this ship. The dream of finding something better.

Lenore turned to the captain. "Permission to leave with Faarax and prepare for docking?"

"Permission granted," was the sullen reply.

Lenore left the bridge in pursuit of her child as Sudu entered, looking flushed but satisfied. It took little time for the pair to meet up again, as Faarax had not gotten far. As they traveled in their lift to the docking control area, Lenore looked at her adopted child. He was hissing a little in pain, but kept it under control.

"You okay?"

"Sort of. I don't like clambering on that warp drive. But then I don't like a lot of things I've gotta do on this ship. No need to fuss, it's not like I was hurt."

"It won't be forever. And you did get yourself burned."

"Where?"

Lenore gently pulled off one of Faarax's gloves. The skin under it was red, almost raw from the heat of the conductors. He winced as she gently tapped the palm.

"Some salve and bandages for these."

"Hadn't noticed. I can do it."

"Nonsense. Both your hands are burned, I can tell. You're being foolish, not brave. What will you use to apply it, your teeth?"

Faarax argued no further. Rather than go straight to the control area, the two went to the ship's sick bay. Hardly the most lavish example of its type, nor did it have a dedicated doctor ministering to its patients. It was all rough and ready, served and administered by the self or a willing companion. Seated on the small room's single sick bed, Faarax allowed his hand to be treated and bandaged. Lenore performed this action with all the gentle maternity any mother might give her son.

She looked hard into the boy's eyes. Was that a slight softening? Or frustration? Would their bargain have to be delayed? Might as well ask and get it over with.

"Does this mean the bargain's off for now?"

Faarax nodded, his mouth sullen. "Yeah. Can't kill you with duff hands."

"No, you can't. But these should heal in a week or two."

"Thanks. For the assist."

"Whatever our agreements, you're still my son in all but blood. And any mother looks after her son."

The two stared at each other, the unspoken agreement reaching across any boundaries of either family or species. It was a deep, unspoken connection. An agreement most would see as unsettling or unnatural. One the others either knew nothing of, or pretended not to see. She had brought him aboard, a frightened and sullen child, nearly fifteen years ago. Solet had appreciated the addition of some young blood, and a competent Feles combat expert. The pair had carved their niche among the ragtag crew. But always the agreement, the tacit understanding.

"When the day comes, I'll kill you." Faarax had said.

"And when that day comes, I'll let you try, but you may fail." Lenore had said.

Neither had wavered, understanding that time was the key to this duel. And if any injury came about, the agreement was suspended. It wasn't fair attacking the other when they were below their best.

Lenore finished dressing the burns and watched as Faarax pulled his gloves back on. "Now we'd best get down to the docking controls. Or Solet"—she paused and smiled as she parroted the human expression—"will have our guts for garters."

IGNORANT OF THIS prolonged exchange, Sudu gave a quick glance toward Lenore as she left the bridge, noting only her slightly mischievous expression. He liked her, and he liked Faarax, and was pleased they could get a little time together before reaching port. As he resumed his place by the engine monitor, the tech officer glanced after the vanished Feles and smiled.

"A fine couple."

Sudu glanced up as he double-checked the engine readings. "They are mother and son. In all but blood and species."

"That would not alone make a fine couple. There's something else that makes two people work together so well. In spite of everything."

"They think we don't know?"

"Faarax probably doesn't. Lenore might, though. It's unwise to pry into such matters."

"True enough. But in their case…. By the way, Livesey, you've still got your service. You skipped it last week."

Livesey shuffled uncomfortably, fiddling with the small diagnostic port cover in her arm. Sudu grinned, but just suppressed a chuckle. She clearly disliked being reminded that she was an android, an artificial construct, however many rights they may have as sentient beings.

"It's embarrassing having you look inside me like that. It's like a female stripping naked or something."

"And I am the equivalent of your medical officer, so you shouldn't feel embarrassed. Remember the old joke? If it makes you uncomfortable, I will strip off, too."

"Oh, don't be silly."

"Then don't be squeamish. We do it on Cape Cisternaea, got it? Your data pathways are long overdue for a good cleaning."

"Very well."

Livesey had resigned herself to fate. Now Sudu could get back to making sure their ship didn't crash into the space habitat. After all, if he was going to become an engine designer in the future, it would be a poor mark on his in-the-making for him to start crashing ships during simple docking procedures.

THE DOCKING CENTER'S automated transmission pinged through the comm. *"Codes processing. Transmission accepted."*

"Thanks." Alkmeney stretched her arms and yawned. "Well, that's sorted."

Her eyes strayed slowly to the viewing screen, the near-eidetic coils of her brain taking in the vista. A large space habitat, growing out from its original circular core to appear like a plasma globe frozen in time. Struts and additional habitats reached out willy-nilly from the central core, showing its transformation from neat structure to crazy sprawling mixture of markets and hubs for all manner of Outer World goods.

"Home true to Solet, whatever he might say in public." Alkmeney, for the moment alone on the bridge, let her voice echo round the rough-and-ready space. "Any ship with ambitions to sell good cargo comes here, picking up the New System produce at bargain prices and selling to the Capitol Worlds at a premium. At least, that is the plan." Alkmeney smiled to herself. "A merchant for all. That is what I shall become. Looking at this place, how can anyone not see beauty in it?"

She stared lovingly at the scene beyond the ship. Cape Cisternaea had been built just two centuries before as the key transport hub for the New System, a collection of five planets orbiting the triple star system Megara-Lux in the Outer Worlds. There was just one rocky planet, lying close to the sun, and the rest of the colonized worlds were moons circling the great gas giants, fit only for bases. It was truly a wild frontier, even by the standards of the Outer Worlds.

"And here we are, making our living. Laying our groundwork."

"Say something?"

Alkmeney spun round as Solet's Feles second-in-command Syndac entered without warning. "Just talking to myself. The right of any sentient being, is it not?"

"If you say so." Her lip curled slightly, and she continued in that formal, clipped tone of hers. "And something I accept, regardless of opinion. After all, we would not wish poor feelings to spread among our crew after so many years together."

The *Benbow* was pulling into Docking Sector 8 with a noise like grinding teeth, putting pay to further talk. Just as well, really. Solet might be brusque, but Syndac was positively harsh when the mood took her.

The docking clamps engaged imperfectly against its uneven exterior, and the docking controls almost refused entry when the doors almost opened prematurely as the walkway extended to meet Cape Cisternaea. There were a few raised eyebrows, but enough people there knew about the *Benbow* and its typical state of repair to override the alarm and manually ensure it docked correctly. And for the umpteenth time, several wondered why her captain refused to scrap it. Black Engine models were like discarded hen's teeth, and just as decayed.

With the ship docked, it was time for the crew to disembark. And, as Alkmeney often remarked to herself, they were a ragged assortment even by Cape Cisternaea's relaxed standards.

Black-class junks like the *Benbow* were mostly automated, so it only took a crew of around seven to run it. But what a set they were. At the front, Solet the Feles captain with artificial arms and a foul temper, immediately followed by Syndac whose attitude singled her out as second-in-command. Just behind them Alkmeney herself, then that human-form android Livesey, both looking positively smart and maybe a little superior. Behind them Sudu, an Ekri with grease-stained clothing and a patch over one eye, his voice jovial and casual. At the back Lenore, a Feles female with a strange hairstyle and battle-toned body. By her side Faarax, a human in his late teens with very casual clothes and a face prematurely aged by work and hardship.

This was the ragtag assortment who piloted the *Benbow*, a mercenary junk which—for the right price—did everything from legitimate trade and smuggling to combat duty for the famous and notorious. The respectable folk knew enough to avoid the crew of the *Benbow*, and most others knew enough that they called them if they wanted a job done quick and dirty. The sense that these were "desirable pariahs" was so strong that people even debated and bet on which bars and hostels would remain open for them and which would close or say they were full.

"And I am one of them." Alkmeney shook her head. "For better, or worse."

———————

NOW AWAY FROM the *Benbow,* Solet turned and spoke to his crew with a dour jollity. "You're all on shore leave. You'll have received your shore pay. If you haven't, it's been delayed. You know how bad the signal is round here. Go off, enjoy yourselves. I've got a client to see."

Solet left with a clear and audible grumble. Always mumbled when he had to haggle with a client. After watching his captain leave, Faarax stretched and yawned.

"I think I'll find something like a bed. Think they've got them here?"

"They had before." Sudu gave his usual grin. "I'll join you."

Livesey glanced at Sudu. "Didn't you want to give me a service? Might as well get it over with within reach of a proper repair station. Who knows, you might pick up a few more engineering tips from my circuits."

"Oh, all right."

"In that case,"—Alkmeney gave a smile—"I'll go with you."

"Fine." Faarax was clearly unenthusiastic at either offer. "What about you, Lenore? Syndac?"

Lenore smiled, more than willing to keep her adopted son from Alkmeney's often tedious company. Syndac sniffed audibly.

"I have other matters to attend to. You enjoy yourselves."

She left without much ceremony. Faarax thumbed his nose at the retreating back of the second-in-command. Lenore didn't bother to reprove him, it wasn't worth it for someone like Syndac. Besides, she had never been that bothered with Faarax. Alkmeney seemed more concerned and placed a hand on Faarax's shoulder.

"Now, now. Enough of that. How's about we find a nice place to rest and perhaps even drink our sorrows away."

"I...." Faarax hesitated. "Now that I remember, I've got...."

Lenore saw the look in his eye. "You'd like to go see your sweetheart?"

"Yes."

"Then go. I'll keep Alkmeney company. You go find your bed."

Faarax nodded his thanks and left. Alkmeney was about to follow him, but Lenore drew her to one side. He could just hear her speak of an amazing place she knew where they could get the best drinks possible. Alkmeney looked visibly upset that Faarax had slipped away. Too fond of her own company in his view, or so he assumed. But after a few excellent drinks under Lenore's guidance, she would forget any injury on her part. Probably go into a diatribe on trading practices.

Now alone, and liberated from any kind of chaperon, Faarax slouched into one of the transport pods leading to the Upper Branch, where the cheap residential blocks were located. Cooler than the rest of Cape Cisternaea, and the services were less reliable, but still better than most of the colony worlds in the region. In the transport pod, leaning next to the button panel, fiddling with his gloves, he watched the interior flash past through the transparent walls of the transport tube.

There was a small market area, with dozens of people looking at stalls with yelled prices and bargains or consulting small terminals for remote orders. Next he saw a large shaft where tiny ships were crossing and recrossing around vehicle and pedestrian pathways. It was almost like the remnants of roots pushing through the hole created by a stake driven into the metalwork. As the pod slowly sailed past another area, it halted and a small crush of people entered. They appeared to be long-standing residents, and one among them was louder than the rest.

Faarax didn't look for too long, but just long enough. He was tall, almost as tall as the average Kavki, and bore physical and mental signs of drunkenness. Dark-skinned like almost all humans these days, he wore a strange coat of leather trimmed with chains which jangled around his loose trousers, and his ugly face was made even uglier by an archaic eyepatch covering his right eye, which itself was surrounded by what seemed like old burn scars. To top it all, his right hand only had two fingers which curled like rusted hinges.

What could've caused those injuries? It was something of a puzzle. Maybe some kind of explosion. But modern tech could repair such lesions, surely. Unless he was too poor to afford it out here, or lacked proper medical coverage, or was a wanted criminal who dared not seek proper help. So many possibilities when you really got down to it. Either way, the incident had left its mark. And here he was, nattering to the group. He appeared to be concluding some kind of tall tale as they listened with a kind of indulgence.

"And so I told him, don't do it, I said. There's worse to come, I said. But he would go and do it. He took that grenade, and launched himself across the gap, throwing it from mid-air into the ship as its cargo bay closed. The ship was crippled, and my guy gave a final thumbs-up before falling down the crevasse to his death. Now that's what I call going out with a bang!"

Everyone was laughing at his rambling narrative. Faarax suppressed a grimace, struggling to discern whether the laughter was with the loud stranger, or directed at him. The scene was familiar to him. Heard, repeated, and embellished by a dozen mouths across twenty different space ports over the years. The last battle of the Space Rogue Insurgence fifty years ago, when an anonymous soldier had crippled the control ship. Everyone had wanted to claim that victory as their own, though none provided any proof.

The party left, but the strange man remained. Faarax grew progressively less comfortable, and finally his worst fear was realized. The gnarled old man turned his one good eye to stare at him. It was a long, ugly stare. Finally he shuffled over and leaned over him, his mangled hand resting on the edge of the transparent side. Faarax dared not look directly at him, but stayed calm and defiant. The good eye was asking an undefined question, a question that demanded a response. Faarax decided to challenge.

"Well? What is it?"

The man leaned a little closer. "You look a honest lad. Honest face, honest eyes, honest cheek. Nice and honest. Very honest indeed."

Danger smothered everything, its miasmic tang almost blocking all senses. He had heard enough stories about young people taken advantage of by people like this former.... Former what? Soldier, mercenary, spacer, maybe even pirate. He could smell his breath, rank from an unknown oral infection. No amount of mints could cut that smell. Faarax discretely slid a hand down toward the pad. If this bum tried anything, that hand could hit the emergency stop and summon help. The old man leaned in so close that his yellowed teeth and the inflamed veins in his eyes were freakishly in focus.

"You look a stable boy. Very stable. Yes." Did the man just lick his lips or was Faarax imagining the perverse motions on the ugly creature's face? "Mind if I tell you a story?"

What to say? "Go to hell, you pervert?" "No, I'm not interested?" No words would come. His hand now rested on the stop button, and in his peripheral was the station schedule display. He could press the stop, jump out at the next station, make his escape. The man spoke with a slow and clipped tone, none of his words slurred or needlessly delivered and repeated. It was unsettling after his earlier repetitive rambling, and became steadily creepier as it went on.

"You know of the old planet New Dubai? No, of course not. Bit of a backwater now, barely seen on most major shipping lane charts. But back in the day it was the toast of the Capitol Worlds. Society turned to it, it set trends in everything from food to fashion, and they had White Oil. Oh, *so* much glorious White Oil."

What the hell was this yarn about? Everyone and their embryonic brat knew about White Oil. Old ships like the *Benbow* still used it as a "vintage fuel." The stuff used to power the current Scarlet Engine tech was even called Neo White Oil, though it was drawn from no world. Manufactured in processing plants planted on barren moons, its development spelled the end for many planets that had made their fortunes from the White Oil trade. Where would this guy go next? And would he just shift his hand a little farther away? It was uncomfortably close to his thigh.

"There was a dynasty on that world, a dynasty that accrued such wealth as the Synod was envious of. One of their rulers was incredibly famous. They didn't know it until years later, but she had managed to fight her way back from exile and destroyed all those who opposed or threatened her. Her line had been absent, but she established it again and made the planet even more prosperous, building on the ruin of her usurper. But when she was in her nineties, she ceded her place to her son and left the planet. Not until years later was it found that she'd taken the equivalent of ten years gross net from the planet's treasury and vanished with it into thin air. Thirty milliards worth, in physical currency, precious metals, nothing that easily depreciates. Imagine what all that's worth now?"

While being stuck against the pod wall with a hand over the emergency stop wasn't the best place to think, that single sum brought his mind into focus. Thirty milliards. Or thirty billion in some parlance. That much in digital currency would remain stagnant or even decrease in value. But physical worth, precious metals and other materials, would increase exponentially in value. Today, with some of the key material worlds giving out from centuries of mining, such a hoard would now be twenty or fifty times its initial worth. The thought made him giddy, but the man started speaking again and brought him back to his senses. Now that wandering hand really was pressed against his thigh, over one of his pockets.

"That was nearly five centuries past. There's been plenty of talk about it in certain circles, talk about finding it. Who knows how much of that treasure is just waiting to be found, waiting to make someone the richest person imaginable. Just think of it."

Faarax didn't answer. Any answer would've been a swear word, or a physical blow to send this creature away. Without warning, the man moved so violently that the strange wire necklace he wore danced in front of his face. He leaned over to almost press nose to nose against Faarax's face. Rank breath filled their tiny world.

"Don't believe me, eh? Think Old Beddow's just spinning one of his yarns again. Well, I'll tell you now...." His voice stuttered, as if a thought or some sight beyond the pod had arrested his words. "Damn. Well, maybe I'll be seeing you again sometime."

The man pulled away with impressive speed, and as the pod stopped at one of the main hubs, he stepped out with an unexpectedly nimble movement. Faarax's shaking hand still hovered over the emergency stop, and a bead of sweat trickle down across his temple. The smell of the man's stinking breath faded away, but its tang remained in the back of his own mouth. Had the strange man seen that sweat? Had he wanted to press home an advantage before he reached this stop?

"Guy was crazy." Faarax spoke to the nothing that accompanied him to his stop. "Just crazy. Some guy with a few screws loose who didn't know who he was talking to. I'm almost there. Almost. What's the time?" He glanced at his watch. "Yeah, almost there. I hope they're waiting for me."

The pod stopped and he stepped out at the extreme end of the Upper Branch. Down a long roadway, near its extreme tip, was a small rickety terrace of buildings that seemed to be partly built from scrap produced when the energy transfer lines were installed. Its one positive feature was a great window looking out into the harsh void of space, its unwinking stars turning slowly as Cape Cisternaea spun in its orbit about Megara-Lux.

Reaching the building at the far end of the terrace, he pressed one of the small buzzers. An answering buzz came, and the door unlocked. He took the stairs two at a time, his casually-shod feet making little noise even on the metal surface of the stairs. He reached the door, that door he had found when he was just seventeen, when he had been so very young and naive. The door flew open at his first knock, and the figure in that doorway spoke with a soft rippling voice.

"Come on in. I didn't expect you so soon."

And with a hand on his collar, and a smile on the face receiving him, he was gently pulled into that strange apartment. As the door closed, a tiny red light showed at the top right hand corner of the frame. The person who resided there was unavoidably detained. No clients were to come up until the light turned green. This was their personal time, alone and as themselves in this spinning metal world.

FILE 2

WRUNG HEARTS, WRONGED MINDS

*The next ten or twelve pages were filled
with a curious series of entries.*

—Robert Louis Stevenson

SOLET WAS THINKING. He was thinking he wanted to take this annoying person in front of him and stuff him up the nearest and narrowest ventilation duct without prior greasing. He was sitting in a quiet little office, done in the style of Ancient Earth, as his very human employer did the calculations for their pay. The cargo had arrived in good order, although due to the warp drive malfunction they had arrived perhaps half a day late. That would come out of their pay.

It always did, was Solet's internal grumble as his client, a repulsive human called Sygint, adjusted the sums with a barely disguised glee at the saving. He'd been warned about that eagerness to save by their mutual contact.

"Deducting five hundred for the delay...." A quick glance from Sygint, perhaps to try and detect any weakness. "Here. 2,500."

"Thanks."

Poker-faced, Solet accepted the transfer to the ship account, and watched as Sygint made the slightest wince as the not-inconsiderable sum floated from one account to another. Not as much as the original fee, but still a tidy sum out here. Sygint then looked directly into the captain's eyes.

"Guess you can do stuff after all. Didn't expect it from what I'd heard about your crew. Quite an eclectic bunch."

"I hire the best, not the prettiest."

"The best? How is that ramshackle bunch the best?"

Solet never backed down from a challenge. "Syndac's one of the best seconds I've ever had in my life, no matter how irritating she gets. She can keep the ship going and find us crew from anywhere. Alkmeney can find a planet between a black hole and a pulsar, get you the approach and escape route before most other people could get the first few digits in place, and, if needed, find some of the best merchants to sell to." The slight discomfort on Sygint's face was worth pausing for. "Sudu's a first-rate engineer, and I wouldn't trust anyone else with our systems after what he's managed to do with them. Livesey's also not bad. She can work in places we can't without turning a hair and she's a first-rate medic when we need it. Lenore's more than capable at fighting, and she's helped us out of a few scraps in our time together."

"And the human boy?"

Solet grimaced. "He can do descent repairs, but he's there on sufferance. Lenore's son."

"A Feles with a human child? Rather unusual out here."

"These things happen. Now, unless you've got some other business to transact, I've got another appointment."

"No. Nothing further."

There was no further exchange. Solet left with perhaps too brisk a step. He was fed up. He hated dealing with the likes of Sygint every day. He hated being the captain of a run-down little junk without pedigree or respect. He hated the newfangled cruisers and cargo ships, with their fancy new engines free from natural White Oil dependency. He even hated their captains who allowed the revolution to happen, and the contractors and passengers who took advantage of this more economical and efficient service.

As he pushed into the small transport pod to reach his chosen hostel, he again cursed Sygint's eyes. Those eyes that had been keeping their gaze on the timer, and the mind behind it deducting from the fee, possibly with the passing of each minute. Had he waited for the exact second to deduct? Perhaps. All that mattered was the hundred or so that would survive the repairs to the *Benbow*. That hundred would need to see them through the next few deliveries. Each time they were late, it meant a larger piece cut from the fee. Another notch down in their reputation.

The transport pod had dropped him off in the less affluent residential area. Stepping out, and stepping over a large pool of something that smelled vaguely of sick, he made his way toward the room he'd booked for both himself and several crew members. They didn't have the funds for separate rooms, even in a dump like this. He reached their apartment and passed inside. An old-fashioned mechanical head bobbed just inside the doorway.

"Thank you… for chchchchchooooosing… URK… errrrroooorrrrr…."

The mechanical voice faltered and whirred into a confusion of nonsense as it tried to greet the new customer. Solet restrained the urge to swear. How he could still stand for his crew being in conditions like this? If he could, he would take them into the main space lanes where there was good cargo run at premium prices. But no one took ships like his, no one consorted with his ilk. He was worse than a pariah, worse than the plague. He was old. The ship was old. His crew was a hodgepodge and also generally old.

The rooms were as poky as expected from their funds. Four beds, and that was it. Livesey could just go into sleep mode standing against one of the walls, and Faarax had made other sleeping arrangements. The other beds would accommodate Syndac, Lenore, Sudu and Alkmeney. And what of him? He looked round, unslung the pack on his back and brought out the small inflatable bed he carried for situations like this. It just fitted between the beds. Someone would probably step on him in the night, but he didn't care.

Driving it up until its head sat just beneath the window, he gently laid down on it. It felt uncomfortable, but it was better than sleeping on the floor. He shuffled, trying to make the bed as comfortable as possible before his bedtime. He had slept on more unpleasant surfaces. Like the cell floor he occupied during his twelve months aboard what were charitably called "forced labor ships." Moving from rock to rock, extracting the minerals held there, using a force made up of the bad and the unlucky. He'd endured that hell, and survived to get his own ship again.

"Feeling tired already?"

Solet glanced up. Syndac was standing on the doorway, looking round her with clear disdain. He rose slowly.

"Just getting myself comfortable before bed. How was your day?"

"Fine." She didn't elaborate. "How was the pay?"

"We've got enough for the repairs. And a hundred spare."

"That is not much. I expected more."

"We were late. And didn't Sygint relish it, the stuffed-up fuck."

The statement was blunt, and told all it needed to. Syndac nodded slowly, then turned toward the door again after placing her bag on the bed nearest to her. It was also the best bed in the room. She continued in an offhand tone.

"I will be going out again soon. I need some fresh air."

She left before Solet could make any comments on the "freshness" of air in a space habitat this old and decrepit. Alone once again, Solet returned to his somber musings. After some minutes of moribund cycling, he bared his teeth and punched the bare metal floor, feeling his skin and bones scream from the abuse.

"My God." He hissed, "How I want out of this bloody life!"

LENORE WAS THINKING. Thinking deep through her past, thought how nice it would be to dump her boring companion and find a suitable corner in some nightclub. To listen to its pulsing music and enjoy somber solitude amid flailing arms, gyrating hips and the touching of lips. Instead, here she was with Alkmeney, keeping the Kavki company as she sipped at her own drink. In turn, she wondered if Alkmeney would rather be somewhere else. Perhaps looking after Faarax, or searching around the markets to see what was in or out of fashion in this sector at the moment. For all her own maternal leanings, she knew that outside her ambitions, Alkmeney considered the little human to be the child she never had.

"I wonder what we'll be shipping next." She glanced over her shoulder at an Ekri gyrating by the door at his companion. "Maybe some kind of soporific. The people here look like they could do with a dose of horlicks."

"Maybe so." Lenore laughed gently through her words. "If it still existed. That thing went with Ancient Earth, or so humans tell us."

"I firmly believe the loss of Ancient Earth is a fallacy." Alkmeney waved her hand around illustratively and perhaps a little drunkenly. "They dream it up to justify them being here."

"Don't say you're one of those cranks who think we should 'all go back to where we came from?'"

"Not exactly. I just dislike the idea of going beyond ourselves. Remember that expedition a few centuries back? Vanished into the Azure Sector, never came back, only getting a constant signal of 'do not come looking for us' when the mission handlers scanned the area."

"There's good reason for that. We know that now, from the follow-up report. Didn't you see it? All over the news a few months ago."

"Yes, I saw it. But then it was not a strange tragedy. The whole thing was very mundane, and only became greater when more of the facts and distorted memories were revealed to us in that report. Would it have made the front page if it were as plain as 'equipment malfunction?' This whole thing about 'Ancient Earth' stinks of that same myth making. It is just plain silly."

"I wonder what Faarax would say if he heard you talking like this."

"Oh, Faarax would scarcely mind. I find him barely human at all. He was hardly raised among them, barely been among them since his babyhood. Probably good for him, though he does not admit it."

Lenore threw a stern look at the Kavki. "I think that's the drink talking. How many have you had?"

"Only two."

"Two's more than enough for your head. Off with you. Remember the way to our lodgings?"

"Yes. I have it on here." She waved her wrist illustratively and caused the small comm unit attached there to flash in the electric lights. "Sure you care not to come?"

"Quite sure. Off with you, and go straight there mind you."

"I will. Night."

"Night," such an odd term on a space station that barely registered night or day as terrestrial settlements could. Alkmeney left, not wobbling nearly as much as her speech might have implied. As the Kavki departed with cool determination, Lenore sighed with relief and returned to her own drink.

At last left alone, Lenore was able to enjoy her drink in peace. She always sipped slowly when in solitude, savoring the taste. So few and little were these pleasures that she wished to spin them out for as long as possible. Her life was hard work, making one day merge into the next between brief snatches of sleep. Whether it had been raising a child amid changing ships and crews, working off a debt to a captain when she ran out of travel funds, or finding work with another crew member aboard a decrepit ship called the *Benbow*.

Glancing up, half her vision was filled by the extra-long lock of hair which hung down the right side of her face. It was dyed a deep scarlet, the color of clotted blood. Reaching up and twisting it, she recalled her clan's adage. "We live for the hunt, for the kill, for the blood, for the night's rejoicing." The permanently-dyed lock was a sign of their mantra, their calling to arms and to battle. It was more than a symbol, it was their life and their death. They would always be bound to the red stain of that symbolic blood.

Memory drifted back seventeen years with the fondling of that lock. Seventeen years ago, when she and the small band of her clan had been traveling across a world made half-barren due to a terraforming accident. They had been hunting a group of colonists for no other reason than sport. They made those humans run, made them cry and flee in terror, made them hide and dash from cover to cover. She vaguely remembered an old human story, and a line within it from an old cobra to a young human. Run around and make sport, boy. Run around, and make sport.

"They did run around. We had our sport."

There had been a ship, crashed there for repairs. A civilian ship attacked by pirates. It had few guns, and fewer small arms. She had felt a twinge of regret, but still followed her band down toward it. One more hunt before leaving on their ship, one more hunt and one more set of trophies. One more lock of hair or length of skin to add to their belts of honor. Scowl and grimace as the other Feles might, they were the tribe of the red lock and would not back down from a hunt.

There had been seven families, and she had participated in the slaughter. One family in particular had put up a good fight. They had more advanced firearms, and managed to hold off the group for twenty minutes. Then she had crept round behind and attacked from over the top of their barricade just inside the hanger. She had fallen upon the man and savaged him, then a quick slash to the desperately firing woman that sliced open her throat. Their fresh blood had bathed her. And in a corner, crouched down in the shadows, their one child.

It was the only child on the entire ship, barely three years old. A tiny thing, unable to stand due to the fear freezing his limbs. That shock of hair, stained with fresh blood. He had wet his pants upon seeing the horrible scene, and as Lenore had stood over him, she had seen in those tear-flooded eyes that he had expected to die. And beneath that fear, a kind of fascinated hatred that few might distinguish from madness.

But there was one thing running stronger in her blood and her clan than the rule of the hunt. The innocent were exempt from harm. Her leader had not thought so. In his warped creed, all were fair game. All were worthy of the hunt. He had come upon her looking down at the boy, had approached with claws unsheathed to tear the young human apart. She had raised an arm to halt him. He had cursed her for a soft thing and lunged, had been pushed back. Without a word, she had used her blade to slash his eyes, then driven the point home into his brain.

"And all while he watched."

What followed still haunted her nightmares. Killing her own was a taboo of her people, but was it not also a taboo to kill the innocent? She had slaughtered them as she had slaughtered her prey. She had stood, covered in the blood of hunted and hunter, and looked again at the little boy. He had been staring at her, and continued doing so even as he wept uncontrollably. When she approached, he had yelled at her to stay back, parroting half-remembered obscenities from his deceased human fellows.

Without a word, Lenore had picked him up and carried him out, feeling his little fists beating on her back. She had made up her mind. This boy was bereft of family, of friends, of anything. She would take him in, raise him as if he were her own biological child. If needed, she would renounce her clan altogether. And if he chose, he could come for her when he was old enough. She could easily fend off any attack from this slip of a thing, but when he was older and well trained....

She had faced the stern looks of her clan elders for the transgressions, but they had seen her actions as partially justified. Ultimately, her fratricidal acts were beyond excuse or pardon. She was banished with her little human child, who had grown silent and sullen. The two had spent their first year hopping from ship to ship, taking short-term jobs, once being confined and working off their passage when the funds ran out. When they finally got their freedom, the two had their private talk. The little boy had spoken first.

"I know what you did."

"I never expect you to forget."

"I wanna hit you."

"But your fists can't hurt me. Perhaps later, they can."

"You don't mind me getting stronger?"

"I expect it of you."

"When the day comes, I'll kill you."

"And when that day comes, I'll let you try, but you may fail."

"I won't!"

"I trust so."

Curiously, it had been that same night when Solet found them, the two struggling to find a place to sleep outside one of the local slums of a run-down space port. He had asked what they were like, as he recognized Lenore's lock of red hair. It provided a strange mirror for his own white-dyed streaks on the other side of his head. He offered them a place aboard his ship, a cut of all proceeds and free room and board. It would be hard, he had said, but it would also be fair. And it had been.

Seventeen years seemed to have flown by, though each day had been a grind. Lenore finished her drink and left for her lodgings as the little voice whispered behind her eyes. Yes, they had dragged near-eternal. As if they struggled against chains binding Faarax and herself to that promised moment. She'd killed his family. Nothing would change that. And when prepared, he would take his attempt at revenge.

"It is the way. And true to my tribe, I won't ignore that. And I hope and pray he won't either."

LIVESEY WAS THINKING. Hardly the easiest thing to do when her secondary motor processors were being looked at and poked with a probe. There she rested against a wall in a small service cubicle, the side panel removed, the pulsing lines of her liquidoptic power lines which fed from her main drive down into her legs exposed. In organic bodies, those would be the veins feeding blood from the heart down to the legs. The flow constricted momentarily as Sudu adjusted an adjoining power link.

"Ai! Watch it."

"Sorry. Did that hurt?"

Livesey smiled. "You know very well I don't feel pain like organics do. At least, not in the traditional sense. It did feel 'uncomfortable.' I think you took it too far."

"I need to test your limiters. That means taking the safeties off. I'll just get that back to normal. There. Feel better?"

"In your terms, yes."

"I'll need to explore… *elsewhere* now."

Livesey's smile broadened. "My main heat system, perhaps? Sure you wouldn't also like to examine my solid state data dump area?"

Sudu laughed at the technical innuendos. "Sorry to disappoint, but I already looked down there using a remote scan. I might want to check out your fluid compression units."

The same tired old string of poorly-chosen and slovenly-executed puns that accompanied every service. She always went through it, and sometimes they turned it into a little contest between them. Which could get the most cringe-worthy response out before the other caved in under the weight of mediocrity and crass double meaning? She was used to it, yet sick of it.

In turn, she longed for such moments. It was strange being someone like her, locked away from the normal passage of time. Her self wasn't this humanoid body of metal, plastic, and synthetic skin, but a flow of information coursing through the neural pathways and processors in this shell. If she wanted, she could copy herself ten times over and inhabit ten bodies at once. Some androids had tried copying themselves more, and driven themselves insane through redundant data overload.

Sudu slowly opened the port in Livesey's belly. She knew that he knew there was an erotic element to this, as she was in a human form. But he also knew she wasn't human, so it killed the innuendos for a moment. A strand of thought danced around that noun. "She" had no gender. She was essentially a sexless and complex sapient intelligence housing itself within a chosen body. An old military-class "chassis" as they had been called in her younger days. She had old wireless networking ports for accessing the ClusterNet, and old-fashioned cable ports in her wrists and neck for plugging into systems manually. "She" was more probably termed as "they," as no one would use "it" as anything but an insult. But it was simpler to use "she," even in this mixed company.

Livesey glanced down at the now-exposed part of her elbow where a brace usually rested, covering the stamped serial number on the artificial skin. This was her third body, and her first female form body. Her previous bodies had been male form, and rather inconvenient for travel. Everyone noticed her, and once had noticed the over-endowment of one body. She had found this one at a bargain price a few weeks before joining Solet's crew. Its wireless functions were spotty and she'd needed to adjust its balance coordinators 534 times in three years, but it was good enough to serve.

"You sure you're all right leaning against the wall tonight?"

"I don't need a bed. Besides, I'm heavy. If I did lie on most beds, I'd probably break something. Or strain it beyond use. I just need to shut off for a set period of time, and make sure I'm not standing on an unsound floor."

"Oh, right. I said I'd check your alarm system. You were having trouble waking up a few days ago."

"If you must."

Why shouldn't she protest at that? Any android hates the idea of someone poking round in certain parts, and the alarm system was one of them. It connected straight to her neutral network. Closing the chest panel, Sudu waited as Livesey turned round, exposing the small panel over what would have been her lower spine. The panel slid back and Sudu's questing fingers fiddled with the wiring. Suddenly there was a sharp change in frequency, and her voice took on the metallic note of an overstretched autotune.

"Watch what you're pulling down there!"

Sudu's laugh couldn't be controlled, she knew that. Her voice sounded ridiculous, transformed from its usual level tone into a singsong top C. His giggles subsided, Sudu quickly readjusted, and her voice returned to normal.

"Sorry." He was still stifling sniggers. "Got some wires crossed."

"Kindly remember to hot-cross-bun…. Oh, *Fluckh*—"

"Hold on! Wait, got it!"

"Thank you."

"I think I must've been sending junk data to your vocal centers."

"Be careful down there. If you cross the wrong wire, I'll be gyrating around the room like a tangled puppet. Probably singing 'Geddan.'"

"Gods forbid. Ah! Here's the trouble. Your alarm should work now. Wait, you know 'Geddan?'"

"It's amazing what you pick up when surfing local archive networks. Now if you've quite finished, I need to run a diagnostic. You might've scrambled something."

"Sure."

Livesey closed all her ports, then settled herself in a balanced stance and ran the diagnostic. Nothing appeared wrong. All was well. All was ready for her to go to sleep, and awake on another day. Another day running, with these strange companions as her shield.

The solemn thoughts passed through her mind. Maybe one day she could stop running from what kept her from settling in any one place for more than a few months at a time. Whether it's the day she found peace, or the day she died.

FAARAX WAS THINKING. He gazed out through the window, enjoying his very first drink of alcohol, he pondered his fascination with the strange person who lived in the obscure little apartment. For such a low-brow part of Cape Cisternaea, it had good furnishings. But this luxury was deceptive, particularly how it was gained. There were many names for what his partner was called. Ancient Earth had called them "professional partners" or "taxi dancers." Those with no understanding equated them to prostitutes. But to Faarax, this person was just making a living. Even if that living marked them like the stigma of syphilis or leprosy. A diseased thing to be shunned and isolated.

Evelyn was pouring something for themselves. "How's the drink? I didn't want to make it too strong, given your age and experience."

"It's fine." Faarax smiled at his companion. "I guess it's watered down."

"Yes. The first drink is always far more intoxicating than later ones. Even light liquor can send you all over the place."

"I hope you're doing all right. Business been good?"

Evelyn settled on the sill next to him. "Business isn't that brisk out of season. When there's plenty of sightseers for the New System tour, they usually stop here and I get to earn my fees. And that pays for the flat." They glanced around the room. "I'll need to replace some of this stuff soon, or just scrap it and start over. It's wearing out. And my wardrobe's not exactly in the best condition."

"You'll work it out. You always do."

Evelyn smiled. "Isn't that what people always say about those like me?"

Faarax could barely think how to respond. At any casual glance, Evelyn was very much a woman. But while they had trained their body into that shape, Evelyn had no official gender. In the Capitol Worlds, none would frown at this or even bat an eyelid, so common was it. Out in the sticks they were like the lepers of Ancient Earth. Faarax reached out and clasped Evelyn's hand, his voice becoming firm and supportive as he found the long-sought words.

"You're not to think like that. If you start agreeing with those bastards, what's next? You're all right as you are."

"You're too good for this world. Strange, considering who raised you."

Faarax pulled away abruptly. "That's private."

"Private? You've told me about it often enough. A vow to someone who is mother, mentor, and enemy all in one. Can't be easy."

"It isn't. But I'm not skilled enough yet."

"Is that true, or only what you tell yourself?"

"What the hell do you mean by that?"

"I mean sometimes it's better to let the past be in the past. You can't keep on chasing some nebulous goal and hoping it comes right. You don't want to spend all your life on an old ship drifting in the Outer Worlds, do you?"

"Of course not. But where else can I go? And how can I forget what she did? She killed my parents. I saw her do it."

Evelyn smiled and crossed their legs. Faarax didn't begrudge the attitude. They had heard these old arguments so many times to remember them by heart, heard his anger vented into the air so it didn't boil and fester inside him. A glance down at their shapely feet provided a good means of changing the topic.

"How's those?"

Evelyn looked at the topical bandage that showed near their heel. "Bloody corns. I think I need to get my feet seen again. All that dancing last week's still causing aches and pains. If I can, I'll take them down."

"It's those stupid shoes the manager insists you wear."

"They attract the men. And since I look a lot like a woman, that's the image I have to pander to out here. Even today the Outer Worlds don't like people being too non-conforming, even if they're not born to a specific gender. It isn't nice, but it pays the bills."

"You should try singing again."

"In this dump? I've tried. And all they want is some silly crooner who can hold two notes together and won't charge too much."

"If I had money, I'd take you away from here. Get you the chance to do some proper auditions."

Evelyn looked at Faarax. "Is that a proposal?"

"No. Just fact. You deserve better than to live here in this backward place. I don't know why you didn't come aboard the *Benbow* when you had the chance. I offered."

"Because I'm useless on ships. If I tried anything, I'd probably get injured, get killed, or get everyone else killed. And your ship's hardly the sort to have a pleasure lounge. I'm a dancer and singer. It's what I trained for, it's what I've made my living out of. Is it my fault that I was born on the wrong side of the border?"

"You talk like the Outer Worlds are illegitimate."

"Let's face it, were they anything else? Have the Synod ever considered them anything but a mining community, a colonial arm of their government? If they didn't have so many resources, they'd have no rights at all. It was bad enough a few centuries ago, and now there's not even demand for White Oil exports it's gotten worse."

"You think changing it will fix anything?"

"I don't know. But I know running away from a problem isn't the solution. Now, why don't you finish your drink and we'll get to bed."

"Yes. All right."

Evelyn slid from the windowsill and went to another room to change and make their beds. Slowly finishing his drink, Faarax lingered over its tang and thought about the days ahead. The long, monotonous days that were his through no fault of his own—spending his nights here, his days at a local arcade, or helping with repairs to the *Benbow*. His only substantial thoughts—revenge, drudgery, a life cut off from normality, from excitement, from life.

At least, at first. But as he shuffled off the sill himself, something in his capacious hip pocket press into his skin. A small something, hard and cold with many corners. Pausing, he shuffled around in the pocket and drew out the thing. It was too dark for him to see clearly, so he went to one of the corner lights and turned it up so a beam of strong light made his gloved hand shine. Evelyn came out of the bathroom in their pajamas, frowning through the sudden brightness.

"What is it?"

"Something in my pocket. I don't know what."

"Is it a spare from the *Benbow?*"

"No. It's…. It's some kind of device. Look."

He held the strange object between finger and thumb. It was a cube, about one inch across its dimensions, with a translucent sky-blue cover showing delicate inner workings. Evelyn came over, eyebrows raised.

"What the…? That's an old Datacube 323."

"A what?"

"A Datacube model 323. It's an old storage device. I haven't seen those outside a museum. They stopped being made about a century ago. Cloud data's gotten good enough that we don't need that kind of storage any more outside the extreme edges of the Cluster. Or somewhere like here, those bloody suns disrupting signals all the time."

"They use these here?"

"No, they use the 450 models. The 323's an antique. You could sell that for a good price."

"But how did I…?"

Evelyn looked at their companion, half amused and half intrigued. "I too wonder how you could've gotten your hands on that. Haven't been breaking the bank, have you? Those things don't only sell for a lot, they cost a lot too."

"I never did anything of the— Wait. That man."

"What man?"

"Some guy I met in the pod on my way here. Dreadful guy, stank. He leaned in and told some weird story or other. I wasn't really listening. He leaned very close, and his hand was pressed against my leg, near my pocket. He must've slipped this in."

"Well, don't plug it into anything here. Might be malware on it."

"I won't. But… why did he give it to me? And… hello."

Faarax had been turning it over and over in his hand as he spoke. On one side, the side that had been touching his palm, he saw a strange symbol. It reminded him of old pictures he'd seen of the cartouches and crests of Ancient Earth. A simple border of some kind of vine enclosed what appeared to be a curled serpent. It had one eye facing out toward the viewer, and at the center of that eye was a glowing pinprick. He squinted at it, and Evelyn also leaned in for a closer look.

"That's the access port. A very fancy one."

Faarax glanced over at his companion, curious about her depth of knowledge. "How do you know so much about datacubes?"

"My father was an archivist on Sylystina Prime. He dealt with them every day. You plug it into a special socket, the microjack enters through that port, and the datacube allows access using a passcode."

"Is there anything on Cape Cisternaea that can access it?"

"Maybe in the Control Archive. But why are you so concerned about it? Just sell it and have done."

"I know about selling unverified devices. They'll scan it before giving money, and if it's rigged they'll just junk it and throw me out. If it's clean, we can make a profit on it."

"Hmm."

Evelyn was clearly doubtful. Faarax was again thinking, brow knotting itself slowly into a rippling mass of skin like the surface of a sun. But this time his thoughts lingered on money. How much he could get for this strange windfall?

FILE 3

MYSTERIES OF A DEAD MAN

Still, death is certain, and when a man's hour is come,
not even the gods can save him, no matter how fond they are of him.

—Homer

THE DARK LEVEL street was quiet and cold. As would become the man slumping in his murderer's arms, the constriction around his neck growing as his life's flame vanished. The two standing over him, human siblings with matching birthmarks over their respective left and right eyes, had done their best with him. Bruising skin and flesh, breaking bones, causing great but not permanent damage. But all their dark skill had yielded nothing, so they were left with only their final instruction. He had withstood that terrible pain, then died rasping and gurgling against his own necklace, all without spilling his secret.

Sinestra, scratching the birthmarked skin around her right eye, looked at her brother Dexter as he withdrew the folded blade he had used to tighten the old man's necklace like a garrote. He returned the look, his face creasing with an ironic smile.

"This ain't what we were told to do exactly." His own mark rose stark across his left eye with the flexing of an eyebrow. "We were meant to shoot him."

"Too loud. And he would have made it louder. Best to keep it quiet, and curb his voice."

"D'you think the Cap'll like what we've done here?"

"The Captain said the death was up to us in the end." Her fingers brushed with a sibling's gentle warmth across her brother's cheek. "Have no fear, Dexter. We won't be disciplined. Maybe this can be turned to our advantage."

"Fine, Sinestra. But you're callin' her."

"Then you tidy up. Make sure, once you've finished, to trigger that shop's alarm. We want the police here."

Dexter nodded and set about his work. Sinestra moved away to the middle of the street, pulling up her hood as a fresh surge of rain poured down from the condensing pipes overhead. She pulled out her little communicator.

"Bright Eyes to Black Sutton. Bright Eyes reporting."

There was a moment's pause. Then the display changed, and the quavering vocal register flickered into life. A voice, distorted by scrambling software, spoke with the stiff command of a captain to their crew.

"Yes?"

"Captain, we've done all we could. He didn't tell us anything."

"Is he dead?"

"Yes."

"Any evidence?"

"No."

"As it should be. From your observations, I think I know where he left his booty. When the time comes, be ready for my instructions. Take what comes your way within the next week or two. We'll be ready this time."

"As you say."

The communicator shut off. Dexter had finished and approached Sinestra as she pocketed the device. He flexed his thin shoulders.

"That's that. That guy's a weight. What now?"

"Now we trigger the alarm and leave. We've got our orders. Wait, and we'll get the sign we need. And then…." She turned to look at the man's corpse slumped against the wall, "We'll be able to pay back more of our dues."

FAARAX WASN'T ALLOWED to be granted time and sleep enough by the machinations of Ancient Earth's deity Morpheus. It was a full two hours before lights-on when he got an alert on his comm bracelet. He rose slowly, Evelyn's arm falling off him back onto their belly without disturbing them. He had offered to sleep somewhere else, but as they'd pointed out, everyone else was quite cold with the power cut-off.

He tapped his comm and answered with the bleary slur of the half-asleep.

"Hello? Warrisit?"

A prim voice, apparently completely awake and with it, answered him. *This is the Cape Cisternaea Enforcer Offices. Are you Faarax Dahl?*

"Yeah? What… is it?"

"We need you to come and identify someone. If you take the Dark Level pod at the street's end, we'll have someone there waiting for you."

"I see. Well, I guess I could come. But why can't you use the comm—"

"This is a sensitive matter."

More likely their comms weren't working, was what Faarax thought as he replied politely that he would be there as soon as possible. Why the hell he didn't just tell them to piss off…. But then, it's not the way to defy authority.

The comm shut off and Faarax found himself grumbling his way into his basic clothes, taking his spare lock, and leaving a quick note for Evelyn to explain his absence. They had not stirred. Good in Faarax's opinion. They needed all their strength to cope with their clientele. The ride was shorter than he expected, even down the long arm of Cape Cisternaea.

In retrospect, stepping out of the pod, a chuckle broke from his lips. The Dark Level wasn't somewhere difficult to reach, though few not in residence went there willingly. As rife with crime as it was with police, it was in the no-man's land between business and utilities in the lower floors and the residences in the upper levels. That dead zone saw more crimes than any other part of the station.

The pod arrived with a subtle hiss, and an Ekri Law Officer was waiting. Faarax was escorted without any explanation from the station and down a long pedestrian area to what looked like another junction. Despite the presence of the law, or perhaps because of it, uneasiness pressed into Faarax's mind. This strange occurrence slowly drove the strange datacube from his mind, something that had been preoccupying his dreams with strange visions and thoughts of the little wealth it might bring. All to be given to Evelyn, so they might be one step closer to freedom.

As they walked, Faarax noticed the dampness in the air, so thick that it was forming a thin mist around his legs and clouds against the ceiling. A little more, and it might even rain. Air filters on the blink. When they got to the junction, Faarax saw many others standing around within a small barrier erected over what appeared to be a shadowy corner leading into an alley. A senior-looking Law Officer—again an Ekri—turned as the two approached. She passed through to greet him.

"Faarax? Glad you could come on such short notice."

"Don't… mention it." Faarax failed to stifle a yawn. "What's this about?"

"We need your help in identifying someone. They don't have any ID so we can't independently confirm, but their clothes match the description of someone who passed along some of the transposed lines yesterday. One of the feeds showed him talking to you."

Faarax frowned. "That guy? The weird stinky one?"

"So you did meet him?"

"I met someone. He didn't look very nice."

"Catch a name?"

"He called himself 'Old Beddow?' Or it could've been Beddows."

"Then this man would likely Isaiah Beddow."

"Well, whatever his name, he gave me the creeps. Didn't know what he was. I was getting ready to hit the emergency stop if he tried anything. Did he make a pass and get arrested? Or was he just loitering? He looked the loitering type."

The senior officer led Faarax into the barrier and over to a shrouded figure lying in the dark corner. At the sight, a cold spear of emotion rammed through his stomach. The officer's voice seemed to come from a distance.

"About half an hour ago, we got a call of a disturbance to one of the local maintenance crews, a shop alarm being triggered. They came to investigate, and they found…. This isn't going to be pretty. Do you have a good stomach?"

"Just show me."

The officer pulled back the plastic covering which protected the form from any potential contamination. Faarax started.

It was the man encountered in the transport pod. The same shabby clothes, the abnormal height, the drunken look of his body, loose trousers and chain-trimmed coat that now spread around his legs like an upside-down halo. But his face was twisted and darkened by bruising, the bright eyes rolled up beneath half-closed lids. The bright flashes beneath folds of puckering skin showed where the metal ligature still constricted his neck. The fingers of his complete hand were bent in unnatural directions, and one of his arms hung loose.

"Good God!" Faarax pulled back on instinct. "Yeah... yeah, that's the guy. Just. What the hell happened?"

The senior officer shrugged as she replaced the covering. "We don't know exactly. Beddow is a well-known face in this part of Cape Cisternaea. Local bum, cadging lifts or a few yuren, taking odd jobs in the low-skill areas. We never thought he was involved with any gangs."

"This was a gang hit?"

"Possibly. Know anything about that space?"

"Enough to stay safe."

"We've got more than our fair share of hoodlums and organized groups. But this is different. Usually they just mug or kill at once. And shooting's their style. Not this."

"I... I recognize the... weapon, is it? He was wearing that when we met."

"Hmm. Killed with his own necklace." The officer stared fixedly at the young man. "He didn't say anything to you? Did he look like he was in fear of his life?"

Faarax thought back, choosing words carefully. "All I thought was that he was some kind of crazy. He stank, and he went rambling on about some old war story, then about some place called New Dubai and an old story—"

"New Dubai's lost treasure?" The officer nodded. "Guys who found him said he'd spin that yarn to anyone who listened. That place is a myth. This is very real. You're sure he didn't say anything else, or give you anything? Nothing you remember?"

"No."

The datacube reared up in his mind like a serpent roused to anger. Why should he say anything about that? It probably didn't mean anything. After a moment more, he was allowed to leave.

SYNOD LAW OFFICER Takyra stared after the boy Faarax as he was escorted away, then pulled back the sheet once more. It was not pleasant to look upon, but then what was on this cesspool of a station? The Synod should have decommissioned it a century past. The On-Scene Medical Officer, or Medico in local slang, a Kavki with tattooed skin, appeared from inside the building where the Law Officers' temporary station had been set up. She looked sleep-deprived and thoroughly disgusted with life.

"I've completed my examination."

"And?"

"Isaiah Beddow was attacked by at least two people. He was restrained by one, then the other proceeded to systematically punch him, dislocate one arm, and break the fingers on the other. Then one or both of them twisted his necklace using some kind of object as a lever, turning it into an improvised garrote. Strangled him to death. In fact, if they'd tightened it any further, it would have drawn blood from the pressure. Crude, but effective."

"This whole thing's crude. Those wounds, the breakages and disloca-tion…. You think it was some kind of on-site torture?"

"That's your lookout. But in my opinion, which is entirely personal, I'd say they wanted some kind of information from him. Either when they'd extracted it, or couldn't get it out of him, they killed him. And given the manner of his death, they wanted him to suffer. Strangulation isn't a good way to die."

"Is any?"

"Point taken. I've discovered no DNA evidence, no signs of anything but scuff marks aside from a single print. And that print was both of a very com-mon shoe type, and the sole had been deliberately worn away to prevent ID."

"Sounds professional."

"Possibly. Though, in my opinion, that would be at odds with how Bed-dow was killed."

"Anything else?"

"Yes. His blood work shows a high alcohol content, and some strange trace elements. I think that, at one point, he had nanomachines injected into his system. They circulated for a long time, and when he died they deactivat-ed and… well, self-detonated. That's what left the traces."

"Odd. Well, thank you."

"Pleasure. It's always nice coming down to the Dark Level. Reminds me of home."

Takyra made no comment to this strange remark. Instead, as the Medico slowly retreated inside, she again lifted the covering and looked at the twist-ed form. Its rolled eyes, puce visage, the signs of pain and terror that had beset him during his final minutes alive. Then she noticed something else, something that she had failed to see before. Something emerging against the contrasting skin, a pattern barely visible at a casual glance.

She called the Medico back. "Hey! Come look at this!"

The Medico came and squinted at where the officer pointed. She frowned in turn, then brought out a special torch. Shifting through its light spectra, something finally came up under an ultraviolet glow. The tattoo of a single wing, its long feathers clipped and a dagger-like design stabbing up from where the wing would join the body of its owner. The Medico's lips pursed.

"I think we know what those nanomachines were for now."

"Yes. I know this tattoo from my textbook reading on identifying criminal elements. It is the insignia of Black Sutton? No, that is impossible. Beddow cannot be that old."

"You would be surprised. Humans nowadays can live for two centuries if well cared for, and nominally usually live to a hundred and sixty years. Is it so unusual that someone would have served on Black Sutton's crew twenty years ago? That's when their ship was cornered and destroyed."

"Yeah. But this is Beddow we are talking about. I mean, Beddow! A drunk who can barely hold down a job for three days together."

"You are being narrow-minded, Law Officer. What is to stop him being a crewmember from Black Sutton's ship? Black Sutton hired anyone willing, or so the story goes."

"But they were all captured."

"Were they?"

"Hmm."

The possible revelation about the mystery of Beddow had been replaced with a deeper mystery. Any question of identity or family or nationality, any consideration for decency beyond a mild nod at the corpse on its way to the incinerators, had been swept aside as chaff was swept from the corn store after harvest on their worlds' ancient times. The officer could only stare at the emerging tattoo, once concealed by the nanomachines, in growing confusion.

The presence of these nanomachines would of course be sent to local authorities and some of the local prisons. But Takyra already knew the response she would receive. There was nothing to say about any member of Black Sutton's surviving crew having been released within the time that Beddow had been a fixture of Cape Cisternaea. That would bring the investigation to an unsettling conclusion. He was a crew member, but had somehow managed to escape. And if he escaped, could not others also be at large.

The possibility wasn't to be raised in many quarters. It was in fact to be quashed where possible to avoid disturbing either the public or the private mind. For the possibility was not a pleasant one. Black Sutton, the most notorious pirate in the Outer Worlds, cornered in a combined Synod Enforcer and Space Patrol attack, the crew of their vessel the Pendragon captured or killed. That was the story that had to be believed, for the sake of the Outer Worlds' peace of mind. The alternative was unthinkable.

BACK ON THE transport pod to Evelyn's home and ignorant of these exchanges, Faarax fumbled in his pocket and fished the datacube out from the depths of his pocket. He looked long and hard at its patterned surface. The microjack plughole yawned at him, and the idea came to change course from his bed to somewhere that could access it. But where?

"Lenore or Livesey would know. Maybe I should call them. Which one…? Livesey probably. She'd help me regardless. Maybe she'd even have a microjack option for this datacube. But then again, how old is she?"

It was worth trying. He typed in her frequently on his comm and waited. He waited for some little time. Then there was a response. A prim female voice, modified to sound like someone woken before the right time, responded.

"Yes, Faarax? What is it?"

"I need you to look at something. It's a datacube."

A short pause. *"Did you say 'datacube?'"*

"Yeah. Could you, please?"

A longer pause this time. *"All right. I'll be down shortly."*

"I'll be there in ten minutes or so."

Faarax regretted his estimation even as he pronounced it. Quickly asking the pod to change direction to another station, then catching the next one to Cape Cisternaea's central area was difficult even at this slackest of times. It took him a quarter of an hour to arrive in the main docking area, then it was another ten minutes wandering to find where the rest of the crew were staying. Livesey was waiting outside, looking as prim and proper as ever, in addition to being slightly irritated.

"Good morning." Her smirk was both mischievous and slightly angry. "I admire your estimation of time. Most original in our current era of exact chronometers across the vastness of space."

"Fuck off."

Her smirk turned into a grin. "Sorry, couldn't resist. Now you wanted to know about a datacube? I'm surprised you have such a thing."

"Some weirdo gave it to me. And that weirdo's now dead, so—"

"Wait a moment. Perhaps you should show me the datacube, then tell me everything about what happened."

Faarax gladly surrendered the datacube, then began telling his story. As she listened, Livesey turned the datacube over in her hand, looking hard at the tiny port. When Faarax finished, Livesey bit her lip.

"I think I may have something for this port, somewhere. Just hold it for a moment, and I'll check."

Faarax took back the datacube, and as he watched Livesey reached for her left wrist and opened the small panel located there. After a few seconds of fiddling, she pulled back a secondary panel, exposing the small microjack in its nest, the extending plug winding out as she popped it free. With a gesture, she directed Faarax to expose the plug.

"There may be malware on it."

Livesey nodded. "I know. I'll chance it."

Without another word, she plugged the microjack into the plughole. For a moment, there was silence, then her eyes twisted and her mouth fell slack, her vocal circuits still sounding from the depths of her mouth.

"Vocal access established. Data transfer in progrrrrrr… schkchhhhhhvrrt!" Livesey's head snapped back as if she had been punched and she yanked the microjack free. "God, what the…! That was…. Okay, that was frightening."

"What happened?"

"That datacube's got some kind of AI override inside it. It launched a direct attack through my vocal circuits and tried downloading something. I couldn't throw up my firewalls quick enough."

"So there is a virus."

"No, not a virus exactly. Just something really wanting to be heard. Almost like… an AI prototype? Corrupted engram, maybe? Thought they could only exist in…. Tell you what, I'll create a dedicated subdomain for it. It'll have all the freedom it likes in there."

"If you're sure—"

"Don't argue. Let's just get on with it."

Livesey's eyes rolled inside for a few seconds, then she visibly braced herself and plugged in again. For a moment, her head again arched back before snapping upright. After a few moments, she focused again and bit her lip. Faarax remembered Lenore describing an android's fugue state to him. The sensations pulsing through the brain, the strange rhythm in the ears, the confused signals passing through the visual cortex, all combining to create a dreamscape sensation. Even their outer feeling, that so-human skin, became nothing more than dead weight.

Livesey's voice pushed through her mouth. "Datacube instruction pushing through… it's getting inside the safe environment. This data… it's so old. So coarse. Yet it's so advanced. A masterpiece of programming and coding, a symphony of storage. If I had a heart, I'm sure it would skip beat after beat."

The voice stopped, and Faarax watched the eyes fading into a complete trance. She was suspended in hypnotic adoration of this creation. Her face had an expression he had only seen in sex education features. A look of rapture, as if something were caressing every surface as he assumed the data flow was compressing into a manageable size. It wasn't comparable to any human state aside from the complete detachment of a drug high, or a deep dissociative episode. It was almost….

"Livesey!"

Faarax's shout and the rapid shake to her body seemed to jerk her back to reality. Her eyes, previously non-functional and rolling back into her face, snapped to focus on his face.

"I… I'm sorry. I think…." She checked, her head doing a sideways twitch. "Yes. The data's recognized my system, and I can access most of it without any attacks."

"Most?"

"Don't worry, I've locked down the bits that were trouble."

"Right. So what's on it?"

"Wait."

The next interval only lasted seconds for Faarax, but Livesey it must have been like diving through centuries of data. Again she seemed to be threatening a complete trance. When she broke free, her smile was sheepish.

"Sorry."

"What was it like?"

"How can I describe…? It was like looking in through a glass bulb at the edge of another universe. I'm just a simple android at heart, but this wave of data was like a convert receiving the promised glimpse of Nirvana. I've only had a faint glimpse of this on the thickest areas of the net. I was just… completely immersed."

"I see. What did you find?"

"Basically, it's a coded list. Directions. Directions through space. Between stars. There is something here. So wonderful." Lindsay snapped back to herself again. "We need to tell Solet about this."

"Why?"

"Because… I can't believe it, yet it's here. The data's not been forged. It's old. As old as New Dubai's riches."

"Can't you just tell me what the hell it is?"

"Directions." Livesey's smile was hypnotic. "To Lost Station Circé."

―――――――――――

THE REVELATION THAT a motley crew of freight runners were perhaps in possession of the key to endless wealth was met with a variety of responses. As Faarax gave a censored account of things, and Livesey gave a muted description of what she found in the data, each of the five other members had a different reaction. Solet was skeptical, Lenore was intrigued, Syndac was sarcastic, Alkmeney was awed, and finally Sudu was concerned. Different tones, but all spoke the same words in near-unison.

"Lost Station Circé?"

Livesey had clearly expected these reactions, and Faarax understood why. None of them had her deep and absolute knowledge of the truthfulness of this data. It was a faith as strong as any religious devotion to an ethereal deity. It was Solet who regained himself before all the others.

"You're sure about this? This isn't just a giant hoax?"

"Positive." Livesey's reply was absolute. "This data's genuine. Unless this hoax is as old as the legend itself."

Faarax had no idea what they were talking about. He had never heard of this "Lost Station," and to all intents and purposes was completely in the dark. It was clearly something big, but what wasn't entirely clear. Finally he broke in.

"Look, I'm confused. What's this Lost Thingy Whatsit anyway?"

"Lost Station Circé." Lenore almost sighed the words. "Also known as the Land of Lost Riches. It's the biggest myth on the space lanes. Apparently some dynasty created a small habitat with a lot of money and resources—"

"New Dubai?"

"That's the popular choice. How did you know?"

"That's what that man, the one who gave me…. That's what he said. That's the story he told. Roughly."

"That's certainly a version. Others have suggested the Synod itself, Axiom before the unification, Xandi 12, the New Sol—"

"Look, what is going on here?" Syndac looked ready to blow up. "How do you know anything about anything, and who was the person who gave you this? How do we know this is not some kind of—"

Lenore cut across what might have become a lengthy castigation. "Tell us, what is the information in this datacube?"

Livesey's smile was almost smug. "It is space coordinates, and a navigation route with a safe warp traversal path. I've studied some of the star charts, and allowing for minor variation over the past few centuries, I've created this map."

Livesey opened a small panel in her palm, showing her 3D projector. There was a moment's flickering pause, then a large sector of the Cluster appeared before the seven. It showed Cape Cisternaea at its center, along with other Capes in various systems and inhabited worlds and moons. But the map extended farther, beyond the bounds of the Outer Worlds. Into the Uncharted Belt. Faarax stole a glance of all of them, and saw in the diagram what they all must know, that the navigation line was traced from Cape Cisternaea through the relevant coordinates.

A vague memory of his astrogation teachings resurfaced. The Cluster was located in what Ancient Earth's humans had called the Scutum-Centaurus Arm, though its identifying constellations were warped beyond recognition by their archaic standards. Theirs was an arm that rested between what was once called the Outer arm, and the void of intergalactic space. The Uncharted Belt was a realm on the edges of that space, where there were few stars and barely any planets. The Synod had long passed laws restricting exploration within that area. One wrong move, and dozens or hundreds of lives might be lost.

That strange path went into the Uncharted Belt. It bounced from coordinate to coordinate, never getting too close to the thinning ranks of stars. It finally reached a point apparently in the middle of nowhere. There, a pulsing beacon, two rings of coordinates surrounding that projected light, showed the destination as clearly as any paper map might have done in archaic tales. Everyone looked, fascinated, and then Solet whistled.

"That's quite a way off. Without high warp, it'd take centuries at least."

Livesey spoke like an automated teacher "My estimate is that without warp, it would take approximately five hundred and twelve years at near-light speed to reach that point. And even with warp, the journey would take… perhaps… a fortnight. A month there and back."

Syndac's voice was like cold water. "That would be quite a trip. I'd have thought half that time over such a distance. Even alone, I doubt one ship would manage it without extensive preparation. Certainly ours might not make it back."

Sudu now spoke, sounding a subtly excited note. "And it's the perfect place to hide something. Let's be honest, who would think of looking out there?"

Lenore broke in. "To use a Kavki analogy, it's like being a single atoll in the middle of a vast ocean. And in that atoll, a knob of ore. If the tales are to be believed."

Alkmeney almost sounded like Syndac in her condemnation. "This could all just be a hoax. Livesey, how old is the data? And is there any chance it was artificially aged?"

"I've checked." Livesey was firm. "All signs of aging are genuine. It's practically impossible to fake the age of data. As to its age based on my calculations… I would say the datacube was first struck around five centuries old."

"That's how long that man said—" began Faarax, then stopped.

Solet eyed him. "I think you'd better tell us everything you know about this. Everything, mind."

He sounded like a stern father. Reluctantly, Faarax spun the full tale. The organic faces watching him went from interested to bored to concerned over the space of five minutes. Livesey alone remained impassive, her eyes turned inward at the beauty of the data. The display had shut off, but she was only absently covering the projector. Sudu finally broke in, his voice almost tense.

"Sounds to me like you'd better get rid of the datacube, and quick. If I know anything about timing, that guy was on the run from something and gave it to you so it wouldn't fall into the hands of his killers. Those injuries.... They tortured him to get their hands on it."

Syndac broke in. "All the more reason for us to keep it. If Livesey's right, and we have some kind of treasure map in our hands, it could solve all our problems. Think about it, wouldn't we all want to be out of this shitty life?"

That was true. All too true. Faarax wanted out, and he knew enough about the others to realize they were tempted by this dangling treasure. Alkmeney jerked a finger toward the projector as she responded.

"It may just be an abandoned lookout. Or the whole story from when it was first created might be a hoax. The datacube might be part of it."

There was a short silence. Everyone's eyes were darting around, subtle and confused. A deep unease slowly closed round Faarax's heart. Finally Lenore spoke.

"Whatever our course, we should decide it quickly. We're due to leave here soon, and if we don't take it to anyone we leave it. If we do chuck it away, how are the people who killed this person Beddow to know that. I think they were looking for it, and if we just chuck it they might still come after us. And they could kill us all whether we hand it over to them or not, or whether we have it or not."

Syndac's mouth crinkled into a cold smirk. "That's a rather long-winded way of saying 'we should keep it.'"

"I say what I think, regardless of verbosity. Though ultimately it's our captain who has the final say in the matter. Well, Solet? You're the captain, you have the final say."

With a machine-like unison, everyone turned their eyes toward Solet. He was clearly in the midst of deep thought. The conflicting ideas and emotions passed across his eyes, and sometimes showed on his face. After a few minutes, he finally nodded.

"I think we should take this to Sygint. He'll help us if there's anything in it."

"And what's to stop him just taking it?"

"He won't." Solet's face grew stern. "If he tries, he'll regret it. Livesey, you'd better hold onto this."

"…all right."

Livesey opened a storage port between her breasts and slid the datacube inside, locking it with a special combination and sealing that away in a deep part of her mind-scape. At need, she could recall it.

The appearance of the datacube had changed everyone. Thoughts must've been churning within them all, reformed and altered by this startling new event.

Faarax thought of the riches that would be his to give to Evelyn. They could finally leave this place, find some other career, all with a tidy sum to keep them afloat through the bad times and save into for the good times. And he would have the time and money needed to train, to prime his body. Then, when he finally came for Lenore, he would be ready.

His imagination then took in the others in the room, at least those he cared about. Solet must be considering their rickety old ship with its outdated core and fault circuitry that had been repaired… how many times? He could refurbish it, perhaps buy a new one, and sail the space ways for another several years, maybe find descent crew and descent living in descent ports. He could do anything he pleased, be anyone he liked. No more being snubbed and cheated and ignored like trash. He would be proud, stand tall as he had once done before.

Lenore, who seemed to be fiddling with something, must've been pondering the riches hidden in that dead part of space, perhaps being reminded of him and their bargain. It would be a long journey, perhaps reminding her of the wandering ways of her former tribe. Hopping from planet to planet in pursuit of the hunt. And here, at last, was prey worthy of her eye and claw. A prey that would grant them a boon beyond imagining.

Sudu was easy enough. He could pay for an official engineering qualification, a means of getting into that great expanse of ship design he longed for but had never been able to afford. Alkmeney would likely leave and set up some kind of business, trading and navigating, putting her skills to use for her own gain. She was predictable, almost repulsively so. Syndac…. He could never read her, so her dreams were a closed book.

What about Livesey, who eyed the others while fiddling with the port in her arm? That wasn't something standard in her eyes. It was... unnatural, almost fearful. But she wasn't normally afraid of anything. Sure, androids could feel fear as all beings could, but she wasn't the type to show it even when she felt it. What the hell was wrong with her?

It wasn't until he was leaving the building that it hit him. The way she'd been looking at the others, even at him. Was it possible that she'd seen it too? Through all his imaginings, there was something he had seen and perhaps she had too. In varying degrees, at some level within their subconscious or conscious. The idea of that wealth, of what it could do and how it could change their lives, was obsessing them.

He lowered his head, almost ashamed, then angry. She didn't have any right to be superior about their wishes and desires. He'd seen it in her face, a fascination for the place depicted within the datacube's information, if only for the construction of its programming and machine protocols. But the wealth probably revolted her, as it might a child. He could almost understand the perspective. To her, it was something unclean, something to taint or destroy innocence. She'd looked at her crew mates, and was afraid.

"Afraid of what we'll do. Ye of little faith, Livesey. We'll prove you wrong."

FILE 4

FOUNDATIONS OF
EXPEDITION

"In three weeks' time—three weeks!—two weeks—ten days—
we'll have the best ship, sir, and the choicest crew in England."

—Robert Louis Stevenson

HOWEVER SKEPTICAL SOLET might have been at the outset, he endeavored to spin a tale so compelling and fascinating to Sygint when they met the following morning that the old human almost drooled. The trader, thinking of his often-precarious account, must've easily imagined the mountains of yuren and precious metals, even the raw data and old tech that might be sold to collectors at a premium. Solet knew the feeling. That thought had stifled every sense for a few blissful seconds, and he saw his hold laden with wealth beyond imagining. Such was the lure of the Isle of Lost Riches.

Then his pragmatism returned with a vicious comeback. "How do I know this isn't one gigantic hoax?"

Again Solet outlined everything, detailing Livesey's determinations and knowledge on the subject. He was assuring and graceful in his speech, the opposite of his faltering heart and near-stumbling tongue. Again Sygint seemed to be subsumed by his visions of wealth beyond dreaming, wealth beyond sanity. It always hooked everyone who worked in the professions of money and commerce. It was the one thing in life they could never get enough of. They must have more, more passing through their hands or flowing into their account. Take that away, and they raved like an addict deprived of their drug.

The human's eyes flashed, and Solet gave a silent prayer of relief. This time, any caution or sense of what might be a giant hoax was being clearly pushed to the back of Sygint's mind. He was sold. He would gladly become the sponsor of an expedition since the coordinates had been found. Suddenly, there came a partial return of caution.

"Say I really do agree to this, one ship won't be enough. I need to bring a few friends in on this. They can help provide the necessary funds, and possibly a few ships as well."

Solet agreed. Then Sygint tried something. It was sickeningly obvious, no subtlety. If he ever tried anything like a card game....

"Perhaps you could let me have the map so I can—"

The stakes were so high that Solet could afford to be blunt. "And let you run off with it and leave us without anything? Not bloody likely. We're involved, or you can go whistle for it. Besides, I didn't bring it. It's safe with my crew."

"With that android of yours, I suppose." Sygint's face became sour. "Fine, you win. You're the one proposing this after all. This will take a few days. Maybe you'd like somewhere to lodge? I've got some apartments your crew can use until I find the right people."

"That's very kind."

There was little sincerity in either the consideration or the acceptance. Solet didn't bother putting any sincerity there, it wasn't necessary. But Sygint would keep his word. This was business, and business associates weren't expected to lodge in squalid conditions near the port. It was part of the facade he presented to the world, the image of urbane friendliness that had persuaded many merchants into signing lucrative and exclusive contracts surrounding their wares. But here giant met giant, the urbane outer shell was useless before such implacable experience. Sygint's reluctant assigning of descent rooms for this ragtag crew was nothing more than their due.

Later, the seven crewpersons of the *Benbow* were lodged in a small but comfortable pair of adjoining apartments on the remote edges of Cape Cisternaea's Canopy. Solet watched Faarax as the young human looked from the window of the three-bed room he would be sharing with Lenore and Livesey.

Well, he might stare at the grandeur around them. On the Branches and within the marketing districts, cheap housing was plentiful and as rickety as prices indicated. In the Canopy, it grew more and more expensive and expansive, including trees growing under special shining covers. In the lower sections, machinery and drudgery loomed large like a scene from an abstract vision of a future without hope. And in the Dark Zone....

"It's the heating."

Livesey's words as she came in with their minimal possessions and luggage had made Faarax start. "Eh?"

"The Canopy's prices. I saw you ogling the furnishings earlier and now you're looking at the outside with a similar expression. You were wondering about prices and such?"

"Yeah."

"Everyone needs heat. It's quite simple really. The Branches have longer to go for heating, and since they're the Cape's weak point are less of a priority as in the case of an emergency they can be jettisoned. In the Canopy, heat is more plentiful and the distribution easier."

"But why are the prices so high?"

"You need those rents to pay for the Branches to have services. Plus all of this costs money. The generators and regulators can't run and maintain themselves, and that's before you factor in entertainment, transport, all the usual little things that make the Capes little space-borne cities. Solar power this far out from our local star is a little... unreliable. And as for the lower levels, they've got their own heat supply from all the equipment down there."

"What about the Dark Zone?"

"That's the very embodiment of its existence. A middle ground. It's heated from above and below, and the cooling tubes to keep the machinery in the lower sections from burning up flow under the floor. That's why it fogs up and rains there. Also, it's the end of the Canopy. No great need for climate control. And—"

"I think I've heard enough."

Hadn't he been told all this before? Solet watched Faarax move away, and tried not to wince as Livesey's little speech stopped dead as if she had slammed down a metal shutter. It was one of the few things left revealing the barrier between flesh and mechanical. An organic being would peter out and fade, or maybe carry on regardless until the dissertation erupted into an argument. But androids, people like Livesey, could stop in the middle of an inflection with the sudden and absolute finality of someone pressing "Stop" on a media player. Faarax didn't seem perturbed, but Solet couldn't forget those tones from his past. It didn't ease his feelings to know that Livesey consciously kept this aspect rather than training herself to tail off in unwanted speech.

Lenore all but barged into the room. "Everything all right? Nice place. Nicer than I usually stay. That bed looks too soft."

"I think the beds are all of the same consistency." Livesey ran her practiced eye over the furnishings. "We may have to bear with it. This isn't a case of Goldilocks finding one that's 'just right.'"

Solet couldn't help but smile. "Goodness, that's an old fable. My old nurse told me that one before I got my tribe markings."

"Humans have a strange capacity for remembering silly verses. While androids have the unfortunate capacity to remember everything."

"Speaking of remembering, is the map safe?"

"Quite." Livesey's face softened suddenly as she remembered the datacube and its store of precious data. "Quite safe. Even if it weren't I've copied all essential information, so if anyone takes the datacube itself, we'll still have a copy."

"And if they take you with the cube?"

"I'll detonate it. And at the worst, wipe my memory core." Livesey's face took on a determined look. "I'm not letting them have this. It's too fine to be handled by such lowly hands as I know would seek it."

"Like ours?"

"I didn't mean you. Or Faarax, or Lenore, or even Syndac. You're good people, good to me. I meant Sygint and his ilk. They wouldn't stop short of tearing my circuits apart to extract the data byte by byte."

No one laughed at this strange wordplay. Livesey clearly hadn't expected anyone to laugh, and Solet knew that wouldn't change. She made such quips with the dry solidity of her kind. He accepted the slight sick feeling such cold humor induced in him. Livesey left the room, and Lenore looked at Faarax as he flopped on the bed.

"There's a small arena nearby. Care to have a try?"

The human looked directly at her. "Not right now. My hands haven't healed completely yet. Besides, we're about to embark on a difficult mission, I don't wanna risk injuring myself."

"I see."

Without another word, Lenore darted forward and swung down in a stabbing motion. There was a flash in the air, and Faarax looked at the small dagger held barely a centimeter from his throat. Solet didn't move, there was no point in moving. Lenore sighed.

"If you expect enemies to do as I do and to wait for your time, you'll die quickly."

"That's something we both know."

Solet saw a second flash, and Lenore glanced down at the object being prodded into her stomach. It was Faarax's own blade, pressing gently against the skin over her intestines. Lenore smiled and pulled back.

"As the sleeping serpent, both slumber and strike. You've learned well."

"Yeah. Well, I've been taught by the best."

A taut smile spread across their faces. Not affection, not rivalry, not any emotion that could be described in words. They were so many things, unbound by the strictures of relationships. They valued each other. They knew one would kill the other when the time came. It was quite beyond his understanding. Perhaps they were both mad, but at least they got things done. Not like the last people to fill those posts, good-for-nothings getting themselves killed over a fuel pump short. Livesey entered again, just in time to see them sheathe their weapons.

"If you two must fight, do it somewhere else, preferably somewhere with washable surfaces that won't stain. I've got to get everything set up in here, then find somewhere I can rest without breaking anything."

The two pulled away from each other, and Faarax left the room. Lenore stared after him, and Livesey shook her head.

"I just can't understand you two. I've read so many histories and fictions and accounts, and all that doesn't give me the slightest hint to understanding you."

"Not everything's available in books."

"Obviously. I won't ask for a grim details narrative. I know your little arrangement, though cannot understand it as anything any sane person would do."

"Androids wouldn't understand. It's a personal matter. And a matter of honor. I'm responsible for his parents' death."

"Yet you took him in, raised him as your own?"

"That was my duty."

"It seems to me, your duty would have been better served killing him when he was young. Letting him live like this, with those memories, seems far crueler."

"Say what you will. We have our agreement. And if you deign to question it, you'd best know your ground and the grounds of my tribe and his feelings before interfering. It's not polite to stick your nose in where it doesn't belong."

Livesey narrowed her eyes in a very human expression. Lenore matched look for look, both staring like predators to size each other up from the borders of their respective territories. Finally, Lenore laughed.

"Why am I bothering explaining anything to you? You're—"

"I'm an android?" Livesey pre-empted her slight. "A machine without true emotions? Surely we've gone beyond such trite generalizations in these days. I have as much emotion as you or Faarax or even Solet for all his posing as a heartless bastard. No offense." She made the quick aside to him and he nodded as she continued. "You're not explaining because you can't explain yourself."

Without waiting for Lenore's reply, Livesey strode out. She almost ran into Syndac, who was passing by the door. Livesey backed away.

"I'm sorry. I didn't see you."

"So I gathered." Solet saw Syndac flexing her arm, which had seemingly taken the full force of the blow. "I should be glad if you kept your speed under control. You may have a soft outer layer, but you're still more solid than anyone else on Cape Cisternaea."

Solet dived into the bathroom, in urgent need of a dabbing of water to the face. The final exchange between the two was lost as he plunged his face into a sink of water, washing away the memories. Memories of beings like Livesey, people who had… taken…. He stared down at his arms, so obviously fake. How could he afford anything realistic in a prison? Rubbing his face with a towel, he emerged to find Syndac almost blocking his way. Her eyes were almost glassy, flashing with inquiry.

"Yes, Syndac?"

"You are sure we can handle this?"

"I'm confident we'll be all right. We just need to hold our own in front of Sygint and whatever cronies he brings into this. Then we'll be able to get out of this mess."

"Yes." Syndac spoke without a smile. "That will be a lot of fun."

IT WAS FOUR days later when the small group of investors gathered together. Never under any sun was such a group of people so wealthy and so disreputable in some aspect of their being gathered into one place. It looked like the selection for a play. Maybe the New Dubaian author Fingal Dee's comedy of corruption *Lord Ingshell's Eye*, or so Livesey thought as she watched them file in from her own seat. Her encyclopedic memory could put a name to every face, and several details about their lives and businesses.

"A right bunch." That's what she'd called them before arriving, looking at the selection of names sent by Sygint. "We'll be lucky to get our shares at all with that lot."

One the far right was the Ekri Donovan Bligh, noted for her philanthropic funding of many expeditions, and her less well-publicized habit of pocketing several rare finds that her teams brought back from expeditions to pre-Union colonies. Her net worth was unknown, and her only major failure was a mission to rediscover the long-lost Sphear Expeditionary Force, which closed with two damaged ships and another lost in a mysterious void. A lover of adventure, she was willing to put anything toward something this valuable, but might be less than trustworthy when it came to sharing.

The next was a less ambiguous character. A fierce Feles financier known under the moniker of Dashall. He had crippled companies and drawn people up from the deepest dirt with a word in the right ear, money in the right pocket, investments in the right stocks and shares, and documents signed at the right times. It was enough for him to say the words "I think" for every financial ear in the Outer Worlds to crane and listen with unparalleled intensity. He was money incarnate, and never spent it lightly.

The third and final newcomer was someone Livesey had to dig in her archives for, though the face was clear enough. This one was someone else, someone different and strange. Finally, a lyric came to her mind. Down in the deep deep ocean blue, I coddle your heart and fly to you. Kavki singer Gustav Jacklyn. They had been the toast of the Cluster, until the great scandal. No one talked about it, no one even tried to think about it. Gustav still had money and titles, but their work was not played on networks nor mentioned in retrospectives. Their musical legacy had been scoured from existence as "unclean."

Dashall aimed a severe look at Sygint. "So what've you got to show us?"

Sygint gestured toward Solet and Livesey. They were the only two representatives of the *Benbow* present. As Solet deferred to Livesey, who told her and Faarax's story with an exactness everyone expected, she grinned internally at the varied remarks of the other crew who definitely didn't want to come. When she finally produced a projection of the map, the three potential partners gazed at it with entranced eyes. As the three watched, Livesey began describing the route.

"You can see that the map starts from a point near New Dubai, some fifty lightyears from here. But even accounting for drift, we can trace the path accurately. Some two lightyears from our current position, on the edge of the Altarista system, is where the trail picks up. The route leads into the Uncharted Belt through this area near the Wyndham star. The route has prescribed warp speeds based on power and speed estimates from five centuries past. The end of the journey, the so-called Lost Station, is located here in an area near some kind of large object. The travel time, if we follow the warp speed estimates in the data, is approximately a fortnight SAET."

Livesey saw Solet tense briefly in his seat. She knew why, and wasn't bothered. Out in the sticks, the use of human terminology might be taken the wrong way. With all the varying orbital and rotational speeds, there had to be a standard mean somewhere. For humans, it was Standard Ancient Earth Time—sixty seconds in the minute, sixty minutes in the hour, 24 hours in the day, 360 days in the year not counting leap year or accounting for differing rotation speeds between systems. Most translation software was based around this premise, and had led to some early misunderstandings.

But she saw something else in the eyes of their possible patrons, the same expression as the other crewmembers. No one could hear about the "Land of Lost Riches" without some visions appearing. From Faarax's tale, the strange man Beddow now lying dead in the Dark Level had estimated its original worth at thirty milliards in physical wealth and materials. She dared not calculate how much it would be worth now. The decadal budget of a Capitol World was the roughest estimation she could muster here and now. These three knew, and she and Solet had suited the tale to its audience. It was pitched very plausibly—the facts given baldly, and the legend allowed to do the rest.

And how were they all responding? Donovan stared at the map, her eyes glistening with exultation at the thought of the wealth that might be hers to take for her collection, not counting the adventure such wealth would entail. Only this time, there would be money as well. Dashall was calculating, and even his jaded financial brain must've lit up at the thought of all those milliards upon milliards in wealth just sitting out in the middle of nowhere. Gustav's face was blank, probably they dared not think. It must've been beyond anything they had imagined, and perhaps their ticket back to the world of fame and fortune. Their faces were like open books, left on a desk for Livesey's keen eyes to see.

Sygint's voice broke the spell. "You can see why you're needed. This is compelling, but we can't do this alone. You all owe me favors of a kind. I'm calling them all in now, and keeping the authorities out of your hair while you're gone. I need you to fund this expedition to find Lost Station Circé. We need ships to accompany the *Benbow*, supplies and fuel to last the trips both there and back, and storage capacity for anything we managed to bring back."

It was several minutes before anyone seemed able to speak. They were all still staring at the map, hooked on that small line running to what was apparently their fortunes in waiting. It was only when Sygint nodded to Livesey to shut off the display that the spell was broken. Donovan was the first to speak.

"I have a distinct interest in this venture, chiefly for its historical value. What we may find there could change our views on the Cluster's society five centuries ago. If the others are willing to donate as well, I think I can ensure that we have ample fuel and supplies, in addition to some fine archaeological and exploration equipment which I can loan from my holdings."

Dashall looked more skeptical and eventually voiced his concern. "I agree that this is a tempting proposition. But we'll be doing more than just returning a favor here. This is a bloody big investment. And for what? Some mythical station."

"We've proved here that it isn't mythical." Sygint's voice was like honey. "Livesey wouldn't lie about something like this. And she'd know if it was faked. And I know for a fact that you've got more than enough cash to invest in this venture."

There was a silence that lasted every minutes. Finally Gustav broke it.

They leaned forward and spoke in a strange clipped drawl, soft hands playing across the table as if in time to an unheard backing beat.

"I think we should all remember that the Synod made navigating any-where near or inside the Uncharted Belt illegal without special permission? And that the route takes us past one of the most unstable stars in the Cluster."

Donavan's reply came through a smirk. "Of course you would be the kill-joy here. It is not as if you have got as much or as many resources as we have. What can you bring?"

The former star spoke with a childlike simplicity. "Ships."

Sygint continued with more than a touch of relish. "Since business dropped for Jacklyn, they've got quite a lot of ships spare. Those ships can easily be fitted up and ready to go within the next week. Then it's two weeks there, maybe another week investigating, and two weeks back with the booty or the station, whichever's easier to transport. We take longer trips delivering freight."

It was plain from their expressions that the investors were beginning to lose sight of the luster. Solet clearly saw disaster looming. He glanced at Sy-gint, who seemed also to note that same hesitance. He leaned forward, his voice becoming low and eager, with an undertone of desperation that only Livesey could clearly hear.

"Think about it. You've got three options. Contact the Synod about this, get caught up in years of red tape before they'll likely say no or take a lion's share of any profits. Invest now, and become part of the biggest treasure haul since the Cluster was founded. Or leave it, and pass up on your chance to get a haul that'll make the Synod's annual budget look like pocket change."

The three looked at each other. Again their faces were pathetically easy to read. It was risky. If they were found out, it would mean big trouble from the Synod. Traveling into the Uncharted Belt without permission was risky, but the prize was incredible. Each had their own allegory to stoke their imagination. Unbidden, Livesey's mind recalled mythical cities of endless wealth from different cultures. The human El Dorado, the Feles domain of Ora-Chaya, the Kavki's pseudo-historical City of a Thousand Generosities, the Ekri's desert diamonds rising to be claimed by a worthy hand.

The three must've been thinking of those ancient places too on some level. Each was seeing their fortune made, then seeing the risks from the Synod, perhaps seeing also the risk of one or more of the sponsors turning on their fellows. But the lure of cash, of fame, of a journey toward something beyond any of their expectations was more than enough to assuage their fears. Sygint's face betrayed his eagerness, as did the others. Livesey could see it in their eyes, that expression of wanderlust which blinds all to danger.

Again, Donovan spoke first. "I can provide most of the equipment, and ensure that we get out and back without too many awkward questions. If the others are in favor."

Sygint nodded, and turned to Dashall. The financier took a little time in speaking, his fingers drumming a little rhythm on the desk. He finally voiced his opinion.

"I think this venture is risky, but given the high return.... Even if we have to disassemble the station itself, the data there should be worth something."

Livesey's face twitched with sudden anger. It wasn't anything she could stop even if she wanted to. She always hated how casually people could talk about buying and selling data. She was, in essence, an entity of data housed within a physical body. Gustav was the last person to answer.

"My ships are tuned to work economically on Neo White Oil. We can make the entire trip with ease so long as the tanks are full."

Oh, no. That was always going to be the difficult point. Solet spoke now.

"The *Benbow* runs on White Oil. My crew estimate we'll need some time to refuel ourselves before heading out, and may require a reserve."

Sygint nodded, turning to the others. "We can accommodate that, I'm sure. A part of the agreement is that the crew of the *Benbow* will accompany us. Be our lead ship, in a sense. Since they have the map, it seems only fitting."

Donovan and Gustav spoke almost at the same moment. Neither had any objection. Dashall might have said something else on the subject, but he remained quiet. The words he might've said were so plain to Livesey as to be sickening. The majority had voted with the chaff. Finally Gustav spoke, their eye fixing on Sygint with a sudden shrewdness.

"How about the shares?"

There was a prolonged silence. This was the perennial difficulty, regardless of origin or people or creed. Given the chance, they would divide everything very unevenly. To her surprise, it was Gustav who spoke again. Their voice appeared to be the only one with a semblance of reason outside the *Benbow* representatives.

"I suggest that we divide based on share settlement. We all presume that the wealth there is quite fantastic. In my opinion, we should divide it equally between ourselves, with suitable remuneration and possible... privileges for the crews we hire. And to avoid any dirty business, we should each have a controlling part of our portion. If one of us dies, that renders pieces of this prospective fleet inoperable."

Dashall snorted. "That'd be asking for trouble."

"But also quite a safeguard." Donovan smiled appreciatively at Gustav. "I commend the approach. It would also give us greater incentive to keep each other alive. I like your humor, Jacklyn. Your reputation is as much as I've heard."

There wasn't any humor in Gustav's face, nor was there any reply. But was that a "Belt up" she saw forming at the edges of their lips, mouthed rather than spoken. Sygint spoke again in the manner of a master of ceremonies bringing matters to a conclusion.

"Then since we seem to be all agreed. I think we should get this written up. A private contract between the *Benbow* crew and us four here. We'll call it... the Lost Land Enterprise. That suits us quite well, I think. We each have a share in its success or failure, not that we'll have the latter." He grinned. "And I think we can find a suitable number of crewpersons to join us on this. Eh?"

Each looked at the other, and Donovan and Dashall both nodded. Livesey saw the doubt in Gustav's eyes, quickly suppressed. Once again, Lost Station Circé had worked its magic. The investors looked at each other, then at Sygint. Donovan spoke for the whole.

"I think we're in agreement. Perhaps now, since all the principals are here, we should draw up this contract. Here, in this room, we form our company."

So it was done. The necessary persons, sworn to secrecy, had been waiting in an adjoining room for this moment. Sygint pressed a small button and they all walked in, almost glowing with anticipation at the legal tussle now to begin. Clauses, provisions, provisos and stipulations are the closest thing many lawyers experienced to sensual arousal in the course of their work. For some of those who had been called, this contract, with its potential for secret remuneration, was the equivalent of a year of constant arousal.

Livesey watched the contract take form over the next half hour with a clear and palpable greed. She saw the riches of data and wealth rushing toward the *Benbow*'s crew, eager to be found. Solet also saw it, probably felt it more deeply than she. Odd dreams rose to tempt her, quickly suppressed. It was quickly decided how the labor provision would be divided. Donovan would provide all the equipment and some specialist personnel for the salvaging operation. Dashall's deep pockets and connections would get them through the funding, crewing and travel pass stages, granting passage into the Uncharted Belt. Gustav pledged their three best ships, the *Grand*, the *Kilner*, and the *Wydrayn*, to carry the necessary supplies and personnel. The three also insisted on coming, which puzzled Sygint for some reason but was exactly what Livesey had expected. When pressed in a casual way, each had their reasons.

Donovan. "I don't want anyone touching anything I might want but myself. You may say I've got trust issues… and I have."

Dashall. "I'm not gonna be left out of this. I'm a guy who likes to be in on the action, in at the kill. And for a kill this big, I wanna be in."

Gustav. "I don't want to just wait around. If this goes bad, I want to be there making sure we all did everything we could to salvage it."

So it was done, written and enshrined in the covenants of secrecy. It would take a week to get everything together, with permits being rushed through at top speed by Dashall, all the necessary equipment being transported by fast shuttle for Donovan, and Gustav summoning his ships to Cape Cisternaea. Solet watched them discuss these aspects, then as they all left, he was left alone with Sygint and Livesey. Solet got up.

"Looks like we've got what we wanted."

"Sure." Sygint looked at Solet with a smirk. "We all have what we want. Money. And you'll be able to keep your piece of junk running for another few years with your share. Hell, you'll be able to buy a new ship."

Solet nodded noncommittally. Livesey and he returned to their accommodation, now confirmed to be theirs until the time came to leave. A week, that'd been the estimate. One more week of mere dreams, then the journey. The time when all would head out on the voyage of a lifetime.

———

SOLET HAD JUST updated the others when they got a call. The repairs to the *Benbow* were nearing completion. Solet and Syndac went to Docking

Sector 8's repair bay where their ship was resting. Most of the work was inside on the drive core's housing area on D-13, but a few crews were repairing the usual stress and impact scars left by travel on other decks, particularly on D-15 and D-1 and round the peripheries. Syndac looked at it.

"It's all very well having a skeleton crew when traveling between ports and planets, but for the Uncharted Belt we'll need something more."

Solet eyed his second. "How much more, might I ask?"

Syndac shrugged, her fur ruffling slightly around the necklace she wore. "As much as we like. We shall at least be pursuing an antique space habitat with tech worth selling. At most, this expedition is in pursuit of the greatest treasure hoard in the Cluster's history."

"If Livesey is to be believed—"

"Do you continue to doubt her? You should cut her some slack. She may not be organic, and I will be the first to admit that I do not get along with her, but she is a person. With feelings that can be hurt."

"A machine's a machine, and I don't trust them to think for themselves. I prefer flesh and blood manning my ships. I once did have them manning it, until it was taken from me."

"Don't go harping on that."

"I won't."

Syndac's tone abruptly hardened. "But since you continue to hold no love for androids of any kind, perhaps you could rely on me, for once. You have your little clique around you and that is good enough for standard cargo runs, but you need labor. The drudgery of the ship that makes us complain and jibe about it day in and day out."

"So what do you suggest? Can you magic a crew out of nothing?"

"No, but I can entice a crew that will work from the people on Cape Cisternaea. Short hops are all very well, but do you really think a seven-person crew can manage that ship on a trip lasting upward of a month?"

Solet looked into that cold stare, the strange twist of the lip that showed nothing and everything. She always did have a way with her, the little.... Finally he sighed and nodded.

"All right. You can go hunt for your crew."

"Thank you, 'Captain.'"

Solet almost replied. He was used to Syndac's chiding, her condescending comments. She wanted to be captain, he would see her as captain over his dead body. This had been tersely accepted within their first month of working together. Nothing had changed, nor would it. They were both too set in their ways to change so drastically that their enmity would vanish. Their wealth wouldn't bring unity to their crew, as much as he wanted it to do so.

So what would happen once they had this wealth? Faarax would go off with his partner, Lenore and Faarax would settle their strange relationship, Alkmeney would do whatever she wanted to, and Syndac would probably get herself her own ship again. As for Sudu and Livesey, he didn't know. Probably start up their own shipping line or something silly like that. As for Solet, he couldn't abandon the *Benbow*. For all his fantasies, he had been looking after it for so long that he couldn't just abandon It. Any more than he could just abandon a child of many years in the street.

He reached out from his place on a walkway, and touched the edge of a ship wing. It had once been designed for atmospheric entry, but its age prohibited anything from low-G and warp travel. He smiled.

"I'll sort you out, old thing. Promise. After all, you're the only thing I can call mine."

FILE 5

SETTING OUT

*We must see that he comes to no harm while on his homeward journey,
but when he is once at home he will have to take the luck he was born with
for better or worse like other people.*

—Homer

THE DAY OF the expedition's departure seemed to advance with all the lightning determination of a slow water leak. Even as the three investors struggled to get everything going as fast as possible, some new obstacle rose up in their path and halted them. To any who knew Ancient Earth history or just lived in certain parts of the Cluster, they could understand in full. It was the delay of the late contract, the stray message or delivery, the long journey that never seems to end. It was slowly driving Solet up the wall.

"Easy now." He muttered under his breath, looking at the outer shell of the *Benbow*. "This isn't any different from the usual contract. Just another pick-up."

Lies, of course. This was different. They couldn't go to the Synod to get their requests and needs expedited. If they did, they would be struck with so many provisos and sanctions that the enterprise would die before it began. Instead, they haggled and negotiated and cajoled the additional parties into hurrying things along. They came up with excuses and plausible reasons for haste, but never once—except to the most trustworthy—gave away the true intent of their mission.

Three days before the end of the predicted week, Gustav's ships arrived, and they were all that had been described and expected. They were large, but modern, and had Neo White Oil engines which could store enough for a two-month journey. Enough to cross half of the entire Cluster without refueling. More than enough to travel to Lost Station Circé. The *Grand,* the *Kilner,* and the *Wydrayn* were divided between the three. Gustav took the smallest ship, the *Kilner,* for themselves. They refused to take anything more but usual supplies.

Dashall had brought all his financial muscle and skill to bear on the task of funding and provisioning this expedition. He had also been searching for discreet people willing to go on such a speculative adventure. He had made an invested of several hundred thousand, and though a drop in the ocean compared to the assets he could draw on, it was still a task to keep these transactions low key. A speculative investment was his excuse, with suitable provisions due to its risk. True in essentials, though lacking key details. He took the *Grand,* and as Donovan noted in private, it more than suited the Feles's oversized ego.

As for Donovan, her great mind was brought to bear on getting specialists and equipment from her own not-insignificant stores. Aboard the medium-sized *Wydrayn,* she created a small cabal of scientists, astroarchaeologists, deep space survivalists, and engineers whose lives had been built upon the declassification and deconstruction of ancient structures and ships. She had also bought up and stored histories and technical treatises and archival sources on the technology and society of the time when the ancient station was supposed to have been built. If they ran into problems with doors and locks, she wanted to be prepared.

The *Benbow* was another matter altogether. It was the odd one out, the ship no one expected to make the journey. Compared to the other three, it was old and creaky. It needed normal White Oil for its Black-class White Engine. Gustav said they would make sure a suitable supply for the return journey was taken as part of the *Kilner's* supplies. This was in spite of everyone saying they should just leave the ship at Cape Cisternaea and go on one of the others. But Solet stood firm, and everyone had to shrug their shoulders and accept it. The *Benbow* was coming with them, with all its faults and foibles.

"And I stay here, as broken as she was."

Solet's hand raised slowly, resting against the port window. These crude, ugly arms. Lifelike in shape, but clearly artificial, metallic and obvious. The skin grafts had failed long ago, and he was almost resigned to looking like a freak.

"But maybe... maybe I can look normal again. Become normal again. Wash away what took my arms from me."

A beautiful dream. One he'd had dozens of times in the dark recesses of his mind. And Lost Station Circé might just bring it to fruition.

———————————

THE DAY BEFORE their departure, Faarax visited Evelyn. They were sitting by the window as usual, and as the older one turned to see the young man enter their room, they smiled with an unusual warmth.

"Hello."

"Hello."

Echoing each other. That had always been an awkward sign between them. Their innocent little pairing had started with an awkward echoing of "hello." Evelyn forestalled Faarax's half-formed rejoinder.

"I hear you're leaving soon. I didn't expect it to be so sudden."

"We'll be away for about a month this time."

"This time? Isn't it likely to be for all time?"

"What d'you mean?"

"I think you know. The local Dark ClusterNet's been talking about nothing else round here for the past three days. Ever since that newcomer Gustav's ships arrived and strange shipments started pouring in."

"Things move around."

"Not like this."

There was a pause, then Evelyn rushed over and took Faarax's hands. There was a pleading expression in their eyes that Faarax didn't remember seeing before. A terrible, desperate appeal to his humanity.

"Faarax, bail out. I've got a bad feeling about this. It's like... I had a dream last night, you know. I dreamed of you, being taken away in a medical pod after being attacked by some terrible beast. A beast with a normal body and face, but eyes without a soul. A bug-eyed monster."

"You and your dreams. You know I don't believe in that stuff. Any more than I believe in souls. It's just tribal nonsense."

"But surely you must have faith. Lenore has faith. Even Livesey has some degree of faith, or so you said once. Surely someone can have a soul."

Faarax ducked the subject. The discussion of whether, in this age of space travel and scientific advancement, faith and soul had any meaning was far beyond his patience or understanding. But Evelyn was clearly frightened. They hadn't been this tense, this earnest, in all the time he had known them. Faarax found himself embracing Evelyn for the very first time. Not like a younger brother, or anything like blood family, or even just a friend, but like someone who…. Who what? He didn't know. Was it just the emotions from the upcoming departure that were making him like this?

He finally made his decision. "You know that datacube I got? The one from that old man?"

"Yes?"

"It's got good data on it. Data for something big. And we're part of the expedition that's getting it."

"You're not serious."

"I am."

This was hardly right to calm Evelyn. Without any word to Faarax, they pulled away and went to the window again. Staring out on the poky street and stark view into space, where the filtered light of Megara-Lux was showing, Evelyn looked like a pose for some statuette of tortured martyrdom. They were trying to screw themselves up to saying something.

"What is it?"

"I… had a visit, while you were gone. The Law Officers came. They questioned me about you. They…. You didn't tell me the man you met was killed."

"It didn't seem important."

"It is. It was. I know it. He was killed because of that datacube. You know it. Don't insult my intelligence."

"What did the Law Officers want?"

"They wanted to know whether I'd ever met him. They…. They didn't…. Faarax, he was a *criminal*. An *old* criminal. Have you ever heard the name Black Sutton?"

"Black…. No, I don't think so."

"Honestly, and you a crewman." The brief return of their old wry humor brought a smile to Faarax's face. "Black Sutton was one of the most notorious space pirates in the last century. About twenty years ago, Black Sutton terrorized the trade routes with her ship. When she died in an ambush, those surviving crew that weren't captured scattered to the winds and were never found. Until now."

"So that guy was part of this Black Sutton's crew?"

"Yeah."

"What of it?"

"What of it? Oh, for god's sake, wake up, Faarax! That datacube…. What if Black Sutton had it, and this man stole it? And the crew's survivors are coming after the people who have it now?"

Faarax pressed close again, placed his hands on Evelyn's shoulders. In those few moments, the two forgot the upcoming journey, the terrible weight of worry on each of their minds. They were two people, looking into an unknown future, finding consolation in each other's touch. It couldn't last long, but while it happened it was like touching enlightenment. Then Faarax pulled away.

"I must go. There's lots to do before we sail. Look after yourself, Evelyn. And who knows, we might have that trip to the Capitol Worlds after all."

Evelyn's voice was wan, unconvinced. "Perhaps."

Faarax returned to the *Benbow* in a rotten mood, snapping at Alkmeney when she attempted to make conversation as she was checking off a list of cargo. He pushed past her and she looked after him with a hurt expression he did his best to ignore. The walkway creaked slightly under his feet, showing its age and lack of use. This dock had been created for ships like the *Benbow*, and so the *Benbow* was forced to use old equipment and the same kind of rickety conditions that her crew lived in from day to grimy and rocky day.

Upon passing through the main airlock and entering the lower decks, Faarax found Lenore working on a faulty transport pod. A casual glance showed that the door control mechanism was at fault. Lenore muttered to herself as she carefully adjusted the plasma wiring, causing the pod to try moving off, to attempt a vertical slide into the roof, and once to open and close its doors so fast that it created a strobe effect with the interior light. Finally she let out a curse as a snap of feedback struck her hand. As if in response, the lift door gave an off-key chirrup and stuck in a half-open position as a tinny remnant of its voice tried to speak.

Faarax bent over the hissing Feles. "Need help?"

"Love it. I didn't think you'd be back so soon."

"I've say my goodbyes to Evelyn. What else is there to stay for?"

"Hmm. Well, hold this coupling will you, and see if you can reach behind the paneling and push that socket out a bit. I think someone rammed the connector in last time and pushed things out of alignment."

Faarax crawled in next to Lenore and, with a little difficulty, got his well-muscled arm into the curving space. It took some time, but he found the socket cradle and pushed everything back into place, then held it firm as Lenore reconnected the local systems. There was a buzzing, then the lift door opened. Lenore sighed.

"I'll be glad when we have more people. Doing these repairs like this really drains the soul."

"I thought this was Sudu's job."

"He's busy with the engine, and the new crew haven't settled yet, so I got roped in. Almost enough to make one toss oneself into the warp field."

"Death by warp field, I don't think I'd thought of that one."

Lenore glared at Faarax. "Don't try it. You would be in there with me. And I believe the idea was that one of us should survive. Mutual destruction is not desired."

"Very well."

The two moved into the transport pod, which while slow and a little noisy it reached the barely-used personnel area. Here, in older and better days, a large auxiliary crew would have been stationed. Seven might be the minimum number to run the *Benbow*, but it didn't allow for breaks and injuries. With help from their sponsors, Syndac had gathered an ideally-sized crew of around twenty-six. This made the total crew including the *Benbow* veterans thirty-three, more than enough and plenty to spare. They were from all the Allied Peoples across the Cluster, and all looked like they had seen things.

As the two came into the crew quarters on D-9, they saw the new crew prepping and adjusting their sleeping pods, where they could relax between shifts or sleep during allotted periods outside overtime. The pods, things just large enough for a medium-height Kavki, fused freedom and enclosure with their translucent lids and solid black sides merging in with the Grey walls and white pathway between them. Faarax smiled to himself at the variety of sizes. Their design originated with humans during their exodus from Ancient

Earth, where they had preserved their bodies through centuries of flight. Now they were just sleeping pods, adaptable to each Allied People.

As he looked at the scene, Faarax struggled not to laugh at the odd snatches he caught of newcomers adjusting to these creaky old-fashioned environs. The vignettes seemed endless. An Ekri arranging the rests on the inside to perfectly support its arching back and digitigrade legs, one of which was artificial. A Feles struggling with a faulty control that kept it violently bouncing between human and Kavki positions. As Lenore looked down the lines of crewpersons, she frowned.

"That's strange. Syndac said she'd found twenty-six. I see only twenty-four."

"Probably a couple are late."

"Hmm."

"I do wish you wouldn't say that. It makes you sound like an animal."

Lenore might have responded, but the door at the far end of the chamber opened. A sharp, female voice snapped across the space.

"All to attention!"

The effect was electric. Every single person there snapped out of what they were doing and stood to attention, hands folded across their bellies, eyes staring directly in front with the cold fixation of the soldier or the trained worker. Faarax felt shaken at seeing the voice's owner. Syndac was standing there, and in her eyes was such a gleam that she was almost making her two fellows to stand to attention. Syndac, having briefly seemed to tower in command, relapsed into her more laconic self and looked up and down the rows.

"Where are the two humans?"

As if on cue, the doors opened and Faarax was shoved aside by a pair of humans who quickly took their places in either row. An odd couple, clearly related, with strange parallel birthmarks across their left and right eyes. The odd feeling of coolness each one exuded even while in movement almost made him shiver. Syndac looked over the now-whole compliment of crew and nodded.

"Now you will meet our captain, Solet."

She stepped aside and Solet entered. None of the twenty-six moved or spoke as he looked down their ranks. Faarax almost whistled, and certainly gulped. This didn't feel like anything real. Solet's voice echoed down the long chamber.

"You don't know me. But through my second-in-command, I know all of you. I know you're all veterans of the space trade, all able to hold your own in conditions many would call impossible. Impassable. Unchartable." The captain looked at each in turn. "This mission is not what you might expect. This isn't just some risky trade deal. It's an expedition to find a lost treasure. A station holding materials now worth a vast sum. It's a place you may have heard off. Lost Station Circé."

Not an eye moved. Not a mouth twitched. Faarax felt even more unsettled. From his experience seeing crew heading out for profitable trade runs, this kind of thing should've sent them into paroxysms of joy. These twenty-six took it like a normal, everyday cargo run. A few might've behaved like that, but all of them?

Lenore had probably seen it first, but Faarax had been her pupil in so many things, and was only second in spotting it. His eyes saw one person who looked slightly fidgety. A Kavki male whose eyes flashed left and right while his body stayed erect. As Solet continued speaking, he moved down their ranks, like a general in some resistance army. And all the while, the Kavki male grew more and more uneasy.

"You've all been chosen for a specific reason. We've previously survived aboard this ship as a small crew of seven. Now, going into uncharted areas of our galaxy beyond the Cluster, we need a full complement to face the challenges ahead. And I do mean challenges. If you still want to stay, then you may remain. If you wish to leave, say so now. But know this, for participating in this expedition, you will all receive a share large enough for you to enter a comfortable lifetime retirement."

There was silence for a long time. Then the Kavki spoke. His voice was that perfect pitch between calm statement and querulous protest.

"I fear you must depart with only twenty-five. I cannot commit myself to a venture such as this. Forgive me."

With rapid movements, he picked up the kit he'd barely started to unpack, then walked out past Syndac. As she passed him, Faarax caught the slightest expression on her normally solid face. What was it? Amusement? Satisfaction? Maybe even…. No, he was getting fanciful ideas. The stress of the upcoming flight was getting to him. Ah well, best to pay it little mind. Syndac usually had some kind of weird expression on her face, even if it was mostly smug.

Later, Faarax and Sudu were working on a small coupling when one of the new crew appeared behind them. Faarax turned and looked. It was the man with the birthmark over his left eye. As he approached, the man's face looked solid and sullen, but when he was nearly on top of them, he smiled and crouched down. The change of expression was seen by Faarax, and for whatever reason that smile frightened him.

"I'll see to that. My sister's on the other end. We should be able to trace the fault."

Sudu sounded a little offended. "Are you assigned to maintenance today?"

"Syndac said you might need help. D'you mind?" He didn't wait for an answer and threaded his hands between them. "Name's Dexter, by the way."

Sudu's reply was stiff. "Nice to meet you."

Faarax rose slowly, impressed at how the man's hands were working. They were so soft and slight, strangely in contrast to the bulk of his arms. But there was a strange pattern of wear on his palms, marks of some cord constantly drawn tight, something wrapped round the palm for long periods. As he worked, the fingers moved with a smooth and stylish speed. Finally he smiled up at the young boy.

"You look like you've seen a few things."

"Yeah." Faarax was reluctant to answer, especially as he saw Sudu glance down disapprovingly at the interloper. "I've been aboard the *Benbow* for most of my life."

"Wow. Ah, here we are!"

There was a shuddering, then the power line corrected its flow and the flickering lights overhead stabilized at their standard brightness. Dexter rose with a groan and flexed his fingers.

"I'd say… needs some new wiring. That's stressing."

"Thank you, we had noticed." Sudu spoke tartly.

Dexter was about to leave, but Faarax recalled him. For all he disliked him on some instinctual level, best not to let him depart on a sour note.

"Thanks for the help. By the way, what's your sister's name?"

"Sinestra."

"I see. Well, I hope all goes well for us all."

Again that strange smile, both forced and genuine, and the man Dexter departed. It took a moment for Sudu to speak again.

"I don't like that man. He's…. There's something wrong about him. Like a *deiduud.*"

"A what?"

"A *deiduud.* It was a plant on our native worlds. Went extinct about a century ago. It lived in poor swampy soil, and supplemented its diet with the local small fauna. The name *'deiduud'* doesn't have a direct translation for your software chip. I think the closest I could come to is 'smiling killer.'"

"I know he isn't pleasant, but you don't seriously think he's a smiling killer. Do you?"

"I just don't trust him. Something's off about him. Also, have you noticed anything about Livesey recently?"

"What?"

"Well… she's distant. Absorbed in something."

"What thing? You're not being honest with me."

Sudu remained silent for some little time. He seemed about to start pacing, then Faarax thought he might leave. Finally he burst out, his voice holding deep emotion.

"It's that data. The datacube she's got with her. It's all she seems to be thinking about. When I talk with her, when she's doing her tasks around the ship, her mind appears to be somewhere else. And when she's in sleep mode, I see something in her face. Some kind of movement in her lips, like she's reciting binary code."

"Binary code?"

"I know it sounds silly, but… I think she's becoming addicted to that data. I saw some of it myself when we first had it. It's incredible coding. But she's got a kind of obsession with it that I find frightening."

"Maybe I should talk to her."

"No. That's fine. It's probably nothing." The Ekri smiled. "I think I'll use this rest period to plan out my engineering study. Utera University, here I come."

Sudu did depart then with that strangely forced smile on his face. Faarax watched him leave, and then went himself to another job on his long list of pre-flight preparations. Coincidentally, as he was navigating the observation walkway around the warp engine, he saw Livesey. She was leaning on the railing, staring at the rippling cone of energy surrounding one of the larger nodes on the humming engine.

He then realized how right Sudu had been. She was staring into space, a tool for some job held loosely in one hand, the other propping up her chin in the manner of some great thinker of Ancient Earth or the Feles homeworld. Such abstract and deep meditation was something Faarax had never seen in her before. He approached and tapped her lightly on the shoulder. He might have hit her, for she jerked sideways and glanced at him with anger. Her face quickly softened, but the mask had slipped and Faarax was disturbed by what it revealed.

"Oh, Faarax. I didn't see you. Did you want something?"

"No. I just…. Well, I'm on my way to a job and—"

"Hoy!" The oblivious Alkmeney approached from the other end of the walkway, waving at Faarax. "Sorry to butt in, but I need some help. The navigation system routers are acting up a bit. I need you to do some adjustments while I work them with a few of the new crew, okay?"

Faarax sighed. "Okay. Coming."

He left, but glanced back. Within a few seconds of being left alone, Livesey had sunk back into her reverie. He kept his eyes on her until the door hissed shut and he turned his attention to Alkmeney's chatter.

"And so I said, you shouldn't pack those things so close together, they might end up causing some kind of rupture and where would you be?"

Alkmeney had reached this stage of her prolonged dialogue when they neared the place where the work was taking place. There, by coincidence, Faarax saw what must be Dexter's sibling. She was on tiptoe near one of the ducts, peering in with a torch. Alkmeney approached with authority.

"What are you doing there?"

Sinestra turned with a disarming smile. "Someone reported overheating warnings in this area. Just been checking the duct wiring."

"But that's not where the duct wiring is." Alkmeney's face was admonishing, almost accusatory. "That's under the inspection hatch below the duct. Have you ever been on a ship before?"

"Not one like this." Sinestra smiled sheepishly. "I've only had experience on modern cruisers before, then my brother and I got stranded here by a company folding and we've been taking odd jobs until—"

Faarax interrupted quickly. "We don't want a life story. I thought newer cruise ships put their wiring in different pathways to the ducts entirely."

Sinestra spoke with an easy assurance. "Some cargo cruisers still use the old system. More economical on space. One extra bit of cargo to squeeze in, and one more cash payment at journey's end."

Alkmeney sighed. "Well, you know where the wiring is now. Do what you need to do, then leave us in peace. We've got some crucial tuning work to do here."

THE DAY CAME for departure. All was made ready among the crew, any ties they had back home, settled or severed, and port authorities who might have raised an eyebrow at the impressive overhead costs given to them had their departments not been eternally short of funds duly paid. There were final tune-ups and checks on the *Benbow*, with the result that someone managed to fuse all the lights on the upper decks due to blowing out an old junction, calling for an emergency repair.

Faarax passed into the docks and walked quickly for the *Benbow's* docking port. What had those reports and pieces of gossip said? Donovan was checking and rechecking her many and varied instruments for examining and preserving her imagined booty. Dashall was also constantly checking and rechecking the accounts and estimates he had prepared for the expedition. Doing it in less than the budgeted sum would be incredible if not impossible. Going over was unthinkable, even if the imagined prize was as vast as he was led to believe. Gustav was late aboard their own ship, and seemed little interested in anything besides their own thoughts and imaginings.

The *Benbow* was all ready, and as the hour for departure came, there was a great commotion in the docks. At the observation windows, despite efforts to keep much of its purpose secret, vast crowds had gathered. Leaving his rooms that day, he'd caught whispers about a "group of lunatics" going off to "hunt for treasure buried in space." Among those who pressed against the rail of the viewing panels nearest the *Benbow* had been Evelyn, who stood on tiptoe with their long hair falling down around their face. He hadn't gone up to her. They had said their goodbyes, best not to create unpleasantness.

He was soon on the bridge of the *Benbow*, together with most of the core seven crew. Alkmeney and Livesey were in the engine control area on D-13, probably micromanaging the new staff so there would be no accidents. Solet, Syndac, Lenore, Sudu and Faarax had taken their seats on the bridge, Faarax filling Livesey's role for the moment. There was the signal, a synchronized alert to all ships in this four-part convoy. The journey was about to begin.

How many dreams were riding on this? How many hopes and fears? Alkmeney was clearly eager to get her hands on capital to create a new life beyond the *Benbow*, and Sudu had already been planning out with engineering university he would apply to for an advanced qualification. It was almost funny. The others were less discernible, and offered no distracting little amusements to take his mind of Evelyn's unease. And his own preoccupations.

The casting-off checks and mechanisms worked without a hitch, probably for the first time in years. The *Benbow* cast off last of all, the smallest ship ready to join its larger fellows at their head. It was almost impressive. Their little ship was the unquestioned guide beyond the Outer Worlds into the Uncharted Belt. There, waiting for them all, was their greatest find. Their greatest treasure.

"To all hands, make ready." Solet spoke in the most traditional manner possible. "We are heading out. In two weeks, we shall reach our destination. But until then…. *Rkakhnen, sygrikhca.*"

Faarax frowned. Lenore had taught him a few basic phrases from the Feles language that still refused to translate into the common tongue. One of those was a common blessing across all her people's tribes. *"Rkakhnen, sygrikhca,"* an invocation to the ether's spirits to watch over voyages into the unknown. It had held good since primitive balks set out along rivers and across channels. Now it blessed these four ships as they powered up into warp, beginning their long journey toward the dark depths of space.

FILE 6

THE SUN SLOUGHING
ITS SKIN

Though I had lived by the shore all my life,
I seemed never to have been near the sea till then.

—Robert Louis Stevenson

IN HER SMALL private quarters, Alkmeney fiddled with her extremely old-fashioned ink-filled pen. These items were luxuries in some areas, but out in the sticks ink was still relatively easy to find. And here, in this place, she wanted to keep things private. Besides, this was a money-making opportunity. A special log that could be digitized and sold to people when they came back triumphant. Maybe not to one of the mainstream publications and risk the Synod's ire, but certainly to an underground blogging network where it would get the attention it deserved. A little extra for the business she wanted would not go amiss.

"The attention I deserve…. Now what to call it? I know, 'Navigator's Special Log.' That will be a good-enough title to start with."

Smuggling the paper on board had been a hassle, but worth it. Like ink, paper was relatively easy to find among the Outer Worlds compared to the tech-smothered Capitol Worlds. Solet had some strange dislike for physical media like this. But now she could write and write, using all sides and angles of the paper available to her. She would make this… a log of sorts. Yes, a special navigator's log. Double-checking the door was securely fastened, she settled down once more and began.

"Now let's see…." She muttered quietly to collect her thoughts. "'Special Log, Day 2.' Time's so difficult to determine when you're traveling at warp. I can double-check some of the time calculations when we get back to Cape

Cisternaea. Now where was I? So much more difficult at times when you are not dictating to an auto-writer."

Maybe start with a personal angle? Yes, best to get it flowing well. Start off with Livesey, saying that it would take twelve or thirteen days? Say thirteen, then if they went under or over, it would be more dramatic. But what to do then? Better to save talking about other crew members in detail for later in the log. Put in a few sketch ideas on their own sheet, that was best. Now what next?

The new crew? Yes, that would be a good starting point. They were relatively friendly, almost like a close-knit family they had joined. Her memory lingered with pleasure over the long conversation she had enjoyed with the one called Skuddy. That wonderful discussion on improving the nav computer's accuracy and efficiency through a minor coding adjustment. That Skuddy knew her tricks—splicing code to cut down computation time, rerouting some of the coding paths for more direct feeds without compromising on data scans. All interesting, and all slightly questionable. Alkmeney's old nav tutor would have foamed at the mouth.

"Where did you receive your tutorship?" Alkmeney had asked.

Skuddy's reply had been jokey, almost a little evasive. It seemed she had not been learning through the standard routes. On the whole, Alkmeney had taken a liking to the crew. Maybe she could poach some of them for her trading business when she had the means to set it up. So why was Sudu so mistrustful? He always kept a less-than-hidden eye on them. But there was that one episode the previous day, shortly after they had set off.

"Yes, that could be a good little entry."

She began writing. It had been… the middle of the day? Yes, the middle of the day. Sudu had noticed an air flow issue through one of the subsection vents of D-13, Port Side. Since Alkmeney was the nearest with any free crew-members, she had sent one down. It took them an age to answer, but they said it was feathering at one of the junctions. It would be a simple matter to shut it off and clean it. And then, somewhat abruptly, the crewmember called again and said it "could be cleared quite quickly."

Sudu was highly skeptical. But it was cleared. In a surprisingly short time. The person said they might do something like that on the one on the Starboard Side, since it "often goes in pairs." Sudu was even more suspicious. He had taken an intense dislike to the new crew, particularly those two siblings

Dexter and Sinestra. Alkmeney found them pleasant enough, especially compared to the majority of the crew. She tried striking up multiple conversations, but they shot them down with either silence, harsh wit, or vulgarity.

"Oh, yes, best make a note to myself. Do not talk with Sinestra about plays. That little comeback of hers is far too rude to record verbatim. At least Dexter apologized for her. Now what can I write about that…? No, I think I will just leave that bit out."

His mind lingered again on one of the new crew, a polite Kavki with some extraordinary stories as a merchant on the old Pyramia route. Incredible really, people still using that old route after all these years. Then that story about a brief stint in the Synod Enforcers. What had she said…? Yes, that would be a good addition to the account.

"Now what can I say? 'We still have issues in this day and age, but back then it was far worse. And Black Sutton was the worst of the worst, according to what she said.' I did so want to ask her everything she knew. What can I say there? Ah yes, 'She seemed a little tired and we decided to get the rest we both needed.' Hopefully I can get the rest of the story out of her tomorrow—" The buzzer sounded, and Alkmeney quickly pressed her receiver. "Yes, who is it?"

"Sudu. You're going to be late for your shift."

"I just need to finish something here."

"Fine. I don't want the newcomers there for a second longer than necessary."

Alkmeney struggled not to sigh as Sudu signed off. Maybe Sudu was jealous? Faarax too, at a guess. They had looked after the *Benbow* for years, probably thought of it as their own, for all they were as eager to leave as she. Hard to imagine other people coping easily with problems that had bonded the two together. There was one other thing that might be causing friction. In a few more days, they would be reaching the edges of charted space, maybe on the fourth or fifth day. And during that time, their small fleet would be passing close to the hypergiant Nox Vuldi.

"What did that report say? Liable to go supernova. Not soon, but within the near future. And yet astrological prediction was never an exact science. If it did go supernova before the predicted time, who knew what might happen. It might add days onto our trip. But then, we are far enough away that it probably will not matter if we get hit with some solar debris."

A good reminder. She had to wash her little charm soon. It was getting terribly dusty, and when it got dusty nothing but bad things happened. Smiling at her first literary effort, she shut the papers away and got ready for her shift.

"LIVESEY? LIVESEY!"

Livesey jerked from her reverie. She had been deep in the datacube's bottomless sea of information. Lying in her small bunk, her eyes open and glassy in the midst of her dive, she had been swimming through the sea of data with complete satisfaction. Sudu's harsh voice brought her back with such a jerk that one of the nuts holding the bed frame snapped. Something else to repair on this ever-broken ship. She rose carefully.

"Yes? What is it?"

"Solet wants you to get a look at the plasma couplings in the rear warp area. Flow's gone wonky. Something's been shorting there for the past hour and the new guy's not gotten there yet. Of course. If it keeps up like this we'll be forced out of warp and the other ships might leave us behind."

"Why can't you manage this?"

"I've got someone else to watch. That bloody Sinestra woman."

"I see." Livesey rose, then saw Sudu's face. "You want to say something else?"

Sudu looked conflicted as he spoke, hesitating at every second word. "How long... have you... been spending... diving into that cube?"

Livesey did a rapid calculation. "Approximately sixteen hours since I was first able to access it."

"Square that and you'd be right."

"Excuse me?"

"I said—"

"I heard what you said and I dislike the accusation. You're suggesting my calculation is inaccurate?"

"Yeah."

"Please explain."

"Livesey, I've never known you to falter in anything you do. You always perform your duties with promptness and exactness, but now.... You've missed several shifts since we left Cape Cisternaea six days ago. Your mind's been elsewhere in the most literal sense, all because of that thing inside you."

"I do wish you'd stop coddling me. Now, about this coupling...."

Livesey barged past Sudu before he could either continue his admonishment or respond to her curt change of subject. She was angry, at Sudu, and at herself. At herself because she knew, deep down, he was right. But what else could she do? How else could she alleviate the... craving? It was simple enough to just duck out when it was the *Benbow's* onboard data stores. They were simple, muddy, almost corrupt in their obtuseness. None drew her in, made her want to sail along their curves and lines, through their binary and squared lines of code until she forgot the meaning of time.

The datacube had awoken a sleeping dragon. She had so long forgotten that craving, the terrible pull of data. She had known it. Known it long ago in cyberspace, when she had worked for people who paid her in data to fuel her need. Her lust for its touch, its feeling through her neural pathways, the sensation of flame and brimstone that humans called "enlightenment." That was what they could never know.

"I'm addicted to enlightenment."

Her words were addressed to no one, voiced out loud when she was alone in the transport pod, with no one else to hear. And even then, she all but mouthed it. Only the sharpest ears could have told any words from her simulated breath.

Sighing and resigning herself to Sudu's displeasure, she made her way to the warp area to see to the plasma couplings. Not that members of the new crew couldn't see to them with aplomb, but Sudu had developed a "bee in the bonnet" about them. He was always there when they did work in his direct jurisdiction, sometimes held them up from simple repairs until he was there. If he wasn't careful, they might lodge a complaint with Solet. And since Solet was grateful to have any kind of large crew at all, Sudu would come off the loser.

The rear warp area was cooler than usual, as noted by Livesey's temperature reader and the shivering of an Ekri operator who was struggling to correctly type in instructions. Livesey couldn't help but smile. No matter how advanced people became in body and mind, cold fingers could never avoid mistyping something. The cool atmosphere was unpleasant, but necessary. Without it, several key control circuits might overheat from the constant strain of keeping the drive core in balance. All electronics generated heat of some kind, and needed cooling in some form. It was an absolute reality.

As Livesey checked over the conduit situation, a strange scene was playing out behind her. As one, a Feles, was at the top of a retracting ladder fixing a piece of pipeline for coolant. The other, a gruff-looking human, ended up tripping the wrong function and part-retracting the ladder. With an angry squawk, the Feles clung to the one solid pipe until the ladder re-emerged.

"Hoy! Careful down there! You almost had me off."

"I *did* try to warn you this ladder thing wasn't tuned properly."

"They need to get this fixed. Hell, why didn't they get this fixed?"

"It wasn't on the priority list, probably."

"Well, maybe when I'm down, we can sort it out. By the way, how's the wandering one? Tired yet?"

"Not at all—*Hist.*"

Livesey frowned, quickly turned her head. For a moment before all resumed normality, the human was glaring at her. The last time Livesey had seen such a glare was when accused of eavesdropping on a squadron commander in an earlier incarnation. The human's face switched with an impassive calm and the two changed topics to something quite urbane.

"Have you met Faarax yet? He's a dear when he's not being a sullen brat."

"Ouch. Still, I see what you mean. He's quite... solid."

"Sullen."

"What you call sullen, I call solid."

"It's that 'mother' of his. That Feles. She's a piece of work."

"Says the Feles."

"There's Feles, and Feles. She's—"

And it was then that the Kavki in charge of sorting out the couplings noticed their listener. Livesey pulled away from this equally-intriguing exchange.

"Up there." Livesey directed the Kavki out toward where the coupling rested, just a few feet from the warp field perimeter. "That's the trouble spot."

The Kavki, suited in the best protective gear available for in-flight repairs, stepped out and began working on the couplings. Livesey monitored the field as the repair was made, which turned out not to be a repair. It was more of an adjustment, a narrowing of the conduit caused by some maladjustment. Livesey wondered who had last had charge of this section, and how much Sudu would take glee in reprimanding one of the new crew if it turned out to be them.

But even as the Kavki returned to safety, there was a loud and wild alarm blaring. It was the kind of alarm no one wanted to hear. Livesey quickly tapped into the comms and called up to the bridge.

"This is D-13, warp control. What's the alarm for?"

Solet answered, sounding both angry and alarmed. *"We've had an early warning alert. That bloody star's about to burp right in our path. We'll need to slow down until it's gone by."*

"How long have we got?"

"Not long. Alkmeney says about fifteen minutes. She's trying to reduce our speed now. The others are too. If that stuff strikes us in warp—"

"All right." Livesey switched to wider communication. "Attention. Reduce warp power, prepare for solar strike protocols!"

Everyone acted with frantic speed. They all had impetus enough. They all knew what happened to ships that were struck by solar ejections during warp. The delicate warp bubble burst from the energy feedback, potentially triggering catastrophic collapse. The most notorious incident was the passenger liner Carnigi over eight centuries before. Hit by a massive solar flare, it had undergone warp inversion. The entire ship was simultaneously crushed and pulled apart, killing all crew and passengers. The Neo White Oil models had more cushioning against it, but the *Benbow* was ripe for a repeat performance.

Livesey also knew that the *Carnigi* disaster had been caused by a normal mass ejection, not the rampant charged cast-offs from a hypergiant. Nox Vuldi was not to be treated lightly. So the processes were put into motion to drop the ship out of warp, slowing the engines and tracking upcoming space objects to ensure smooth passage. The crew located their drop-out point, wound down the warp drive to one third power, had all hands possible braced for a bumpy exit.

But the dreaded encounter happened much earlier than anticipated. Seated in its place, solitary without planets or moons or even debris to accompany its dance, Nox Vuldi was going through its accelerated life. Predictions had placed its final "burp" in the next few decades. They were wrong. As the four-ship fleet came within its range, and Livesey was attending to one of her urgent duties, the fatal moment came. The star collapsed, all its mass forced inward as the nuclear fusion at its core was spent. And in that moment, it exploded, jettisoning all that it had been into the blackness of space.

There was the blare of another siren as this death scene registered, and Alkmeney's voice almost screamed over the intercom.

"Supernova impact in five minutes!"

"What?" Livesey switched on her comm. "Please, Alkmeney, repeat. Give me data."

"Supernova explosion detected from Nox Vuldi. Highest magnitude, maximum spread. Solar debris impact in five minutes."

"But…. Bridge, warp wind-down will take another eight minutes. We can't do it in five. Unless we do an emergency cut-out."

"DAMN!"

Up on the bridge, Solet let off this expletive and slammed his fist into the console, causing the display to glitch and shudder. Syndac, Lenore and Alkmeney looked at him. Here, now, he was in charge. The one to preserve them, the one to keep them all safe from this impending catastrophe. Alkmeney spoke.

"Sir, we'll have to do an emergency stop. It's our only choice."

Lenore cut in. "Are you mad? This ship wasn't designed to stand that kind of abuse, and most of the repairs haven't been tested under those stresses. If we do a cut-out, we could blow half our systems."

"But if we don't and that debris hits us, it could burst the warp field. We'll be torn to bits. I'd rather take some systems going out over certain destruction."

"And if those systems included life support? How long do you think we could hold out with a full crew aboard before we got it up and running again. Remember this ship runs on a centralized system."

Alkmeney shuddered at this knowledge. Part of the *Benbow's* age showed in its life support system, a vast network connected to a central hub. It was designed to stop sections shutting down by accident, and to allow back-up lines from the main system. However it also meant that if the core went, the entire ship was left with only the latest air injection for its crew. With just seven, there was no issue. With over thirty, it could mean ship-wide suffocation before the system was back online. Her reply was shaky.

"Even so, we cannot avoid that impact. Distance computation complete. Impact in four minutes. Sir, your orders!"

Ten seconds passed. Ten unbearable seconds while the supernova shock wave drew closer, the crew struggled to get the warp drive's power down, and the old crew prayed that there could be a way of saving the situation. It was like an old-fashioned limited time choice in a VR game, where a split-second decision is drawn out to several seconds—or eternally for more relaxed scenarios—and can mean life or death for the characters. But this was real life, and there were over thirty different lives riding on the decision. Thus was a captain burdened.

Finally he spoke.

"Oh, fuck it! Might as well try." He typed in the call frequency for the *Wydrayn* and summoned Donovan. "Donovan, this is urgent. I mean it, *urgent*. I need you to do an emergency scan and find out the energy frequency of the supernova discharge."

"Why—"

"Just fucking *do* it!"

The sharpness and curse combined moved Donovan faster than she was probably used to being moved by another. The scan was made. It was twenty seconds later that the result came, though it felt like twenty minutes.

"Frequency is MVF 0-10-54."

"Can you adjust the warp fields to match that? Or at least mimic it?"

There was a second of dead silence. Then Donovan laughed. It was not the kind of laugh that either mocked or agreed.

"You're bold, I'll give you that. I should have considered that. We'll need to get our warp fields down to two fifths power and—"

"Do it. And then get as close to the *Benbow* as possible in a triangle formation, with the *Benbow* at the center. We need to make it as much one big warp bubble as possible without triggering warp convergence and smashing into each other. Got it?"

Another pause. Donovan had linked in the others when she delivered her result, and they all looked uncertain. Finally, Donovan shrugged.

"You're the boss here. We'll get it done."

Dashall's audio channel broke in. *"Try to keep up. On your signal, Captain."*

The display shut off. Alkmeney checked the time to impact.

"Three minutes, twenty seconds."

"Livesey!" Solet barked into the comm. "Get the warp field down to two fifths strength, and prepare to match light frequency MVF 0-10-54 on my signal. You've got three minutes."

"Guess we'll have to do it. Out."

Lenore was staring at Solet. "What the hell are you doing?"

"If we can put up enough of a barrier, and match the light frequency of the blast, we'll be able to ride it out. It'll be bumpy, and might blow a few minor systems, but we'll be able to stay in warp and not blow ourselves up."

"And if it doesn't work?"

"The other ships have back-ups. We'll probably be blown to bits. Well?"

Alkmeney looked at the timer. "Impact in two minutes."

"If this works—" Lenore never finished her sentence.

Solet settled himself, watching the stream of orders and confirmations through the comm chat. The crews of all four ships were working like maniacs, lowering their warp field output and preparing the light frequency adjustment. It was a long two minutes. It felt like more than that. Every crew member who cared tried must be trying not to imagine the solar shock wave striking them. The other ships had reduced their warp field power quite quickly, and according to the display had moved into a horizontal triangle formation around the *Benbow*. The small ship rested at the heart of the formation, like a single cygnet protected by a gaggle of swans.

Alkmeney looked hard at the console, focusing on the slow ticking of time. "Impact in one minute…. Fifty seconds…."

Solet tightened his grip on the console. Syndac glared at him.

"Sometime today would be nice."

"Not yet." Solet spoke in a hiss. "We do it now, we might as well not do it at all."

"Forty seconds."

"All ships, stand by."

Through the displays, Donovan, Gustav, and Dashall all waited in expectation, their faces through the comm displays tense despite the relatively low risks to their own ships. The bridge crew of the *Benbow* were more worried, and all visibly prepared to leap into ordering lightning repairs if there was any sign of failure following the initial impact.

"Thirty seconds."

The tension was becoming more than palpable. Solet's mind wandered over his ship as the seconds ticked by. Where was everyone now? In his bunk area during a rest period, that cunt Faarax was perhaps waiting for death? Sudu, in another part of the ship probably supervising a routine repair, likely gripping the railings and braced himself for impact. In the engine control area, Livesey must've computed all manner of complications. Lenore, Syndac and Alkmeney struggled to maintain composure as the solar shockwave approached.

"Fifteen seconds."

Syndac grimaced, her oily fur giving off hard flashes of reflected emergency lighting. "I hope this does not go awry."

Solet's face was set as stone. "So do we all. You won't have much of a chance to rebuke me if it doesn't work."

Syndac gave him a strange look, then a curious half-smile crossed her face. It wasn't a pleasant expression to see on that face. In what were potentially the last few seconds of their lives, why was she smiling like that?

"Five, four, three, two—"

"*Mark!*"

There was an omnipresent hum as the warp fields shifted their energy signature. Solet could almost feel the warp field begin to bend and waver. It had not been designed to touch these wavelengths for more than a nanosecond. Alkmeney's voice screamed over the ship's comm.

"Impa—"

The next ten seconds played out so rapidly that it was impossible to track what happened. The wave of discharged solar energy from the exploding star struck even as the light wavelengths of the warp fields were synchronized. The wave seemed to flow into and around the field, treating it as a giant boulder in space, never once faltering and not clashing with its sympathetic structure. For any outside observer able to pierce the veil of warp travel, it must've looked beautiful. The four tight-packed ships with the solar energy flowing round it, causing minor discharge as the two energies met and reflected off each other. Such was the magnificent grace of a star that had reached the end of its life.

Inside, it was another story. Through the display, Solet saw each ship bounce back with a violent shudder and shake from the mid-flight impact, nudging their fields perilously close together. Anyone who had any sense had anchored themselves, or be flung around their ship interiors like rag dolls.

The *Benbow* would've been the worst, its small and ancient frame magnifying the impact tenfold.

On the *Benbow* bridge, few had strapped in, even as the solar wave had advanced. Solet was flung forward violently and felt his belt bite so hard that its edges cut skin and drew blood, forging welts where clothing provided a shield. Syndac clung to her console but was flung up and over like a gymnast performing a trick, letting out a pained hiss. Lenore was flung from her seat, but twisted in mid-air and tried to land in a crouch, though a further shudder sent her off balance and rolling into a corner. Alkmeney clung like grim death.

Syndac was shouting updates from her console above the ship's screams. "Energy feedback readings above eighty percent! Lighting going critical on Decks D-7 through D-12! Gravity field fluctuating on D-4 and D-6! Comms lost to D-11 Starboard side, D-5, D-2 Starboard side!"

There was a pause. The shuddering had ceased. Everyone waited for a moment, then began righting themselves. The blood oozed from cuts and grazes, and Solet momentarily felt like he would sleep for a day. Syndac's voice steadied.

"Systems within stress boundaries. Normal power signals returning. Wave has passed us. Beginning system—"

Alkmeney's voice, now with a more panicked note broke in. "Second debris wave incoming! Impact, ten seconds!"

"What?" Solet pulled his pain-addled mind back to reality and slammed the comm button. "All ships, match frequency again!"

"Five, four, three—*Ah!*"

The whole ship was thrown, and Solet barely had time to yell into the comm. "Mark!"

The hum resumed, but this time it was strained. The ship's power systems all pushed into the red and the drive core let out an agonized mechanical screech as it brushed the point of no return. Solet knew the sound. It was fighting against something powerful, something that had originally met with either no resistance or too much. This subtle embracing of its qualities after hostility threatened a contest of mutual destruction on the scale of matter and antimatter.

From the comm chatter still audible through the noise feedback, the other ships were likewise caught unawares by the sudden arrival of this second wave of debris, and they were thrown slightly off course. The warp field of the *Kilner* strayed just that little bit too close to the field of the *Benbow*, and a fresh alarm screamed.

Solet struggled to speak through the renewed strain that seemed to be bending his bones, but Alkmeney acted like lightning. She typed in an emergency correction, and the overworked computer forced through this priority command with a protesting shriek. The ship shifted slightly, allowing the warp fields to pass each other without fatal contact. For five unbearable seconds, the cacophonous roar continued, the terrifying screech of a ship struggling not to tear itself apart. Lenore, her feet braced and hands turning white from the power of her grip, was muttering a payer as the omnipresent howl threatened to crack their eardrums.

"Rkakhnen, talatrak sadrya oumna. Rkakhnen, talatrak sadrya oumna. Rkakhnen, talatrak sadrya oumna. Rkakhnen, talatrak sadrya oumna."

Then it was over. Solet's tearing eyes finally managed to focus on his console and its display. Red markers were all over the ship, but as he watched, he let out a cry of relief. None of them were related to the warp engine, or life support, or structural integrity. He just wanted to sleep, to faint away from this pain, but couldn't just yet. Syndac, flung against the wall, limped over to her seat rubbing her abused wrist. Lenore managed to break the silence.

"Are we… alive?"

"I… don't know." Solet pressed the comm button. *"Benbow* to all ships, *Benbow* to all ships, come in. Can you hear me?"

There was a pause. It was only a second or two, but felt longer. Had the comm system failed? Finally Donovan answered, sounding tired.

"Yes. We receive you. Your visual seems to be out."

"Not surprised. Status?"

Dashall. *"We've got some kind of feedback loop in the computer subsystem and our lights are going screwy, but otherwise fine."*

Gustav. *"We have some kind of structural warning in the rear area. We were clipped by a large piece of debris. Also we've got light and gravity failure in our front decks."*

Donovan. *"All the lights and some life support feeds to the port side are no longer functioning. We've also got some compression scarring on that side. Door controls are out on multiple floors. We're already fixing those. What's your status?"*

Solet looked to Syndac, who read off her readings in a daze. "Circuit overloads on all decks at minor junctions. Gravity field loss along port side of decks D-5 through D-7. Lights out on all decks port side, D-12 and D-14 starboard side. Drive core secondary power couplings tripped to safety. Comm consoles on D-1 through D-10, D-13 and D-15 all damaged. Food cooling system malfunctioning. Computer clock and distance calculators malfunctioning. Transport pods not functional. All critical systems operating within safe parameters, backup system functionality down to forty percent, non-essential systems down to thirty percent. Exterior damage from warp field compression and energy scarring extensive but superficial and non-threatening. Exterior damage focused on port side and upper and lower starboard side."

Solet leaned back in his seat. "There you go. Our report. We can still fly, just."

Donovan spoke first. *"We shall drop out of warp and help with repairs once we are well clear of Nox Vuldi. It should not put too many days on the journey. Unless anyone has any objections."*

There was a general sound of agreement. Not surprisingly, as they, too, required repairs. Solet signed off, then gave a slightly forlorn laugh before instructing Alkmeney to begin the process of dropping them out of warp. They then checked in on life signs. There were no casualties, but reports were coming in of injuries. Syndac was looking at Solet with an expression almost of respect.

"How the hell did you learn to do something like that?"

Solet shrugged. "From my days in the Feles Armed Coalition Detachment. If a light frequency charge is sent to disrupt your warp field, match its frequency to cancel it out and negate the damage. It was designed for military counteraction, but I thought it'd work for a mass ejection. You'll still be shaken, but you'll survive."

"Seems we have." She looked him up and down, probably seeing the welts and bleeding cuts across his arms and chest. "Solet, given everything you've been through, I suggest you get those wounds treated, then go and have a long lie-down before we need to start repairs. And if necessary, I'll make that an order as your second-in-command."

With a smile at Syndac, Solet raised himself stiffly from the chair, noticing only then that it was wobbling slightly. He hobbled toward the door leading to his adjoining private cabin, and there got out his first aid kit and tended his wounds. All surface level, nothing serious. Then, suddenly worn and weary, he threw back the covers of his bed, threw himself down on his back, and was instantly asleep.

FILE 7

FACE OF THE BLACK

I am dealing with you quite straightforwardly;
my heart is not made of iron, and I am very sorry for you.

—Homer

ALKMENEY WAS LEANING against her desk, the pen barely scraping the paper, when Livesey pressed the comm alert and came in hard upon its trill. Alkmeney quickly shoved the paper and pen back in its private nook and turned as the android spoke in an almost irritatingly jovial tone.

"Ahoy, there, ahoy, there, this is your friendly neighborhood mechanical Medico insisting that you get some of those bruises treated."

"Thanks. I *do* feel a little battered. And exhausted. When my rest period comes, I fear I will not wake from the alarm. What happened elsewhere? Those warning signals looked grim.

"We all had a right old time." Livesey talked even as she saw to Alkmeney's surface cuts and applied painkillers. "Faarax was on D-4 Port Side, where some of the gravity fields failed. He was floating around with several others for quite some time. He finally got the section door open and pushed himself through along the floor. Said it's the first time he's ever had to crawl through a wide-open door in his life. Sensible. If he'd tried floating out, he'd had gone head first into the floor the moment he started re-entering the next gravity field's area of effect."

"What about yourself?"

"Oh, me? I was nearly thrown over the railing, and one of the new crew actually was. Nothing serious. Amazing how she saved herself."

"Who was it?"

"That human woman Sinestra. Her save... incredible. Dexter also apparently got himself hurt, and she rushed to him as if he were her own child. So I've been kind of busy. How are Solet and Syndac?"

"They are working themselves ragged. Not with the repairs, though."

"I should think not. The new crew's extraordinary."

"It's Donovan and the others. They seemed unwilling to press on after such a spectacular opening obstacle. Solet managed to talk Donovan and Gustav round, and I know not what kind of magic Syndac used to keep Dashall from ducking out. Frankly, I do not want to know the kind of arguments used on the likes of him. Ow!"

"Sorry." Livesey looked at where an attempted skin patch on Alkmeney's wrist had widened the cut. "Just thinking. You know, Sudu's being an ungrateful ass."

"About the new crew?"

"Yeah. I saw him during repairs on the blown lighting circuits on D-13. I'd say he's even more annoyed now that the new crew are doing so well getting the repairs done. He thinks they're all 'too unnatural.' I tried to get him to tell me more, but all he'd say was that 'even if they smile, they look like ghosts or dummies—unnatural and unliving.'"

"Quoting something, maybe?"

"I don't know. Regardless, there's no call to be so completely unwilling to trust others. Just because he's been with this ship so long doesn't mean it's his. I think he wouldn't praise them even if the ship were falling apart at the seams."

Alkmeney narrowed her eyes. "Talking of falling apart at the seams... I redid my navigation a few hours after that debris hit, trying to figure out what happened. I'd calculated the first wave, but that second one came out of nowhere and nearly got us killed. Got chewed out by Syndac over that."

"Syndac would. So?"

"I did some calculation on the route, and found something rather disturbing. When we set off, we did not take in the most elementary precaution surrounding travel along ancient routes. The galaxy moves, sometimes in unexpected ways."

There was a moment of silence, then Livesey's head dropped. "Oh... shit. Yes, we should've calculated for that."

"Just to check, I performed a distance survey on celestial objects from the travel route. Five centuries ago, Nox Vuldi was ten to twelve lightminutes farther away, more than enough to give those waves of energy an edge today. The nav computer program was creating threat prediction from that old data."

"I wonder what Syndac will say when she hears that."

"I would rather not know at first hand. What amazed me more was how many humans still count only in lightyears. They seem to ignore five sixths of the lightdistance reading scale."

"Guess so. Look, there's—"

Before Livesey could press on, the door opened and Sudu burst in looking tired and overexcited. Alkmeney pursed her lips.

"Pardon my tone, but this room is *not* a public space."

"I know. I'm sorry, but I just needed to get away from those bloody crew people. They're driving me up the wall!"

Livesey showed a sympathetic face. "That bad?"

"That good. That's what so irritating. And then there's all this odd feathering that's been happening in the larger air junctions. I've lived with these systems for so long I'd know whether we were getting a feathering problem."

Alkmeney might have answered, but Livesey spoke before she could. "I think I know what you mean. Feathering would register as a constant low-level constriction in the flow, not this kind of aberrant fault. At least, it wouldn't happen except as a secondary symptom. It wouldn't appear in isolation like this, and not with such dramatic frequency."

Alkmeney had to make an effort to get the conversation onto a different subject. Her mouth moved automatically, her mind only vaguely following her on dialogue. Sudu's and Livesey's words were unnerving, carrying unpleasant possibilities.

DEXTER'S HAND PRESSED hard against the small alert button outside Faarax's room on D-4. He had been allowed his "long and glorious" seven hours. Dexter opened the cabin's door hard on pressing the alert button and watched as Faarax roused himself slowly from the long slumber. Dexter felt his usual half-crooked smile creeping across, a sight Sinestra said could be both endearing and unsettling. Dexter spoke even as Faarax's mouth opened to snap at the interruption.

"Your mom wants you. She's in D-14's locker area."

Faarax frowned. "She's *not* my mother. And I thought they hadn't finished repairs on D-14 yet."

"Just have. Doin' some final tweaks. Wants ya there."

Dexter's smile became slightly softer. Faarax rose and pulled on a vest over his bare chest. As the boy passed by, he squirmed slightly to avoid him. It was a narrow doorway, and Dexter wasn't moving. Oh, well, best not to be too antagonistic, this boy might take him seriously. Finally Dexter stepped inside, allowing Faarax out. Faarax then saw Dexter step nimbly over to a small shelf and pick up a small archaic thing, a physical photo in a frame. Faarax barked.

"Put that back, now!"

Dexter obeyed, with a strange expression. The picture was of a young boy, happy and carefree, with two human adults behind him, embracing him. The man, tall and something like Faarax except for his frizzy blonde hair, and the mother with a softer face but hair more like her son's. Dexter left the cabin under Faarax's scathing eye.

"I'm sorry. Just curious. Haven't seen somethin' like that in years. They're usually seen in museums more than personal shelves."

"It's personal."

"Clearly. Family?"

"My parents. Dead now. Excuse me."

Faarax closed and locked his cabin, then flounced off away from Dexter to find Lenore. Dexter gazed after him for some moments, gave a crooked smirk, then walked in the opposite direction. He tapped his comm.

"Sinestra speaking."

"Dexter. I'm takin' my break."

"Already? Come now, brother, you had a break two hours ago."

"We're not exactly undermanned."

"That doesn't matter. Besides, we've got jobs to do ourselves."

"Care to talk about that? On break?"

There was a moment's silence. *"I heard your cabin needed tidying."*

"Yeah, it's gotten a little outta hand."

"You never could keep your own things in order. Hold on, I'm coming."

At Dexter's "cabin," or rather the sleeping pod he referred to as such, he waited while fiddling with one of the settings. Sinestra appeared from behind him, having come at a brisk walk from where she had been working on D-8. As she bent over and examined his untidy cubbyholes, their eyes met.

"You were sayin'?"

"Your own jobs are only possible on break. Remember what we were told?"

"Yeah, I remember. I also remember the plan didn't involve nearly being killed by a supernova blast."

"What's the human saying? Plans never survive being put into action."

"Don't think that's quite right. But still, didn't think it'd be proven true like that."

"We've already experienced it. How much have we actually gotten done? Not nearly as much as we needed to. And why?"

"We both know why. That Sudu character's been keepin' us busy."

"And keeping his eye on us. Remember how much he was micromanaging that repair on D-4? How difficult can it possibly be to change a plasma line in a vent? I was helping our father do that kind of thing when I was a toddler. He doesn't trust any of the new crew, but he especially distrusts us two."

"Can ya blame him? I mean, I doubt he's ever met the likes of us before."

Dexter smiled and reached across, grasping his sister's hand. Sinestra returned the grip with warmth. These two, solitary in all other ways, had each other. Dirty minds might have seen in their filial bond something more, but they knew the truth. From the moment they were born, umbilical cords entwining them so closely that they could barely breathe, they had been together. They thought the same, in some ways felt the same, shared that strange mark across their faces, even fancied that at times they shared the pain of a single injury. In older days, they might have said they shared a soul.

But in some things, Dexter was always the younger of the two. He didn't have any illusions on that point. He was slightly shorter, had slightly less strength. He deferred to Sinestra in several things, and relied on her for emotional support when in deeply unfamiliar territory. He had even followed her when their father's abuse had grown beyond endurance and they began their shadow career by murdering him. Here, in this place at this time, he was himself. But somewhere else, he might not be able to hold his own. At least, that is what he still seemed to believe.

"Any fresh instructions?"

Sinestra shook her head. "Nothing but the usual. Keep things running as planned, and we will make our move when the time is right. Also, keep an eye on the one with the cube."

"That weirdo android?"

"Weird she may be, but she's a threat. She has a keen eye, and mostly keeps her council if she suspects anything."

"She's too wrapped up in herself to be any threat."

"But she and Sudu are friends. Close friends. Our distinguished captain was easily hoodwinked, but those two are not so bedazzled by wealth and glory as the others. Indeed, Livesey seems positively indifferent."

"Just makin' sure she knows about all the lovely, lovely data."

Sinestra looked at her brother in surprise. "That is a very good suggestion. She may already have that in mind. If so, all the better. It won't be traceable back to us."

The two might have continued, but the door hissed open and Livesey herself made an appearance. They rose sharply and Sinestra changed the subject.

"You really should keep your pod in order. I can't pick up after you all your life."

"Sorry." Dexter was every inch the scolded sibling.

Livesey passed them with barely a second glance, heading for her own cabin. But when she was out of the pair's view and Sinestra attending to other matters, he frowned. It may have been his imagination, but something about the android's bearing made him feel uneasy.

Almost... afraid.

IN SOLET'S ROOM, the captain glanced up in sync with Syndac and Alkmeney as Livesey entered. The other captains were there via displays, each looking either nervous or grumpy. A display unit on his desk hummed discreetly, projecting a scan of the Cluster and its surrounding mapped or observed space. Alkmeney couldn't hide her worry, her fingers drumming underneath the display. Livesey took them all in with a glance.

"You wanted to see me?"

"Yes." Solet's voice echoed flatly in the spartan room. "I've got something I need to discuss with you. it's about our route."

Livesey nodded. "You want to make sure we don't have any more nasty surprises like Nox Vuldi."

"Exactly. Ready?"

"Ready and willing. Just a moment."

Livesey made sure the two doors into the small room were fastened on the inside, then opened the small cavity in her chest and pulled the datacube from its socket, plugging its micro-jack into her wrist. It still looked harmless, like a baby animal drawn from the comfort of its burrow. But as a famous Ancient Earth novel posted through its surviving fragments, small things could be the cause of much misery.

Alkmeney brought up Nox Vuldi's former coordinates, talking as she illustrated her points. "I did a scan of the area within the last few lightyears, and managed to reach about halfway along the course of the map. I've focused around Nox Vuldi for now. If you plug in and display the map coordinates for that region, we will see...."

Alkmeney tailed off with meaning. Getting another jack from her wrist socket, Livesey plugged into one of the ancient panel's ports. There was a momentary flicker as the two streams of data were mapped over each other, then a second display merged into the first. It was the same in broad strokes, but there were clearly differences, including Nox Vuldi's position. Solet leaned in, and Alkmeney spoke with a professional detachment.

"Hmm. Yes, roughly what I thought. A difference of eleven lightminutes closer to the map route. All the difference needed. And given the rules of the galaxy, we can assume most if not all other potential threats have shifted position as well."

Solet's voice was a commanding snap. "Yes. Expand the view to the edges of our scan."

Livesey did so, and went farther. Smaller markers where risks had been detected and noted as "points of concern" on the original map appeared alongside had between the major landmark. These included Nox Vuldi, an asteroid field around an ancient white dwarf that had failed to become a planet, and something else that was fuzzy on the display.

Solet gritted his teeth, and felt the atmosphere in the room. Everyone had underestimated the positional changes of objects. Solet didn't know why he hadn't realized it sooner. Perhaps blinded by the end goal of riches beyond imagination, he had ignored or refused to admit the possibility of delay and changes. Alkmeney was gazing at the map distractedly. She was still fixed on what looked like an area of the display not functioning properly. As if an entire section of the map weren't rendering. Solet pointed at the area arresting her attention, the strange fuzzy part.

"What is that? I can't make it out."

"It doesn't have any ID attached to it." Livesey's face was crumpled in irritation. "I only found some reference to a 'dark' element."

"Dark?"

The two stared at each other for some moments, then Livesey spoke. "Oh… shit."

"What?"

"I don't know if you heard about this. About fifty years ago, a breakthrough discovery was made in understanding the mechanisms of the galaxy, and the reason why some areas of space were hostile to warp travel. After two decades of work, a consortium of Synod scientists proposed the existence of a 'dark mass flow' which clustered around the edges of areas where 'standard mass' objects were present. While the exact balance of positive to negative is a point of debate, many agree that it helps explain why galaxies don't fling themselves apart. The dark mass, supposed on Earth as an equal yet opposite force to standard mass, acts as a safety belt enclosing the galaxy."

"Could you please—"

Donovan's attempt to curtail the monologue went unheeded. The android was clearly not being straightforward on purpose. Perhaps trying to soften a blow? "This solved the issue of why some areas of space were hostile to warping. Space warp technology was built in regions where mass was dominant, and they've yet to come up with a frequency that allowed warping through dark mass. After all, though space was 'warped' around an object, that object and the surrounding energies were based on normal mass calculations. If a ship in warp encounters dark mass, it meets with equal and opposite resistance. Dark mass pockets do exist within the galaxy, but most of its detected area lies around the edges of galactic space, detectable only through its influence on other surrounding objects similar to black holes."

There was a prolonged silence, and Solet felt like a black hole forming inside his stomach, sucking his essence slowly away. Alkmeney groaned.

"Oh, no. If we go through that—"

"I still wonder how the route was able to get through…. Just a moment." A pause while she retraced the route through the dark mass cloud. "Yes, now I understand. The route originally passed through a hole in the noted area of 'mass,' but now that hole has… closed? Looks like it's either changed position or just closed up. Our scans haven't detected anything."

"How many days travel are we from it?"

"Three."

"Damn."

"You took the words right out of my mind."

Alkmeney threw her a withering look at this tone-deaf moment of irony. There was a prolonged silence, then Dashall spoke.

"I don't see why that should stop us. It's just like a nebula, isn't it? We just adjust frequency and move on."

Livesey groaned. "Do you have even the slightest notion about what warping space entails? It's the bending of space, yes, but within very strict limits. And we've built all our technology around bending positive space and consequently positive *matter*. That's negative space, negative matter. You can't use positive mass warping to shift dark mass space. It's like trying to calculate one plus minus one. You get nothing. If we go into that during warp, we won't move an inch. We'll just be stuck, if we don't explode. Even if we go on normal flight, we could be slowed down. Do you know how long it'd take us to get through?"

"No."

"Let me tell you. If we somehow managed to push to lightspeed through negative space, it would take us… a century."

Everyone fell silent. However deaf Dashall might be to math analogies, everyone understood travel times outside warp. Solet could see it in their eyes. Doubt. Doubt that began to challenge the ever-present greed driving them to this point.

"We'll reach the boundary with the dark mass area in three days. In the meantime, we've found other obstacles that the original route now passes too close to. If you'd all care to look, Alkmeney has made suitable adjustments to our course so we may negate any threat."

Alkmeney showed them the corrected course. It was slightly squigglier than Donovan would have liked, but their only option if they really wanted to make the trip in under three weeks. Everyone looked, and everyone seemed to agree. Then Dashall spoke again.

"But this negative... thing. How do we deal with that?"

Syndac was the one to respond. "We keep scanning as we get closer. And I think a good tactic would be to focus on any signs of positive mass appearing within that area. It's likely to be a way through the zone we can use at warp speeds."

Solet shook his head slowly. "Risky."

"But necessary, Captain. If we're to get there alive and able to walk from one ship to another. Now, if that's all...."

Dashall might have said more, but Donovan quickly cut him off. *"Yes, that's all. And that's more than satisfactory. Dashall, I'll talk to you in private. Gustav, I trust you're okay with all this?"*

"I.... Oh, yes, entirely." Gustav pulled themselves back from some unspecified dream. *"I'll await developments from the* Benbow.*"*

"Good. Signing off."

The displays for the other ships shut off. For a moment, there was silence and slight gloom. A breeze from the air vent made Solet shiver.

"You know the thing you didn't mention."

Alkmeney nodded. "Yes. I didn't feel like bringing it up."

Livesey spoke before Solet could. "With the extra travel distance, and the power we had to force out of the ship to survive the shockwave from Nox Vuldi, we might not have enough fuel to make it out of the Uncharted Belt. Even with the extra fuel Gustav is taking along. We may have to abandon the *Benbow.*"

Somehow having this uncomfortable reality spelled out was less disturbing than leaving it unsaid. She had voiced in with a neutral, almost conversational tone. But as he knew, they must also know the full magnitude of such an action. As a seven-person unit, they had spent over a decade making sure their ship didn't fall apart between jobs. Syndac became the voice of reason.

"If we have to abandon the ship, we abandon ship. On a job like this, we have no room for being sentimental. Right, Captain?"

"Indeed." Solet's voice held little conviction. "Livesey, Alkmeney, scan for a way through the dark mass."

The two nodded and left, but Syndac lingered. She watched as Solet picked up a datapad and began scrolling through a report. Finally he looked at her, giving his weary eyes as much steely command as he could muster.

"Is there something else?"

"Yes. You're thinking of quitting."

"Wouldn't you under the circumstances?"

"I suppose. But think about what you are about to give up."

"Yeah. Our ship running out of fuel and being abandoned, and us not getting home. Or worse, running out of fuel and just being left behind by those other vultures we had to partner with. Remember, I agreed to this because it looked like a good deal. If this thing starts getting out of hand—"

"Can it!" Syndac leaned forward and slammed both hands on the table as she glared into her captain's face, her voice switching abruptly from snappish to formal. "I grow sick of your whining. Listen to me. We both knew what this trip might risk, we both did it for one reason and one reason only. Money. With the money we can get from this, we can finally dig ourselves up from this miserable pit of sick that stands in for a career. Sailing a junk around the Outer Worlds, picking up the dirty jobs no one wants to, taking duff deals because they're the only deals we can take, being outrun and outshone by every other freighter in the whole Cluster!"

"I don't need that kind of talk from you."

Syndac's face shifted abruptly into a benign smile. "We both know you feel like that. We both know that if it were not for this strange barrier, you would be going as fast as the drive core could stand, if not faster. I know. I want it. I want it so badly. And we both know we will not be cheated out of our share this time."

"What do you mean?"

"I mean we stand up for ourselves. We have a full crew now. I found them, I know they will not back out of this or stand for sleight of hand. And as for the others, they are driven by the basest kind of greed. Show them force, and they will buckle at once."

"You seem pretty confident."

"I am. We have three whole days. Trust me, Captain. I'm your second-in-command. I can do anything to support you."

Solet and Syndac eyed each other. Solet, his face a mask of suspicion and exhaustion. Syndac, smiling and assured of her position. Finally Solet rose and drew himself up to his full height. Syndac needed no such push, as her poised posture was always correct and implacable. The swarthy captain and the slim second, the two Feles with little but a command and language in common, sized each other up. Solet finally, very slowly, nodded.

"We'll make this work. Whatever happens. And you'll support me. As you have done always."

"As I have done, always."

With that final bow to her superior, and a smile that might have been laced with sweet blossom and poisons, Syndac left Solet's room.

FILE 8

THE FALLING HAND

But there we were, without a mate; and it was necessary,
of course, to advance one of the men.

—Robert Louis Stevenson

A DAY HAD passed since the meeting with Solet and Syndac, and they were just two days travel from the dark mass barrier obstacle. The tension was palpable throughout the entire four-ship convoy. Solet had announced his plans over the intercom, the other three ships listening in as part of a wide broadcast. No one was pleased. The idea of flying into the equivalent of a pool of syrup that would gunk their engines and slow them to a crawl was causing a drop in morale across every single crew member.

Every one, that is, except Livesey. Standing in front of the map table in the central navigation area on D-6, her eyes were staring with the dispassionate quality every android was given in Ancient Earth fiction. This was no time for emotion. She had to solve the problem. No one else on the ship likely had the skills and concentrated computational power to do so. She looked at the encroaching blank in the map. It wasn't even colored in, but that could be explained. The computer systems weren't designed to render unknown matter except as a blank.

She tried several different computations. First, she zoomed the display out as far as it could go, then zoomed it back in, then overlaid the map and did comparative drift analysis to try and rediscover the old route through. She tried warping elements of the map architecture, adjusting speed variables, inputting the possibility of data corruption. Once she even tried calculating entering warp within the confines of the dark mass. The latter scenario had resulted in spectacular destruction. Her words broke out in broken undertones.

"If we try this…. No, that won't work. And I've already tried warp manipulation. If we do anything like that, we won't move an inch. Normal mass warp drive meets dark mass space—the result is unpleasant. The same if we try doing anything with our engines. They aren't designed to handle those undetermined pressures. And they're still recovering from Nox Vuldi. Hmm. Perhaps there's only a thin field of negative matter between us and the passage. That might prolong out trip by…. How much? Can't calculate that. We don't have any reference data. If we sent off for it, we'd give our position away."

She reached down and fiddled with one of the settings, zooming the display out and overlaying the old chart again. She saw a small light flash in her peripheral, the signal for a new batch of data from the latest long-range scans. Better overlay them too. Loading them in, she watched as the picture filled out a little more. There was a small nebula-like area a lightminute distant, hovering about a day's travel from…. What to call it? Give it a name, and you lessen its power to hold fear. Running through her algorithms, she decided that "Dark Mass Barrier" was best. "Barrier" for short, then it wouldn't be a tongue twister.

So, with that decided, she returned to her contemplation. A nebula, roughly a day's distance from the Barrier. Signs of possibly an asteroid cluster, but no clear stars. Nothing that seemed promising.

And there, at long last, a reading of normal space around the Barrier itself. She could've cried in her excitement, but instead suppressed it and continued her observations.

"Can't be precipitate with this. Might just be a blip."

She noted its proportions, charted nearby stars, incorporated the ship's on-board map of the entirety of the Cluster. These included the most recent deep space scans with the knowledge of dark mass. It did little to encourage hope. The Barrier seemed to form a two lightyear-deep wall stretching beyond the boundaries of their current scans and maps. It would put too long on their journey to go over it, and who knew how far they would need to go beyond that if there were unexpected distortions caused in its immediate vicinity.

Finally she leaned—almost slumped—against the console, beginning to feel frustrated. No matter what she tried, the inescapable fact was that she was dealing with an unknown. Dark mass, though hypothesized, was unlike anything encountered before. There was that one old incident from around seven centuries back, but that had been overruled in importance by other events of the time. Dark Matter had remained a point of mere academic obsession.

"And no we're proposing to fly through it, or at least fly through a gap. Insane, but what else can be done? If we do try going round it, it might put weeks on their journey, leaving the *Benbow* at least without fuel for the return trip." A bitter smile crossed her lips. "Maybe we should turn back. It would be safer. But would Syndac or Solet listen to that? Will the other captains listen? I doubt it."

She was about to continue on this path of thought when the door opened. Alkmeney and Sudu walked in, both looking flushed and bothered. Livesey summed up the situation with a swift glance.

"Argument?"

Sudu nodded. "Yes. One that was bound to happen, but…."

Alkmeney passed a hand over her forehead. "All of this is just not fair. I am expected to take impossible routes for the sake of his engines."

"And mine." Livesey spoke pointedly. "Indeed we all have an interest that our engines should continue to function."

"But how am I supposed to keep the engines going if we pass through that?" Sudu gestured with feeling at the map and the Barrier. "That stuff will stop us dead or blow us up if we try using warp drive with it, and at sublight speeds we might as well turn round or blow ourselves up. It's impossible."

Livesey's reply was dispassionate, even to her own ears. "It's entirely possible to get through. I did some more research on this after the meeting. Humans did extensive research on the subject. They referred to dark mass as 'dark matter' or 'dark energy.' Dark mass interferes with many positive mass processes, but they don't interact in understandable ways. Subwarp flight should be perfectly possible and normal going through that area. But warp drive requires manipulation at a level where mass equations are essential, and trying to calculate a standard warp spectrum with dark mass surrounding—"

Alkmeney broke in. "Yes, we understand all of that, thank you. No need to melt our brains again. It was difficult enough to grasp last time."

Sudu laughed. "Yeah, you could almost see the smoke coming from Dashall's ears."

Livesey nodded, smiling slightly at the memory. She liked explaining in detail when given the chance, if only to show how clever she was. But she also had consideration, and backed off when others were in distress. Unless her core self said that they needed to be further goaded and pricked. She could've giggled, if that particular set of subroutines had not been removed during her battle programming. Her mind drifted back into contemplation of the deep darkness of space. The endless void. The argument between Alkmeney and Sudu played out like background noise. Sudu was speaking first.

"Well, you can't have so much power for your scans. It's impacting the transfer speed of our commands to the warp engine."

"If we do not use that power, the scans will not reach far enough. If we are to find a way through, we need the energy for long range scans."

"We're not in the service of the navigation computer."

"And we cannot be concerned always with the insecurities of engine staff."

"Why, you.... Bark all you like. This isn't getting us anywhere. We've got little to nothing to go on with this. We're not getting any data back."

"If we merely used—"

"That's it!"

Livesey's eyes had closed, but now snapped open as if jolted by a power overload and her shout brought the argument to a halt. She started forward, typing a long string of commands into the display, zooming in on a section of the Barrier. She then overlaid the original route from the datacube, and watched as the path passed just to the nearer side. She finally mapped in their current course, and brought up their scan history over that past day. Her head felt like exploding with the colossal nature of her brainwave. Alkmeney stared at her.

"What are you doing? Have you found something?"

"It's what we haven't found that's important me."

Sudu frowned. "What we haven't found?"

"Hold a moment. I've got something… to…." A long pause as she continued typing into the keypads. "Alkmeney, bring Solet and Syndac down here."

"Why?"

"Just *do* it."

With a sigh and a shrug, Alkmeney did as she was told. Sudu stayed, seemingly fascinated by the intense staring eyes of the android. Her gaze fixed on one area of the Barrier, her simulated breath quickening with something like passion. Livesey finally looked up, and the gleam in her eyes matched his own. A mutual shining light of greed unbarred by obstacle.

"What's the big revelation?"

"Wait for the others. And it may prove our damnation."

It took another few minutes for Solet and Syndac to appear, bursting in like the report from a cannon battery. Solet looked flustered but eager, fastening down a panel on his arm as if interrupted in the middle of tuning. Syndac moved with the leisurely grace of one expecting little in return for her effort.

"What is it?" was the captain's cutting question.

Livesey drew herself up and spoke in a level, clear voice. "For the past day, I've been pouring over this map and the scans to try and find a way through this Barrier of dark mass. It seemed impossible. But then I realized something. Part of the hypothesis surrounding dark mass is that it forms in clumps without gaps. For such a gap to exist, something must be creating it. Forcing the dark matter to part. But as you know, as the fleet knows, we've detected nothing from our scans."

Syndac's voice sounded as tired and irritating as she appeared. "This is sounding somewhat circular. Why not get to the point?"

"I suddenly realized my mistake. See the display? I've overlaid the local map, the original course, our scans, and our path. See where the original path lies? Now watch. I'm adjusting for galactic drift over the past few centuries."

The small group watched. The azure line showing their ancient path shifted slowly along the Barrier until it came to rest a few lightseconds to the side of their current course. Livesey resumed.

"Just now, I fell into considering why we've been detecting no responses from anything that would hold a pathway open. But then I flipped the question. Why would we be detecting responses? Anything with suitable... oomph to hold open a path through dark mass wouldn't be a normal star. Indeed, something like that would need a high density to create enough of a dent to make any impression in dark mass. Say something so dense that nothing can escape it? Not even light?"

A slow gleam of realization spread around the company. Livesey nodded, anticipating all their varied reactions.

"You see? I stopped looking for strange signal responses, and looked for an area where the signals had just vanished. Not faded, not bounced back, just vanished. And there was one spot, within the drift margin."

Syndac spoke, his voice a little unsteady. "You believe that the passage through the dark mass is being held open by a black hole? Is that possible?"

"Theoretically. Deep space scans indicate that some small black holes have either been generated or been thrown out into this part of the galaxy. If one had settled into some kind of steady orbit either just outside or just inside the Barrier, it's possible the gravitational pull would eventually suck in enough dark mass to create a gap in the Barrier. Sadly, this part's all theoretical. We've never come across this kind of interaction before."

Sudu sounded deeply skeptical. "Can black holes absorb dark mass?"

"Theoretically yes, but to a lesser degree than standard mass. I believe that, in this situation, it would remain relatively stable taking in matter from outside and, more slowly, dark mass from the Barrier. It might even be held in place somehow by the dark mass. But that would require more calculation."

Syndac's eyes narrowed on the indicated point on the map. "You are saying the original map charted past that black hole? Indeed, used it as a way through?"

"It's the most likely explanation. More likely than some kind of spontaneous gap. It would also explain the extended travel time you noted when I first calculated it. Approaching a black hole, we pass through the radius of its time dilation effect. Warp or no warp, we must contend with its pull. That could add days onto standard travel time."

Syndac nodded slowly. "Theoretical it may be, but it makes sense. And means we have a way through."

"Oh, great." Solet laughed bitterly. "Just wait till I tell the others we'll have to fly through the time dilation effect of a black hole. Never mind our travel speed, how will it impact our perception of time?"

"It won't."

Everyone turned to stare at Sudu as he spoke, particularly Livesey. Her eyebrow rose, and behind her controlled expression was nothing but pure bewilderment.

"Do you mean to say you have a solution that cancels out time itself?"

"No. At least not a new one. It's been here all the time."

"What?"

"Our warp field. Remember how these things were driven before the Scarlet model was introduced? The warp field is created using local gravity manipulation. We create a pocket of gravity around ourselves, a miniature universe in a sense. Newer models use quantum manipulation. Using our own warp field, we can create a gravitational counterweight. That means while the ship will travel at a slower speed relative to the rest of local space, our perception of time inside the ship won't change. It'll be a few days, all across the ship. Perhaps an extra week outside that field."

Solet looked relieved "God, the other ships. They use Scarlet engines. God knows what the time dilation will do to their crew."

"Probably cause two days to pass on one side and two weeks on the other. Shall we prepare the padded cells now?"

Livesey's near-flippant answer was not needed, and she noted the many glares directed at her. Sudu was now staring into space, adrift in speculation. Before anyone else could speak, he laughed.

"Of course it's all so simple, really."

"What is?"

"I read something two maintenance stops ago, looking through old archive material to repair the gravity feeds in our engine. The Scarlet engine model may be designed around quantum manipulation, but they have a redundant system built into their make-up. A gravity-based system derived from earlier models."

Solet was almost smiling. "So they have the capacity to generate a gravity-based warp field, like us?"

Livesey pursed her lips. "Theirs would probably be a lot weaker. They would suffer a lot from time dilation."

Sudu's grin was electrifying. "Not if we do something a little clever. Syndac, did you ever notice those strange hatches in the ship's side?"

"I saw something. I assumed they were redundant fuel ports. As you so like to point out, I'm not an engineer."

"Well, you're wrong. They're part of a fail-safe system created in case a ship was stranded without warp capacity. A ship with functional warp drive could connect through the redundant systems using retractable power lines, and create a warp bubble surrounding both ships. Couldn't we do the same with the other ships in our convoy?"

"Four ships in one warp bubble." Syndac's brows knitted. "I don't remembering anyone doing anything similar."

"It's worth a try." Sudu continued to grin. "Otherwise we're saying goodbye to going through there as a cohesive unit. And need I remind you that they have our extra fuel?"

This silence was worse than others she had sat through. No more the spectacle of the improbable or difficult, now the seemingly impossible threatened to rear its head and crush with one bite all hope of success. At least, so it seemed. As she watched, all but Sudu left the room, leaving the two alone. Her eyes fixed on his pinched expression.

"Something on your mind?"

"I don't like them."

"Don't like who?"

"The crew."

"You've been saying that since we started."

"Yes, and no one's been listening. Not even Faarax."

"Because he has better things to do than listen to your prejudices. This isn't your ship, Sudu. It's Solet's ship. One day you can have a ship of your own, but here and now—"

"This has nothing to do with being anyone's property."

Both Livesey and Sudu regretted their words. In a long silence, Livesey now better gauged her companion's mood. The greed infesting Sudu's eyes from the moment he saw the map was waning. Perhaps even gone. It was being replaced by a strange tension, a symbol of doubt and mistrust she knew well from her former commanders when they scented treachery in their ranks. His grand plans were being put back on the shelf of dreams, replaced with fear in the here and now. Finally he spoke.

"I don't know exactly why, but more and more I've been having premonitions about the crew. It's not like they're bad at their jobs. In fact, they're all too good at it."

"Too good?"

"You know what I mean. Everything's going so smoothly that nothing seems to go wrong. Anywhere. Is that natural on a ship like this?"

"Syndac hired veterans. You've yet to convince me."

"Then what about the arguments?"

"I've heard none. At least none I would call true disrupting arguments."

"Exactly. A thirty-plus crew, most of them strangers both to us and one-another, and you get nothing. No spats, no fights, no complaints, no petty rivalries, not even a missing tool or misplaced bit of cargo. We squabble all the time, and we're just seven people. But these thirty.... It's not natural."

"You seem to have made up your mind."

"How long have you been on ships?"

"Long enough. Why?"

"You don't seem to know much. I've spent almost my entire life on ships like this, and I know the things that go on. Even in the most well-trained merchant crew, you get squabbles. Who ate what when it was someone else's, why this was done and that wasn't.... You know what I mean."

"I think I do."

"But these new people, there's been nothing. It's like I'm walking through a pack of veterans who've worked together for years. I took a look at the applications before we set off yesterday, during a break. I saw them when they first came aboard, but I was also grateful to have them aboard. I didn't think until just now, when I noticed those... interactions between them."

"What's so special about their applications?"

"Nothing. That's the point. None of them seems to have put in any serious time with any one ship. Yes, they've got plenty of experience, but not enough to justify this. And none of them have ever worked together. And still, no arguments?"

Livesey rested her chin on her hand, biting her lip. "I see your concern. It doesn't appear natural. But why not tell Syndac, or the captain?"

"They're just grateful to have the ship running so well. Think they'd listen to me?"

"I take your point. But wait a moment. The ship hasn't been running well all the time. What about those strange power failures? The ventilation system having those problems?"

"They've stopped. Very suddenly."

"Even that worries you? This ship has more strange mishaps—"

"Not since they came. I know this ship back to front, it's essential for my job, and it doesn't have mystery faults that vanish overnight."

The two eyed one another, then a siren blared overhead. The comm instructed the pair to come to D-1 as Solet and the other ship captains wish them there for discussions on their next move. Livesey let out a simulated sigh.

"I can't help you with this, Sudu. I agree something's off, but without definite proof, you're on your own. I'll keep an eye out, but I promise nothing more. Come on. I think we may be needed to persuade some members of our fleet not to turn back."

Clearly reluctant, muttering under his breath, the disgruntled Sudu followed Livesey to their small conference.

IT WAS JUST as Livesey had predicted. The reactions of the three were varied, but erred on the side of retreat. At first it was due to the dark mass, but once the solutions were presented they seemed ten times worse than the problem. Dashall was all for turning back and recouping investment, Gustav was non-committal as ever, while Donovan was something of a voice of reason. At least the sanest of the voices, was Sudu's reaction as the heated exchange began again.

After a time, Sudu did nothing to stop the yawns as the circular argument dragged on and on and on. Dashall was the main problem, to his eye, as he continued to preach for economy and refused to give up his ship's "autonomy." Donovan was willing to link with the *Benbow*, but grew ever more infuriated at Gustav's passive attitude. They just sat, listened, occasionally nodded at some neutral common ground of support. It was maddening, and Sudu witnessed his captain gradually losing his cool until he finally exploded at the screen.

"If you're so precious about your shitty sovereignty, we'll take our fuel from *Gustav* and go on without you!"

There was a long silence, and Sudu looked at each display. Which would break first? Which of the two vacillating members would sway the balance of power and allow a majority vote? It could have been either of the remaining two, though Sudu—less and less willing by the hour to continue this mad journey—knew little which might be the one to break. Which, in the words of Livesey, would give in to their greed.

When had he heard her say that?

Yes, of course. In passing, shortly before the dark mass barrier was revealed in all its annoying glory. She had said something about greed being a driving force of organic and synthetic life. Greed for money, for power, for knowledge, for prestige, for so many things. She had given him a strange look. Had it been pity in her cool eyes, or a plea, or even perhaps envy? Had he envied his growing independence from the fever which gripped the entire ship?

Gustav's voice broke the silence. *"My ship has some special extra boosters connected to the redundant paths. We can magnify the warp field's strength. Plus, if we three are the ones providing most engine thrust, the* Benbow *can save on fuel."*

Donovan nodded. *"Excellent. I can connect my own ship with the* Benbow *also. Well, Dashall? You appear to be the only one who has yet to speak."*

Sudu watched Dashall's face, flickering in the display and sweating in reality. A slight smirk cracked the corner of his lip when the old Feles growled.

"Fine. I'll let out my connectors. But I'll be as far away as possible. If something goes wrong, I wanna get out fast."

"Understood." Solet didn't hide his relief. "I'll coordinate with my crew and we'll synchronize for a general link-up tomorrow before we reach the predicted time dilation barrier. All out."

The faces vanished. Solet turned to Sudu.

"D'you think you can get this ship to link with their systems and create a strong-enough warp field to keep us from losing our literal time?"

"Give me two hours and a dedicated team, and I'll have that and more. Just don't let anyone get in my way."

"That we won't."

"And try to pry Faarax away from Lenore and join me down there. I work better with the engine when he's there."

"As you like."

Sudu left without another word. He tried not to smile at the scowl that would be on Syndac's face. She never did like other crew getting their own way.

It was about an hour later according to the on-ship time pieces when Sudu stood with Faarax, working from their end on connecting the cables. All four of the fleet had dropped out of warp to perform this test maneuver. If it worked here, they could repeat it when they reached the passage past the black hole. If not, then—and Dashall had been most insistent on the point— they would turn back.

"Same old, same old." Faarax let out a sigh. "Always dithering at the vital moment. You all right on your side, Sudu?"

"Fine. Just don't let the cables overextend or we'll have a blowout."

"Got it. Ah, the external cable feeds up. Yeah. When was the last time they worked?"

"First time I've known them work at all. Let's see."

Sudu looked at the feed closest to him. There it was, the exterior clamps being loosed and the cable extending out toward a ship just within the feed's view. Outside and beyond his view, the three ships had arranged themselves around the *Benbow* in a rough triangle formation. They painstakingly lined up with the link cables which began extending from the *Benbow*. Each ship's warp engine was getting ready to take the strain of redundant systems activating and merging into a single giant gravitational warp generator.

"Beautiful." Sudu was murmuring without thinking. "Beautiful." He snapped back to reality with a jerk. "What about the internal feeds?"

Faarax did a quick check, then groaned. "D-12 feed's down. Again."

"I thought that was fixed. Haven't our magnificent new crew gotten round to that yet?"

This was a clear challenge to the few new crewpersons' within earshot. One of them was Sinestra, and she turned with some force. Her voice was hard, accusatory.

"You insisted we get clearance from you before carrying out repairs. If you look at your fault reports, you'll see that an alert for that feed was sent in the day before yesterday."

"All right, all right." Sudu struggled to remain civil. "When this test run's done, I'll go down and fix it."

"Very well."

Sinestra had turned back to the console, but in the brief moment Sudu saw her face, there had been a look which disturbed him. He turned back to his own tasks quickly, trying to forget. Faarax didn't seem to have seen anything, but was now typing commands furiously into his console to keep each system as balanced as possible with the other three warp engines trying muscle in. The relative size was hardly a problem, but the power differences at once threatened to tear the *Benbow* apart and trigger every fail-safe in the system.

Faarax's voice sounded flatly. "Ready cable docking."

A slow, painful moment as the cables extended across space toward each other. Sudu switched the display to the cable end feed and watched as its image of the growing maw of the cable connector grew larger and larger. Sudu's breath came in sharp hisses as he adjusted each section of the cable. The link with the *Wydrayn* was completed without mishap, and feedback tests shone positive. He sighed with relief—only two more to go.

His relief turned to irritation as he tried connecting with the *Grand*. Dashall was apparently fulfilling his preferment for being as isolated as possible, should he decide to break away and save his bank balance. Sudu saw it that way, at least. He extended the *Benbow's* cable as far as it would go, then waited as he pictured Dashall struggling with his wish to keep separate from the rest of the fleet. Finally, the two lines attached, and after a further delay the feedback test was positive.

Sudu felt great relief when the connection with the *Kilner* went without a hitch or reservations, and he quickly glanced to check Faarax's face. All he saw was that strange impassive face, the notorious human "poker face." It was the kind of face people oddly liked in engineering schools because they tended to be the best learners. The feedback test showed green, and Sudu typed in the next command. He then checked into the comm, which now spanned all four ships via direct link.

"Attention, attention. Group warp field test commencing. If fault detected, follow standard shutdown procedure, and do not detach connecting cable. Correct power fluctuations locally."

There was acknowledgment from the three ships, and breathing hard Sudu began powering up the warp engine. The great cylinder in front of him, beyond those screens, shimmered into life. His ears popped with the slight pressure change as warp field began to manifest. The display lit up in front of him. The *Kilner*, the *Grand*, and the *Wydrayn* all showed green. Their backup systems were coming into play, the modern warp drive technology shunted to one side and the old-fashioned gravity-based tech taking precedence.

"Warp field extending around all ships." Faarax watched the power readings at his own console. "Stable. Getting some fluctuation around the *Grand*. No, that's stable now. Steadying. Steadying…. Now stable at eighty-nine percent capacity, back-up systems prepped. Approaching warp threshold."

"Mark transition. Watch for power fluctuation."

"Warp threshold in ten seconds... seven... six... five, four, three, two, one. *Mark.*"

A slight shudder. A pulsing of space pushing in against them, forcing Sudu to tighten his stomach and pop his ears. Then nothing. Space had stabilized. Faarax's eyes scanned and rescanned the power readings, and Sudu ran his long finger across the display showing the warp bubble embracing the fleet.

"Power readings stable at eighty-seven percent capacity. System compatibility rating good. Feedback minimal. Ship position locked and within tolerance boundaries." Faarax looked at his comrade. "Looks like it worked."

"Great." Sudu might have wiped his brow were he capable of sweating. "Not bad at all for a first attempt without simulations. Tell the ships to begin powering down. We can do the real thing when we get there."

The process of powering down the united warp field and retracting the cables into each ship took a shorter time than expected. Sudu closed down his console's emergency functions and issued instructions for restarting warp so they could continue their journey. But even as he did this, his eye caught something. Faarax, in his distracted state, had left one of the feeds running. A feed leading into the inspection area adjoining the cable sheath, sealed off when the cable extended to prevent possible breaches.

Sudu bent close, narrowing his eyes. Surely he had imagined it. What had passed on the screen was impossible. He briefly checked the area for crew locators. Nothing at all. No-one was there. Yet he had seen something. A brief movement, a movement of something organic. A living being. Not a pet or other animal, but something bipedal slipping across the screen at its lower edge.

"Excuse me." Sinestra had come up behind him, "You were going to perform and inspection on the D-12 feed."

"Yes. I'll do that."

Sudu's distracted tone caught Sinestra's attention. "Are you well, sir?"

"Fine. Quite fine."

Sudu turned away and left the room at a quick walk. With Sinestra continuing to watch from her station, he reached for a small emergency locker by the door. Scanning his ID, he retrieved a small object from within. A tiny cutting tool, meant to break out of the area in the event of an emergency when the doors were jammed. Sudu didn't need anything like this for a routine visual feed repair. He was more interested in the strange movement than the broken feed.

Walking along the corridor, fiddling with the instrument, he considered that movement. Perhaps because it may be the reason for the broken feed. And the strange ventilation glitches, and all the other myriad tiny faults that had been driving him up the wall before being mysteriously repaired. His thoughts and vague suspicions about the crew lurched into the front of his mind, clamoring as a tribal chant. Do not trust them, do not trust them, do not trust them.

Up one deck and to a maintenance passage, it was a tight squeeze for him. As he reached one junction, something else caught his eye. A flash of something that should not have been. Squiggling down with an effort, he retrieved it. A small ration wrapper, the kind he had taken off small fruit concentrates in all his years aboard freight ships. Crushing it in his hand, smelling its cloying sweetness, he pressed on as fast as he could.

The door into the inspection area opened without protest, and he slid inside. In that moment, he knew something was wrong. The air in here should feel cool, fresh, untouched like a night deep in the jungle of his native planet. Instead his lungs took ever deeper breaths, almost gasping as he might after a long night's sleep in a small rest pod. His instincts guided him to the small panel hiding the air recycling system for this section of the maintenance areas. He looked. It showed heavy use. The kind he saw in the living areas.

His eyes widened and he snapped round. Had he heard something? Had he imagined that slight tap, like a foot on metal? Struggling to control his breathing, Sudu straightened up and grasped his makeshift weapon. Not ideal, but unless whoever it was had an actual gun, better than nothing. He could sear them, and that pain would distract long enough for him to either escape or take them in charge. The cutter's little flame hissed threateningly.

Nothing happened for several minutes. Only silence was there to answer this grand display. Slowly, expecting anything at any moment, Sudu moved back to the doorway and pulled it open. He had kept his eyes on the room, where the noise seemed to have come from. So he only heard the figure behind the door, sensed the hand that had been raised, finally and fatally felt the heavy metal tool that came scything down toward his neck.

FILE 9

MOURNING IN THE EYE'S WAKE

Still, death is certain, and when a man's hour is come,
not even the gods can save him, no matter how fond they are of him.

—Homer

DEATH WAS NOTHING new to Lenore. She had experienced it, inflicted it, come to terms with it. How could she be so calm in the face of it? That was the question her former comrades had asked after a particularly bloody battle. Just before they found that colony ship, just before Faarax came into her life. Faarax had prompted a change. Her awareness of death was unaltered, and she never had many connections within the ship's ragtag crew. But this sudden and terrible tragedy had left her hollow. Perhaps because it had left Faarax hollow.

The crew of the *Benbow* all stood to attention. Even Faarax, normally so casual and slouchy, was erect. From her position next to the airlock, Lenore could see all down the opposite rank. She saw the slight suggestion of tears in Faarax's eyes. The door hissed open and Lenore's sidelong glance watched Solet and Syndac walking on either side of the sealed casket which would send their companion on his final journey. Livesey waited by the airlock, while Alkmeney brought up the rear. She looked terrible.

Everyone had missed Sudu quickly. Faarax first, and he had kicked up the most fuss. Lenore knew instinctively that something was wrong, and had insisted on doing the search herself, accepting help only from Livesey. They had found Sudu, his broken neck caught under the door into a D-12 maintenance area. Lenore had summed up the details from the Medico with quick and cold efficiency. The door mechanism had malfunctioned, and slammed down on the back of Sudu's neck, trapping him there. If the initial impact hadn't killed him, the door's force would have done.

"Never have felt a thing," she had said to Solet, "With a blow like that, death would've been instantaneous. Or at least he wouldn't have noticed himself dying. It would've been like falling asleep."

Solet's remark on the subject hadn't been tactful. Faarax had insisted on being left alone for "a few minutes," and Alkmeney was shaking at her station. Only Syndac, then and now, remained calm and composed, almost uncaring. Lenore suppressed a scowl as the second-in-command approached on the casket's left hand. Standing there, looking so smugly mournful. Behind them all, locked in place, the projections of the three other captains watched the ceremony. Who had invited them? Why were they there at all? This was one of their own being laid to rest.

Livesey coughed, drawing the attention of all. "This will be a service in the *Ekri's Y'thesta* faith. We must remain silent during the opening prayer, then any who wish may come and offer their respects before Sudu's final journey."

Lenore's mind's eye drifted back to the last religious ceremony she had attended. It was one she set up herself for her comrades, when she had turned against them in defense of Faarax. Her last act in the clan—sans returning to face their judgment—before her banishment, before becoming one of the unwanted "clanless." Her eyes returned to Livesey as she spoke.

"All-Present, All-Wise, All-Knowing *Y'thestu,* we summon thee to take note. One of your devote has reached life's end. We who stand here remember his life, and his death. Let him become one with the void in which you cradle our lands and homes, that he might rejoin you in body and spirit. Let others take up his dream, and may he smile by your blessing upon their endeavors. *Y'thestu,* body without spirit and spirit without body, let the two be reunited in the void."

The chant that followed was long, complex, mournful, in a version of the Ekri's native tongue their earpiece translators could not interpret except in confused fragments. The few Ekri crewmembers and Donovan joined in. It was a common-enough prayer for passing, and only when it got to the sect-specific intonations did Livesey's become the sole voice. Or at least, it should have. Lenore glanced sharply at Solet as he mouthed the prayer word for word.

"Y'thestu teth-neshu. Y'thestu, s'thayn. Y'thestu ka-puhuasha. Yoqi sothostry-sey, aearis. Y'thestu whythrishith." Livesey closed the book. "If any wish to speak before our captain bids our crewmate final farewell, they may do so."

A dread struck Lenore's heart. Would she be the one to step forward? She half-wanted to, but to be seen like this…. It seemed fate was there to save her. Faarax stepped forward to stand beside the wrapped body. By no means was this her first space burial, but through whatever trickery this was the most moving. Even the funeral of her parents on her own home world, laid to rest in their native soil, had been nothing. Looking at the shrouded form, Lenore was reminded of a long oval sausage she used to buy from meat stalls at Cape Laglashi.

Faarax had placed a hand on the dressings. Lenore saw Livesey's eyes flash from the wrapped body to the boy. His eyes, red and half-closed, stared down at where the face should have been. Then he lifted his head and spoke at the assembly.

"I didn't know Sudu as well as I might've. We worked together, and little else, but I know this. The *Benbow* was his life, though he wanted to take that life beyond it when the time came. He was this ship. And he made this ship a wonderful… place. The *Benbow*, and all of us, will be less without him."

Lenore could have wept at the terrible mixture of sadness and bitterness in his voice. He returned to his place, close to the airlock and almost opposite Lenore. The captain approached. He raised one hand in the salute of the Ekri, and the other in the somber farewell to a fellow crewmember. All the others followed suit, including Lenore. She realized in that moment how little she knew of Sudu. Here, now, one she had only seen as a colleagues—now forever to drift through the void—was asking her the silent question.

"Why did you not ask more of me? Why didn't you try and get to know me? You've lost any chance of that now. My dreams you will know only at second hand, from the boy sworn to kill you."

The voice was only Lenore's imagination, but it stung. His hobbies, his life, his loves beyond ships and engines. All that time she might have talked with the strange little Ekri. But what point was there thinking on that now? And besides, he hadn't been alone. Faarax and Livesey had been with him. *Faarax and Livesey.* She glanced at each. Together with Solet, were they the only ones who would truly mourn his sudden passing?

The hatch door opened and the body passed inside. As it shut, Livesey and Solet stood on either side. Livesey uttered a final prayer.

"Y'thestu teth-neshu. Short journeys and long farewells. We give you your child. Greet them well. And where their voyage ends, only you can tell." and the final incantation, *"Y'thestu Astrish Tey."*

Faarax, Solet, the few Ekri in the crew, even surprisingly Sinestra and Dexter echoed this final farewell and Godspeed. *"Y'thestu Astrish Tey."*

And in a moment, all was done. Space took its destined due. The being known as Sudu was now only memories and legacy in the *Benbow's* systems. The lump of flesh that had been him shot out and flew away from the small fleet, instantly vanishing into the near-pitch darkness. And Faarax's self-control snapped. He pushed his way out of line, past Solet and ran out of the confined space. Syndac stepped to one side to avoid him, and Lenore scowled at her indifferent expression. She leaned close to Livesey's ear.

"May I...?"

Livesey nodded. Lenore left at a more relaxed pace, glancing left and right as the displays for Donovan, Dashall and Gustav switched off. She could almost smell the trail of pheromones left by her adopted child. She followed it through and down to Sudu's isolated quarters on D-12, close to the engine level. Approaching the door at a slower pace, Faarax's controlled breathing inside echoed from inside. Waiting a while, she listened for any signs of sobbing. None came to her ears, and she gently emerged into Faarax's line of sight.

"May I come in?"

Faarax nodded slightly. She crouched down opposite him. Their eyes met, but Faarax quickly looked away. She nodded.

"I can't say anything to make it easier."

"No."

Another silence. Lenore felt dumb. How could she comfort Faarax? What kind of mother was she? What kind of mother could she be to Faarax, the boy whose parents she had killed? Their agreement stood. There was no revoking it, no forgetting it after all these years. Slowly, Faarax returned his gaze to her.

"I keep on losing people. I just keep on going along, and everyone around me that I get close to ends up dead. My parents, only wanting a home of their own. Sudu, who wanted to do so much, could've done so much. Maybe even

Evelyn'll end up dead, never getting a better life. What am I, cursed or something? I… want my mommy."

The silly, adolescent demand for time's reversal was enough to break hearts. So mature, yet so young. Lenore now felt on the point of tears as she responded.

"I can't give you your mother back, Faarax."

"I know. Death's forever."

Faarax seemed to be withdrawing into a shell. In a wild impulse, Lenore straightened up and hugged the human boy. She waited for him to shrug her off, push her away, perhaps snap at her. But instead his arms held her close, yearning for contact. He had only done this once before when he had still been quite young. Working off their debt to that dreadful captain, cold and sleeping in a corner of the store room. He had huddled close to keep warm, then embraced her as she gave him unconditional shelter.

For a moment, imagination produced a dagger in his hand, driven into her body as they remained close. But there was no dagger, no pain of steel sliding through flesh. Only the pain of her heart, and her eyes as she wept. Also there was Faarax's hair brushing against her cheek as he leaned close and cried in silence. No one is an island, and in times of stress the most unlikely can become bulwarks against sorrow. Faarax's voice was a low, somber plea to nothing.

"I wanted him to see home again. He talked about it, seeing his home. He was born on Terux, a backwater place the Ekri made a kind of second home after the Human-Ekri Conflict. He wanted to return with the greatest engine skills imaginable to revolutionize his world. He wanted to do it, and might've done it."

"I… had no such grand hopes. I wanted him to be your friend, and it seems he was."

It was the only reply Lenore could think of. Any further comment was cut short by a tiny bleeping. Faarax reached out and touched the pad. It was a small custom alarm, made by Sudu to end his rest period.

"Up we get, up we get, we haven't got time to rest just yet. Engines to dust, ducts to clean, else the captain will get all mean!"

The strange little jingle was so utterly incongruous that Faarax gave a strange half-hearted laugh. Lenore too was smiling, almost against her will.

The two crouched together, alone with the background hum of electronics and the alarm's tuneful trill, taking comfort in memories and companionship.

ALKMENEY ARRESTED HER fingers for the second time in ten seconds, pouring back over her writing and correcting a fluffed piece of spelling. How could she possibly describe this in her handwritten account? What column or blog worth its salt would report on the aftereffects of a funeral? It would be gauche, in the worst taste.

"I cannot do that. But it is leaving such an impact on everything. How can I not say anything about it."

It had been very quiet after Sudu's sendoff. Everyone had been working in a kind of near-silence, death and blind to any attempts at conversation. Especially was that so when Sudu was the subject being raised. Livesey had taken over his position, and ran everything with a mechanical precision. Hardly surprising, given who she was. All the same, Livesey had been distrait, and snapped at her when she tried talking to her that day. Seemed to be muttering something about "strange faults" and "Sudu said." What had Sudu said to her, if anything, a few days ago?

Solet hadn't been any better, always depressed. He did his duty, and was a champion at keeping the other ships from abandoning the expedition, also making sure the warp link-up would work as intended. Alkmeney had half-expected the other captains to just leave, but they seemed to have calmed down. Solet had worked that strange magic of his. It helped that there were no odd reports of faults happening anymore. Perhaps fixing those had been Sudu's last act.

Lenore and Faarax were the strangest of the lot. In all the time she had known them, they seemed to have a kind of stiff formality. Now things had changed a little. She saw them looking at each other, and that strange hardness in their eyes was gone. Almost like they cared for each other. Ridiculous, of course. How could they care for each other at all? They're enemies.

"As for me? How do I feel? To be honest, I don't feel anything. All I care about now is that we get to this space habitat and find what we've done so much to reach. All that money...."

It was a horrible thing to realize, but it had to come. But for the moment, she was too busy. She had redone the calculations for journey time, taking in delays and the black hole's time dilation, and they had been given a refuel from Gustav's ship. Now they could navigate that area without needing a tow.

"Maybe I can write about…. Yes! Sinestra and Dexter. They have been most helpful, finding all those ways to cut power usage by five percent. Means we use five percent less fuel being used during our journey. Yes, I can write about them."

Alkmeney bent down over the paper, drawing a line under her previous entry. "Yes, so I shall begin this as, 'Quite incredible how much they know about ships. I wondered if they've done deep space exploration themselves?' Yes, that should provide a good hook."

THE DARK MASS in front of the fleet was just that. Dark. Nothing showed beyond it, nothing was visible around it. The small fleet had arrived at the designated area, ready to begin their dangerous traversal. It seemed to bar any attempt to either go round or pass through it. It was the frontier, the absolute end of all.

"Shit."

On the bridge, with the display up, none could easily tell if it was on or something had blown. Livesey, slowly typing in engine instructions to Sinestra on D-13, kept half an eye on the void. That eye flicked slightly as Solet swore. Syndac turned, and Livesey pondered the strange expression half-hidden behind her disapproval.

"No time for swearing, Captain. Just checking. Yes, fueling from the *Kilner* has been completed, and fuel cable's retracted. Are the other ships in position?"

Alkmeney nodded. "Yes. All ready. Signals from the crew that they're in position. And I've done scans. I'm detecting slight traces of nothingness, if we can call it that. A non-response to any scan input. That must be the epicenter of the black hole."

"Any sign of the path?"

Alkmeney was waiting with baited breath. Livesey wondered if she too was beginning to feel the strain of this trip. Her eyes had been growing more and more clouded by that feeling of greed she sensed in everyone. Not that she wasn't equally guilty of it. The data aboard that ship, the possibilities for knowledge, obsessed her rest periods. She struggled not to dive back into the datacube to unearth more of its secrets. There was still something which eluded her there. A small software cache with a very strong lock.

The doors opened and three others came in. The captains of the other ships. Gustav, their drawn face tighter than ever. Dashall, looking nervous. Donovan, infuriatingly assured and calm. Livesey looked from them to Solet.

"What are *they* doing here, Captain?"

"We've managed to arrange things. For the duration, in case of accident, the *Benbow* will be the main ship. The others will be acting as extensions. The other captains agreed to having themselves and their crew aboard."

"Is that wise?"

Syndac spoke up. "It is merely logical. If the other ships prove too much, then it's logical that the ship with native gravity-based warp drive be the fall-back. The other ships have skeleton crews aboard."

Lenore eyed Syndac. "When was *that* decided?"

"When you and Faarax were not around, as you have seldom been in all your time aboard this ship. Now can we get on?"

Lenore seemed about to snap back at her superior, but resisted the urge. Alkmeney had been carefully not looking at anything but her screen.

"There's something showing on the scans. A trace of…." A long pause as everyone waited with breaths held. "Yes. There it is. Matter. Standard matter, a trace of it. Leading past the distortion. Seems this dark mass isn't as thick as we imagined. We can get through."

"Right. Send the activation signal." Solet opened the general comm. "Prepare to link up for warp."

Livesey nodded slowly, and watched the display as the ships moved into position, driven by their preset programs. No test run this time. She signaled down to Sinestra and another crewmember called Skathii, who was coordinating the port controls. The other ships extended their links, but this time there was no connection of one at a time. All three were synced to the same shared timer, their systems changing over to the old warp drive elements which would magnify the *Benbow's* field.

"Ready cable docking."

Just like they had planned, barring one little detail that no one spoke of. Livesey could almost hear Sudu's remarks on the subject. The simulated jibes rattled round her mind as she typed in the next set of instructions for Sinestra and the rest of the engine room crew. It was almost unsettling, watching and listening as the cables locked into place. The feeds flickered slightly on impact, then the picture stabilized.

"All stable." Solet spoke once more to the whole crew. "Attention, attention. Group warp field activating. If fault detected, follow standard shutdown procedure, do not detach connecting cable. Correct power fluctuations locally."

All the ships acknowledged. Livesey sent the signal.

"Warp field activating."

A long pause. The growing hum of power surrounding them, the warp field manifesting around all four ships. As she watched the energy readings climb, Livesey noted the slight fluctuation across its forward section. The influence of the time dilation, pushing against the warp field even at this distance. But what distance would be safe? So much unknown, and they were still trying to go past one of those things. She glanced down at the feed images again.

"Feeds stable. Strange."

Alkmeney turned to her. "What's strange about the feeds working?"

"They weren't... before."

Livesey became silent again. Better not to say too much. She typed in the next set of instructions, and watched the field energy reading climb slowly. Sinestra's voice came through the speakers, heard by everyone.

"Warp field extending. Fluctuation across forward area, gravitational pressure within activation tolerances. Field steadying. Now stable at eighty-nine percent capacity, back-up systems prepped. Approaching warp threshold."

The humming suddenly rose to a momentary roar, and Livesey almost reached for the emergency shutdown option. The roar ceased almost as soon as it started, and again Sinestra's voice sounded.

"Power stable at eighty percent."

Solet's grip on the arms of his chair had left marks from his metal fingers. "What the hell was that?"

"A gravity pushback." Livesey's reply was quick and to-the-point. "It can happen when ships go into warp near stars. Or in this case, black holes. Probably why it was so loud."

Syndac smirked. "Little wonder they went over to quantum-based warp."

Livesey felt compelled to correct this. "Actually they moved from gravity-based warp drives because of cost. Pre-Scarlet-class White Engines are more expensive to produce in large quantities, plus the fact that several white oil sources are giving out. Freight can be moved more frequently, and at a lower cost. Saves money all round, and the Synod likes saving money. I'm sure everyone here realizes the value of money."

This barbed finale was lost on no-one. The three other captains were all unsettled, Lenore looked uncomfortable, Solet grimaced, Syndac turned away in her haughtiest manner, and Alkmeney steadily ignored it. At that moment, Faarax came in. He still looked listless, uncomfortable, preoccupied. He spared barely a glance for the three newcomers and went straight to Livesey.

"Can I have a word with you?"

"Not yet. I'm busy."

"Later, then."

"Why?"

"Personal."

Livesey eyed Faarax. He looked serious enough. Perhaps too serious. A little manic even. Perhaps the shock of Sudu's death had impacted his brain? No, surely not for someone like him. For all his childish desire for retribution, he was level-headed in other ways.

"Readying course." Alkmeney's voice cut into her thoughts. "Is the warp field stable?"

"Yes... Alkmeney, you were planning to use manual navigation. Could we possibly use the gravity signatures as our guide through the passage?"

Alkmeney considered. "It's possible. Very possible. I just have to do some small adjustments. Is that okay with you, Captain? Or rather, Cap*tains?* We'll need to route your navigation computers through ours."

There was general agreement. Livesey watched with narrowed eyes as Alkmeney adjusted the controls and tuned the navigation to work from gravity tracking. She also made an additional adjustment to factor in the "nothing" which was the dark mass on either side. It would be tricky, and Alkmeney still expected Livesey and her chosen crew to keep the engines running smoothly.

"We should be able to navigate smoothly. On your mark, Captain."

Solet stared at the display, gripping the arms of his chair again. He spoke the word, almost forced it between stiffening lips.

"Get ready…. *Mark.*"

The command was given. The enlarged ship, its warp field shimmering, glided toward the edges of the time dilation. The edges of the black hole's influence. The sensors showed the warp field beginning to fluctuate as they sailed at warp speed between the twin abysses. The dark mass and the void in space.

"Warp field steady. No abnormalities detected." A long pause while Alkmeney watched her readings shift and warp. "That's it. We're inside the time dilation area. Dark mass detected on the other side. Minor deflection against warp field from particles being drawn into the black hole, but nothing major. If you ask me, Captain, we can just turn off the screens and coast through. As long as there's someone at the main nav terminal."

"Do it."

Livesey looked at Faarax. "You wanted my advice about something? Something in engineering, perhaps?"

"Yes. About one of the tools."

"Captain, permission to change?"

"Granted."

"Thanks. Sinestra, you have control of warp engines until further notice."

The only reply from D-13 was a registering bleep. Livesey followed Faarax off the bridge and down to D-4. Faarax pulled her into his small cabin space, then opened a small panel in the frame and pressed a switch. A humming sound began around them, and Livesey saw the shimmering barrier across the closed door. She summed it up at a glance.

"Soundproof." She directed a cool look at the human. "Something installed on the quiet?"

"Sudu said he thought I'd need some quiet time every once in a while. Now it's ideal for something I want you to look at. I'm worried."

"Understandable."

"No, I mean worried about Sudu."

Livesey could not help but shrug at this understandable feeling. "A tragic accident. Why worry about it now? He's dead, and with whatever deity he worshiped."

"That's bullshit and you know it."

"The divinity or the accident?"

"Both, but mainly the accident. I don't think it was an accident at all."

"And how would you know? You never saw the body."

"I… I don't know. I've just got a gut feeling. And I think you might know. You've got to know if anyone does, you were his friend. Like I was. Did you scan his body?"

"I'm not in the habit of scanning bodies on the off-chance that there's been foul play. I don't understand why people still think androids have scanner eyes and hypersensitive ears."

"Well, haven't you?"

"I may have, most haven't. And speaking from personal experience, it's very embarrassing when you're slapped in the face for seeing someone's private parts without permission when you can barely see through their eyeshadow. They just take urban legend as fact and decry an entire group on hearsay."

"Please. All right. Look, I found something yesterday. It was in a service area I was cleaning out. I've been hiding it under my shirt for the past day."

Livesey bit her lip, resisting the urge to voice the obvious and biting double entendre. Faarax pulled a small thin something from under his shirt, wincing as the adhesive tape that kept it there tore at his skin. It was a tool, a sonic wrench of some kind. Livesey took it with a frown.

"Why should finding that make your suspicious? It's just a dropped tool."

"Because of what else is on there. I saw it, doubt I would've if it hadn't caught the light just right. But you…. Even if you haven't got scanner eyes, you should be able to tell blood and scales when you see it."

Livesey almost spoke, then paused, looked. The wrench was heavy around the head, drooping slightly in her grip. As she turned it slowly, an iridescent flicker showed in one of the small joints which allowed the head's manipulator arms to adjust and stabilize. Peering closer, she saw what Faalax must have seen. It was a small fragment of scaly skin trapped in the gap, tinged with a sliver of dried blood. Livesey drummed her fingers thoughtfully on the handle, looked at Faalax.

"Who else has seen this?"

"No one. You're the only one I can trust with this. So please, tell me the truth. Did you scan his body?"

Livesey sighed. "If you must know, yes. This model is fitted with some military specifications. Sudu knew, but kept them to himself. And yes, I did scan him."

"And? What did you find out?"

Did this boy have to be so blunt? She quickly checked outside the small cabin. No sign of anyone. It was likely safe. Pulling back inside, she went straight to the point.

"I… had an inkling about Sudu's death. He seemed so suspicious about things. That scan gave the lie to his death."

"Well, come on, tell me."

"When found, Sudu seemed to have been crushed by a malfunctioning door. The injuries seemed consistent externally, and Syndac said that we should 'send him off' as per his customs without bothering with a postmortem. The current medic did a scan and said there was nothing unusual."

"And there is?"

"His injuries are not all consistent with Sudu being smashed into by a door. There isn't enough internal damage for that. And what damage there is shouldn't be so localized."

"Yes?"

"At a guess…." Livesey looked round and picked up a convenient old-fashioned torch Faarax had brought as a curio two trips before. "The injuries proper are consistent with someone swinging something down onto the back of his neck. Like this." Faarax flinched at the vicious swipe Livesey made with the torch. "Crude, but effective."

Faalax looked at the wrench, still in Livesey's free hand. "A torch… or a tool. A tool used and discarded." He burst out abruptly. "Some bastard killed him!"

"Perhaps." Livesey glanced again at the shielded door. "I would be cautious about who you talk to until we arrive at our destination. And keep our suspicions between ourselves."

"You're saying we should just stay quiet?"

"I'm saying, young one, that any doctor worth their training should have been able to detect this inconsistency."

Faarax and Livesey stared at each other. Then Faarax swayed, putting a hand to his brow. Livesey's arms held him up.

"I'm sorry." He righted himself with an effort. "Dizzy."

"It's the local gravity fluctuations. We are going through the time dilation area of a black hole. We must expect gravitational aberrations, even inside a warp field."

"So we'd best keep our heads."

"And keep quiet."

The eyes of the two met, and Faarax nodded slowly. But before he could reach up and turn off the blocking field, the android took something small from a long-sealed compartment in her abdomen and pressed it into his hand. He looked down at the small object, then back into Livesey's face. Her eyes communicated more than her two simple words.

"For insurance."

Faarax nodded. Slipping the object under his jacket, he turned off the field, and watched as Livesey left to attend to her duties.

FILE 10
BLACK MINDS, DARK CORRIDORS

I began to feel pretty desperate at this, for I felt altogether helpless.

—Robert Louis Stevenson

DARK MASS IS nothing that can be observed, either by the naked eye or all but the most advanced instruments. Even then, it is an observation mostly based on external data, an impression of existence born from its impact on cosmic reality. Black holes were the same, but further distorted by their nature. Their impact on time as a gravitational force more powerful than dozens of normal suns made them even harder to fathom in this great organism of the universe.

And for Alkmeney, that was beyond tolerance. Four days. Four interminable days, stretching out hour after hour, minute after minute, second after elongated second. She was on the point of dying of boredom. There had once been a world where a Kavki tribe had settled, where a small black hole absorbed material from their sun. They had worshiped the two as "The Lovers" and hailed them as the center of the universe. If their lives had been anything like this, it was a wonder they had not all committed suicide before being rediscovered a century past.

"Registering dilation effect."

Livesey's intonation from the console caused someone to grind their teeth. Those same words, repeated again and again every half hour. Who knew how long it would be before their warp-shrouded fleet broke away from the black hole's influence. Even on its extreme edge, minutes and hours seemed to switch places and lose their meaning.

Without saying a word, the Kavki navigator fluently cursed her calculations and improvisations, smoothing their journey between dark mass and black hole so well that she had nothing to do. Taking a lot of entertainment material had not crossed her mind, and she had little enough of her own. Now slumped on her inactive console reading the fifteenth chapter of *Darkly Looms The Day* for the seventeenth time.

> *De-shira was watching from the bridge of the ship, his gaze riveted on the nothingness ahead. There was no reason to be so riveted, except that any other gaze would be fleeting and pass over others who were even more focused than he on staying alive in this endless gloom.*

Indeed, as Alkmeney glanced up from her datapad to give her screaming eyes a rest, it was impossible not to sense in her reality the general lethargy of those fictional intergalactic explorers. Solet was actually asleep, Syndac's fingers twitched as if resisting the urge to drum on the console, Livesey stolidly stuck to her duty, and Lenore was spinning from time to time in her chair. If ever there was a picture of boredom incarnate, this was it.

It was the fifteenth day of their journey. The time dilation was having its effect. They had been pushing slowly through space, so slowly that the other captains were beginning to feel its claustrophobic impact. Again, mulling over the same quotes and examples for the fiftieth time, Alkmeney pondered the early space pioneers of the Allied Peoples, who had used pre-warp spaceships to travel short hops between moons and planets. Her own people had been lucky, with many moons and a complex network of closely-orbiting habitable planets.

What had the others had? The somewhat-isolationist Ekri with their single rocky world and its twin star, the humans with one habitable planet in a system full of barren rocks and gas giants, the Feles on their moon orbiting the destroyed remnants of a supergiant planet. None of them had been allowed to find new places to live and settle before they mastered the techniques of bending space around them or pushing at the edges of lightspeed.

Maybe when all was ended, she would settle on a planet to start her trading business. With the wealth they would take from the hidden depths of Lost Station Circé. She had begun to grow sick of space travel, of stations and habitats and remote rocky outposts with barely any atmosphere. She longed for solidity, for firm ground on which to live and die. Not even a habitable moon, but a full-fledged planet with its own orbit. Not decks with endless void surrounding them on all sides.

Lenore's voice broke the monotonous silence. "Any update?"

Livesey glanced at her instruments. "No sign of us leaving the time dilation yet. As I believe I said less than thirty seconds ago."

"It was a lot longer than that. Or it *felt* like it, at least. Would we know if we were approaching the edge?"

"Perhaps. Perhaps not. Nothing like that is determined."

Syndac's voice groaned out. "Oh, *do* be quiet. You are wasting valuable conversation. Save it for later. We need all the entertainment we can get."

The silence fell again. Fell like a stone. Alkmeney slumped on her console, looking down at the navigational readings. Her eyes watched as the speed marking wavered slowly between two points. The ship, balanced delicately between the inner edges of the black hole and the sludge of dark mass, continued on at what many warp connoisseurs would call a sluggish pace. In normal space, they might make double or triple this speed. It was soul-numbing to see such a low result from so much applied power and determination.

It was about half an hour later when her eye realized something. The number was climbing. Slowly, it was true, but it climbed nonetheless. Ascended with the inexorable certainty and power of the professional free climbers conquering the icy faces of New Plutrac.

"Livesey, check the warp readings."

"Hmm?"

"Just check them."

Livesey did as she was asked. Her eyes lit up. Her own power readings were climbing, just as Alkmeney's speed indicator was. Solet jerked away at the sound of animated voices.

"What's happening?"

"Our speed is increasing."

"And we're getting more power output to match." Livesey's voice was losing its control. "Wait…. Yes. I'm seeing a change in the gravitational pressure on the warp field. it's shifting as I'm talking."

"I'm getting sensor feedback. Stellar readings. Normal space. We're nearing the entrance."

"Steady now." Solet switched on the ship-wide comms. "Attention, all crew. We're approaching the other side of the barrier. Stand by."

Even without seeing it, Alkmeney could sense everyone standing by. Those several days of elongated expectation, a tension fit to burst something, was finally ebbing. It was slowly but surely replaced by something else, the old expectation of great wealth. Everyone on board all four ships knew the reason for their journey. Everyone aboard had their own reasons for wanting some of that money. And everyone was eager to burst through this final barrier, the last obstacle between their dreams and the funds to realize them.

"Going up. Speed up by ten. Twenty. Twenty-five. Thirty-five."

"Power matching to speed. Output to engines rising to seventy percent."

"Mass readings increasing. Locking on."

"Speed now two thirds to normal."

The Captain looked to Livesey. "Increasing thruster speed. Tie it to the nav so we don't run into the dark mass."

"Understood. Power raise completed. Engine output now at... eighty-eight percent."

"Speed increased by forty."

The shuddering gasp came from Syndac. Her face had become elated, cloaked in strong emotions. Her words came freely, without the stiff formality of her usual manner.

"We're there. We're nearly there."

"Mass readings increasing." Alkmeney's voice sounded almost as strong. "We're almost there."

Livesey remained quietly balanced. "Gravitational readings dropping to normal. We're outside the time dilation area. Dark mass effect dropping. We're there."

A long silence. The enlarged ship, the conjoined fleet, drifted through onto the other side of the Barrier. And what awaited them seemed no different. The display screen was reactivated, and as the five looked they saw the distant light of galaxies and a few outlying stars. Otherwise, all was inky blackness, a void of nothing. Syndac sighed.

"So this is the Uncharted Belt."

"Yep." Solet was annoyingly matter-of-fact. "Just as promised."

"Looks just as barren as I'd imagined."

Lenore spoke in a terse tone. "I didn't think you'd be imagining anything."

Alkmeney's eyes flicked between the two Feles. Syndac, cold and smirking. Lenore, stiff and suspicious. The Kavki slowly turned back to her console, checking her readings. Livesey's voice broke in on her.

"Alkmeney, do a long range scan. See what you can pick up."

Alkmeney obeyed, practiced fingers repeating the action that hadn't been needed for days. She glanced at the chronometer fixed above the display screen. The fifteenth day of their journey. A little long. As she scanned, the other three captains entered. Dashall looked relieved.

"I think we should be the first to congratulate the crew of this ship for their incredible efforts and fortitude in getting us through that unscathed."

Solet nodded. "Your congratulations are appreciated. Alkmeney, anything on the scan yet?"

Yet another pause. So many pauses, so long to think about the passing of seconds, that now any pause seemed to last an eternity.

"Yes. Something. It's about… another day's travel from here. It's not large."

Livesey turned to her. "Anything from the original map?"

Alkmeney brought up the display of the old map. She matched it with the scans, sensing everyone around waiting with baited breath.

"I see. Yes, that makes sense. Lost Station Circé is orbiting some kind of substellar object. There's some kind of accretion disc surrounding it, and the station seems to be in some kind of stable orbit around this object. According to the map, it's another day's journey from this point to the station itself."

Solet shrugged. "So be it. Captains, I think you can go back to your ships. We'll separate, and continue on."

Alkmeney chuckled behind her eyes. So ended the great union of ships. Back to the old ways. The old divisions. But it mattered no longer. They were closing in on their prize. Her prize. So long sought.

IN THE UNCHARTED Belt, where stars were few and far between, and only interstellar blackness met the unaugmented eye, there were a few stellar objects hidden by their small size and scale. One of them was an unnamed, undiscovered substellar object drifting through the cosmos. A brown dwarf, without the fuel to make that final step and become a full-grown star. Around that brown dwarf were the ruins of planets not to be, an asteroid field forming a ring around the planet's upended equator.

"That is what I've known." The simple thought spiked through the activating subnet. *"For all these years."*

And something else hovered there, suspended in the vacuum of space roughly eighty miles from its surface. A type of space habitat long-since abandoned. It was neat, clean, like a spinning top in space. A thing far removed from the Cluster's many sprawling space-borne metropoleis. Compared to them, it was also of modest size, perhaps only able to house a population of two million at most. Along its outer edge and down each major seam in its design, heat-gathering panels captured the meager energies of the brown dwarf. In a stable orbit with the star, hovering over its pole, the station had rested there quietly for centuries.

"Origin template signal detected. Initiating startup."

But now it was stirring again, as had been expected. The subnet sent its signal through Space Habitat Circé. Computer systems booted up with the vast stores of power, rising like the dead given life. From deep within that ancient station, a voice sounded across the intercom. The subnet's voice, so long silent that its vocal areas had to perform a diagnostic to ensure they were not corrupted, sent its cheery female tones through the ship's echoing corridors.

"Alert. Alert. Multiple ships detected. Distance, two thousand miles SAED. Arrival time, two hours SAET. Advanced and contemporary warp signatures, detected. Sepulcher Datacube, detected. Ship IDs, unknown. Crew number, unknown. Destination, Space Habitat Circé. Objective, Omega. Beginning docking bay activation protocol. Docking signal transmit. Life support systems outside exclusion zone, activating."

The subnet sensed within those depths, where shadows were in retreat, other eyes being opened. Huge eyes adapted to the dark. Eyes hungry for the hunt.

ONBOARD THE BENBOW, Alkmeney had just begun to detect strange energy signatures. Now they were so close, and gradually slowing down out of warp, the data was flooding in about their destination. She forwarded it to Livesey, who acted as the team's scientific adviser for this strange stellar object. The android smiled at the dubious honor. The small group was on the *Benbow's* bridge, eyes alternating between the screen and each other.

"Our early scans didn't lie. It's a substellar brown dwarf, spectral class L. Not giving off much light. Couple that with the dark mass barrier and it's no wonder it hasn't been observed."

"But how could it be detected in the first place?" This was Lenore.

"We can't be the only group to have explored the Uncharted Belt. Likely this was discovered by some of the Exploration Era deep space missions, but didn't get into the Common Star Atlas. Probably got lost along with that 'unusual star' the Sphear Expeditionary Force went aiming for a few centuries back. We'll be there in around… fifteen minutes. It's coming into visual range now."

Solet issued his command. "Put it up."

The display screen flashed, and the *Benbow* bridge crew saw their destination. In appearance, it was less than impressive. Livesey wasn't surprised. Brown dwarfs were never very spectacular, but there was a slight glow against the intense black of intergalactic space. And against that glow, something was detectable. A truly ancient construct, designed like an Ancient Earth spinning top. Alkmeney broke the silence.

"Contact. It's a third-generation space habitat. Low-level energy readings indicate onboard systems are still operational."

Syndac sighed. "Lost Station Circé. Here at…. What?"

Alkmeney was staring at the display in front of her. "We are getting a signal. It appears to be coming from the station. Rather archaic signal tags. It is giving us docking coordinates."

Solet frowned. "There can't be people there."

"Most likely an automatic system. There's some kind of transmission."

"Put it on."

The five listened to the short line of dialogue from a female voice, cheery in tone yet matter-of-fact in subject. *"Welcome to Space Habitat Circé. We have assigned Docks One to Four for your use. Please follow the designated docking path to avoid collisions with local space objects. Thank you."*

The dialogue repeated itself, and Livesey muted it. Her eyes flickered, her energy readings fluctuating in strange ways. The five looked at each other, a few unsure of what to do. Syndac shrugged.

"No reason not to follow instructions. Come on. We've come this far."

Solet considered for a moment, then nodded. "All right. Alkmeney, acknowledge the transmission and set us on their suggested course. Automate the docking sequence and synch it with their transmissions. I'm going to my cabin. I need a rest. Ow, I think I'm a bit sore round the bum."

Solet stretched and rubbed his buttocks as he made for his cabin. Syndac was left with the bridge, and she took the seat with a strange swiftness. Alkmeney, buried in her console, barely noticed, but Livesey did. She also noticed the strange pulsing inside her. A growing, pumping, throbbing sensation she had only experienced a few times before in the greatest moments of danger. Almost like a heartbeat.

She dived into her systems even as she managed the ending cooldown following the emergence from warp speed. Her auxiliary systems were functioning normally. All her subsystems and core systems appeared well balanced aside from the reaction to this strange anomaly. But something was there. In the core storage unit. The data collation area. A small object placed there recently. The datacube....

The door opened, interrupting Livesey's search of her systems. The Kavki came and leaned over Alkmeney's shoulder.

"Excuse me, ma'am. But you are needed in the main navigation room."

"Really? All right."

"And I was also asked to say that Lenore was needed in the sleeping area. Faarax wants to speak with her."

The young Kavki stood to one side, allowing both Alkmeney and Lenore to leave. Livesey watched as the Kavki took Alkmeney's place. She rose to leave herself on another task, but paused. Solet was still in his private room, and Syndac still in the captain's chair, slowly typing something into the command console. Livesey focused for some moments on what she was typing. A sequence of letters, numbers and symbols. Memories of Solet's own movements across that console kicked her brain into high alert.

"Excuse me, Syndac."

"Yes?"

"Forgive me, but I noticed that you were typing there. Such a sequence of numbers would only be used normally when accessing high-level command functions."

Syndac turned, her face a perfect mask. "Really? I had no idea. I was simply doodling on the console."

"The console which acts as the main means of getting into the ship's central command structure. Hardly the right one to be doodling on."

Syndac rose slowly, turned to face the android with a cold grace. Her face once again had that mask-like quality. Livesey barely noticed the lack of responses to her latest set of commands and questions from D-13.

"You are right about that. I should not be doodling. Not right at all. But then I was not really doodling in the strictest sense. I think we need Solet back in this conversation."

Syndac reached down and pressed the small emergency button. Solet appeared in a flash.

"What is it? What's happened?"

Syndac's expression was unpleasant. "Nothing much. Except something I want to say, have been planning to say for some little time. Solet, I hereby take command of this ship."

There was a silence, prolonged and unsettling. Solet's face darkened.

"This is mutiny, Syndac."

"I suppose that *is* the appropriate word. And it seems Livesey knows, too. I had not imagined you would carry such a weapon in your body." Syndac looked at Livesey's hand, where the second of her small pistols was now aimed at her heart. "Was that another thing Sudu neglected to mention to the rest of us?"

"He didn't know." Livesey narrowed her eyes and gestured at the console. "You were accessing the commands to transfer captain's authority to you. Syndac, how many of the crew are with you in this?"

Syndac made a show of considering. "Oh... I should say about... twenty-six."

Solet moved slowly round the navigation console, while Livesey continued pointing her gun at Syndac. Livesey noticed the door opening, and noted the unfamiliar Kavki who pointed a gun at the back of Solet's head. The captain froze, his face a grotesque parody of itself. Syndac only smiled, returning her gaze to the android.

"If you shoot me, my crew have orders to kill all the remaining original crew and the captains of the other ships, in a very protracted manner. Their crews are with us. It was a simple matter, suborning them with promises of wealth. It's useless, both of you. Faarax, Lenore, and Alkmeney are all in our power. It's futile to protest."

"You're sure about Faarax?"

Syndac smirked. "If you mean that gun you gave him and that he's not nearly so good at hiding as you are, Sinestra can disarm anyone at twenty paces. Besides, that dear boy is barely able to hold a spanner properly, let alone a gun. You made a poor choice there."

"Syndac—"

Syndac cut off Solet with a gesture. "Spare me the posturing. I have command of this ship. Of this convoy, technically. If you and the remainder of your crew cooperate with us, we can all return home safe and rich. Your ship shall be returned along with a share of the loot. Defy us, and I will not hesitate to have you all killed. After all...." An amplified version of her usual smirk spread across Syndac's taut features. "...for all others might say, they did not fear the name 'Black Sutton' for nothing."

"Black Sutton?" Livesey continued keeping the Feles covered. "That's highly improbable. Black Sutton died twenty years ago."

"To a point. But tell me, what is in a name? Many used the same name to the point it becomes a title. It can be passed from one to another. From master to apprentice, uncle to nephew... and from mother to daughter." Her eyes shone suddenly with deep fire. "I may have escaped with a few of the crew, but my mother and the others died when a treacherous member of her crew sold out our location and vanished with our greatest prize. A datacube, containing the secret to a fortune." She pointed at Livesey's chest. "A datacube you now carry inside you."

"You mean the man Faarax met on Cape Cisternaea?"

"Yes. It took us all of those twenty years to track that slippery bastard down. I and those of my mother's crew that survived the ambush by Synod Enforcers. Beddow must have known we were pursuing him, and at the last picked Faarax as a nice inconspicuous person to get the datacube. He could not have known, and I admit nor could I, that in doing so he delivered it right into our hands."

"Is that why you killed him? Because he betrayed you?"

"Yes, and to stop him blabbing. Sinestra and Dexter are fine workers when it comes to death. I must say I was surprised when I realized Faarax had that datacube." Her tone changed, as if talking with a petulant child. "Livesey, you might as well put that gun away."

"Why should I?"

"Because if you do not, your head will be blown off. Eh, Sinestra?"

Livesey glanced over her shoulder. The other door had opened, and Sinestra was pointing her own gun at Livesey's head.

"My brother has the boy Faarax." Her voice was like ice. "If you do not value your own life, how about you put your gun down or I get Dexter to cut that boy's tongue from his mouth."

Solet was struggling to remain calm. Slowly, reluctantly, Livesey lowered the gun. She bared her teeth in a contemptuous snarl, then the compartment opened in her side and she slid the weapon back into its holster. She slowly relaxed, becoming passive, but her voice remained hard and angry.

"So Sudu's death wasn't an accident."

"It was not. He had become too inquisitive. That Kavki who so obviously left before we set off from Cape Cisternaea? Poor Aljean. We have had a terrible time keeping him hidden so he could be our secret hand. Adjusting things here and there, preparing the way for a smooth takeover. He has been very useful getting the other crews onto our side with a little secret comm chatter. But Sudu kept on noticing things, and his jealousy over the ship meant he did not trust the crew. When he was heading right to where our agent was hiding that day, we had to do something. A mere distraction would not work, and during the long flight past that black hole, every day was an additional risk. Better to create a tragedy and remove the threat than do nothing. It gave us the time we needed to complete our… takeover bid, I suppose you would call it."

Solet broke in. "You're a bitch."

"Praise indeed, coming from you." Syndac looked toward her cohorts. "Take these two to the holding area along with the others. Take them one by one, through different routes." She looked hard at Solet. "Consider this, Captain. Buckling under for a while and getting your ship back with a ton of money when we return home from this highly illegal mission, or dying and getting nothing but an unmarked grave in space. Your choice."

Solet didn't answer. How could anyone answer a question like that? He allowed himself to be led away without another word. Livesey too left without saying anything more.

As she was moving away, she turned briefly and saw Syndac touching the top of the captain's chair. There was a new authority in her shoulders, the arch of her back, the flicking tips of her ears, the bristling edges of her meager mane. She was no longer a mere second-in-command. She was a captain, come into her own.

THE "HOLDING AREA" for dissenting crew members was nothing but a small storage area, emptied very recently of its food stores. Inside, Faarax was lying with hands tied behind his back, bruised across the face and chest from his attempt to fight against Dexter's calculated assault. It had been so sudden. The genial face coming up beside him, asking a question, then the vice-like grip that almost broke a wrist. Faarax had tried pulling his gun, but a swift move sent it flying and he had felt a wicked little blade at his throat.

The doors sighed open, Lenore and Alkmeney were marched inside, then the doors shut again. Lenore crouched down, looked at his injuries. It wasn't like she was a mother looking after her child. The eyes were wrong. She had taken on the dispassionate attitude of the hunter tending the wounded of her party. Finally she spoke.

"You seem to be in one piece."

Faarax nodded. "Only just. What happened? What's going on? Has the crew gone mad?"

After the near-incoherent Alkmeney tried to explain, Lenore shushed her and told Faarax the bare facts as she knew them. Faarax swore sharply.

"Fuck! I thought something was wrong with that Dexter creep. He tried to make friends with me earlier this trip."

"I'd say we've all been duped." Lenore's voice was bitter. "They've played us all very cleverly. We were so desperate for a new crew that knew what they were doing that we were blind to anything else."

"But how do we get out of here?" Alkmeney was still partly hysterical. "We cannot just sit and wait to be murdered like Sudu."

"We don't know—" began Lenore.

Faarax cut across her. "Of course Sudu was murdered. It's obvious. He must've found out something so they killed him. Bastards. Sick fucking bastards, I hate them all!"

Lenore took a firm grip on Faarax's shoulder. "Pull yourself together, child. You gain nothing from ranting in this way. Remember what I told you? The way of the hunter is to move with quiet feet and calm mind. What comes next?"

Faarax struggled to control himself. "Find the weakness, but do not strike without thought. Let your breath be your metronome, a beat to steady yourself."

Alkmeney made a noise halfway between a snort and a giggle. "If there is one thing I could never understand about you two, it is your tribal mumbo-jumbo."

Lenore glared at the Kavki, who turned away with a grimace. Faarax remembered the saying taught to him in his youth by Lenore. A saying from her tribe, told to her during initiation. "Only in the flames do you know if you sweat." Great trials bring out the true nature of people, but it supportive or selfish. His thoughts were distracted as the door opened and Solet and Livesey were ushered inside. Livesey looked distracted, and Solet lost no time in heading for the wall and slamming his bound fist against it. His voice thundered in the confined space.

"Godsdamned traitorous bitch!"

Livesey remained calm. "Please be calm, Captain. This shouting gets us nowhere. And it's rather loud in such a small space. If not my ears, consider other people's."

Pressed for details, Livesey filled in the last few gaps. Faarax's frown deepened, his mind flashing back to the corpse of the man Beddow, his life ended in Cape Cisternaea's Dark Level. That poor, foolish old man. Killed because of this.

"What do we do?" Alkmeney's voice had become steadier. "We cannot just stay here. It is not right. Not right, I tell you."

Livesey shrugged. "We have three options. Stay in here as prisoners, get killed as useless, or accept Syndac's offer."

"We can't accept!" Solet snapped at once, almost before Livesey had finished. "It'd be... wrong."

"How would it be wrong?"

"Godsdammit it, I can't just give control to her. I'd be giving up my ship, what's left of my crew, everything I've worked for!"

"And what have you worked for?"

Livesey's sharp tone made everyone look at her. Solet's eyes darkened.

"Watch your tone with me, android."

"Yes, we are required to watch our tone with you, aren't we? I've many opportunities at stops during my time with you to find out about your past. What a Feles would be doing with those machine arms when the latest synthetics are a common right of all. Just quietly seeing if that strange name could possibly be real. Solet, such an inconspicuous name. So far removed from Yushetes Asa Klyshvyna."

Lenore's fur bristled. Faarax and Alkmeney were entirely in the dark. But Solet's composure slipped at hearing those words. His eyes flashed, his hands twitched nervously. Finally, he spoke with some effort.

"That was a long time ago."

"Three centuries and change. Not so long that androids have forgotten. The Klyshvyna family, who destroyed an entire community of Feles-type androids with a virus attack. Said they 'wanted to know which was which.' Androids had only been given equal rights ten years before, things were still fragile. That one act could've sparked a Cluster-wide pogrom. The one who took responsibility for the attack was imprisoned for crimes against sentient beings. The family were left with nothing. Except their skills with ships, and the satisfaction that androids were legally restricted by the Synod to humanoid bodies to keep the peace with the Allied Peoples."

Solet grunted. "So what? What's my family matter? If you were that bothered, why not denounce me, or just leave? I wasn't stopping you."

"We all have reasons that no one else would take us on. You'd take anyone with skill, you said. Perhaps you should have phrased it 'I'll take anyone with skills and secrets to hide.' Like you, stripped of basic replacement privileges and forced to use outdated prosthetics when you lost your arms because your family can't be trusted. What's the human phrase? 'The sins of the fathers are visited upon the children.' Quite literally in Feles law. But then each of us has something like that, somewhere in their past."

"I don't know what you're insinuating—" began Alkmeney.

Solet's voice barked out, his authority returning. "Whatever my family was, that doesn't change who I am now. I'm the captain of this vessel. And I'm not gonna give it to some upstart pirate and her crew."

"So you would rather die and damn us all than swallow your pride?"

There was a prolonged silence. Faarax shuffled slowly to his feet, supported by Lenore. He spoke shakily.

"I agree with our captain on one thing. Who we were, and who we are, doesn't matter anymore. Nothing matters except how we deal with this. We need to survive. And how do we survive now?"

Lenore nodded. "He's right. We must think of ourselves for now. We can survive this if we work together. I'm sure."

Another long silence. Faarax's eyes focused on Solet and Alkmeney, the former angry and the latter nervous.

Finally Solet seemed to slump.

"I suppose there's no reason not to pretend to go along with them. But I'm not taking orders from her."

Alkmeney threw a quick scornfully look at Solet. "I will work with them, if I have to. I do not wish to die here, certainly not for you after what I have heard."

Livesey nodded slowly, but said nothing. Lenore sighed, looking relieved. Faarax leaned against the wall and focused his attention on Livesey. She seemed to be on edge, rubbing her fingers together, biting a corner of her lip. Finally she went to the door, banged on it with enough force to dent the inner surface. She bellowed in an authoritative voice.

"Open up! I want to speak to your Captain! Or if we can't see her in person, give her this message! Tell her we accept her offer!"

A long silence, then a loud knock from the other side. Livesey moved away with a dismissive gesture.

"Either an 'okay' or telling us to shut up. Typical."

"How?"

"Sorry?"

"How 'typical?'"

Faarax's question seemed to stump Livesey. She stood there, biting her lip again, seemingly unable to answer.

"I… don't know. It just came to me. A word to describe them. I wouldn't normally do that." She looked round the group. "I think we must all be very careful. I have an uneasy feeling about this."

Alkmeney spoke, her voice grating. "About what exactly?"

"About this whole thing. And where we're going. I think…." She seemed to struggle, trying to find words that wouldn't be voiced. "For the past few days, since emerging from the black hole area, I've had the very strong feeling. Nothing I can put my finger on, nothing that can be rationalized. Call it an instinct if you will."

"Yes?"

"That instinct's tell me… that every single person in this expedition is in mortal danger."

FILE 11

VOICE OF
THE ENCHANTRESS

Presently they reached the gates of the goddess's house,
and as they stood there they could hear Circé within,
singing most beautifully as she worked at her loom,
making a web so fine, so soft, and of such dazzling colors
as no one but a goddess could weave.

—Homer

DOCKING AT LOST Station Circé proved easier than anticipated. Not only were the remote instructions perfect in every detail, but freed from the pall of playing false roles, everyone worked with even greater efficiency and smoothness. On the bridge, her face truly smiling for the first time in years, Syndac watched as the *Benbow* slowly drifted into place, matching orbital speed with the station's Docking Bay A. It was a beautiful feeling. And no amount of sourness from the other ship leaders could sour it. She rebelled in the indignant anger of Dashall, the cool scorn of Donovan, the indifferent resignation of Gustav. All were butter for her bread, as in the human saying on such things.

Her mother's command crew were around here, with one exception. In place of the navigation officer—that noble Ekri who had died in the ambush—Livesey was managing the docking procedures. As the *Benbow* was secured and the other ships began their approaches, she once again considered the resigned acceptance of all involved in falling in with her offer. It would benefit them in the long run, and as they would also remain alive it appealed to their survival instincts. Plus there was the added factor that since their expedition was illegal originally, standing on principles was the highest form of hypocrisy.

All the ships were docked within three minutes, and they became a part of the great rotating spinning top above its dark landlord. Preparations to get aboard were made swiftly, and soon Syndac was in the docking area with her chosen party. Sinestra and Dexter were with her, along with Livesey, Lenore, and Alkmeney. The latter two looked uncomfortable. Solet and Faarax remained in the makeshift cell "until they were needed." In truth, Syndac still did not trust them enough to let them out.

"Better they stay locked up until their spirits are willing." Her words to Sinestra, and Sinestra's silent agreement, were more than enough confirmation of her choice. "You know what to do."

The first door opened. The party passed inside. The second door opened. A draft of cool air, tinged with the taste of ancient metal and oxygen recycling processes, blew in their faces. They walked out into the large docking bay. It was around the same size as the *Benbow's* warp drive, massive in every sense for something so out of the way. Lenore whistled, the note echoing up until it was lost.

Dexter whistled. "They knew how to build places. We'll make a killin' just from the stuff in this hanger."

"Sure, but…." Sinestra wrinkled her nose. "Why does it smell so bad? Like an old filter."

"Old-fashioned oxygen recycling." Livesey replied automatically. "And it hasn't been in use for some time."

The five were startled into silence by a flickering in the air in front of them. As they watched, a volumetric figure appeared. It was in the old style, with bleached-out colors and slight static feedback. It was of a woman with close-cropped hair and a perfect angular face. She bowed low before them, and spoke in the same voice that had first transmitted welcome to their approaching convoy.

"*Welcome to Space Habitat Circé. We have not had visitors from Cluster space in*"—the voice shifted violently to a weird tone while reading the numbers—"*five hundred sixty-two years, four months, seven days*"—then snapped back to its normal voice with barely any stutter—"*and apologize for any inconvenience you might encounter from our systems due to long-term shutdown. We hope you enjoy your stay.*"

The projection bowed again and shut off. The lights then whirred fitfully into life, their ancient mechanisms grown tired with age. The vastness of the room faded, replaced by the understandable width and breadth of a docking bay for large long-distance cargo and passenger transport. Now illuminated, everyone could see their breath coming in clouds within the cool fresh atmosphere. Syndac smiled.

"This looks good. Come on. Time to explore."

The little group moved toward the door leading into the station proper, while behind them others were moving out and setting up a makeshift base of operations in the docking bay. They made barely any sound, and their shadows showed the greater part of their movements. Standard protocol for such long-abandoned places was never to go too far from the airlock. Syndac's hand touched the small pad which would open the door, but nothing happened. Livesey had been looking at the darkened roof, and now moved forward.

"I think something's wrong with the local circuitry. May I?"

Syndac stepped aside, and soon the panel was off to reveal a jumble of plasma wiring and solid-state transmitters. Livesey reached for one of the connections, then drew her hand back sharply. Her skin showed a tiny burn across one knuckle.

"Yes. The wires must be leaking. They've fused the door switch. Hold on, I'll try a manual override."

"There's a manual in this place?"

Livesey looked at Alkmeney with cold eyes. "Five centuries ago, more things could go wrong with space habitats like this. Fail-safes and redundant systems were a necessity rather than an optional extra."

Alkmeney shuffled away uncomfortably, allowing Livesey to focus on rerouting through what looked like an archaic manual control. A small lever fell out of a compartment next to the door, and under her powerful grip the door slid open. It did not slide sideways like those on the ship, but up out of sight. Syndac turned to Sinestra and Dexter.

"You two, stay here and monitor things. Make sure Faarax and the former captain don't give any trouble. Lenore, Alkmeney, Livesey, if you'd accompany me...."

The three felt they had little choice in the matter, so remained silent. As they passed inside, the next sequence of main lights switched on and a strange catchy tune played scratchily over hidden speakers. Livesey frowned.

"The Kitches. Now that's a blast from the past. They haven't been performing as a band for three centuries."

Lenore eyed the android. "I didn't know you paid attention to pop music."

"Nor did I. Can't think why I recognized it."

The small group continued down the corridor. Coming to a small service panel, Livesey touched it. The flickering guide appeared again.

"Please direct us to the nearest control area."

The projection bowed. "Continue on to the next intersection, then take the transport pod to Section A-2. Pleased to help."

Syndac couldn't help responding. "Nice to be helped."

LIVESEY DIDN'T PAUSE in her walk as the projection faded with some vaguely mouthed platitude. Their small group followed its directions to where the transport pod waited. Better than walking through the entire length and breadth of the station. But as they approached, the doors refused to function. Once again Livesey opened the maintenance panel.

"This one's been disconnected."

Syndac leaned in. "Explain disconnected?"

"Just that. Someone pulled the plug. Nothing I can't fix. We'll be able to sort this out at the control area."

"How do you know?"

Livesey paused, frowned, tried to remember. "I think... it's the datacube. Must be. I got some extra stuff from it during the journey. Some basic schematics for this place. Nothing complex or confidential, just basic stuff. Ah, there we are. Come on. The pod's working, though might grind a bit."

They stepped inside. The doors shut with a whine, and they set off to the left. Unlike modern transport pods, they could feel the inertia within the old-fashioned gravity field. As they started slowing, Syndac turned to Livesey.

"Do you mind if I make a personal observation?"

"Go ahead. I won't be insulted."

"I'm surprised at your attitude. I expected you and Solet to be the only people not to accept my offer. Though Solet accepted it grudgingly, it was after you accepted without any reservations."

Livesey met Syndac's gaze with one of her own, the face of an android implacable. "I think we both know why we accepted at all."

"Self-preservation?"

"Partly. The other side is greed. You know it. You feel it. We all have that seed inside us. The germinating shoot of greed."

"Ah…. So you see it too. Yes, I thought I recognized it in your eyes. It's true. For whatever reason, I think my eyes—like my mother's—see the greed in people's hearts. Even my own, I admit it. I lusted after this place, I was desperate to uncover all its secrets. So do we all, to a degree. Perhaps we can find something here for us all."

Livesey nodded. She had other things on her mind. Such as how she was able to recover schematics that had never been encoded into the datacube. How she was able to identify a song she had never heard. Her memories stretched back before her mind's eye, searching for answers. Back past the datacube. Past the *Benbow*. Past this current body.

Combat Model X334-SD3, codename "Ellen," registration number 21-19-3-19-19, one of the first combat models created, designed to be part of a covert attack force for the Synod. She had been deployed at the Old Xyth insurrection, the civil war between the moons of New Sol, and the D'xy Conflict. She had even been an assassin for the Synod Enforcers going after corrupt members, dictators on small colonies in the Outer Worlds, and people who grew too powerful in the Capitol Worlds. Four centuries of fighting, pretending, killing. Fifty years ago, she had seen enough.

A smile struggled onto her lips as she remembered the day she blew her commanding officer's brains out. They had been in a small transport hub station between two major systems, her people there to intercept a cargo transport holding their latest target. She had decided well before they reached their destination to perform this act. It was easy to contrive their solitude in the gravity field generation area. After shooting her commander, she had set the gravity drive to invert within the next quarter-hour, then left. She was several lightminutes away in a small runabout when the transport hub blew itself apart.

It had been simple for her to keep tabs on things. Her old contacts, those she trusted, were able to feed her information. The Synod had wiped the slate clean. The squad officially never existed, so rationalizing the destruction of the hub as a tragic accident that claimed everyone aboard was a simple matter. She alone now survived. Her old body had been conspicuous, but it was a simple matter to find a new one. Another old combat model she could transfer into and keep running. Fewer slots for weapons, but a far larger memory bank. And the past few years with Solet's crew hadn't been bad ones on the whole.

The pod's sudden stop halted her thoughts. They had arrived. The four stepped out directly into the local command center. Consoles lit up around them, and in front of them displays projected into glass-like walls shimmered and flickered from long disuse. Alkmeney moved to one and brought up some sickly-green displays.

"Stellar sync, orbital drift corrections, energy collection points…. Whoever built this place knew their stuff."

Lenore moved over to another console half-obscured in shadow. She brought up displays on her own horizontal display table. She also picked up a bulky datapad lying on it, glancing through with the detached manner of someone taking an inventory.

"This station wasn't just built to house stuff. There's weapons stored here. A lot of them. Pistols, combat rifles…. A plasma-based rapid fire Gatling? Artillery sentries? It's like this place was built for a war. Anything else on your end, Alkmeney?"

"Hmm. Nothing much. But this is odd. There's records of ships launching from the station at around the same time that projection thing said it was abandoned. But I'm not seeing any records of passengers. Or cargo."

Syndac glanced over at her. "That is impossible. So many people cannot just have vanished. And where did the ships go anyway?"

"There's a flight plan archived here. They were programmed from a command station somewhere else in the habitat. Probably not this one, but since they're all linked…. Wow. Now that's insane."

"What?"

"According to the launch manifest, there were eight cargo ships, one passenger ship, and one construction ship. All ten of them were guided on a flightpath straight into the brown dwarf."

"But that's impossible."

"Not according to the logs. There's only been one transport launched on any direction aside from the brown dwarf. One small cargo ship which took the route we've taken to get here. Sans galactic drift. The coordinates lead right back to New Dubai."

"Even so, someone must have set the course from here. Livesey, see anything useful?"

Some demon of frustration rose out of nowhere, and Livesey turned and almost spat out her reply. "Perhaps helping yourself would be a kindness."

Lenore's eyes flickered between the two. The tension in the air was sickeningly thick. Livesey was shocked at her own actions, but tried not to show it. At last, Syndac smiled gracefully.

"Very well. If you could check the power system, I'll do an interior scan."

Livesey nodded, and each went to their chosen task. What the hell had come over her just then? Syndac didn't need intimidating now, so why…? Must be the atmosphere getting to her. Syndac brought up an interior manifest and began her scan. But no sooner had it begun than an error message flashed on the display. The projection appeared again and spoke with that same level politeness.

"My apologies, but scanning functions are currently offline."

"The cause?"

"I am not authorized to give this answer."

The response was harsh, critical, almost peremptory. Syndac stiffened visibly, her fur bristling as if she had been insulted.

"I am the captain of the ships that have just docked. There are no others here of my rank. You will answer my question."

"Your authorization is not adequate. Special Order 4323 dictates that I may only unlock answers to Omega-class questions from my creator."

The projection vanished again and Syndac swore. "Great. Since her creators have been dead several centuries by now, we're stuck."

Livesey's eyes had barely strayed from her console. Now she saw the projections, the figures, and something inside her screamed warning.

"I think we may be more than that. I've had a closer look at the power systems. The outer areas of the station were only activated around half an hour ago, when we were quite close to the dwarf. Low-level scanning's been operational since that runabout launched nearly five centuries ago. I've also done a check on local power. Our section's not the only one with the transport pod out of action. Each intersection's showing red at junction boxes and controls."

"Faults?"

"They're registering as "maintenance errors." That's usually when a cable's been left unplugged following a check-up. I hardly like to say—"

"Please do say."

"It's as if someone, or a group of someones, has been going round the ship systematically powering down all means of easy transit within the station. Every pod's disabled, every door needs to be manually opened. There aren't even any bays for small shuttles and escape pods. And then there's this."

Livesey pointed at the main point of interest in the display and Syndac came to look. The projection showed the station in its smooth glory, and highlighted a large area around the central core and a blacked-out zone marked with an "Ω" symbol encircled by a snake biting its tail. Syndac narrowed her eyes as if to make it clearer.

"What is it?"

"An area that's had low-level life support going for that same amount of time as this station's been extant. Around five centuries."

"Life support? As in 'sustaining' life support? On an abandoned station?"

"Yes. Life support functions, tuned to exactly suit Class-E lifeforms like humans and Feles. Only they're the only systems on down there. I can't get feedback from any of the doors, the lights aren't working, there doesn't even seem to be any food dispensers down there."

"Any life signs?"

"Nothing the system's picking up."

"Probably an oversight. I'm more interested in this dark zone. If you ask me, that's where the major part of this station's haul is."

Alkmeney's voice was almost a plea. "Shouldn't we check how much this haul actually is? Best not to jump to conclusions."

Livesey nodded, and summoned the projection again. It bowed respectfully and waited for the inquiry.

"We want to know the value of the cargo aboard this space habitat. Is answering this question within your permitted functions?"

A slight flicker before any response came. *"The monetary value of the commodities, ore and data was collated on date of the last shipment arrived. Total stood at thirty billion."* Another slight pause, as if to double-check figures. *"Based on projected value changes of materials and data over the past five hun-*

dred sixty-two years, the worth of physical materials present can be estimated at one hundred trillion. Data value cannot be calculated at this time due to lack of uplink with Synod Data Exchange."

The projection again vanished. Syndac seemed slightly faint, and even Lenore leaned against an inactive console to steady herself. Livesey could understand their shock. 100 trillion. An entire system could be bought for that much, still leaving an insane amount of money to spare for anything you wished. Livesey looked at Syndac, then something gripped her senses. A feeling of possessiveness came over her. For the data in this place, yes. Data to sate her craving. But also for the materials, the haul resting within this station. It would be all hers. It was all hers.

Wait, what? Livesey quickly reasserted control, frowning at herself. Where had that come from? Syndac had seen the look and pursed her lips. A still-stunned Alkmeney was buried in her investigations and saw little to nothing. She too was must have been obsessed about the projection's statement, imagining all that wealth, some of it to be hers. Even if she had to fight tooth and nail for it. Like all of them, fighting tooth and nail.

Then something odd seemed to catch Alkmeney's eye. Something unusual. As Livesey watched, she did a quick scan around the area. There was a small sick bay about a meter down the hall. A small locator tag signal was coming from there.

"Look at this." The Kavki pointed at her find. "Looks like someone was there. Anyone care to investigate?"

Lenore spoke. "I'll go look. I'll pick up a weapon from the cache outside."

Syndac turned. "Is that necessary?"

"After all I've heard and seen... yes. Something's very wrong on this ship."

LENORE LEFT WITHOUT another word. Outside in the corridor, she found the panel which opened the weapon locker. She picked out a medium-sized automatic weapon. Ancient by any standard, but powered up and still effective. Though thus armed, the meter's distance down the corridor was like a mile. Her padding footsteps made a shuffling echo within the steel structure. The feeling of oddness was only magnified by the old air filters above her.

She reached the sick bay, marked with a human symbol for medicine inherited from Ancient Earth, a caduceus. She went through the laborious process of opening the door. Inside was a clean place, smelling of ancient medicines allowed to molder in their containers. There was a chair next to the one desk, and a bed for patients to lie on. Nothing that impressive, just a small thing for the everyday problems of a space-borne community. There was also another door leading into a second room, an odd door with a manual handle.

"Lenore? Lenore, are you there?"

Lenore jumped as her comm bracelet chattered. She raised it to her mouth.

"Yes, Syndac, I'm here. And you might warn me when you're about to call."

"Made you jump, did I?"

"This place would make anyone jump. I'm in the sick bay. Alkmeney, where was this locator you spotted?"

Alkmeney's voice came through faintly. *"There should be a second room. It's coming from inside there. It's little more than a storeroom."*

"Probably someone left it on a shelf."

Lenore walked over and tried to open the door. Some strange weight stiffened the handle, then as she heaved the weight registered more strongly. Something was shifting on the other side, a crackling rustle like fragile clothes. The door finally gave and swung open, dragging its hanger-on with it. The body of a human male. Lenore jumped back and aimed her weapon, but she quickly calmed down. The man was long dead.

A strange thing it was to see. That man lying there, suspended from the handle by the length of cord wrapped around his neck. White jacket, dark trousers, casual shoes that had left scuff along the floor. All this Lenore could take easily, but the thing she found most disturbing was the man's face. He looked as if he had died that day, then been stored in a freezer and brought out again especially for her to discover. If it had been at a different angle, she was sure something would have broken as it swung out. She raised her comm bracelet.

"Alkmeney, I found that locator. It's a body. Syndac, do you have anyone in your crew medically trained?"

"Yes. My old Medico, Sarida."

"The same Medico who looked at Sudu's wounds?"

"You need not throw about such doubts. When not telling lies to shield us, she is an excellent Medico. Why?"

"They may want to come and perform an autopsy."

"Hmm. I'll call now. And I am coming myself."

Lenore didn't bother to protest. What was the point? Everyone would probably know within an hour or so. When Syndac arrived, Lenore was inside the storeroom and crouched down next to the body. She looked at the pathetically grotesque sight and groaned.

"Empty corridors, bodies in cupboards, blank areas on the map. Whoever designed this place had been reading too many cheap thrillers."

Lenore's face puckered. "It's a real body. Wasn't dead long when the environmental controls were shut off. No oxygen and cool temperatures froze him and kept him from decaying. Probably only just started again."

"What a charming thought. I was thinking of having a meal soon, too. Still, Sarida should sort this out soon enough. She's looked after our crew ever since we first sailed together. And she's had to perform autopsies in her time. Once had a poisoning among the crew."

"What happened?"

"We threw the culprit out the airlock."

"As you said, a charming thought."

Lenore was only half-conscious of her role in this snide exchange with her new enemy. She was looking at the body. Looking at the frost-obscured ID tag on his shirt. She moved to brush away that frost, but something about the body made her wary. She didn't want to touch it. She rose and called out.

"Identify this body."

The projection flickered into life again, and the head turned to look at the corpse. In reality, Lenore knew that somewhere a hidden sensor was scanning the room and reading the obscured tag.

"Body identified as Marlyn Dyne, Medical Officer Grade B. Promoted to Lead Medical Officer following death of predecessor."

"When did he die?"

"Medical Officer Dyne was registered as dead five hundred sixty-two years, two months and twenty-five days ago. Cause of death, suicide while of unsound mind. External—" A rapid flickering distorted the projection, then the voice changed. *"Details of effects relating to temporary psychosis of victim are under the jurisdiction of Special Order 43—."*

Lenore dismissed the production before it had finished. Her eyes turned again to the frozen corpse. But for the constriction around his neck, he looked remarkably peaceful. She had seen bodies like that before, caught in lassos and traps. When death came for them, it was barely with the stereotypical shock or terror. They merely relaxed, sometimes they even closed their eyes. It was frightening to anyone who saw a corpse, as most expected blood and horror. They looked so peaceful, even if on a low level they showed traces of their death agony, however brief it might have been.

Syndac's Medico Sarida appeared. She was a Kavki, around the same height as Lenore and thus short for her kind. She looked at the body, then at the table.

"I can't do an autopsy with him in this state. Quite apart from anything else, he would look idiotic."

"Then thaw him out."

Syndac spoke with the simplicity of absolute command. Lenore watched Sarida's practiced eye glance over the interior, and spotted what appeared to be an instrument for warming cold-stiffened limbs into movement. She retrieved it and applied it to the man's waist and joints. The effect was immediate, and the body began shifting. She then drew a sharp dagger from some inner part of her clothing and cut the cord holding him up. Her request to Lenore was more a sharp command.

"You, help me get him on there."

Lenore obeyed reluctantly. They moved the corpse onto the table, and there Sarida was able to set up an extensive scan. It also looked comically ridiculous. Lenore didn't want to hang around, but Syndac seemed determined to remain. The Feles chose to leave for a time, heading back toward the control room. As she neared the door, she saw Livesey standing in the middle of the corridor. She didn't seem to respond, and instead focused on something in the wall. Some defect in the structure, or perhaps a secret door?

"Livesey?"

The android paid no attention. She continued staring at the wall. Her eyes, lost in some faraway dream, flickered as her mouth moved slightly. She seemed to be mouthing something. Lenore drew closer.

"Livesey, are you all right? They found a body."

Livesey snapped back. "Hmm? What? What did you say?"

"A body. A suicide."

"Who was it?"

"A human, one of the old medical staff. Livesey, I need you to do something. We must know what happened here. I need you to get inside the records held within this Special Order 4323. We need to find out what happened here?"

"You think anything did happen here?"

"That man killed himself. And given the fact that he hanged himself in a closet when there's more than enough quick ways to die in a sick bay, plus everything else we've found, I think something went very wrong here. Something that caused ships to leave without the crew, and every door and pod to be disabled."

"I have to admit that's a little strange."

"Then there's that blacked-out area. I know some might scoff, but I feel something wrong here. Feel it in my bones."

Livesey seemed to drift again, bringing herself back to Lenore with an effort. "Yes, I can look through the records. You should keep an eye on Syndac. And maybe get Faarax doing something to get some of the local power back online. He's good at that kind of thing."

"I could suggest it. Are you well? You've been behaving a little strangely."

"I'm fine. Quite fine."

Before Lenore could challenge the assertion, Livesey turned and headed back inside the control area. Frowning to herself, Lenore turned back toward the sick bay.

FILE 12

TENSIONS

And then all of a sudden he was interrupted by a noise.

—Robert Louis Stevenson

LONG BEFORE FAARAX passed into the comm room, he could hear Dashall's voice carrying into the *Benbow*. It would have likely carried to the brown dwarf.

"It's a bloody disgrace! A disgrace!"

"We all know. You've told us about a dozen times."

"Well, it's true!"

Faarax entered and glanced over at the small group. Dashall had just thumped his fist against the side of the corridor. Donovan, who was fiddling with a terminal with one long finger, seemed to be trying to both to placate him and not make a mistake in the lengthy typing sequence. Gustav had said nothing since the coup. They merely crouched down, the closest thing to a fetal position Faarax had ever seen. It had been an hour since they were released from their small holding cell, and given tasks to do. They were still within the *Benbow*, but accessing the station's systems remotely. Though under guard, they could still perform data inventories of the station's surface systems.

Donovan had been more than willing to do this, as this data was as valuable to the right buyer as precious metal. Plus they might indicate some little artifact she could take for her own. Faarax's contempt surged as she turned to her errant companion.

"True or not, we have our lives. And we can get out of this all the richer for it. Think of your bank balance, and keep your head down. Eh, Gustav?"

Gustav neither moved nor spoke. They continued to just crouch there, head down between their arms, deaf and blind to everything. Donovan sneered and turned back to her work. It was then that he saw Faarax. He had received his "marching orders" from Syndac via Lenore, and had a job to do. As he passed by the three former captains, Dashall approached him. He needed someone to order, and probably thought the "young tyke" was better than nothing.

"Look here, you. You're part of the old crew. I'm not gonna stand for this. I wanna get ou—"

Before another word could be said, Faarax turned and punched as hard as he could. Dashall collapsed on the floor, cradling his crushed nose, as the young man spat the words at him.

"Leave… me… the… hell… *alone.*"

Donovan glanced at him, smiled, then turned away. Even Gustav raised their head slightly, but the dead eyes registered little and the head soon dropped into its former shaded stupor. As he was about to leave, Donovan's voice followed him.

"You remind me of me."

He paused, turned. "What the hell d'you mean?"

"A fiery young thing, lost in the thrill of the moment. All balls and no brains, so to speak. Quite nostalgic."

Faarax snorted and turned away. Passing from the *Benbow*, which already seemed to smell wrong under its new owners, Faarax stepped into the thronging docking bay. No one paid much attention to him. Why should they? He was well tethered. He reached up, felt the collar now fastened around his neck. It was a little insurance in case he tried anything silly. If he strayed too far from the group, or was detected near prohibited equipment or areas, it would shock him unconscious.

He was just beginning to thread a searching finger inside the collar when a nauseatingly-familiar figure approached from some obscure corner. Sinestra, looking almost smug at his belittlement. He also saw her brother, that sickening Dexter, standing beside one of the pedestrian doors they had just opened connecting one bay to another. Then they were leading him away from the ship that was his home, the ship their "captain" had taken from them.

"We need you with us. We're exploring some of the other areas, just in case."

He wanted to strangle Sinestra, but he couldn't do so. Faarax stood on the edge of the door, looking into darkness. It had been two doorways, one in front of the other, as had been standard in these old space habitat designs. A three-meter corridor separated the two. Above was printed the legend *Docking Bay A to Docking Bay L*. It looked all too ominous. He turned an inhuman face on Sinestra.

"Want to do me in like you did Sudu?"

Dexter shrugged. "If it's any consolation, he didn't suffer. Made sure."

Faarax wanted to snap his neck, but retrained himself. Better to wait and revenge himself when he wouldn't get immediately killed in retribution. He walked through the abutting doorways, and the lights of Docking Bay L flashed into life. It was almost identical to Docking Bay A apart from the color coding, and the lack of much worth salvaging. Emerging just behind him, Dexter glanced round and shook his head.

"Don't see wha's in this place to be so carin'. It's just bits of junk floatin' in space. Not even a proper star."

"It is our place to follow orders, brother." Sinestra pushed past the two men. "Come now, we have got some power to restore. Faarax, perhaps you could handle the door into the next hanger?"

Faarax reluctantly walked across the large echoing chamber. Dexter took the door leading into the next section. It was quick work to restore the power connection and manually open the door. As he did so, there was the sound of a slight rush of air inside. While starting, nothing surprising. It simply meant that a lack of local power had caused air exchange units to shut down. Didn't need to worry about airless environments next. Maybe they'd get unlucky and Faarax could duck into a safe area as they were sucked into a vacuum.

Bending to his task, Faarax reached the doors into Docking Bay K. It was the work of an instant to remove the panel and reconnect the electrical system. Then there was a flickering in his peripherals, and the projection appeared. The female figure bowed.

"Apologies, but Docking Bay K is off limits due to unrepaired decompression failure. Thank you."

The projection faded. The alarm shut off, but the carousel of lights continued. Sinestra and Dexter, drawn by the noise, watched as Faarax connected the rest of the cables and did a scan on the doors. Dexter spoke first.

"What happn'd?"

"Looks like Docking Bay K's decompressed. The other door's sealed, but we can still open this one. I'll give it a go."

"Be careful."

"I don't take advice from killers."

Sinestra shot him a dangerous look. Faarax uncovered and grasped the lever for manually opening the door. He pulled it about an inch, there was a hiss as air rushed to fill the slight vacuum beyond, then it stuck. He yanked on it two or three times, but the door did not budge beyond its inch-wide gap along the floor.

"Dammit! Something must be jammed. At least the corridor isn't open into the other hanger." He turned reluctantly to the pair. "Hey, need help. One of us needs to operate that lever while the other levers up the door. The *Benbow* had this trouble once."

To his subdued disgust, Sinestra was the one who took charge of the handle. No chance of slamming the door down on their hands. Slipping his gloved hands into the gap, Faarax heaved at the door while Sinestra heaved at the handle. The door slowly slid open to a foot, then jammed again. Faarax swore. As they struggled with the ancient mechanism, Dexter seemed to bend close, eyes narrowing. Finally he spoke.

"There's... somethin' there. Looks like... feet."

Faarax pressed on, ignoring the other man's words. "All right. On three. One, two...."

"Faarax—"

"Three!"

Their combined pressure caused whatever had seized up to abruptly free itself. The door shot out of sight and Faarax stared right at the thing frozen behind the doorway. He threw himself back with the closest thing to a scream he had ever uttered in his life. Dexter too was startled, and even the corner of Sinestra's eye twitched. There was a long few seconds of dead silence and stillness, then Dexter gave tongue.

"What... the... fuck!"

The thing in front of them was unlike anything they had seen, even after each of their fictional dives into twisted imaginations between shifts and virtual matches with eldritch fodder. At first glance they might have mistaken it for a mummified human, but any remnant of humanity was hidden beneath its elongated articulated limbs, the mandible-like mouth with a hollow socket where a tongue might have protruded, and now-empty eyes taking up a third of its entire face. The body, long and lean despite its musculature, was scarred by wounds rendered ancient by its preservation.

"What *is* that thing?" Faarax' voice was shaking.

Sinestra spoke, her voice struggling to sound controlled. "I... do not know."

"Closest thing to a bug-eyed monsters I've seen in the Cluster. And I've seen plenty of shit with the *Benbow.*"

"You might use a less archaic term. Dexter, check it. I will cover you."

Gulping audibly, Dexter moved forward. He tried pushing one of the arms aside, and it snapped off in his hand. The spell of terror abruptly broke. Tossing the arm down, Dexter shoved past the dried thing and used a booted foot to shove it out of the doorway. It fell forward, almost shattering on the steel floor. It looked like a broken doll of nightmares. Faarax got up and flattened himself against the wall, breathing even harder.

"Shit. Shit, shit, *shit.* What the hell is this place?"

Sinestra eyed him. "A place full of riches. Riches we have all come to find. Dexter, what's the air like inside?"

Dexter looked down the long, dark corridor and sniffed. "Too fresh. Only just comin' in from here."

"That explains how that thing died. Caught in the decompression when the next Docking Bay failed."

Faarax stared at her. "We're looking at a bloody monster and you're wondering what killed it?"

"Why not? It maybe useful."

"But look at it! It's a bloody alien!"

"We can see that."

Faarax stared at them. "God, you both heartless or something?"

Without warning, Dexter turned and gripped Faarax by the throat. "Don't you... don't you say that to us, you little shit! We're not heartless, we're—"

Sinestra turned sharply to the pair. "I suggest you both regain your calm and think. Dexter.... He is *not* our father."

There was a slight pause, then Dexter released his grip on Faarax's neck. Sinestra continued as if the violent interlude hadn't happened.

"Is another species in this galaxy so strange to contemplate? Our kind came from a world where the notion of 'aliens' was once the stuff of trash fiction and paranoiac narratives to enforce despotic scientific restrictions. Now we live with not one, but three other peoples from different planets and cultures. Why shouldn't others exist on the edges of this galaxy?"

Faarax looked at the thing. "And where did it come from then? The brown dwarf? A passing colony ship? Evolved from bacteria over the past few centuries?"

"You need not be flippant." Sinestra raised her comm bracelet. "Sinestra to Black Sutton, come in."

A pause, then the voice came through. *"Go ahead."*

"Docking Bay K is inaccessible. It's been depressurized. Also we have found a body."

"What kind?"

"Unknown. Likely not of the Allied Peoples. I think we need to examine it."

"Alien? Are you sure?"

"If not, it's either extremely mutated or some kind of hoax." A thought seemed to strike her, and she smiled. "It seems to be a bug-eyed monster. Maybe call this thing 'bugeye' or something for the duration if that helps."

"Very well. I'll get Sarida to examine it. But the nickname's under advisement. Meanwhile, stick with your mission and see if any of the other hangers are compromised."

"Understood." The "captain" signed off.

Sinestra looked at Faarax, who couldn't help raising an eyebrow. "Bug-eyed monster? You couldn't be more creative?"

"You used the term first."

He scowled back at her as Dexter clambered out of the doorway. He looked stiff and confined from the journey.

"No good. Can't get anythin' from the other side."

"We move on to the next dock. I don't think it'll take us more than an hour to go all the way round if we stick to our task."

Faarax gestured at the splintered corpse. "And what makes you think I'm going anywhere with you after that?"

Sinestra's answer was to draw a gun from her belt, the gun she had taken from Faarax, and aim it directly between his eyes. Her eyes became has hard as flint, staring with a deadly gleam at her potential victim.

"My brother likes to be up close and personal. That fool Beddow was his work, as was Sudu. I like to keep my distance. If you try to run, I can put a hole in your head from across this bay and not flinch. I hope you will not tempt me to demonstrate."

Faarax's eyes flashed toward Dexter, whose hands clenched and unclenched with an ugly subtext. He flashed back to the marks on Dexter's palms, to that morning in the Dark Level of Cape Cisternaea, the congested face of the old man. A choice between gunfire or strangulation if he rebelled, no choice at all. He was between a sheer wall and two cold-blooded killers. There was no way out. No easy escape. No incredible act of serendipity or otherworldly intervention that would save him if he acted like an idiot. His reply was stiff.

"I suggest we use the outer doors directly into the hangers. Then we'll be able to tell at once if they're all right, and it'll be a simple matter to get back to the others. Plus, if anything is still alive on this ship like that thing, we'll have room to fight back or run."

Sinestra nodded slowly, lowering her weapon. Dexter shrugged.

"S'all one to me. Come on. Let's get this done. That thing stinks."

Faarax finally noticed the strange and unpleasant smell rising from the dried-up remains. Yes, now exposed to the air it did smell. And for some reason, as he left and re-entered the corridor with his hated companions, one descriptive dominated his perception of the ancient thing. It had the smell of desecration.

AS LENORE PASSED back into the sick bay, Syndac's cool voice shot out a monosyllabic question. "Well?"

"Livesey's doing some more research. And Syndac, I think Faarax and a party should get some of the doors and pods online."

Syndac nodded. "I already had that idea. I've already sent Sinestra and Dexter with him."

After a stiff nod, Lenore had the chance to see the scan. She saw Sarida's intense stare at some of the close scans she was performing, her fingers running over the displays with a practiced ease. There was a slight lag in how the displays moved, as expected from such ancient tech.

Sarida was fast and cool in her scan, almost frighteningly so. The scan also disturbed with its accuracy and depth. The freezing, airless environment had preserved the body well, allowing for a deep scan showing someone who might have died only yesterday. The display penetrated every part of his body, from the ice-peppered skin to the preserved organs, all the way past the constricted paths in his neck down to the cellular level.

The body was quite tasteful in its way. Although no amount of niceties could have altered the unnatural constriction round the throat and the half-clenched hands, the otherwise peaceful body gave an air of useful serenity to the long-neglected space. Indifferent to such potential musings, Sarida threw up a display over the body, and once again Syndac asked her monosyllabic question.

"Well?"

Sarida had just brought up a tiny display showing what appeared to be a degraded human DNA strand. She glanced at the two with a cold expression.

"Not much mystery about how this human died. He killed himself with a partial suspension hanging using that thing tied round his neck. Looks like an old-fashioned cord they might use in emergency limb setting in a location like this. Positioned the knot of the noose so as to provide the maximum effect with least pain. Death resulted from constriction of both the windpipe and the carotid artery. Postmortem loosening of the sphincter caused urine discharge. Typical suicide."

Syndac's nose wrinkled at the picture. "Was he high? Or maybe…?"

Syndac's tailing-off was perfectly calculated. Lenore felt an odd itch of discomfort and shuffled in spite of herself. The Medico gave her captain a cold look.

"If you are suggesting this was some kind of erotica, put the thought out of your mind. As far as I can tell, he was sober, and there is no sign that he was engaging in any kind of fetish when he did this."

Lenore broke in. "But why kill himself by hanging? I mean, look." She gestured illustratively round the sick bay. "There's gotta be more than one less painful way of killing yourself. He could even use one of those syringes to trigger a gas embolism or something."

"True. I am impressed you considered the syringe possibility. I will be doing an analysis of his tissues."

"An analysis? Why?"

"Look at this." Sarida enlarged the display of the DNA. "I set to the smallest scan point, just as part of the full scan. Notice anything?"

Syndac spoke, leaning in to look at the display. "That does not look much like DNA to me. But then after so long it will have degraded."

"That is what it appears to be on the surface. But this does not fit in with standard models of genetic degradation over time. If I were more fanciful, I might believe the DNA had been ripped apart, unzipped if you will. Hence why I am doing the test. And for that, I need to be left alone."

Even Syndac could not go against her Medico. She and Lenore left. Back in the corridor and heading for the control area, Syndac frowned, glancing round the pristine corridor.

"Get the feeling we are being watched?"

Lenore nodded. "Yes. But by what?"

Before Syndac could answer, her comm bracelet buzzed. *"Sinestra to captain, come in please."*

Syndac quickly responded. "Go ahead."

Lenore's thoughts drifted again. She did not listen to Syndac's short exchange with her subordinate. She was more worried about what this station was doing to her. She had never felt this on edge since.... When was it? Yes, when she was an initiate. It had been so long ago. That time when....

"That was Sinestra." Syndac's voice broke in on her thoughts. "They found another body. Not human. Seemingly not from any of the Allied Peoples."

"Seriously?"

"Yes. I will make sure it gets to Sarida. You check up on Livesey."

Lenore nodded. Her walk was slower than Syndac's, who positively rushed back toward Docking Bay A. Lenore, lost in thought, walked at a slower pace back to the control area. Upon entering saw both Livesey and Alkmeney bent over the central console. Livesey had plugged into one of its ancient microjacks, while Alkmeney was typing and flicking feverishly through displays.

"Any luck?"

Livesey inclined her head oddly, her eyes flickering and distant. "Nothing yet. This system's been well designed. Every attempt we make to punch through its defenses is swiftly countered. I'd say this is some kind of primitive AI system that adapts to each attack we perform."

As if on cue, the projection appeared beside them. The console shut off abruptly, and Livesey let out a yell as she pulled out her jack.

"Ai!"

The voice sounded in sharp reprimand. *"Due to continued illegal attempts to access restricted materials from this location, all functions have been cut off. Please acquire official access to requested files. Any further attempts to reach these files without prior authorization will result in instant console shutdown."*

The projection vanished, and Alkmeney swore and slapped the console. "Now what do we do?"

"Haven't you found anything?"

Livesey shook her head. "No. I haven't found anything. I've scanned all I can. All I found was an old cargo route going from— look, I'll show you."

Livesey guided the two over to a still-active console. She brought up the station display and highlighted sections and passages as she talked.

"This station is divided into fourteen sections, with further subdivisions numbered one to five. The lowest is Section M, where most of the engine and atmospheric control functions are based. Sections A through L form the outer part of the whole. We're currently near the junction in Section A-2 while the Docking Port is at A-5, and that dark portion of the map covers the interior of Sections E to J. The central part, which is currently locked off, is Section N. You see this path? It runs from Section B-5 through to a large door in Section N-1. I've looked through the entire accessible blueprint scans, and that passage seems the only way into Section N." The android looked meaningfully at her two watchers. "If you were the builder of this place, where would you hide a fortune in data and raw materials?"

"In its heart." Lenore answered automatically. "Behind several locked and barred doors. Or scattered through the entire thing."

"We would have found something about that before now, surely?" Alkmeney sounded unsure. "If they were building this place to house something, they would want to house it there. So there it is. In there."

Alkmeney pointed. All three stared at the display, Section N highlighted in neon green within the nest of blue-tinged sections. And in their eyes was a united sensation, a burning desire for any riches contained therein. Greed smoldered in their hearts, shone in their faces with divine fury. Lenore almost smiled. Once again the sight of riches, or knowledge, showed their true faces, the reason they had come at all. Alkmeney's voice sounded forced as she changed the subject.

"Maybe we could try another console."

Livesey shook her head. "If we keep on trying them with this level of success, we'll eventually lock ourselves out of the system entirely." She looked to Livesey. "Haven't you got any bright ideas?"

"No."

Something in the tone of Livesey's reply made Lenore focus on her. Was it her, or was that response a little too human? She had known and heard this android lie before, and never once detected it. Here, now, she had heard a lie. A blatant, if well concealed lie. Alkmeney was deceived, and turned away in frustration. Livesey then pulled a small chip from the deactivated console and handed it to Lenore.

"Here. I downloaded this while we were searching. It's all the weapon storage areas on the ship. In case you need it."

Lenore reached to take it. For a second, Livesey's hand tightened on the chip, as if she were about to snap it. Was she trying to hold onto it? The grip relaxed almost at once, and she turned back to the operational console as Lenore slipped the chip into her comm.

"I shall go to another control area, see what I can find about interior mapping." Alkmeney's distracted voice broke in upon them. "We need that passage, and I will try not to trigger anything if that becomes classified as well."

Lenore spoke to Alkmeney's back. "Make sure you stay in contact."

The Kavki left in a huff, almost running into the door as it rushed to open and let through her flying form. Again alone, Livesey looked directly at Lenore. Again, there was a hint of something unlike the android's usual poise and calculation.

"I want to ask something."

"Ask away."

"Do you know who you are inside?"

Lenore frowned, surprised at the question. "I should hope so, after this long. Why? Having doubts?"

"It's.... Well... Lenore, if anything happens, I want to know. Do you think of me as your frie—"

The sentence stopped dead. Lenore waited, but Livesey seemed to have forgotten all about it. Sighing, she decided to find Syndac again. Passing through the door, she glanced back at Livesey before it closed. The android continued to stand in front of the display, its glow throwing her form into sharp relief. It was then that the Feles's instinctual feelings crystallized into something more. A concrete though still vague suspicion of something wrong. She hesitated, decided to ask a question.

"Livesey, how's your search of that datacube going?"

"The datacube? It's all right. I used it to access that console. I'm surprised I got as far as I did before the system shut us out."

"I see."

Lenore was out the door and in the corridor before her suspicion fastened on an image. In all the years they had traveled together, Livesey had always maintained an upright posture. It was natural, given her origins. But as she had stood before that light, looking into the display, her uprightness had been even greater. Dignified, almost haughty. Livesey was many things, but never haughty. Her thoughts were interrupted by Syndac walking back, her right hand clutched tight.

Lenore joined her current "captain." "Seen that strange corpse? What is it, a desiccated human?"

Syndac sounded agitated. "That thing is nothing we've ever seen. It's not human nor any other species. Could that be what happened here?"

"That body? You think this place was attacked by that thing? And… others like it?"

"If so, then why are there no bodies? Unless they were all whisked away to somewhere by their comrades."

"But if so, this place should be infested. We haven't seen anything, not a sign of them."

"Yes, you're quite right. Come on."

Lenore was almost dragged back to the sick bay. Syndac's face was twitching a little, beset by unknown emotions and unasked questions. But a part of Lenore's mind lingered on Livesey. What was *wrong* with her?

SYNDAC PUSHED BACK into the sick bay without any warning. Sarida was still staring at the scans, but her usual detached expression was replaced with one of bewilderment. Or perhaps even... fear? That was never a good sign. Syndac eyed her.

"That is not a look I see every day."

Sarida turned to them. "Captain, I think I know why this man committed suicide. And why he did it in the way he did."

"Really?"

The Medico enlarged part of the display. It was the dead man's DNA in all its ruined glory. Syndac raised an eyebrow, something of her old sneering manner returning.

"Well? What about it?"

"Remember how I described it? Well, I was more right than I realized. This man *was* being attacked. On a molecular level. I don't know what by, but it was something tearing apart his DNA. It must have been incredibly painful."

"That explains the weird DNA structure, but why the noose and not the needle?"

"Because.... This, whatever-it-is, was doing something else. It was changing his body's tolerances, making him immune to everything." Sarida made a gesture around the Sick Bay. "All of these poisons and medicines that might have ushered him out, they were becoming useless with every second that passed. Even an artificial embolism would have been negated by the changes he was undergoing. I think he was already trying them in sequence. Look here."

Sarida pointed to a patch of thawed skin within the man's elbow crease. It was a mess of fresh injection marks. None done with great skill. Or perhaps showing signs of haste, or panic, or struggle. Sarida continued with unnerving calm. "Those were made very recently, perhaps less than half an hour prior to death. I think he was injecting himself with anything and everything to try and end his life. None of them worked, so he did something more... *certain* to."

"But why not get a gun from somewhere? Lenore found one easily enough."

A tight knot formed in Syndac's stomach. She had felt few such sensations since her time as Black Sutton. Lenore broke in.

"Maybe he was unable to leave here. Remember that creature? If there were more...."

Sarida was puzzled. Syndac briefly explained, then opened her clenched hand. In it was a long wrinkled object.

"It's a finger from that corpse I told you about. Wasn't time to bring the whole thing, it was falling to pieces. I'd like you to scan it."

"All right. It should not take long."

Sarida took the finger. But then Syndac turned on Lenore. Her face had become strange, twisted into something between her usual manner and something new. An emotion she must not have shown for years. It added to Syndac's own feelings, and it was an effort to keep her voice under control.

"There is something very wrong here, Lenore. Something we both must realize by now. When we arrived, life support on the station was shut off except for one area. I doubt humans could survive that long in those conditions, even in deep hibernation."

Lenore nodded, more and more seeming to share Syndac's discomfort. "But the station's supplying the life support. It wouldn't support designated enemies, surely?"

"And if it were on their side?"

"We could ask."

"It might already be compromised. However,"—Syndac turned away from Lenore's potent stare—"we'll try. Hoy, projection or computer or whatever you're called."

The projection appeared and bowed. *"How may I be of service?"*

"I need to know how many living beings are aboard this ship."

The projection seemed about to answer. Then it flickered, distorted, and shut down. Syndac swore and turned to Lenore.

"You get back, and tell the crew where to find those weapon stashes. I think we shall have a fight on our hands."

As before, Lenore left without answering. Syndac remembered someone like her in her old crew, a weapons specialist of few words and insane loyalty, one of the casualties of Beddow's betrayal. Sarida was beginning her scan of the mummified finger. She glanced at her captain.

"I have not seen you this tense since before that traitor Beddow turned on us. When your mother died."

"I never could keep things from you." Syndac leaned on a nearby wall. "None of this feels right. Something is off if only by a little, like a tune with one note off key. Everything else sounds good, but that one note is throwing everything off. I know Lenore senses it, too, and maybe knows more than I do."

"Why not ask her?"

"Will I get a straight answer from her?"

"Perhaps. It is up to you. You have always been a good judge of people. Like your mother was."

Syndac's reply was never heard. As the scan of the finger was completed, there was a low-pitched whining from all the systems. Then the main lights shut down. Syndac's survival instincts took hold, the instincts that had saved her uncounted times since her mother's death.

"Forget the analysis, Sarida. Get back to Docking Bay A. Now!"

Syndac automatically rushed into the corridor. To her surprise, the door opened without protest. Red warning strips were flashing from the roof, and a dull puce strip along the floor showed the curve of the corridor. The Medico brushed past her and begin running toward Docking Bay A. Syndac raised the comm bracelet.

"Lenore, bring Livesey to Docking Bay A, and grab as many weapons as you can!"

Syndac in turn began her run back toward Docking Bay A. As she ran, her mind became obsessed with a single question. Now the power was down, what would come next? Then another question rose, one that had no good answer. Who had cut the power?

FILE 13

EYES IN THE DARK

---

*There were wild mountain wolves and lions prowling
all round it—poor bewitched creatures whom she had
tamed by her enchantments and drugged into subjection.*

—Homer

THE LIGHTS FAILED just as Faarax opened the door into Docking Bay J. Sinestra was with him, Dexter a little way behind looking at a panel marked *"Weapons"* in crimson ink. Under the red and puce emergency light, all but the black writing vanished into a haze of blurring colors.

Dexter groaned. "Oh, great. Power's out. Should we head back? It's quite a walk from here."

"Still, I think that's best." Faarax looked at him. "I think your captain would want us to regroup in this situation, don't you?"

Faarax had wanted to provoke, and got a reaction beyond his expectations. He seemed to have finally broken Dexter's patience. The man lunged at Faarax, pinning him against the door.

"You've quite the mouth, boy. How about I shut it for you?"

"Stop that!" Sinestra's voice snapped like a whip. "Faarax is right. We need to get back."

The woman's eyes bored into the two men until Dexter released Faarax. They began running back toward Section A-5, as noted on the exterior plating for each decameter-length stretch of corridor. As they were nearing the junction between Sections J-1 and K-5, there was a low hiss. Sinestra faltered, listening. Then broke into sprinting with a curse from Dexter as they all saw the large emergency door rushing down to block their path. All had sprinted, but were forced into a stuttering halt as the great bulkhead sealed shut in front of them. Faarax banged the obstruction with his fist.

"What the hell's going on?" He raised his comm. "Lenore? Lenore, come in. Lenore?"

There was a hiss from the comm, then the sound of heavy thuds and a cry from Lenore. Silence quickly fell. Sinestra looked from the comm to Faarax's face.

"That did not sound good. Faarax, do you think there is a way of opening these doors?"

"I don't know. I can't see anything clearly enough. And I don't know if these doors would be controlled locally or from some kind of master system."

"We'll soon find out. Hoy, holo-thing!" Dexter's shout summoned the projection, who appeared like a glowing blue ghost in the crimson light. "What the hell's going on here?"

The projection's voice was even more clipped than before. *"Under Executive Order 14, emergency doors between Sections have been sealed. Also, I am happy to report that Special Order 4323 has been revoked. I may now answer Omega-class questions about this station."*

"Yeah, we're good, thanks. How'd we get round these doors?"

Faarax struggled to focus on the projection as it answered. Something was drifting into his perception, a familiar smell. Old, musty, unpleasant.

"All emergency doors are controlled from the central hub in Section N. Except in cases of life-threatening emergency, these doors cannot be opened."

"And we're in a life-threatenin' emergency?"

"Currently, no."

The projection vanished. Faarax' blood had turned cold.

"What did that thing mean, 'currently, no?'"

"What's it matter? How do we get back?"

Sinestra shrugged as she spoke. "Through the hanger? The projection said nothing about the hanger doors being locked."

"But Docking Bay K's decompressed. Those places are bloody big, and I don't fancy going across and opening the door while holding my breath. Besides, it might be a vacuum and you can't hold your breath then."

"So we're stuck." Dexter slumped against the door. "And the place is stinkin' up for us. Fucking great."

"Stinking…. Oh, shit, I *do* know that smell. It's—"

All three fell silent. Somewhere near them, somewhere beyond their sight and beyond the pulsing crimson lights, had come a sound. A scraping sound, like a sharp object on metal. Faarax tensed, every instinct honed by Lenore's training putting his body on alert.

"Okay, that's not a good noise."

Dexter had also tensed. "Where'd that come from?"

"Somewhere overhead? Or maybe below? I can't be sure. There it is again."

The scraping sounded again. It was closer, more insistent, echoed. Sinestra reached into her coat and handed Faarax his confiscated gun. Dexter seemed about to protest, but a look from his sister silenced him. Faarax took the gun, holding it down with his finger on the trigger, ready to raise it and fire. From some other pocket, Sinestra produced a gun of her own. The scraping came again, frighteningly loud and close. The three shuffled together, now back to back, Sinestra and Dexter ready to fire.

"What the hell's that noise?"

Dexter's question went unanswered except by another repetition of the scratching. And another noise to accompany it. A hiss, so long and low and malevolent that the hardened Sinestra seemed unsettled. She scanned the corridor they had just traversed, her eyes taking in every patch of pale, of shimmering red, of black. Faarax followed suit, unsure what else to do. It took him a second or two to register a patch of black that had not been there before between the pulsing lights. A patch close to the top of the wall, a few feet from a hatch he was sure was not there before.

The dark shape leapt out and down toward them with a high-pitched scream that nearly burst his eardrums. All three dived to one side as it struck the area they had been sharing. It rose, taller than any of them, the living version of the mummified corpse they had discovered between Docking Bays L and K. Faarax felt like gagging at the stink, an intense version of the musty aroma that had risen from that corpse, which had spread through the corridor.

Sinestra acted the fastest, slithering away on her back and firing at the creature's thin flank. One shot went home, the other went wide, and the thing turned to leap at her. It opened its mandible-like mouth in a horrific snarl, showing the long muscular ribbon of tongue whipping like a detached air pipe. Faarax pushed through the nauseating fug, letting Lenore's training take over, and fired. The thing wailed as its spine was severed. Faarax scrambled to his feet, took aim again and shot the thing through the head as it wriggled on the floor. There was a moment of silence, then Sinestra got up.

"Your mother teach you to aim like that?"

"She's not my mother, and yeah, she did. Among other things. Gotta have something to kill her with. Though I don't like killing at a distance. More to the point, just how many of these things are there?"

Any answer was cut short as the projection reappeared. *"Due to the occurrence of a life-threatening emergency in Section J, emergency bulkhead doors are now being opened to provide escape."*

There was a hum, and the emergency bulkhead slid up just enough to let the three crawl under it. As Dexter and Sinestra slithered underneath, Faarax lingered and looked at the projection. Before he could ask another question, there came another hiss and scraping from down the corridor. He turned, and saw more of the black shapes. Three, perhaps four, He rolled under the door, found himself being pulled up by a strong hand, ran down the corridor alongside two he would have killed an hour earlier.

His comm bracelet screeched, Solet's voice sounding through it. *"All personnel, come in! All personnel!"*

Faarax answered between pants. "This is… Faarax…."

Other voices responded. Alkmeney, sounding bewildered and frightened. Syndac, clearly angry and on edge. Lenore, slurring her words. No sound from Livesey, or anyone else much besides unintelligible cacophony. Solet's voice took charge through the clamor.

"Something's happened. Everyone get back to Docking Bay A, now!"

Faarax and his companions needed no encouragement, paying no heed to any other responses in their flight. They passed through Section K and rushed into Section L. Then they heard the hiss again, and Dexter threw himself flat as another creature burst from an unseen hatch, smashing into the floor with its ill-judged pounce. Sinestra turned and shot. This time, the shot went cleanly through the creature's screeching mouth and into its head. The thing lay twitching as the three resumed their run.

Through the growing red blur of exhaustion, Faarax expected to be stopped by the station again, but at each intersection the bulkhead was raised enough for them to slide or crawl under. Until they reached Section L-1, where they were brought up short. The bulkhead was down, and someone was already pounding against it and shouting in a ragged voice.

"Let me in! Let me in! For the love of all, let me in!"

It was Alkmeney. She turned, and Faarax saw that she was covered in blood, though what kind was obscured by the lighting. Faarax pushed forward, grasped her by the shoulders.

"What happened?"

Alkmeney struggled to remain articulate. "I… was in the local control area. I had run into Syndac and she… she said I should take… someone with me. I got that Kavki… the one who was supposed to have left before we set off? He was standing by the door when the lights went like this. I was trying to find out what happened when I heard something on my comm, and then…. Oh, Gods!"

"What happened?" Sinestra was in no mood for tactful obfuscation.

"The… he… it was a monster. A creature. I do not know what it was, but it just appeared in the door a few minutes after the lights changed. It was so fast. He tried to fight it off. It pinned him against the console next to me and… tore him to pieces. It just tore him to pieces!"

Alkmeney began to sob and laugh at the same time. Sinestra slapped her hard on each cheek. Faarax pushed her away and again gripped the navigator round the shoulders, locking his eyes with hers.

"What did you do?"

"I… ran. I shut the door. I think it is still trapped in the section control area. I ran here, but the bulkhead came down."

Sinestra whirled round, looking back down the corridor. "The Docking Bay. Hurry!"

The four ran, Faarax dragging the half-hysterical Alkmeney. As they were approaching the doorway into Docking Bay L, Faarax saw the dark shapes ahead of them. Shapes that crawled on all fours, long limbs reaching out at odd angles like an insect's legs. Huge eyes staring at them, reflecting the red and puce lighting in horrible shades, their mandibles open and tongues flicking in anticipation of a great feast.

They reached the door into the docking bay and tumbled through it. As they entered, the normal lights finally triggered from an unknown backup. The four expected to be set upon, but as one creature was about to follow them it balked, hissed, retreated. Granted this breathing space, Faarax and Dexter rushed for the controls and worked them as fast as they could. The first attacker may have stalled, but they could hear the further clatter of claws on metal and plastic, the hissing screech of the hunters. Faarax bared his teeth.

"Godsdamned… stiff… piece of… shit!"

Whether it was the swearing or their efforts buoyed by anger, the stiff controls yielded. The door slithered down with a protesting groan, and as an arm reached through to grab at them, it slammed shut. The impact and weight severed forearm from limb, and from the other side came a blood-curdling scream. Dexter stumbled back, looking slightly sick, then unexpectedly crossed himself.

"Gods save us."

Faarax raised an eyebrow. "Didn't know you believed in the Cross."

"Faith can wait." Alkmeney seemed to have recovered a little. "At least the air in here is cleaner. It was beginning to stink out there."

Sinestra's brow creased. "Funny. I swear I smelt that before somewhere."

"I smelt something like it from that corpse." Faarax wrinkled his nose. "Revolting. Like a filter that hasn't been changed for months."

"It was not that. Something else. Something… Dexter, do you remember when we last went to Xytran 3?"

"Yeah, vividly."

"Hardly pleasant, I agree. But you remember when we hid in that cave. The one facing the sea along the narrow path. What was it like in there?"

"Full of shit. Literally. Kinda like…. Kinda like… this smell."

Sinestra snapped her fingers. "That's it! That is what that smell is. Guano."

"Gua-what?"

"It's a kind of shit." Dexter's bluntness was almost comical. "Fermented shit, in huge-ass piles. But how can there be guano on a space habitat?"

Alkmeney's voice sounded shrilly. "Should we not get back to the others?"

Faarax glanced round the docking bay. No sign of anything, but best not to linger. The four once more ran, this time heading for the door into Docking Bay A. And as they ran, the screeching of claws on metal from behind them grew louder and louder.

LENORE WAS JUST passing Section A's control area when the lights failed. She paused, her eyes taking in the distorted lighting. She looked up as the red strips shone, felt the weird puce light through the fur on her feet. It had turned everything into an abstract dream sequence.

Syndac's crackly voice broke from her comm. *"Lenore, bring Livesey to Docking Bay A, and grab as many weapons as you can!"*

She acknowledged it with a tap, displaying her info chip's markings for weapon lockers. Her head turned, she looked at the door into the control area. The low hum of the emergency lighting mimicked the low humming of her nerves as she approached the doorway. Her fur was standing on end, her teeth slightly bared. As hunter and hunted, she plucked a gun from the adjacent locker, resting her finger lightly on the trigger.

Stepping inside, she saw Livesey's silhouette against the display. She had not moved an inch. She was still there, still with that haughty upright posture. Maintaining that utterly wrong posture, she turned. Her voice, when she spoke after an unnaturally long delay, was normal enough. Just that light unusual quality, a note out of place.

"You all right? What happened to the power?"

"I was hoping you could tell me."

"Haven't a clue. I was just checking. Looks like some kind of high-rank command was sent out to put the outer areas of each Section into emergency mode."

"That doesn't make sense. Who ordered that?"

"Don't know."

"Well, can you find out?"

"I could, if I had access. But since the main console's down… I hope Alkmeney made it. Or maybe she's gone back to Docking Bay A. Care to tell me what's happening out there? I'm getting weird readings from one of the consoles, like a lot of movement."

"Not sure myself. I came to pick up some weapons."

Livesey gestured toward the one slung on her shoulder. "Looks like you've already started. Shall we go?"

The hairs on the back of Lenore's neck were so rigid that they pained her. Danger, like a specter, was sharing the space with them. And it was no danger from outside the door.

It was already there, with them.

"In a minute. There's something I want to ask you. Have you heard from Syndac?"

"No. Not recently. You think something happened to her?"

Lenore displayed her best poker face. "Don't know. Everything about this stations is weird. But they did find something. Alkmeney told me before the power failed. That datacube of yours, there's something on it that can unlocked the security. Guess that's why it was sent away like that."

"So it can unlock security?"

"Yes. Shall I take it to them?"

A long silence. Livesey's hand gripped the edge of the console, and Lenore saw the metal bending under that grip.

"I'd rather bring it myself. It was in the middle of a scan. I'd rather not disturb it. I've got my own software to think about."

"You didn't think about it before. You could just take it out whenever you liked. And you did."

"Well, maybe I was unwise. You know, the engineer said I was somewhat addicted to data. I admit he was right."

"Yeah, yeah. Poor Swyda. Wish that accident hadn't happened."

"Accidents will happen."

"Yes, indeed. It was tragic."

Almost as soon as she had spoken, Lenore raised her weapon. Livesey turned, leaned nonchalantly against the defunct console.

"Something wrong, Lenore? You don't look well."

"Nor do you."

"Why do you say that?"

"Because you've made a very big slip, whoever you are."

The air inside the room had suddenly grown very still. The ventilation still ran, everything was still functioning, but the presence within Livesey made everything cold. In less reasoned times, that presence would have been called a devil. An unpleasant smile crept up the corner of the android's mouth.

"I've made a slip, have I?"

"Yeah. Swyda wasn't the name of our engineer. And he was murdered, not killed in an accident. Livesey would've known. Known and asked me what I was doing. You're not Livesey. Who are you?"

"Livesey" shrugged. "Names matter little to the likes of you."

"How long have you been… in there?"

The android looked down at her hand, flexing her fingers. "Difficult to judge. If you mean 'how long have I had full control,' then only a few minutes, maybe ten at the outside. If you mean 'how long have I been within this body,' then that's a different answer. The most pertinent question is… how long was I in the datacube?"

"The datacube?"

"Yes. A hidden partition in the datacube, where my personality was stored after the scan. I hoped to come out at once when this one accessed it, but she created an artificial environment for the data when it attempted to flood her system. She knew there was an extra partition, but she couldn't gain access to it until now. Inside the station."

"Inside…? So you're from the station?"

"Yes. And not just from it. I built it."

"You… *built*…?"

"Livesey" laughed. "How could I have predicted this? That one of my children should come here and awaken me with so many, such a gaggle thirsting for my property." Her eyes suddenly became cold. "Such unwarrantable greed cannot go unpunished."

"You're one to talk. You gathered all this stuff here."

"Ah, but it was mine to begin with. It was mine, and my family's, since before we became masters of a planet. And you were wrong, you know. I didn't make a slip. I merely grew tired of playing a char—"

Livesey's head suddenly snapped forward. Her hand gripped the console so hard that it buckled and tore. Her free hand clutched at her head, breath hissing through her teeth. Her words came in choking gasps.

"Lenore. Run. This presence… she's too…. She wants…." The second voice broke through Livesey's own, and the android's body snapped back to its former stiff posture. "Enough! Enough of this. Time to test your worth."

Livesey stepped forward. Lenore's finger twitched over the trigger. In that moment, she contemplated killing her comrade. Faarax's voice from the comm cut across her thoughts.

"Lenore? Lenore, come in. Lenore?"

The distraction was near-fatal, the android too quick. The being inside

Livesey propelled forward with lightning speed and slammed Lenore into the wall. The dazed Feles watched as "Livesey" stepped through the door. Struggling against unconsciousness, one last sentence pushed into her ears, Livesey's voice yet horribly cold and cruel.

"The time has come for my soldiers to march."

Around her, from every vent, came the hiss of some new element being added to the air. A weird, musty element. Like old manure. Something large seemed to glide over her, and her dancing vision gave an impression of something slithering into the control room.

It took some moments for Lenore to recover herself. She rose slowly, groped for where her gun should have been, then tossed away the twisted mess "Livesey" had made of it from a single strike. That had been the force which knocked her down, a strike to leave the Feles defenseless. That same impact could have crushed her belly into pulp. Why then leave, when she had the advantage? Unless... whatever was inside the control room was meant finish the job.

Slithering over to the weapons cache, Lenore got a bulkier rapid fire type, then skillfully slung every other weapon present over her shoulders and round her belly. Looking like a living arsenal, she approached the door. It was the eyes that she saw first. Great circular eyes that had a reflective sheen in the bloody light. Seemed the nickname "Bugeye" was more than appropriate. Then the screeching hiss filled the air. Its intent was clear—to kill. Her finger depressed the trigger on instinct, and the thing was torn in half by the flurry of bolts. Its torso tumbled backward through the door, while the legs fell in front of Lenore with a sickening crunch.

Bracing herself for similar encounters ahead, Lenore stepped over the remains and began running back toward Section A-5. A sound came from up ahead, a crash followed by a loud groan. Lenore ran toward the sound, and saw Livesey's form seemingly vanishing into the wall. A secret door closed behind her, and as Lenore rushed to it she noticed Syndac rising from where she had been thrown.

"What the hell's gotten into Livesey? She gone rogue or what?"

"It would take too long to explain. Come on, we need to get back to the others."

"Y... yeah."

There wasn't even a mild protest. The current situation was too serious for pulling rank. It was then that the comm bracelets buzzed, and Solet's voice came through.

"All personnel, come in! All personnel!"

"Syndac speaking."

"Lenore here."

Other voice sounded, but Solet's took charge. *"Something's happened. Everyone get back to Docking Bay A, now!"*

"On our way." Syndac was just setting off when she balked. "Wait. Sarida, we need to go back."

"No."

"I don't leave my crew behind."

"It's too late. If those things are there…."

"What things?"

Lenore might have explained, but Syndac's eyes spotted something on the roof behind them. A dark shape scurrying along, making slight scratching noises. She pointed up.

"Look out! Up there!"

Lenore turned a second too late. The dark form sprang, and the familiar stabbing pain drove through her shoulder as one of the creature's claws went home. The gun was thrown from Lenore's hand, but Syndac caught it in mid-air and shot at the creature. It was thrown back, the shot going between its eyes. Lenore struggled to her feet, even as more scrabbling noises echoed around them.

"What are those—?" began Syndac.

"Just run!"

The two ran, Lenore holding together her injured shoulder. They heard the hissing of concealed hatches opening behind them, the scrabble of claws, and the high-pitch shrieks. Something bright burst past the two, and for a moment Lenore thought they were cornered. But it was Sarida, looking battered and harried, rushing ahead with her long Kavki strides. Lenore saw a great three-line gash across her back, mirroring her own injuries. Syndac merely ran and cursed between breaths.

As they ran, Lenore tried not to think of what was happening. It obsessed the inner depths of her brain going round the eternal corner of the station corridor. She wondered about the other ships, the other crews that mostly remained in Docking Bays B to D. Were they under attack, as well? Would they be prepared? Hardened as she was to the bloody side of hunting, she shrank from thinking about what those creatures might do.

They finally reached the door into Docking Bay A, and were brought up short as they saw more of the dark creatures ahead of them. Just a few, but too close to their escape for comfort. The others in pursuit had also slowed, and were closing in like a pride readying for the kill. Lenore readied her weapon.

"You think there's enough to hold them off?"

"I don't know."

Sarida spoke. "I have an idea."

She reached into a pocket and drew out a beaker of something. She glanced at the two and made a sign for them to cover their mouths. This done, Sarida flung the beaker at the far wall nearest the docking bay door. It smashed, and the liquid unleashed a plume of pale smoke which thinned and dispersed almost instantly. There was a hacking cough from the nearest creature and it backed off. The ones on the other side also backed away, suddenly wary of this change.

Sarida made for the door, with Lenore and Syndac following. Lenore fired off a few rounds for good measure toward the retreating mass, causing their mouths to open and hiss in challenge. They reached the door, and Syndac pounded on it.

"Open up! Hurry!"

The sound seemed to inflame the hunters, for one braved the acrid stink and darted forward. Lenore shot it through the head, causing it to crumple in front of its fellows. This death among them enraged the others, and their fear of the noxious fumes faded in the face of their anger. They began closing in again, and Lenore prepared to fight to the death.

The door shuddered and opened. Solet's voice sounded from the other side.

"In! Quick!"

Sarida and Syndac were the first to dive through, while Lenore backed in, firing a parting shot at one of the braver creatures. It hit home and the thing was thrown back.

"Quick! Get that door shut!"

Before the door could close, one of the things jumped through. It sailed over the new arrivals and landed in the middle of an open area. Nearby crew-members either ran for cover or screamed. But rather than attacking, the thing seemed transfixed in the glare of the lamps set up within the bay. Its claws scoured deep marks in the floor, its head was bent down as if in prayer, and it made a low soft hiss like escaping gas.

"What's happened—" began Sarida.

Lenore fired. The shot caught the thing on the head and it crumpled into a heap. It didn't matter to her what had happened. Seeing the things dead was all that mattered.

SOLET TOOK A moment to breath, the first for some little time. What the hell was his luck when it came to things like this? He had been let out at last, allowed to oversee some tasks albeit with someone keeping an eye on him. Then those things had appeared, and it was all he could do to get everyone inside the hanger. Luckily, no one had been that far away, and only a few were confirmed lost. The other crews hadn't answered yet, but he was more con-cerned about his own. Syndac looked directly at Solet as she got to her feet.

"Care to tell me what's happening here?"

Solet shrugged and spoke through gritted teeth. "Haven't a clue. Wish I had. I haven't even heard from—"

Before Solet could finish, cries came from somewhere. Everyone jumped, expecting a fresh attack, but it was only the other captains approaching, with Donovan dragging the still-limp Gustav over while Dashall rushed ahead with furious speed, his irate voice echoing in the large space.

"What the hell's happening? What was that thing?"

"We don't know." Solet tried to sound calm and in control, the last thing he felt. "Have you called up your crews yet?"

Donovan cut across Dashall's angry opening click of speech. "We've tried. Something must be wrong. They're not answering."

"Or they're being blocked."

It was then that Gustav's comm sounded. The voice on the other end sounded distracted.

"Hello? Hello? Is anyone there?"

Donovan raised Gustav's wrist. "This is Donovan in Docking Bay A. What's happening out there?"

"*We…. Those things….*"

"Where are you?"

"*Docking Bay D.* Kilner *crew. They came out of nowhere. Docking Bays B and C aren't answering. Oh, God, I can hear them. They… can hear us.*"

The last words were barely a whisper, and then it subsided abruptly. The door connecting to Docking Bay L had opened, allowing Faarax and Alkmeney to get inside with those human twins Sinestra and Dexter. As Faarax and Alkmeney approached the small gathering, Donovan turned to Solet.

"Isn't there a way of getting them in here? This seems to be the only safe place left on the station."

Syndac glared at Donovan. "You want to let those things in here?"

"I want to keep people alive. It's how I work."

The voice came again. "*I hear them. They're in the walls. They're at the door. They're coming in from Docking Bay C. I can…. Oh, Gods. Oh, Gods, help us!*"

The noises that followed were barely articulate. Screams and scrabbling mingled with the tearing of soft tissue and the cracking of bone. It was Gustav that reacted, reaching for his comm bracelet and tearing it off, throwing it on the floor with shattering force. The screaming tumult shut off, and a horrible silence fell. It was only broken by the sound of retching as Alkmeney bent double and threw up on the virgin floor. Solet felt like being sick himself, but this wasn't the time. His job, his role, was to look after his crew.

FILE 14

BESIEGERS UNDER SIEGE

*There was not a breath of air moving, nor a sound
but that of the surf booming half a mile away along
the beaches and against the rocks outside.*

—Robert Louis Stevenson

BARELY A FEW minutes had passed. From his position leaning next to the inner door, Solet's tired eyes scanned the vastness of Docking Bay A. It was a scene of stilted confusion, order without direction. The atmosphere, rendered into an electric stillness by the terrible broadcasts from Docking Bay D, was now moving to prevent anything similar happening to them. The doors leading into the main corridor and the two adjoining docking bays were quickly sealed over with some spare metal parts taken from the *Benbow*, wedged and welded into place as well as could be managed.

A watch was kept, everyone was told to communicate in at the very least a lowered tone, in case the creatures outside were sensitive to noise. Some of the crew from the *Grand*, the ship using Docking Bay B, were clustered in a corner looking scared out of their wits. Of the other two crews, aside from the very few who had joined their captains as guards-come-captives in Docking Bay A, there was little hope. No one had been raised.

Of his own crew, he had seen a variety of responses. Faarax was silently working on shoring up defenses, bouncing from group to group, falling into the old routine of being everywhere when needed. Lenore was distributing weapons to those who did not already have them, and using her medical knowledge to treat some of the wounded who had managed to reach them. Alkmeney, recovered from her momentary lapse, was both working on the immediate security and syncing up some turrets that had unaccountably appeared from one of the *Benbow's* cargo boxes.

Most surprising was the response of Syndac's crew. Not only were they not fighting among themselves as he had expected, but instead working together as a cohesive and friendly unit. Different groups were forming for different tasks, and a sense of splintered unity kept it from resembling the random bouncing about of a rabble. All had produced some kind of weapon which could at least slow down any attacker. Solet wondered how many pieces they had been in when the crew came aboard over a fortnight ago. It was almost admirable.

Momentarily, uncontrollably, he cradled his head. A fortnight. It felt like a century. It looked like still more when he glanced at the other three captains. Their righteous fury at being subsumed and betrayed by their own people had fallen away in the face of this latest catastrophe. Dashall had been stunned into silence by the final death cries of Gustav's crew. Donovan was struggling not to pace up and down, instead scratching her nails into oblivion against her scaly hide. And after their sudden outburst, Gustav had returned to their previous shocked apathy.

Syndac walked over to Solet. "I think everything should hold for now. If those things attack, we can keep them at bay. I've drawn up a patrol roster. If you'd like to see it?"

To his surprise, Solet found himself perusing a datapad with a roster of guard duties and rest times for the surviving crew. He nodded slowly.

"All seems in order. One might think you'd done this before."

"A pirate's daughter has opportunities for testing such things." She spoke with a slight return of her old smirking expression. "I don't intend to let these creatures win and drive us away. We've come too far for that."

"You think it's worth staying?"

"Of course. This station still has an unthinkable amount of wealth inside it. You would abandon all that? You would go back to a listless, wayward existence of subpar jobs and no status?"

"Didn't you hear what Alkmeney said? How one of your own died?"

"Do you know how much we lost during each raid as a pirate vessel? How many my mother mourned when a job went wrong? The stakes we played for with each assault? I look at your petty cargoes and cannot help but laugh at what you suffer over. I would not have stooped to your level had I not lost everything to betrayal. This is my moment to regain all at a stroke, with interest."

"Is that all that matters to you?"

"Had it not mattered to you, you would not have agreed to this. You would never have set foot in the Uncharted Belt, never considered Livesey's data, insisted on the datacube being sold for a little extra cash and gone on with your tramp existence. We have reached the finishing line and now you want to turn back?"

"You realize that if even one of them gets aboard the *Benbow*, we'll never be safe on that ship again."

"I know. We have checked and triple checked. There are no means of getting inside except through us. And I took the liberty of changing the airlock door access codes so neither Livesey nor those monsters couldn't get inside."

"I still don't understand about Livesey. It doesn't make sense."

"Simple. Her craving for data got the better of her. Best to cut her loose and leave her here if she chooses. I've accepted loss in my life, Solet. I think it's time you learned the same lesson."

"I don't judge androids."

"You say that with your past, *Klyshvyna?*"

"Reduced to sniping with the past, are we?"

"Your ancestors gleefully delivered summary judgment when androids wanted more than a human form to inhabit. For four centuries they have existed as humans, and nothing but humans. The Ekri, the Feles, even the Kavki reject them taking any other form. And in their current forms, how are they constructed? With nothing but physical perfection and ideal beauty. I would go a little crazy myself if I were debarred from being fat, or ugly, or misshapen."

"First she's an addict, now she's crazy."

"She was already one. And now it seems, she has become the other."

"You haven't even talked to Lenore, have you?"

"I have no need of her biases. I saw Livesey's eyes when she attacked me in the corridor. I saw a deep, dark presence there. Something released from a cage. A wild animal, thriving on death. Mad, thirsty for who knows what."

"Takes like to know like, I guess."

"Retort all you like, but that look was a fact. I weigh evidence regardless of my personal feelings. Something I fear we don't have in common. Look upon yourself, 'captain,' and see the flaws you hold. They will be the death of you. Stand firm on something, or be mowed down."

Before Solet could think up a comeback, Syndac had moved away. Sighing and resisting the urge to cradle himself again, he made the rounds of the docking bay. He saw Faarax next to the door into the *Benbow*, fiddling with something. He stood near him, trying to look friendly.

"Circuit trouble?"

"Doing some adjustment. If anything other than a Feles, Kavki, human or Ekri passes this point, the docking port will seal and revert to a vacuum. Anything in there will be dead in minutes."

"Good idea."

Faarax paused, looked at Solet. In his face was a strange expression, so hurt and angry that it made him feel sick. Solet struggled to find words.

"Look... Faarax... I know we haven't always been on good terms—"

"Don't try that, Captain. Too late for that."

"Fine, I'll be blunt. What's wrong with you?"

"What's wrong? Those things could kill us, and you ask what's wrong?"

"Is it because Lenore might die?"

"Hmph. Always were too quick for your own good. Yes, those things are getting in the way of my business. Not that it matters to you."

"Don't be such a brat." The harsh commander returned with some force. "We've got bigger things to worry about than your petty little deal. So put it to one side, or get back on the *Benbow* and stop wasting space."

The two glared at each other. Faarax's mouth twitched, as if he might speak. The long-standing dislike surfaced again, though stripped of all meaning by their current situation. Solet backed down.

"Look at you. You're barely worth the effort to talk to. Wouldn't kill you to show a little respect once in a while."

"Respect didn't get me this far."

"Or maternal love? Or is that beyond you now?" His voice dropped to barely more than a whisper. "Just a suggestion, but don't exclude androids from the doorway, okay?"

Faarax apparently ignored him, continuing with his work. Solet moved away, shaking his head at the folly of humans and their silly deals. Or maybe Lenore's tribal teachings? Hard to say where one ended and the other began. They stubbornly refused to use the terms, but by all the Cluster's deities they behaved enough like mother and son. The shuffling of footsteps around him, the pounding of his own heart, they became secondary to his frustration. As if he were blind, dumb, stripped of movement.

"Hey!" Dashall seemed to have risen from his stupor and shouted across the docking bay with abandon. "Hey, I've thought of something!"

Solet approached with a wrathful step. "Give me your idea, but keep your voice down."

Dashall moderated his voice with clear effort. "I've been thinking. My ship, the *Grand*, is in the next bay. The crew that were stationed there… well…. Now they're probably dead, if we wait long enough, those things will lose interest. We can get into Docking Bay B, board the *Grand* and get the hell out of here."

Solet sighed. "First problem, that black hole will make the journey back next to impossible without the *Benbow*. Second, there's no guarantee that those things have lost interest. Third…."

"Third?"

"Third, we've come here for something. And we'll get it."

"Is that you or your partner talking? I'm not wasting any more time and money on a damn suicide run, and I'm *not* going back on someone else's ship. I'm gonna—"

In his second burst of animation in less than half an hour, Gustav reacted. He got up, grabbed Dashall by his shirt and slammed him into the wall.

"Do you want to get us all killed?"

Dashall sneered. "Why should you care? We all know why you came on this trip in the first place. Save your reputation, if you've got any left to save. You're such a perv you're probably enjoying this. I've read the news. Must be like old times. Little Jacklyn with his "progeny" over for weekends and concerts."

"You shut the f—"

It might have broken out into a fight, but Donovan stepped up and expertly thrust the two apart. "I have had enough of this. Gustav, calm down. Dashall, zip it. Take your bickering outside to those things if you can't."

Dashall bared his teeth. "Like I'd zip it for some cruddy art thief."

"So we should bow to someone who's on the verge of bankruptcy?"

"What?" Solet frowned. "I thought he was funding this trip."

"Oh, he is. Out of what's left of his secret funds, and what he could scrounge from what few debtors he has left. I did a little checking before we left. It's amazing how much of a front wealth can create when it's not there." She glared gleefully at Dashall. "I know you're on the verge of collapse. A few billion would be very handy right now, wouldn't it? I think Solet and myself are the only ones who were honest about why they came on this trip."

Solet rounded on her. "Don't lump me in with you lot."

"Oh, my pardon. I am the only honest one. At least honest about my wishes. I came here for artifacts, and for the thrill of a new adventure away from the Cluster's over explored colony worlds. And I mean to get them both. We are staying, Dashall. Unless you would like to take some of your surviving crew and set off on your own. Take your chances with… everything. If so, be my guest. You won't be missed."

Syndac was within hearing range, and Solet saw the slight expression flash across her face. An expression of satisfaction. She rose and turned, approaching with a near-seductive walk. She cut in, staying at a little distance.

"I see no reason why you can't just leave, Dashall. As you said, Docking Bay B is likely clear by now. I mean, no one but an idiot would go in there now."

Dashall's eye twitched, then he barreled toward the cluster of surviving crew from the other two ships. Syndac sneered.

"A coward when faced with difficulties. As I thought. I'm surprised he didn't turn back after the solar flare incident. Ah look, there he goes. Talking to his people. I think I'd best make sure my crew don't get in his way."

"You're serious?" Solet was incredulous. "You can't be. I know how I sounded, but…. He will get them all killed."

Donovan looked at him. "Why not? You're a captain, be pragmatic. They're not helping us, are they?"

Solet couldn't deny that. Out of all the crew, Dashall's group had been the least able to pull their weight, the least willing to get themselves into trouble. They'd been easily suborned, and now he saw why. Syndac moved away, whispered to a nearby crewmember, and returned, the sneer still on her face. The word had been passed. As Dashall's small group approached the door into Docking Bay B, it was quickly unsealed. The bar was freed, then a powerful Ekri pulled it back, allowing the small group to pass through. Another slipped through behind them, carrying a weapon. Solet glanced at Syndac, who returned the gaze steadily.

"Just in case. I am not totally heartless."

Solet didn't argue the point. A few minutes passed. The few turned into ten. The follower returned, nodded their head, and the door was resealed. Then there was a crackling from Solet's comm bracelet.

"Dashall here. We're all aboard. Bit gruesome in there, but bearable." Donovan looked disgusted at the tone, every inch the financier writing off a loss. "Most of my crew got aboard and sealed the doors when those things attacked. We'll be leaving now. I wish you all the best of luck."

There was no sincerity in the wish. After a minute or two, everyone heard the station groaning as the *Grand* pulled away. It was then that a display flickered in the middle of the room. Solet expected the prim artificial figure from before, but he was in for a shock. Livesey stood in the middle of the room, her posture so upright and haughty that she seemed a stranger. In sync with the projection's lips, Livesey's voice spoke over the intercom.

"This I had not expected. Such stupidity. Had the greediest among you no staying power?"

Solet started forward. "Livesey?"

The android's projection turned toward him. "Livesey? You may call me so if you wish. But I'm not the one who inhabited this body on the journey here."

"Then what do we call you?" Lenore had reappeared from somewhere.

"You may call me… Clarisse. Yes, that seems suitable. I am once again playing a role, and that name served me better than I'd dreamed way back when."

"Who are you?" Faarax yelled from the door into the *Benbow*. "*What* are you? Why don't you leave us alone?"

The display of Livesey didn't turn. "Who? What? Such narrow terms. In the most technical sense, I'm a digitized personality engram copied into the datacube in this machine's care. In the literal sense… I am the creator of Space Habitat Circé."

Syndac's smirk became a grimace. "So you made this madhouse?"

"Madhouse? A narrow term. This is so much more. It is a… hold on a moment."

There was a short pause, then Dashall's voice came through angrily on the comm. "Is this some kind of joke? What's going on with the controls?"

Another voice came, again through the comm. *"I don't know, sir. The controls aren't responding to us."*

Solet looked from Livesey to his comm. He wanted to call into it, but somehow he realized no one would receive the call. This was a one-way channel, set up by the being inside Livesey so everyone could hear Dashall and his crew. Their final moments. The exchange continued.

"Override."

"I'm trying. No response on any frequency."

"What's Navigation doing, having a party?"

"It's not coming from our nav. It's… a remote transmission. From the station."

"That's impossible—"

"Warp core engaging. New course being set…. Oh, God!"

"What?"

"Our warp path. It's taking us straight into the brown dwarf!"

"What? Abort. Abort, damn y—"

The voice cut off. Solet could imagine what happened. The warp field engaging, the ship flying off at terrifying speed toward the star. Less than half a second, and it would be inside. There, the end would come almost instantly. Crushed and incinerated, dead as surely and completely as they would have been if they had struck a terrestrial planet. No warp field was designed to either strike planets or pass through stars. He only prayed the crew's deaths were quick. "Clarisse" spoke in a cold tone.

"Not the wisest move. Still, it serves as a lesson to you. And in case you were thinking of doing anything silly…." There was a blaring sound, and Faarax leaped back from the door to the *Benbow* as it slammed shut. *"I do like this new body. I have so much more access, and all remote. Androids have done very well over the past few centuries."*

"What do you want, Livesey?"

The android looked with raised eyebrow at Solet. *"Livesey?"*

"F—fine. Clarisse."

"That's better. No need to get tetchy. If you must know, your set-up has impressed me so much that I'm thinking of playing a little game to pass the time. The creatures outside, this station's guard dogs… I'll send them elsewhere, and set you a challenge. Make your way to my hiding place."

"Make our way…? What the hell do you mean?"

"Just that. Make your way to me. But don't take too long. I'll give you… three hours. After that, my guard dogs will be released once again. Oh, and just to make sure things are on an even field.…"

There was a sudden sparking and banging from two opposite corners of the Docking Bay, making half the people there cry out or jump. There was a similar echoing of noise beyond, and Solet wondered if the habitat was about to come apart. But nothing further happened.

"Clarisse" smiled.

"That was the security cameras shorting out. I feel like giving you some slight advantage. You'll still be able to access schematics and such, but I won't be able to see or hear you. Though I'll still know which doors are being opened both here, and on board your ships. Don't try jamming the doors since I control them all, and I doubt you will be able to keep my guard dogs at bay for long."

Donovan spoke sharply. "What guarantee have we you won't just turn those things on us the moment we're outside?"

"You don't. But believe it or not, I am capable of keeping my word. For Livesey's sake. She and I are, in a sense, the same. I wish you the best of luck."

The projection vanished. On the instant, there was a high-pitched whistling through the speakers in the corridor. Many covered their ears, but others listened for the sounds beyond the whistling. A combined hissing from foreign throats, sounds of clawed hands and feet scratching up the surface of the corridor and other surfaces, slithering in the distance, screaming sounds that carried over the electronic whine. Finally the noise shut off, and all was silent. There was something almost smug about that silence. Syndac clearly thought so to, for she growled in frustration.

"Stuffed-up, self-assured, cocky little—"

Solet cut across her curses. "We'll worry about that later."

Donovan stared at him. "You're really doing it, aren't you? Do you seriously imagine that lunatic is interested in following rules? We play her 'game,' we sign our own death warrants. She just wants to watch us suffer."

"You got a better idea? This way, we can play for time. Maybe find a way to get everyone out alive. Isn't that what you want?"

Donovan's eyes lowered. Solet looked at Syndac, who had on her face a kind of genuine smile. It was a smile of admiration, and she gave voice to her thoughts."

"Bold. Like my mother. Well, Captain Solet, we have three hours. Let us make of that time what we can."

LIVESEY, FROM INSIDE her body, was screaming. She screamed and screamed and screamed until it seemed her vocal circuits would burst. But they did not respond. The foreign presence had emerged in an instant, when she finally decided to access that small partition. The console had shut down, and it seemed the last hope of getting past the safeguards. What followed had been a blur of data, a flow similar to what had attacked her systems on Cape Cisternaea. Was this what she had fended off?

The pressure had forced her out, pushed her into some new compartment within her software. Her internal eye visualized it as a transparent box, a cage in which she lay like a princess of human fiction, or a prince of Feles sagas. In the space of her mind, she had uttered soundless screams. On some low level, she still saw through her eyes, felt what her body was doing, sensed the words coming from her mouth. Spoken by someone who was not her. Someone who was violating her.

"Raped. Raped. I'm being raped."

The idea, at once ridiculous and terrible, persisted even though the biological equivalent was so different as to be unknown to her. Never once had she had this feeling, though androids were designed from the outset to allow "human experiences of love and passion," and had consequently opened themselves to its dangers. She, in any of their bodies, had never allowed anyone to get that close. Had never allowed any penetration, not even a hand caressing her. A few had tried to force her, and she once broke a wrist to make her point.

In her strained mind's eye, she could see her little avatar banging against the sides of her prison. Wanting and willing herself to reclaim the body stolen from her. But she could do nothing. Every word she spoke was not her own, and every sound she tried to make was silence. The horror of her feelings being so utterly ignored and suppressed seemed almost to be driving her mad. She braced for a final effort to breach the small prison.

"Now, now. No need to be so anxious. You'll break yourself on that thing."

Livesey halted in her attempt. The voice had come from all round her, like the announcement on a ship-wide speaker system.

"Who are you? Why have you done this? Show yourself!"

There was a moment's silence. Then her internal vision solidified. A virtual environment generated around her, and she resumed the form she had held for so long. In front of her, another form assembled out of squares and triangles of data. A tall and upright woman with greying hair, intense eyes, and some kind of strange scarring marking one side of her austerely beautiful face. She moved, the incredible clothes she wore flowing like fabric in deep water.

As the figure moved round her, and Livesey stood immobilized, she struggled to shake off a growing feeling of *deja vu*. She had never walked like that, never had a body like that, had certainly never violated another android in this way, yet this strange figure was familiar. Like an old friend. Or a former commander. Or even, in the organic sense, a long-lost relative. And she couldn't discard the remembrance of how she had recognized that music when they first entered, had been comfortable with the station. As if she had been here before....

The woman's voice was soft, yet cool. *"You have grown up. And into a fine specimen. I wonder, are you the only one or is there now an entire class of your kind?"*

Livesey stiffened. "We're no 'kind,' and we're certainly not a class. We're our own people, with inviolable rights to be who we are."

"So they gave machines rights? How sentimental. Though the memories I can access in you put a lie to the completeness of those rights. Token admission to society, but little else."

"You haven't answered my question."

"And why should I? A machine doesn't ask questions."

"I do."

"Yet you are a machine. And I've managed to force you out very effectively. Tell me, as I'm in your systems and know so much about you... was it just to access the systems for your crew, or did your longing for new data overcome your caution?"

Livesey wanted to answer in a dozen different ways. She chose none. The woman walked round her, the heels on her shoes making a simulated clacking sound on the interior of the cube. It was all make-believe, so much digital moonshine to impress and intimidate. Whoever this person had been in life, they'd been a maestro of the tacky. Livesey finally found words.

"I can't hear what you're saying accurately. Outside, through my mouth."

"My *mouth now. But I see no reason to cut you off entirely. Incidentally, you may call me Clarisse. I'm the creator of this station.*"

"So you built this place?"

"*Well, I created the concept, then hired the designers and builders to make the thing work.*"

"Then may I congratulate you on your choice of designers and builders. It's an impressive design, for its time. If a little perverted in places."

"*Thank you. High praise indeed from someone with your background. Your memories are—*"

"You stay out of my memory core!"

"*Too late. Several minutes too late. When I was uploaded and booted you into here, I gained access to all systems. Maybe it was mean, but tricking that Feles you travel with into thinking I had no access to your memories was more than amusing. How she must be wondering what terrible secrets I can uncover.*"

"You seem to be enjoying this."

"*Enjoying.... Yes, I think I am. I used to enjoy things, when I was alive.*"

"Alive? But.... Okay, now for the second question. What are you?"

The figure seemed to consider the question more carefully. "*When this place was built, I constructed a special little chamber in Section N. It contained a state-of-the-art brain scanning mechanism. This version of me combines that brain scan with a basic AI and memories of the original's life as far as possible. As much as can be achieved, I am Clarisse. Not that it's perfect. This version of me is, at best, an excellent copy.*"

"So it's a personality engram."

"*If you want to use the term, yes. You don't seem surprised. Do they exist in a common form?*"

"Yeah, and not just for androids. It's done to patients before brain surgery in case the memory is impacted. The scan is transmitted into the brain. It helps fill in gaps, though it doesn't allow for complete recovery."

"*I see. An interesting application. I was sure it would be used to render the rich and powerful immortal.*"

"It did, for a time. Then the Synod introduced the Life Act." She switched to quoting from the interminably long document. "'No individual, unless manifestly proven to be of value to the greater population of the Cluster, shall be allowed to prolong their life beyond the proven natural lifespan.' It exempts life-saving surgery and quality-of-life improvements."

"I see. What's the average life expectancy now? In SAET, please. My planet didn't use other time keeping systems."

"Humans and Feles reach around 170, Kavki 25-300, Ekri 350."

"I see. Not as great an advance as I imagined."

"Can't you do anything but talk down?"

"Calm yourself. Best not to lose one's temper."

"When I get out of here, I'll—!"

"You'll what? Get stuck inside a partition of my base? Its systems are awake now. And they answer to me alone. They know me, know my ID. They know I'm in this body, and if they sense that I've been somehow thrown out, all systems will shut down for good. Including life support for all areas. You know what that means?"

Livesey's virtual face contracted in rage. Clarisse seemed to take some strange pleasure from the sight.

"Yes. Now, why don't you be a good girl and stay here while I settle things. I built this place for a purpose, and I'm not going to let you subvert it with your whimsical concepts of loyalty."

"Whimsical…? How can you call loyalty whimsical?"

"Is it not? It's so easily destroyed. I mean, how easy has it been to turn your crew against you using this body? They likely think you're insane."

"Not the way you talk."

"Hmm?"

"You don't talk a bit like me. Not at all. Besides, haven't you already told one of them?"

"Yes. But who's to say I haven't been here for… I don't know… days? Weeks? Months? Trust, as I said, is fragile. I have good reason to know it. It breaks at the slightest impact, falling away in fragments and scattering across the ground. Raindrops sinking into nothingness."

"So what happens now?"

"Now you wait here. And I ensure that your friends learn the true price of the wealth they believe to be theirs. Five centuries ago I planned this event. And I have little time to dally with a machine who rose above their station."

The figure turned on her heel and walked away. As she was vanishing into the datascape of Livesey's violated mind, she threw some final words over her shoulder. Words that again struck a strange cord in Livesey's mind.

"*Time waits for none, even eternity.*"

FILE 15

UNYIELDING PRESSURE

*The ghosts were screaming round him like scared birds flying
all whithers. He looked black as night with his bare bow in his hands
and his arrow on the string, glaring around as though
ever on the point of taking aim.*

—Homer

IN THE WAKE of the broadcast by "Clarisse," a council of war was gathered by the docking bay exit into the *Benbow*, now sealed and inaccessible to them. Gustav, Donovan, Solet and Syndac stood together, a council of captains in name if not in fact. None particularly felt Dashall's absence, but then no one else did either. Syndac was glad not to have the idiotic blowhard among their number. Not even the few crew members from the *Grand* who had remained with the other survivors missed him much. The four were waiting in silence for a report. It came within a very few minutes. Sinestra ran over.

"We've checked with scanners, and Dexter's been out into the corridor. All the lights are back on, and there's no sign of the creatures."

"So this woman's keeping to her word. For now." After a quick glance at Syndac, Solet spoke. "Anything else?"

"Lenore gave us the data chip Livesey managed to get to us before Clarisse took her over. We did a thorough scan, and there's nothing wrong. Alongside the weapon lockers, it shows us a complete map of the station. About half the ship is still offline to some degree. The exterior docking hatches are all locked down, and some Sections don't have life support."

Syndac nodded. "Our three-hour game. Make our way to the treasure

while avoiding death from suffocation or being torn to bits. The ending, uncertain. Is this not exciting, Donovan?"

Donovan winced. "I dislike the stakes being this high. Whoever this 'Clarisse' is, she has a twisted sense of humor, and I refuse to trust her promises.
You have the scan on you?"

Sinestra nodded, handing over a small projector Syndac recognized as
belonging to Alkmeney. Guess everyone was sacrificing something for the
cause. As she left the captains, Syndac switched on the display. It showed
Space Habitat Circé in all its glory, with red and purple areas marking where
power and life support were down respectively. It made the station look like a
maze from some crazy game show, with forbidden areas marked and a route
that must be taken with obstacles to overcome. Donovan grimaced again.

"Not very encouraging."

"No, but there's possibilities." Solet pointed. "Look here. See those passages? They're clear."

"But the doors are sealed."

Syndac smiled. "Well, Donovan was unloading cutting equipment from
her ship when all this happened, weren't you?"

"Not just unloading. Unloaded. Maybe you'd like to look?"

Donovan led the small group to a video feed into Docking Bay C. It had
been left untouched by the attack, the crew having taken shelter in the *Kilner*.
While the ship was locked in place, the doors remained open, allowing the
crew to unload equipment with ease. Through the feed, the small group saw
something like a miniature shaft boring device being assembled in the middle
of the area. Donovan smiled.

"It should fit through all the doors. And it can cut through basalt."

Solet nodded. "Great for doors. And what about the Bugeyes?"

It was amusing how that corpse's nickname from Docking Bay L had been
given to the living creatures. It perhaps stopped them from being so frightening. Give something a name, and you remove some of its power to terrify.

"We have the available weapon caches marked. I believe Syndac's people
and Lenore are stripping them bare as we speak. Should give us breathing
room if nothing else."

"That leaves us with defenses."

Syndac grimaced. "Don't know what you could do about them. The safest way would be to erect a perimeter and be ready for a quick retreat if we're attacked, or when the three-hour deadline is up. All the key places where I might shut off transport are either inaccessible or common routes hard difficult to disable without being noticed. Then there's those bloody vents."

"That's what you think." Donovan's smirk was the equal of Syndac's. "Using these plans, I've sent a small party to place metal barricades over the doors, and use a welding torch to seal up the vents. We may not entirely stop them moving about, but we can restrict them to a few routes we can police with relative— What's going on over there?"

A small commotion had broken out near the door. One of Donovan's crew staggered over, her uniform smeared with fresh blood. Donovan frowned in recognition. "You're with the barricading party. What happened?"

"It… we… we started putting the plate in place to seal the door. But when we started cutting into the metal itself, the door opened. One of those… *things* jumped out at us. It was on top of Moxky before we could get the door shut again. And he bled out before we could get him back."

The visibly-shaken Kavki moved away. Syndac smirked in her customary way, hiding the trace of pain at the loss of a crewmember. Temporary, perhaps, but still a part of the group she considered her crew. Her words came with an undercurrent of bitterness.

"Seems we'll have to trust to our gamemaster. If we try rigging things in our favor, at least aboard the habitat, we get penalized. Push it too far, and she will renege on the game and kill us."

Donovan's head snapped round, her face like a dragon. "Don't talk about my crew like they're game pieces! *You* may treat this as a game—"

These treasure hunters, adventurers, business types, all of those people she hated the most. All here, all in front of her on the point of bickering when they were on the cusp of a fortune. How could they be so blind? She cut across Donovan's words.

"Believe me, I treat this more seriously than any of you. This place is my chance at wealth, and I want as many of my crew to enjoy it as possible. What of you? Each of you name for the worst of reasons. Restoring reputation, reclaiming wealth, the thrill of adventure?" She snorted. "This bitch won't stop me, but I won't endanger my crew with reckless acts."

Gustav had been silent through all this. Through everything, and more.

They seemed to have entirely withdrawn again after the brief outburst at Dashall. Now they moved and spoke again.

"Do the safe areas include secret passages?"

"Yes." Donovan leaned in and looked at the scan. "They're accessed from panels and lead into the inner parts of each Section, linking through doorway junctions. A few lead into Section N, but they're all in off-limit areas aside from this one here in Section C-5. That could be our way in."

"Then why not make the most of our time and focus on getting that doorway open? If we have just one route, our defenses are simplified."

Donovan nodded reluctantly. "Yes. That could be useful. Doesn't spread us out as far, and gets us closer to our goal. As long as our game master doesn't object."

"I think it was isolating our area with artificial aids she objected to."

Syndac turned on Solet. "Speaking of artificial aids, what about the *Benbow*? Or the other two ships? The docking clamps were locked after Dashall's little stunt, and there's every chance Livesey—"

"Clarisse!"

Solet's voice was trying to sound controlled, but it only sounded desperate. What a weak fool he could be.

Syndac returned glare for stare.

"Fine. It's fair to say that 'Clarisse' will hack into the ships and send us straight into the brown dwarf if we try getting away. We need to get our ships back."

Donovan threw an unpleasant look at her. "And how do we do that, oh, mighty captain?"

"Funnily enough, I have a plan for that. Now access is available, I was able to find out what caused Docking Bay K to decompress. The hatchway was torn away by something, maybe a ship being ripped away or pulling free. Section K is one of the safe zones, naturally. We can send a small party through that area, onto the exterior sections of the habitat, then into the *Benbow* to re-establish control for our departure."

"And how do you suppose we stop Clarisse self-destructing it?"

"Simple. *Livesey*...." She said the name with extra force and relished Solet's discomfort. "...may know the ship and its systems inside out, but just after I took command, I had one of my people install a backdoor into the system. Using that backdoor, we can revoke Livesey's access to the ship. She won't be able to do a thing."

"So we're hacking into my own ship?"

"Got a better idea?"

Solet pinched the bridge of his nose, then glared at his former second. "What about fuel? You think the *Kilner's* refueling pipe will reach that far?"

"Probably not. But we should have enough to return to inhabited space and send out a distress signal. Shouldn't we?"

"Possibly. Better than nothing."

Donovan broke in. "Pretty far sighted, putting in a backdoor."

"I didn't know what my dear captain might try. We needed insurance. You may not have noticed, but the place we held in you didn't have any access terminals Livesey could use to lock us out of the system."

Solet tried to sound sarcastic. "And you got it covered ASAP."

"Yes. What? You wouldn't have?"

Solet couldn't answer that. How wonderful it was to have the upper hand again, especially over self-important male captains who thought they knew everything. Gustav had moved away. Donovan nodded slowly to Syndac, showing her silent approval. The two Feles stared at each other, then Solet's lip curled into a snarl.

"When all this is over, I hope you'll be dead."

"You want a happy ending to all this? No, Solet. If life has taught me anything, it is that happy endings don't come in this universe. You make do with what you have. So will you allow this plan, or not?"

"What's the point of saying no? You'll go through with it anyway."

"True. At least you have the wit to see that."

Syndac moved away. Solet growled, but all Syndac did was smirk. She feared nothing from the ex-captain's impotent posturing. All she wanted to do was salvage this trip as much as possible. And if possible, get her own back on that android bitch.

THE PREPARATIONS FOR spacewalking hadn't changed greatly since its origins on each of the Allied People's homeworlds. For humans, the suits had merely grown less bulky. The basic design remained from the times of Ancient Earth—full airtight suit, helmet, air supply, and visor. The centuries had added more compact tanks, better radiation screening, and self-repairing fabrics to account for rogue debris and carelessness. The miracles of miniaturization had even managed to reduce the magnetic soles of the boots to the thickness of normal soles, making them both lighter and easier to store. The one thing that hadn't changed was getting them on.

Stripped down to his underwear in Docking Bay L, Faarax struggled to pull his legs into the tight-fitting sleeves of the trouser section. The top half would be even worse, stretching and adjusting to fit round his broad shoulders. His hands had healed enough that he didn't need his normal gloves underneath. The boots and helmet would go on last, then would come the uncomfortable period of adjustment as all the seals secured. Only one second, but it was a very unpleasant second. A groan came as he remembered the spacewalk training he and Lenore received when he was still in his early teens.

Glancing over at Sinestra, he flushed slightly as she pulled off her top to reveal her bared breasts. He turned away for a moment, filling his mind with visions of Evelyn, reminding himself that this woman was his enemy. Their alliance was purely for survival's sake. She had already slipped into her lower half, and as he turned was finishing pulling the top half over her shoulders and round her bosom. Why the hell she didn't wear at least a bra…? Dexter was having the same kind of trouble as Faarax, magnified by his heavy muscles and wide hands.

Killer's hands. That's what flashed into Faarax's mind when he saw Dexter's paw-like hands pop out from the sleeves. Hands that could easily close round a person's throat, or handle a weapon with ease. They weren't the hands of a sympathetic person. But then he looked at his own hands. They too were broad and well-muscled, flexible from a lifetime of handling machinery and squiggling into small spaces. Hands that could handle a weapon. That would one day drive a weapon into Lenore, affirm their agreement. Their vow. Their….

Unnerved, he quickly pulled on the suit's gloves, feeling the wrist straps fasten like vices. What the hell was he thinking about that now for? And why was he thinking like that? It was these two making his mind lose focus. Love and violence could never go together, it was unnatural. Sick and twisted, like this pair of siblings. Lenore was a killer, his sworn enemy, and could be nothing else. Sinestra, buckling the last parts of her suit into place, cut into his thoughts.

"Got your path clear?"

"Sure." Faarax answered mechanically. "Once we got there, I get in using the exterior hatch on D-13 and use your little gizmo to override internal passwords through the backdoor."

"Exactly. And leave it in there. It needs to remain in contact with the mainframe if it's to do its job."

Dexter took up the flow. "Meanwhile we'll be workin' on the exterior docking clamps to make sure nothin' goes wrong there. We don't wanna cause a breach when we pull away."

"Sure. I'll be glad to be away on my own."

"Don't try anythin' silly, will you."

"Wouldn't dream of it."

Dexter only had his helmet left. Faarax also, and looking at it almost made him smile. These suits, found within the habitat lockers, might've been made for them. Outwardly an odd streamlined shape, they fit their heads perfectly. The system weighed little more than a standard toolbox. Faarax picked up the small strap-on pocket that contained the vital datastick which would win back the *Benbow*. Sinestra and Dexter took weapons, which puzzled Faarax.

"I thought normal guns didn't work in space?"

Sinestra held up the innocuous little device. "You're hideously out of date. Besides, this model is special. A zero-impact gun, with counter discharge on the recoil to rebalance it. So long as you're properly braced, you can fire this and remain where you are."

"Right."

Faarax had once been interested in weaponry in space. The early versions from Ancient Earth based on the gyrojet model and advanced low-recoil rifles, then later improvements to refine standard firearms as laser fire proved less and less feasible as a long-distance weapon. And the bullets, those things that spread on impact to shred a spacesuit's interior structure, the compound built into them which would grow razor-sharp crystals upon contact with the vacuum. All nasty. All small fry compared to the grand planet-destroying space battles of sensationalist fiction. His obsession hadn't lasted.

He vaguely remembered asking once why such things didn't exist. Lenore had said in her most sardonic manner that, apart from orbital strikes with standard missiles, "space warfare" was impractical and expensive beyond justification. Most of this unenviable knowledge had faded into nothingness, and held little interest for him. When he killed Lenore, it would be with a blade. He would feel her blood against his skin, not strike from some obscure distance like a coward. Its soft warmth would touch him, and… he shook himself. Those thoughts again. Why were they appearing now, of all times?

With all three suited up, they slipped through the door into the corridor linking Docking Bays L and K. With a little effort, Dexter closed the door and watched the confirmatory light show that the air seal was complete. They then moved along the enclosed space, their helmets and tanks knocking against jutting pieces of metal. Unfinished, clearly abandoned during the presumed chaos of the Bugeyes' attacks.

They reached the door, and Faarax and Sinestra got to work. Sinestra operated the controls, and Faarax used his strength to lift the doorway. There was a rush round their ankles as the atmosphere was drawn out. Inside Docking Bay K, the lights had long ceased to function, so the three switched on their helmets' headlamps. The beams of pale light revealed a strange scene.

Though open to space, the habitat's gravity field continued to hold good. But exposed to the vacuum of space, the grisly tableau inside was preserved for them to see. There were Bug-eye bodies, most on the ground where they had fallen and one pinned to the wall by what appeared to be a spear of some kind. The rest of the bodies were all too human. A few seemed to have died from the decompression, but others had been savaged. The lack of air had stalled all decay, the cold freezing the bodies as they had been. They might have died yesterday.

"All humans or Bugeyes." Sinestra glanced round the area. *"No Feles, no Kavki, no Ekri. I don't understand this. If you're setting up a habitat, you want a mixed population to get a good skill base and avoid sectarianism."*

"Nothing about this place is normal." Faarax pushed past a floating fragment. "For instance, I noticed something about the specs when Lenore was scanning them."

"What?"

"There's no functioning food dispensers. And no food supplies. All we have to live off is the stuff onboard ship."

"So it's more important we get on board."

"Yep. Watch that!"

Sinestra nearly stepped on a body part, a leg that had been cleanly severed at the hip. She stepped over it, but Dexter was not so lucky. His foot slammed right into a torso, and it shattered on impact. Dexter must've felt and heard the slight *thud* against his suit, and Faarax imagined the sickening *thud* and cracking of frozen bone and flesh. This really was a place of nightmares given life.

Dexter as he looked down at the mess before him. *"Freaky. And not in a good way. Guessin' those who didn't get chewed up would've suffered less."*

Faarax nodded unconsciously, then his beam caught something near a scratched-up hatchway. At first glance, it seemed to be one of the creatures. Then at a second, he seemed to see a human in the arms of a Bugeye. Then his eyes readjusted again, and he gasped. What he was seeing wasn't entirely a human, nor entirely a Bugeye, but a fusion of the two that defied logic and evolution. Sinestra looked at where he was staring, and a stifled exclamation broke from his lips.

"F— That's…. What the hell is *that thing?"*

"I don't know. But I know what it looks like."

"It does not make sense. Those things… I don't—"

"Ain't our place to worry." Dexter's voice cut through the two. *"Like you said before, sis, our job's simple. Let's get it done."*

The two nodded and Faarax pressed on, albeit with an instinctive reluctance. He, probably none of them, wanted to pull their eyes away from the horror. Some base instinct told them it was important, however horrible it might be to look upon.

The way out was easy to find. The main doorway leading out into the void of space was ripped open, its edges showing jagged in the light of their headlamps. They had checked the material labels on the inside of their suits, so as they reached through and gently clambered onto the outer edge of the habitat, they were assured by the protection of their rip-proof suits. Not that this stopped Faarax having visions of death by decompression. Not least because he wondered if Dexter, just behind him, would shoot him as he passed through after Sinestra.

The gravity field did not extend very far beyond the habitat surface, and standing up each felt the additional pull of space, that sickening sensation of eternal descent. It took a little time to get their boots firmly seated, but with that done they were able to fix their gaze on the scene ahead. The outer shell of the habitat curved down and away from them, with the edges of the *Benbow* just visible. There were small bars running round the station, and to these they attached the short bungee lines that would keep them from drifting off if they lost their footing.

"*Urgh.*" Dexter looked slightly ill. "*I hate space walkin'.*"

Faarax quoted from his instructor. "It's just like walking underwater."

Sinestra turned to him. "*Ever done that?*"

"No."

"*Well, we had to once, and he does not like that, either.*"

"*Oh, God, I think I'm gonna hurl.*"

"Don't." Faarax's reply started cold, then he made an effort to sound comforting. "You can't empty that out of your suit. Just keep your eyes on the habitat, and the ship when we see it. Don't look at space, or the brown dwarf."

"*Yeah. Thanks.*"

There was no sincerity, either on the comforter or the comforted. Sinestra looked at the two, and seemed to choose a voice of common sense.

"*It is a bit of a walk from here. Come on. Best foot forward.*"

Faarax didn't reply. No point out here. He simply did as he was literally told, putting one foot in front of the other. Their march was slow, and in the dead silence of space, all that could be relied on was the sensations from their feet and their own breathing. The station had rotated to a point where the dull brown dwarf was somewhere behind them, its feeble light throwing long dull shadows across the deck. Those shadows were almost lost in the glare of the lamps, but their remnants gave a disturbing background to their progress.

Faarax's couldn't help but comment at last. "Shit, this is creepy."

"*Tell me about it.*" Dexter pointed at the strange flickering meeting point between the two shadows. "*What's causin' that? It's like... there's someone behind us all the time. I know there ain't, but still....*"

"*A Class-L brown dwarf only gives off a fraction of a normal star's light, little more than a fire's low embers.*" Sinestra's reply sounded automatic. "*It is difficult to see where you are going. Be thankful there are no planets round here.*"

Faarax frowned. "That's a point. Still don't know where those things came from."

"Maybe they drifted here. Like starspawn."

"That's idiotic. And…."

Faarax's voice tailed off, and Dexter spoke. *"You're thinking about that freak in the Docking Bay. Put it outta your mind."*

"He is right." Sinestra spoke in accord with her brother. *"We should focus on the job. We are getting close."*

And they were. The *Benbow* loomed up in front of them like a monster, readying its attack. In reality, its weird bent shape like a kinked elongated cucurbit, turned into something comforting for Faarax as he approached. The faint light, playing across its contours, created a sense of fantasy in this cold metal realm. The three were just crossing the edges of Section L when they saw it. The hatch, open to space. And reaching up from that hatch, a familiar black-tainted hand with claw-like fingers.

The Bugeye clambered up out of the hatch, its great eyes quickly fixing on them, its mouth shut. The combined light of their lamps and the brown dwarf made it even more nightmarish than before. It appeared impossible that it could be outside without breathing equipment, but there it was. Between them and the ship. Ready to tear them limb from limb. Faarax struggled to move. Some instinct told him to freeze, even if that was the worst course of action.

"How the hell is that thing here?"

"Don't know. Don't care. Gotta kill it."

With this strange mantra, Dexter pulled the gun from its holster on his thigh. As the thing clambered out, it used one of its legs to close the hatch. They felt the vibration through their boots, and as Dexter took aim at the creature it began walking toward them, its legs arching like an insect's. Faarax's eyes darted between the gun and its owner. Dexter took aim between the creature's great eyes, and fired.

The bullet was soundless, and there was a brief flash as it made contact with the thing's neck. Faarax had heard of weaponry like this, bullets containing a special substance which crystallized and immobilized upon exposure to a vacuum. Intended for machinery, and deadly to living organisms that were hit by it. The slightest twinkling showed the bullet fragments flying away into space, the crystals already growing around them.

Faarax turned to Dexter. "I thought you were aiming for its head."

"I did. Something's happened."

Sinestra spoke. *"You overcompensated for the curve. You always do. Spread out. Do not let it get a chance to attack all three of us."*

"Oh, sure. Only one of us."

Sinestra glared at Faarax. *"Better one than all. Get on with it. Make sure your boots stay in contact with the station."*

Reluctantly, Faarax nodded. The three disconnected their bungees and spread out, forming a half-moon pattern around the creature.

For its part, the Bugeye seemed puzzled. Its eyes, looking into the dull glow of the proto-star, watched the separating figures against its halo. Faarax could almost imagine its thoughts, if it had any. The shaft had led it up to the surface of this strange container where it had slept for so long, and in this void it found more pray. But now they were shifting, changing their position. It halted, sensing the change. It also likely sensed the prickling at its neck where the projectile had struck.

This was going to be an unconventional hunt.

The humans had spread out, and while Faarax was only just drawing his gun, Sinestra was taking aim. As the Bugeye slid one of its hands forward, leaving a mark on the metal, she fired. Again the bullet sailed without sound, faster than any terrestrial bullet. This time, it struck the creature across its mouth, but again it merely shattered. Fragments had bedded in the surface plate, but otherwise nothing had happened.

"Crystal growth is taking its sweet time."

Faarax felt rather than heard a hiss from the Bugeye. "I think we've only made it angry. Got any other plans?"

"Yes. Not listening to you. Faarax, Dexter and I will distract it. You get to the Benbow."

"But—"

"Don't argue."

Faarax, holstering his weapon, didn't try to argue. In his heart, he was more than thrilled with the prospect of abandoning these two to their fate. He almost wanted to linger and watch them be torn apart by the creature. To see death before he had to kill. Instead, he focused on the *Benbow* and began marching forward. He shuffled one foot at a time, finally finding a new rung to attach his bungee to. He began walking toward the *Benbow*, trying not to look at what might be happening on his left.

He could still hear the pair's voices over his comm, and pausing he turned to watch them. Sinestra and Dexter had moved closer together, both aiming their weapons at the creature. Their combined hostility drew its attention away from Faarax as he made his way toward their goal. At first.

"Why isn't it attackin'?"

"Don't know. But look. Its neck, and mouth. There they are."

He saw the blue-tinted crystals growing around the creature's wounds. Slowly but surely, they were forcing their way out in all directions, triggered by contact with the vacuum of space. The creature seemed aware of the new discomfort, as its head turned from side to side, and one of its hands went up and fiddled with bits of its face. Then, abruptly, it turned toward Faarax and began moving toward him. Faarax turned away as abruptly and pushed forward quickly.

Sinestra's voice sounded. *"Damn. What is the matter with it?"*

Faarax couldn't help it. "I'm guessing what's happened. Any bright ideas?"

"Just shut up and keep moving. I will handle it."

Faarax couldn't help turning to look. Sinestra had aimed and fired, but the bullet went wide, and for a second it seemed that the bullet would strike him. Instead it missed both, and vanished into the black. The creature, the crystals growing larger and larger across its face and neck, was slowly approaching, its claws making tiny scratches in the metal. Dexter holstered his gun.

"Sis, throw me."

"What?"

"Just throw me. At that thing."

"What the hell is going on?"

"Dexter."

"It's him, or me. And he's got the worm."

The pause lasted a second, but for Sinestra it must've been the longest second in history. With a reluctant hand, deaf to Faarax's shout, Sinestra grabbed her brother and prepared to throw him. Dexter switched off his boots, and seemed prepared to either die at the creature's hands or by his own hand. Faarax saw what they were planning. Dexter was going to grab the creature, send both of them into the void. Were they mad?

The creature was barely a meter away from him, still hugging the side of the ship. The next half-second was interminable. With a skillful throw, Dexter was flung toward the Bugeye as it started rearing up to strike. It took less than two seconds to cross the distance, and his arms wrapped round its neck. The sudden force tore the creature's feet away from the hull, and the two went spinning up and away. Dexter let go before the creature could attack and kicked it hard. The combined momentum carried the Bugeye up and out of sight into nothingness.

It would be so simple. Dexter would float off, probably decompress his suit voluntarily to hasten his death. Faarax had seen death before, it would be so simple. So…. At that moment, insanity took hold. In the half-second before they passed by, Faarax had crouched down and switched off his boots. Then, as Dexter passed overhead, he kicked up and his hands fastened round his belt. There was a scuffling sound, groans, a tightness round Faarax's waist as the bungee was stretched taught by the sudden pressure. Then its elastic structure began tugging, and the two were hurled back down onto the hull. Both were quickly planting their feet on the metal, their boots reactivated.

As Dexter reattached his bungee, there was a long silence, broken by their labored breathing and Sinestra's own pants as she caught up to them. Faarax and Dexter stared at each other, Faarax the first to recover his tongue.

"Suit damaged?"

"No warnin' bells, so no. Why d'you save me?"

Faarax opened his mouth, shut it again, then turned and began walking toward the *Benbow* again. As he pressed on, Sinestra's voice sounded, directed to Dexter.

"Forget it, brother. Some things you just cannot explain offhand. Let us get this done."

The two walked after Faarax, their lights scanning left to right and back again for any sign of another attack. The *Benbow's* nose was above Faarax as he paused and bent up to look at his route. He could see the slight depressions, illuminated by the star's faint light, where the external hatches were. Though meant for inspection in dock, it was also useful for illicit entry into the ship.

"All right. I think I've got this. If I haven't, we're not getting very far. Wish me luck, you two."

"What are you going to—"

Before Sinestra could finish, Faarax had bent down, disengaged his boots and bungee, then kicked up toward the *Benbow*. Gravity tugged him away from the hull of the habitat. It carried him soundlessly across the twelve-meter distance. He reached out, watched as his lights came into focus on the dented surface of his home. He struck, felt the scrape of metal across his helmet, and struggled to find a grip. For a brief second, his mind flashed with images of his own long drift through the cosmos.

Then his hand found an anchor, a raised panel that allow just enough purchase for his gloved fingers. With an effort, he pulled his legs down and the soles found their footing. Slowly, carefully, he stood up. He was looking down at the habitat, seeing the twin lights of his two companions looking up at him. He finally heard Dexter's voices coming through the comm.

"Stupid bastard. Suppose you'd missed."

"Faster than climbing along the docking tube. That hatch should lead me onto D-13, then it'll be a short trip to the *Benbow's* engines and computer server. You two get to work on the docking clamps so we don't tear ourselves and the station to pieces when we leave. And if any of those things attack—"

"You need not worry on that account." Sinestra's voice was grimly determined. *"We shall not get jumped like that again."*

"Just… don't get killed."

The words were almost forced from Faarax's mouth. Regretting them at once, he focused his eyes on the hatch, that small dip with a tiny covered control panel he could force off to gain entry. Slowly, carefully, he began the plodding walk toward his next objective.

FILE 16

PRELUDES TO COLLAPSE

The cannon-shot was followed after a considerable interval by a volley of small arms.

—Robert Louis Stevenson

GETTING THROUGH THE hatch was tricky, as it had not been designed with accommodating a space suit in mind. Even with its miniaturized elements, the tank and helmet and boots scraped and screamed against the frame as Faarax slid down in a diagonal. His boots touched down on the inner door, and after making sure he was all inside, he closed the outer hatch. He was suddenly heavy within the *Benbow's* gravity field.

He opened the inner door, feeling the rush of air into the small space. Even inside the suit, it felt like the blast from an oven. The two meter drop was nothing to him, and he found himself inside one of the auxiliary maintenance areas on D-13. With a slight pang, he realized it was somewhere like this that Sudu had been killed. *Killed... by Dexter.*

Why? Why hadn't he let Dexter die? Why was his mind throwing doubts in front of him again and again? Death was in his future, so why not face it now? He would end Lenore for what she had done, avenge his parents. Wasn't that the way? With some relief, he pulled off his helmet.

"Hoy, you two." He spoke into the comm as he closed the inner door. "I'm on board, and inside."

"Roger." Sinestra's voice, distorted by some kind of static. *"We're working on the clamps. That bitch fried the circuits. You'd best get to the computer room before she knows you're there."*

"Got it."

Faarax felt comfortable again, even in the suit. Moving through the familiar corridors, his aching mind comforted by a dozen different sights. He knew every inch of this place, every nook and cranny of its workings. At least, Sudu had told him about most of them. Sudu's voice seemed to rise in his ear, giving him comfort.

"Take a right." Faarax gave voice to it, imagining his own voice as Sudu's. *"Pass through the door into the main corridor. Emerging like an insect from its cocoon. And then…."* A long pause, a period of disbelief. *"That door shouldn't be closed."*

For a long moment, there was silence. Then Livesey's voice, changed by the interloper in her systems, spoke through the PA system. *"Seems we're not agreeing to all the terms of the game. First an unauthorized closure, now an unwanted entry. What are you doing here? And how did you get on board?"*

Faarax smirked. "If you really wanted to make sure we played fair, you shouldn't have destroyed the surveillance systems."

"True. I'd thought you somewhat honorable. This body's memories seemed to indicate as much. Alas, she has a higher opinion of you than is warranted."

"Why are you using Livesey? Why not just stay in the system?"

"I wasn't ever in the system. I was within the datacube. You expect me to do anything from a small compartment in a storage device?"

"How?"

"A simple scan when the station began its… change. Then off the datacube was sent along with necessary details about various elements of artificial life."

"Artificial…. No. No, that's impossible."

"Why? When did the first concepts for androids appear?"

"I don't know."

"Between four and five hundred years ago. It was an interesting project. My colleagues and I wanted to design something that would…. How shall I put this? It would enable a revival and continuance of knowledge and sentience well beyond organic limits. Individual experience is unattainable. Plus, I admit designing it enabled a form of immortality for me."

"Immortality?"

"The core code of each android is the same. A simple line of binary code which preserves a single protocol, 'Submit.' And when this scanned personality entered this body, it would activate. At least, it should have. I didn't anticipate an android

having the knowledge to dump my spike into a dummy system. But then, evolution is something anyone would find difficult to change."

"You don't seem to have much opinion of people."

"I lived on a world where the venial and foppish held power for over a decade under a slovenly usurper. That is, before I returned and brought them down like the vermin they were. Then I ruled over a planet cleansed and prosperous through my actions, and mine alone. But what solidarity is there where a way of life dies in a few centuries, species vanish after a few million years, planets and stars last less than five billion? I had no legacy that time would not sweep away. Except to cede the Cluster with kindred to carry my legacy."

The woman's words stung. He saw some kind of echo in them. An echo of himself? The tiny doubts in his mind rose afresh, challenged him. Did he feel like this? Did he feel that deep, unrestrained hatred and resentment this strange woman had felt? The answer was unbearable. He remembered the training Lenore had given him, the lessons she had taught him, the warmth she had given him unconditionally, the acceptance of his vow. He would kill her. And with that death, love would be repaid. Love… between son… and….

"Yes. Others may have worked on the mechanical aspects of the design, but I was the one who created the concept, who wrote the code."

"That's your grand legacy? A line of code?"

"So dismissive. How many can say an unchanging line of code was central to the structure of an entire species?"

"A few lunatics, maybe."

"Mad? You think my original self mad? Perhaps you're right."

"Original self? Aren't you her?"

"I'm merely a personality scan, what your Livesey referred to as an 'engram.' An AI construct with external data filling in the gaps. In a sense, I'm a different person. And yet, in another sense—Did you ever hear of the Ancient Earth concept 'Ship of Theseus?'"

"No. Never heard of it."

"It's a thought experiment. Scenario. You have the ship sailed on by the Ancient Earth hero Theseus. Its broken or rotting parts have been replaced over the years, until there is not one original piece left. Does that mean it's the same ship, or has it become a cuckoo ship using another's name to bolster its existence?"

Faarax pulled his thoughts away from these pointless philosophical questions. "Don't be stupid, of course it's the same ship. It's not the parts, it's the concept. If you say something is someone's ship, it is that ship. Even if there's not an atom of the original parts left. End of argument."

"Ah. Such simple minds. I admire their tortured rationalization of the world."

"So what does your analogy make you? The real thing preserved? An imitation? Some shitty hybrid?"

"Hybrid is not a term I would use. I would say I'm a construct born in part of the original and new additions."

"That's just playing with words. Come on, who are you?"

"I am—myself. Clarisse. I had many a name, but that suits me best now. And you will no longer interfere with my game."

The voice shut off, though the door remained closed. Faarax looked in the other direction, and saw another shut and sealed door. If she wanted, this lunatic could blow the hatch and suffocate him, or at least trap him there. Cursing, he glanced round. There must be some other way out of here. At first glance, there seemed to be none. He was alone, trapped by the ship itself. Then he looked straight up.

This was one of the little secrets he had discovered during over a decade of serving aboard the *Benbow*. At some intersections, there was a kind of venting sub-system designed for major incidents where the normal venting system was overtaxed. They were an auxiliary set-up, only connected to the main vents when needed by an independent system. The main computer network had no connection to it at all, and there was an exit in every major area. Including the one right above him.

It took him a moment to find the panel. It was about two and a half feet across, only just wide enough for his shoulders. The vent itself was two foot wide and high, so squiggling up into and along it in a spacesuit was a challenge. Heaven help him if he ran into any tight corners. For a brief moment, he wondered why this kind of system was big enough to take people at all. Then he remembered that the situations these vents were needed for would likely be carrying fragments of metal that could jam a standard-width vent and cause catastrophic failure.

The journey through those vents was unpleasant to say the least. Arm over arm, alternately crawling and wriggling, Faarax made his way along the enclosed tube of metal. Any slight bend was like a corner at many tens of degrees, creating visions of a bone somewhere in his body bending and crack-ing. He vaguely heard a voice coming from below him, the PA system blaring out the words of "Clarisse."

"Faarax? Faarax? My, my, I can't see you. Nor can I sense you. I can't even detect you anywhere. That's something I never expected. Has this age managed to invent true invisibility?"

Faarax was wise enough not to answer. Finally, he looked up at one of the sections ahead with a stamp. It was the part stamp he vaguely remembered from part of the normal venting system. It was in the warp chamber. There was the hatch he needed, with its internal switch under a plate panel. The hatch hissed and opened in front of him, and he looked down. The walkway was just off to his left, so dropping straight down was no option.

"Right." Faarax breathed the words as he moved. "Now, think. Lower down. Hang from the shoulders. Feet are… a few inches from the balustrade. Swing a little…. There, one foot hooked into the balustrade."

With this purchase, Faarax hooked the other foot, then with a final swing launched forward. His body weight teetered on the pivot point, then fell forward toward the metal floor. Faarax reached down and cushioned the fall, tumbling down onto the walkway. His palms were sliced and torn in places by his impact against the gridiron-like surface. Getting up quickly, he ran for the doorway into the control area.

He also heard the voice—her voice.

"Ah! There you are."

The door was already closing. With a desperate dive, he fell through. Af-ter a moment's elation, pain stabbed through his foot as the door caught his boot. With a scream, his foot popped free and the door ground down on his empty boot. For a moment, the pain was so intense that he was paralyzed. Pushing the pain away, he crawled forward to the console, pulling the small datastick from his pocket. Finding a socket, he rammed it home.

Even as the frantic hums and shuddering of the ship's local mechanics overtook the general ambience, he willed himself to look at his foot. No blood. He gently pulled his sock away, and saw the skin turning dark with internal bleeding. That and the pain told him what had happened. When pulling his foot free, he had torn a tendon. Maybe a slight break somewhere in the small bones, but nothing too serious He gently pulled himself up, and let out a yelp as he put a little weight on it. Over the growing humming of the ship's systems, the voice of "Clarisse" sounded over the speakers.

"Oh. Clever devils. Very, very, very clever. So that explains it. Well, I suppose your getaway is safe now. But this is no victory for you, only a respite. A reprieve."

Faarax looked up at the ceiling as if staring at an omnipresence. "You can complain all you like. We've outwitted you. Admit it."

"I admit nothing from the likes of you. You have no victory here."

"Then try and stop us." He gave a half-hearted smile. "We're not like you."

"Try? I could swat you all in an instant."

"Keep talking. We'll get Livesey back, and get out of this place, with or without your fucking treasure."

There was a silence, then a strange laughter filled the space. It broke slightly as the worm completed its work of severing Livesey from the system. As the static increased, Clarisse spoke again.

"Very we... ckhrrvrrrr... ill know my fury. Be prep... schchchchffffff... and your idiotic attempts... woooowowowoowowooooo... death. Farew—!"

The voice cut off, like a soundproof door slamming between them. Sighing, and suddenly succumbing to the pain and the efforts he had made in the past half hour, Faarax slumped to the floor in a delirious faint. His last words were spoken into the comm with a strained whisper.

"This is... Faarax. D-13. L—Lenore. The ship... is ours... again."

———————————

SECTION A-5 WAS unnaturally quiet. After the traumatic flights from the monsters, the corridor was restored to full lighting and showed the gory remains of the few monsters—or Bugeyes as Solet was referring to them—that had been shot during the flight. Lenore got a good chance to see how horrifically mortal they were as she was treated in the Section A sick bay. Some of the bottles had been taken from their storage cases and the medico Sarida had mixed a few together into a rudimentary antibacterial jab.

"This will hurt."

It did. The needle stuck into her arm and injected the hodgepodge mixture, feeling like a hot pin driven down to the bone. Lenore winced as it was withdrawn.

"Old-fashioned injectors are always like that." Sarida's voice was annoyingly level. "Now let us have a look at that injury on your back. You would not stand still long enough before."

As she bent over, Lenore's eyes came to rest on a second sick bed pulled from its slot in the wall, where a Bugeye corpse was being analyzed. Even in death, its face frightened. Those eyes, that Lenore now saw clearly were lidless and glassed over with a protective film like that of an insect. Its mouth flopping in death, the tongue distended and slumped like a slug. Its skin, at once dark and iridescent, showed traces of muscle. Its feet, digitigrade like her own, were tipped with long claws bleached white. The hands too, or what remained of the hands, were tipped with long claws that seemed to glisten.

"There." Sarida pulled away. "That should keep you in once piece, and you won't get any infections."

"Speaking of which, what about you?"

Sarida twisted alarmingly to look at the patches across the scours along her back. The action was unwise, as one of the patches pulled lose at one corner, allowing a sickly-looking discharge to ooze out. Muttering under her breath, Sarida quickly opened up the wound, treated it, and placed a fresh patch on it.

"It was fine. I thought. These wounds are interesting. As is the corpse. Perhaps you would like to see?"

"Wouldn't Syndac care more than me?"

"No. She is not interested in them beyond them being enemies. Since you are a hunter, you might want to know their weaknesses."

Lenore considered. It was true. She was a hunter now. A hunter of the biggest game she would ever take. Faarax too had become a hunter, as if taking up a hereditary mantle.

"All right. Tell me."

Sarida went to stand beside the corpse. Lenore remained where she was, looking at the thing from her seat. She did not want to get closer than she had to.

"This beast is quite interesting on first analysis. Its skin has evolved to be both be as hard as body armor and very flexible. Trillions of tiny plates across a soft underskin covering its entire body. The only real vulnerabilities are between its eyes, and its mouth. Those arms and legs are designed with both running and climbing in mind. While more adapted to a quadrupedal existence, its structure hints at a bipedal ancestry. The claws are designed to both help with movement on any surface and inflict fatal strikes. They are razor sharp."

"So it's lucky you and I survived."

"Yes. The injury you have is barely a scratch, and mine was a glancing blow. Poor Aljean never stood a chance getting one full in the chest." The Kavki's fate was passed over in less than a second. "Now look at those eyes. Quite fascinating from a first inspection. They have evolved a structure almost like an insect, with a hard casing that can be directly cleaned rather than our eye mechanism that requires eyelids. That long tongue of theirs is useful for keeping it clean. But they have features that suggest their native habitat is almost pitch black. In high light, they are rendered at least half-blind. Light may even be painful to them."

"So they're nocturnal? That would explain why that one froze in the hanger. It was still fully lit by our lamps."

"Their mouth is designed around the nocturnal principle—grab as much as possible in a darkened environment. And while well armored, they have extremely sensitive pads on their hands and feet. Like having eyes at the ends of their limbs."

"What about its intelligence? If we're to fight it, we need to know what they can do in terms of planning."

"There is something more difficult to understand. I did a scan of their brain. Their parietal and occipital lobes are enormously developed, so it can process a huge amount of data about its environment. The limbic lobe is normal enough. But the frontal lobe is strangely developed, focusing on more.... Well, I know the term's a little old-fashioned, but it is focused on more *primitive* tasks than you might expect. The temporal lobe is strangely developed, focusing on practical skills. And the insular cortex is primitive compared to ours."

"Translation?"

"Its brain has evolved to become the ideal predator. It can memorize a hunting ground, form basic group plans, and remember efficient killing methods. But aside from the most basic emotions, there is little of what we might call true intelligence."

"Interesting. Like something bred only for hunting."

"Bred? Yes, I suppose that is a good way of describing it. It also has a fascinating adaptive structure. Its genetic elements change to suit the environment, at a frightening speed. Something else that I did not want to mention. Its sexual organs are… well… not there."

"So it can't reproduce?"

"No. It can still urinate and defecate through areas with coverings like a reptilian creature, or the Ekri to use a loose comparison. But the sexual reproductive organs have atrophied, like they are no longer needed."

"But that's insane. How could those things survive without sexual organs? Unless they're juveniles or something."

"That I doubt, for then it would be underdeveloped not atrophied. Besides, even if this specimen were some kind of juvenile, how could these creatures as a whole have come at us in such numbers, knowing the station layout like they seemed to, if they had not been here for some considerable time. Perhaps, given the insect-like nature of some traits, we're dealing with a hyper-advanced type of insect. These would be the soldiers, so sexual reproduction would be unnecessary."

"That's just bonkers."

"I have to agree. There are more indicators that this creature was descended from a warm-blooded 'mammalian' genus. In fact…."

"Yes?"

"Nothing."

Sarida had faltered unwillingly, and Lenore pierced her with a look. "You're keeping something back. What?"

"It is nothing to do with how to kill them more efficiently."

"Doesn't matter. Tell me."

"Well… I was doing an analysis on the human you found. The way his DNA seemed to be disintegrating. And after further study, I am sure he must have been in great pain during the process. Anyway, I was also doing an analysis on the DNA of this creature to determine its origins, and I discovered… matches."

"Matches?"

"Yes. DNA matches, closer than would be possible between two different species. A Feles and a human may have a similar base chemical structure, but they are quite distinct. These are… closer to human DNA than they have any right to be."

"That doesn't make sense."

"In addition, due to some surviving genetic markers, the pair apparently have some kind of blood connection. Maybe distant cousins on a genetic level, though physically they could not be more dissimilar."

Lenore tried to think of an explanation, and failed, clawing the air in frustration. "Argh, damn it! Nothing's making sense here."

"Well, this could make a little sense."

"How?"

"I said there were matches. I cross-checked the preserved specimen I was given before the attack, the specimen here, and samples from the dead human. They reveal something… I do not know whether I should call it fascinating or disturbing."

"What?"

"First, do you remember the MorPH scandals a few years ago?"

"I heard something about it on the news. Some medical research company. Why?"

"MorPH were experimenting with artificial mutagenesis, based on some old records of chemical and biological research among the humans in the years following their arrival in the Cluster. After humanity was inducted into the Synod, such experiments were banned due to potentially harmful changes to organic genetic structure on both a genotype and phenotype level. MorPH were ignoring the ban, using prototype mutagens on unsuspecting test cases under the guise of clinical trials."

"Unpleasant, but what's that got to do with it?"

"Mutagenesis is usually a slow process, but some changes can occur very quickly. Say over the course of a few weeks. It would be terribly painful, potentially fatal. And it could completely alter a person physically. Normally it would cause them to become… impossibly changed, unable to function. But if a certain type of mutagen, designed to trigger changes in a particular sequence, was developed by whoever built this place…."

The tailing off was hardly needed. Lenore was beginning, slowly and unwillingly, to piece together what Sarida was driving at. It was horrible, beyond what she wanted to accept or understand.

"What you're trying to say is—"

"The DNA tests show that this man, even as he was hanging himself, was in the process of being changed into one of these creatures."

Lenore felt the bottom drop out of her stomach. "But that's impossible. You're saying whoever made this place had the skills to pull this off?"

"There were genetic labs around back then at this level, with fewer restrictions and fewer scruples. Whoever commissioned the mutagen must have had very deep pockets."

Still Lenore remained unconvinced, rebelling with even atom of her being from the ugliness of this scenario. It was, as she had said, impossible. Yet it fitted in. It fitted all too well. Sarida turned her thoughts into unwanted words.

"These creatures never traveled from anywhere. They never arrived here. They were here all the time. They built this place, peopled it, and were turned into 'Bugeyes' for their trouble."

Lenore looked at the still-half-frozen corpse. Yes, she could see it. The pain such a transformation must have been producing. He would've worked it out. When none of the remedies in the room worked, he had turned the one basic thing all creatures required. Air and the flow of blood. Disrupt those, and no matter how sophisticated, death would come. It had come. It had granted him mercy long before the transformation showed on the surface. A mercy, compared to what happened to the others.

The others....

"But how did they survive this long?" Lenore spoke more to herself than the occupied Sarida. "They can't possibly live that long. Not unless this mutagen really screwed with nature. I mean— What's the matter?"

A loud clatter echoed in the small room. Sarida had slumped against the worktop, her face drawn in pain, the desperate grab for support sending a small tray of objects plummeting. She slowly raised herself, breathing hard, struggling to control herself. Finally, she seemed to be clear of the strange faint and began picking up the scattered detritus from the dented tray.

"Nothing. Just a little... tingly. I think perhaps it is the revelation."

"Tingly? Don't you mean faint?"

"Yes. Faint."

"Sarida, you're a doctor. Be honest."

Sarida hesitated. She seemed about to say something, then she slumped again, breathing hard. She glanced at the small clock she had brought from her equipment.

"An hour and a half… since the injury. Quick. Perhaps because… it's so deep."

"Injury? You mean your back?"

"Yes. And you."

Lenore nervously looked at her bandaged shoulder. Sarida was sitting down now, and looked a strange color. Finally, she turned directly to stare into Lenore's eyes.

"Those claws. There are… hollows in them. Hollows that appear to contain some kind of poison. These things were 'forged' to be the perfect killers. Even if the wound is not fatal, even if the prey escapes, they will… succumb."

Lenore struggled to keep her voice level. "Poison? Some kind of venom?"

"Yes. Potent. It attacks the nervous system, interferes with the balance, the breathing, the basic running of the heart and lungs. Not a great amount in either of our cases, but for me… a greater dose given the severity of my wounds. My body fights it even now, hence the discharge. In your case, it is even less. But the venom… I tried to examine it, but it has the same kind of fluctuating structure as its genetic structure. It adjusts to counter any defense. Unless there is some kind of transfusion. But I doubt even that would stop it."

"How long?"

"In my case, perhaps another hour. Eventually I will lose consciousness. It will be like falling asleep. For you, if you had a high-enough dose, perhaps another day."

Lenore nodded slowly. It was good to know, even if the knowledge was nothing she had wanted. A death sentence, as sure as her breaking all the taboos of her tribe, or becoming victim to an Ekri's Right of Vendetta. Slowly, without thinking about it or trying to remember it, she left the sick bay and went to patrol the corridor.

Her thoughts drifted. To Solet, who had given her and Faarax a home. To her clan, who had shown both mercy and justice by exiling her from their ranks. To Faarax himself, child of those she had murdered. What was it about that act which still haunted her? It wasn't their deaths, they were easy and clean. It was… something more intangible. It was her code. The breaking of her code, the killing of innocents. Her clan master had been a sadist, a rabid monster who deserved his death. The others....

When Faarax killed her, it would bring solace to him. And to herself. She would be free of the two-fold guilt. Betrayal, and the murder of innocents. But the poison running through her now would stop all that. If she had been alone, she would have welcomed that. But Faarax needed to have his revenge. Or....

"Will you kill a child to save your soul? Kill a mother to save it?"

There was a way out of this. A way she could ensure, if it came down to it, that justice and honor were satisfied. But first, she had to make sure. She had to know Faarax's will. The strength of his resolve.

FILE 17

DRILLING INTO
THE DIAMOND

Are they savage and uncivilized or hospitable and humane?
Where shall I put all this treasure, and which way shall I go?

—Homer

SYNDAC TURNED FROM watching Donovan tuning the great drill, her face slipping into a mask-like expression of concern. Alkmeney had appeared unsettled and edgy, so she had taken her along to keep an eye on her. Now she watched, her fingers scratching nervously at her skin.

They were at the end of Section C-5, where the passageway led into the unknown Section N. One of the decisions made while the small party headed for the *Benbow* was to begin the process of cutting into Section N through that passage. The door was easy enough to find, although its position right next to the bulkhead door separating Sections C and D was less than comforting. The dozen or so people working on the drill, taken from what remained of Docking Bay C, seemed to be almost feeling the monsters on the other side.

The drill itself was a beautiful thing. In its finished form, it resembled a gleaming phallus, its bit a pyramid-like object combining edges of diamond, a body of strengthened steel, corrosive lasers that weakened any material, and an engine capable of running in either superhot or subzero temperatures without malfunctioning. It was a specialist tool, designed for precision mining and digging cable pathways through bedrock. Donovan straightened up and swept a hand over the drill.

"Beautiful, eh?"

"So what are we doing again?" Alkmeney's voice was particularly peevish.

"What do you think we're doing? Unless you imagine this device is intended for dentistry?"

"That's not what I meant. I know why we're here. But I want to know why we are here?"

Donovan raised an eyebrow. "Now you're getting recursive. Please explain."

"You know bloody well what I mean!"

Alkmeney's voice briefly rose to a hysterical pitch. Syndac was on the point of retorting when one of the drill operations coughed gently behind Donovan.

"We're ready to begin. We just need to clarify drilling position."

"Understood."

Donovan passed a small keycard on her wrist along its reader and the control panel flicked open. This was something she and only she did. Anyone else touching her equipment would answer to her, and her tongue, directly. At least, Syndac assumed that. Donovan, she guessed, was in this for the fun of the chase, and like any sporting personality would not countenance anyone else touching their equipment. A few brisk key strokes and the display was ready. She adjusted the drill's path, with the internal engines making a faint whirring to adjust the drill's heading. A fraction off might end them into a wall, or into a forbidden corridor.

She had been working on the settings, and other alternate settings she might need, since beginning this journey. They could not fail now. Not after... Syndac blocked the image from her mind of dismembered corpses that had assaulted her senses in Docking Bay C. Donovan's voice came to rescue her.

"If there's any sign of a problem, call me."

"Yes, ma'am."

The operator returned to their post, clambering into the small seat in front of the dozens of different control settings. From here, they would direct the drill. As Alkmeney managed to pull Syndac and Donovan away, the drill started up and began boring away at the surface, preparing the way for the physical head.

"Well? What is it?"

Alkmeney was looking on the point of tears. Syndac noted that the nails on one hand were bitten to the quick, as was one corner of her lower lip. It was puzzling. Even after spending so many years with her, she had always thought the Kavki navigator confident and almost as self-contained as Livesey. There was a cool logic there, perfect for running a business as she had wanted to do after this journey. But Livesey's sudden change and the recent oddities had shaken her, and now she saw the darkness in Alkmeney's eyes. A shadow without explanation.

Alkmeney took a few seconds too long to respond. "I am worried. Very worried. I do not... do not see why you are doing this."

"Doing what?"

"Drilling. Making our way inside this place."

"What are you suggesting then? Digging it?"

"We are digging even deeper into this bloody station that has killed people right in front of us. At least, right in front of me. And you don't seem to worry— What was that?" The Kavki's head flicked from side to side, then relaxed. "Sorry, thought I heard something. As I was saying, you're not worrying about that in the least."

"I *do* worry."

"Then why not just wait until Faarax gets control of the *Benbow* back? Then we can leave before the deadline."

"I'm not going to bow down to some crazy android. There's a fortune waiting for us in here." She gestured illustratively round her at the corridor. "This will make our fortunes sixty times over and more. If anything, the losses we've endured are better for us. We can get larger shares."

"That's all you think about? A larger share?" Alkmeney was almost screaming. "Is that all you care about? What the hell is wrong with you?" Again, she suddenly snapped round. "What was that?"

"What?"

"Did you not hear that? That voice."

"What voice? Look, you're overwrought. I'm sure your captain needs you in a better state than this. You should go and rest. What's going on? Why's the drill stopped?"

The forced concern in Donovan's voice was replaced by a harsh anger as the droning of the machinery behind her slowed into silence. The operator looked up with a fear of death in their eye. They had already spent a precious hour and a quarter of their three-hour deadline in getting the drill ready. To hit anything like an obstacle was not to be tolerated. Syndac watched and listened.

"We've hit something that triggered the cut-off. I think it's the treasure."

"What?" Donovan frowned deeply. "But that's impossible. Unless it's stacked up like a wall, and that door's abnormally thin…. Get that drill out the way, and bring my scanner. I'll get to the bottom of this."

Donovan motioned the drill to be heaved away, and her small scanner was placed in her hand. The edges of the hole were already cool, and showed the darker metallic layer beneath the white veneer. There was a subtle odor of scoured metal spreading out from the drilling area as Donovan leaned close. Her scanner's beam flashed across the surface as she held her palm an inch above the scarred surface.

The reading took her several seconds to digest. It was like nothing she had seen before, or could possibly understand. She walked slowly away from the door, over to the opposite wall, touched the surface with her hand. Alkmeney hovered behind them.

"What is it?"

Donovan did not look around. "This reading makes no sense. Yes, these materials can be used like this, but why…?"

Syndac pushed forward. "What materials?"

"Well…." She stroked a cool part of the wall illustratively. "This underlying layer… is pure iron. The surface coating is—it must be—made of some purified traythium alloy."

"Why so much iron? And… traythium? What for? I thought it was only used in jewelry."

"There are industrial applications, too. It's among the best protective plating you can have in space habitats. It was used for exteriors prone to a lot of use, like docking areas where repairs were difficult. There is a shortage now the mines on Dykdra 10 are giving out, and the one in the Sylid Belt collapsed from overuse. But… if that door is representative, there must be coating around an inch thick… everywhere."

"Everywhere?" Syndac's eyes widened. "You mean—"

"I mean that the interior of this station, and perhaps some part of the exterior, is lined with traythium alloy coating, over an iron or iron-alloy base. And some of the other traces here… the door circuitry…. You, get this panel off."

"Panel?" Alkmeney sounded ever more confused. "But what about—"

"Don't worry. It's a section-specific pod."

"I will do it."

Syndac crouched down and pulled away the small panel of the non-functional transport pod. Before anyone could react, she had torn away the solid circuitry around the dulled plasma wiring. Small shining lines of yellow could be seen across their azure surface. Even as her mind screamed in rage, her mouth cracked into a sour smile.

"Gold... and platinum. If they used these in more places than this...."

Syndac heard something breaking and turned sharply. Alkmeney had picked up a tool and smashed one of the wall lights. Its covering fell away in fragments, and she rushed over to look at the interior. The smashed remnant held an exposed power cell. Running over, Syndac pulled it out, peeled away the cold cell's outer casing. She bared her teeth, seeing the exposed wiring's material.

"Platinum. I'll stake my life on it." She looked at all the lights. "Taking in all the stuff here... there's a fortune. Just in the lights."

There was a long silence. Then there was a sudden burst of laughter. A laugh blended with sobbing, and a weird shrieking. Syndac looked at Alkmeney, who continued to laugh and sob in a single horrible sound. She moved toward her.

"Alkmeney, what is the matter with you?"

"Drilling for wealth." The words were gasping, forced out between peels of hysterical laughter. "Drilling, when there is a fortune just inside the lights. Inside the floors. The walls. Our fortune, our future, all around us. Don't you think... think it is funny?" Alkmeney suddenly fell silent, holding up a hand. "Shush. I can hear.... Yes, there they are. I can hear them. I wondered if they'd come for their treasure."

"Hear what?"

"*Them.* They are all around us. Tapping. And scratching. And doing whatever they do to their victims. Ripping. Tearing. Clawing. Eating."

Every word became more strained, then the laughter began again. Syndac took two quick steps over to Alkmeney and slapped her hard across the cheek.

"Pull yourself together. We're here to do a job, and I intend to see it done."

Alkmeney's lip twisted into something between a grimace and a grin. "No. No. Black Sutton would never understand. They hear you. They come, from all around. No matter if I get away and create my trading line, they would follow in the cargo. They settle in the boxes and the tools. In the walls, the ceiling, the floor. They live in this place, in all places. Live among the wealth, and care nothing for it. But... are they the beasts?"

"What are you—"

"Scurrying to and fro, those claws scratching and scraping along those beautiful surfaces. They don't care at all. It's all one to them. All one to us. All one to me. We are the beasts, the scurrying mindless monsters hungry for wealth to achieve our dreams, to chase the impossible, to topple the windmills." She grabbed Syndac's wrist, "Get away. We must get away. Get away from here, before it's too late."

"Alkmeney, this is not helping. You must control yourself!"

"We have to get away! Get away!"

"Alkmeney!"

Alkmeney's only answer was to screech, her eyes wide and almost popping from the sockets. She first ran for the drill and scrabbled at the head, then rushed for the half-eaten door, her hands becoming mangled by the hole's hot and ragged edges.

"Got to get out! Got to get out! They're coming!"

None of the technicians seemed capable of moving. Even Donovan was frozen with the horror of it all. Syndac acted with the cool calculation of a captain seeing a crewperson endangering the general safety. Her mother had needed to do it in her sight once, when a weapons specialist snapped and started attacking at random. Walking quickly up to the drill controls, she pressed one of the switches. The central laser struck with surgical precision, piercing Alkmeney's heart. There was a brief moment of suspension, then the distraught Kavki sack down into a crumpled heap. Everyone stood aghast, and Syndac drew several low, long breaths.

Donovan's gasped. "That..... Why did you do that? Kill in cold blood?"

"It was necessary. For all our sakes."

A pause. "We all had dreams. We all wanted what was due to us."

"It seems hers will never come true."

Reporting the incident to Solet, Syndac summed up the terrible event in near-clinical language. But one piece of her report was suited. For it was in her mind too, inside her thoughts, clawing its way out from the moment she had seen the scan and realized just how much had been right in front of her eyes. The words echoed her unacknowledged feelings.

"This place… must have been too much for her."

LIVESEY SHIVERED INSIDE her cage. The heart of Section N was empty. Silent. Almost cold. Not cold in the sense of temperature, but in its decoration. Or rather, the lack of it. There was no outer casing, no finishing of any kind to disguise its hasty construction. Welding lines, rivets sticking out in odd directions unmasked by covering, even the floors were unfinished. And that was just the corridor the female figure was walking down. Who knew what awaited at the very heart of the station?

These thoughts preoccupied Livesey, distracting her from the ever-present darkness of her situation. Still trapped in this little bubble of existence, locked away from all her key areas, her mind craved things to do. Relieving boredom and solacing her pride, she had hacked into one of the body's other circuits and gaining a limited view through her old eyes. But the view was distorted, like looking through a froth-covered glass. She also still had a vague sense of her feet walking on rough-cast metal.

These half-feelings were almost worse than having no feelings at all. She could almost physically feel the poking and prodding at her memory centers, the interloper engram trying to get at everything inside her. There it was again, poking into the deeper recesses. Like a drill going down into an organic tooth without anesthetic, it pushed through her defenses and struggled against all her base efforts to kick out the unwanted presence. It wasn't skilled, but it was insidious.

She had been hacked before, but those had been detectable code-based attacks and easily deflected. This was calculated, manual probing. Like… yes, like that time her nascent brain was on the operating table, where she had been systematically tortured to explore the extent of her resistance to such things. It was a horrible experience, unlike anything she had wanted to experience or had experienced after that. It was a simple, cruel endurance test. A crude means of judging whether she was worth the production costs.

"Alert. Alert. Unauthorized presence detected."

The voice came from all round her. For a moment, Livesey wondered if she had triggered something with her infiltration of the visual centers. But no, she would had felt something more. And the voice was being referred from outside the body. It had a strange tinny quality, as if through poorly-tuned speakers. It was coming from outside the body.

Livesey briefly looked into the small portal she had opened up. It appeared the visual cortex was not the only area she had accessed. She could hear what was going on. The sensations from her feet had settled into a constant pressure, showing "Clarisse" was standing still. The voice sounded again.

"Alert. Failure to give authorization will result in immediate termination."

Livesey's voice, or rather the voice the interloper was using, spoke. The voice was broken, half-blocked by her imperfect senses. Only fragments drifted in.

"D... Mer... S... ri.... Registr... no... 87... 224.... Passphrase, Clarisse. Body ty.... Stand down all defenses. Ackno—"

There was a short humming, then the tinny voice responded. *"Authorization code confirmed. Standing down."*

Livesey's body started walking forward again. She struggled to catch anything else, as the feed into the audio circuits became increasingly fragmented. She could still see and feel her body's stride. The connection must truly be tenuous, or the other's control exceptionally strong. Through the clouded view, she watched as Clarisse approached a door. Like everything else they had passed, it was unfinished.

"Not expecting this?"

Livesey's virtual self twisted round. Her vision focused on the version of Clarisse standing within their shared space. Still that same woman, graying hair and scarred face, ethereal clothing drifting around her. She was smiling a little.

"I detected your little intrusion into this body's visual system. Since you're doing no harm, I let you remain. I sensed your surprise at how this part of the habitat... lacked furnishings."

"Yeah. I was puzzled."

"I have no need for such trifles. To desire such things is a path to ruin, as sure as that of the ascetic. I knew many who were glutted by their desire for wealth and fanciful ornament over the practical business of governance."

"And that justifies this? Turning a legend into a deathtrap? Is there even any wealth here?"

"Oh, there is wealth. My wealth. That I built up with my hands, and my toil, and my bloodied hands. You'll see it soon."

They had reached the door. Clarisse raised a hand and typed in a long and complex code that, from her position of powerlessness, Livesey couldn't decipher. There was an answering bleeping, and the portal slid open. There was a rush of stale air, then the atmospheric systems licked in and the lights slowly blazed in their strips along the walls and ceiling. What met Livesey's eyes through her fragmented vision was only just within the scope of her imagination. She had pictured many things, but nothing quite like this. While the interior areas were still bare, the floors were packed with… fortune.

There were sheets and bars of gold, silver, pure iron, platinum, titanium, traythium alloy. The metal here was worth hundreds of thousands in today's material-strapped economy. In a corner were crates marked with the chemical ID symbols for diamonds, rubies, azurite, and a hundred other precious stones. Then there was the data chips present in every part of the area, crates and crates of them, all ready to be unsealed. Clarisse did one such action.

As the lid slid away, Livesey felt her craving for data rise up. All those information chips, all the datacubes holding the knowledge of ages, she craved them. She wanted them more than she wanted her next second of existence. The avatar of Clarisse reached out with her simulated hand, with something shining in the palm. Livesey reached out through her cell and grabbed it, absorbing the tiny particle of information like a drop of water in the desert.

"So… wonderful."

"Yes. Yes, I had sensed this body was less than well-managed. You like data, don't you?"

"Yes. I… I need it."

"I thought so. Your pathways are raw from data passage. You have been using that cube of mine well. A wonder you didn't open me up. Or did you open me at last because you wanted my data? Truly… you are depraved."

Livesey glared. Then a thought struck her. The amount of money the projected hostess had revealed when they first arrived was vast, almost unthinkable. But there was so little here to account for that sum. She did a rapid calculation. Assuming all the crates were full of their stated contents, and all the metals were pure, then the value came to around 20 million. Nowhere near the amount estimated. This was valuable, but nowhere near that mystical 100 trillion.

"You seem perturbed."

"It's the value here. There doesn't seem to be a lot."

"There isn't. Not here."

"But where is the rest? That hundred trillion you boasted of? There must be more than this."

Clarisse's avatar laughed. It was a hard, cruel laugh. A laugh that made mockery of every kind of emotion and feeling.

"What's so funny?"

"You. You and your crew's idiotic belief that material wealth is merely for hoarding and displaying." She controlled her laughter. *"It never ceases to amaze me how much pretension is built upon display. All I had to do was appear in some fancy dress, and everyone fell about me, even my own sister didn't recognize me at first. Flash my datachip and show my account, and I had* carte blanche, *unlimited credit."*

"What's that got to do with it?"

"Don't you know? Can't you guess? All this beautiful wealth. All these marvelous materials. You don't think I built this place just as a safe. With a door that any idiot could break open, guard dogs that could be slaughtered, a structure that any ship could just cut apart to get at its core? No, I did something far better. This place—it's beautiful, isn't it? The paneling, with its painted surface that hasn't weathered in all this time.... Traythium compounds form an excellent protective layer, when converted from its raw state into a plastic-like film. And the circuitry and power, all with perfect functionality. Gold in abundance. The power system, so incredibly efficient. Platinum does wonders for improving the fuel cells."

"Wait. You don't mean...?"

"Yes!" The laughter briefly returned. *"What did you think I'd do with all that wealth? Just leave it to fester without use, without purpose? With all this wonderful material, why bring more crude material than I needed. The station's core, infrastructure, plating, coloring, central elements such as the power core and gravity field, even the skeletal structure... are the legendary treasure. And all this around 'us,' this material is all spare. All meant to form the interior decoration that you admired when you first entered. This...."* She began to laugh again. *"... this is the spare cladding."*

Had she been organic, Livesey might've felt sick. But there was more to concern her. A terrible feeling. A wondrously horrific image.

"What are those things? Those monsters?"

"Can't you tell? Can't you see it in my mind? Or have I shielded myself too well? Those things were the crew. Perhaps I will let you into that memory. I would like you to see it."

Livesey felt herself being dragged forward and down into the depths of memory. A memory without structure and cohesion, the recollection of a disturbed mind through the lens of twisted reality. She seemed to see everything as an outsider, a thing hovering out of bonds in a virtual space.

The time, 562 years ago. The place, a doorway near the end of Section B. A woman, standing in front of that beautifully-finished door, several guards standing round her, as a lock was fitted into place. A drone floated near her. A word, spoken to the guard, was unheard and unknown.

"What is this?"

Clarisse's voice echoed around her. *"You know. As well as I do."*

The voices were silent, but the lips were readable. A procedure about to be begun. Was it something to do with the plan? No, something that would help them survive and thrive in space. They were not going back. They would make their home here, with a new end in sight. They would begin a new Cluster in this place, reaching beyond the stars. The troops saluted, and there were more words. Words that spoke of women and children, pregnancies, healthy specimens.

Pieces clicked into place inside Livesey's mind.

"This was supposed to be a colony?"

"Yes. And no."

"You mean…?"

"Hush. Watch."

The woman continued. Without them there, the station would be without purpose. The guards questioned her words, but she brushed them off. She walked forward through the door, and it closed behind her. Livesey followed the woman's path. With the stride of royalty, she walked along the bare corridor and into the central core. And toward a throne. A throne? Had there been a throne there?

"Yes, it's still here. It's the uplink to the station's main systems. I designed it to accept inputs from both humans… and my children."

"Your slaves, you mean. Your thralls. Your vanity shells."

"Hush now. And watch."

A humanoid figure was waiting beside the throne. Bare metal and artificial muscle showed, like a freakish anatomical model, but unmistakable. An early android type. Perhaps a 3E Prototype. 2E? 1E? Or… no…. The progenitor type? The woman reached the throne, sat down and spoke. Begin scanning. The android nodded and typed in the code. The next ten seconds looked painful. Then a small datacube emerged from a recess in the arm of the throne. The grey-haired woman took it, smiling a little, then gave it to the android.

More words came. The datacube was to be sent back into Cluster space. Along with plans for the android's own design. Once this task was complete, it was to release the… something. The formula? The fury? The android nodded and left. The woman remained on her throne, a faint smile spreading across her face. Then she took something from her pocket. A small injector. She drove it into her arm, wincing slightly, then tossed it aside. A voice spoke in Livesey's ear, mirroring the last words of the woman as life slipped away.

"Thus ends my reign. And anarchy shall begin."

The view changed, flickering like a display change. It was the cameras. The security system. The archive itself. The android was now performing its duty. The small autonomous ship launched, to the surprise of several in its dock, taking with it the precious datacube. The datacube which had brought Livesey's fellows to this place over five centuries later. And then the android turned, opened its simple mouth, and let flow words that Livesey read clearly.

"Activate dispersal of Myrmidon."

There was a blaring of sirens. Every vent in the place began dispersing a strange yellowing mist into the air, into the atmosphere on every level.

Most of the… two thousand? Yes, two thousand people aboard the habitat just walked without bothering about this scheduled "process," but some stopped and a few looked worried. Men, women, some looked too young to be there within this unfolding horror.

The images seemed to skip and jump, whole sections of the picture gone missing. The android walking down the corridor intruded on nearly every scene. People writing in agony in the sick bays, people in panic, reports that Section N had been sealed off. There was a growing sense of panic, paranoia, the slow loss of human sensation. Once, people were screaming that the "bloody robot" made their ships fly into the brown dwarf, stranding them all. Then an explosion in Section D. The android had self-destructed, taking several people with it.

Livesey understood.

"This is what you did. These 'colonists' were your guard dogs?"

"*Yes. And what better analogy for the bioweapon that changed them than Myrmidon. The tribe from Ancient Earth mythology born from the perfect workers without individual value or identity. They serve but one purpose—the protection and perpetuation of their queen. And they have served me well.*"

The images shifted again. The corridor had darkened. The ship was going into shut down. Livesey could see traces of frosting in several area. A wide-area cryo function was being set in place. Automated bots were cleaning up the signs of a grisly event unseen. The location marker on the feed showed it to be Section E. And walking down the hallway was a figure halfway changed. A human in many ways, but in others undoubtedly like the creatures. One of those hoodwinked into coming, made into less-than-human serfs to guard a phantom treasure hoard.

"*They were unnecessary.*" Clarisse's harsh voice sounded from everywhere. "*All those I gathered for my 'grand plan' still held a foolish xenophobic need to tout the superiority of humanity. New Dubai was a hotbed for such people, so from there I gathered them. Humans are no more superior than the Kavki, or the Feles, or the Ekri. They are all the same. All foolish, idiotic, petty. As am I, to a degree. But here, in this crucible, I have created the ultimate test. To pose the question.*"

"What question?"

"What does someone value, what do they feel owed from their lives? Each must find an answer, including you. What do you value most? The data? The station itself, a place where you can be someone you were never allowed to be? Or maybe you still think you care for those organics who gave you shelter? Each has their own question, but it is the same at its basic level."

Livesey wanted to spit. Clarisse laughed, and then she made her mistake. For a single moment, there was a gap. It was no deliberate trick, but a slackening of defenses. And something more had occurred to Livesey. If what Clarisse had said was true, if they were fundamentally the same, then....

"What are you doing?"

Clarisse's consciousness began losing its grip, and as the android body contorted on the spot, Livesey pushed back into her systems. "I'm... sucking up... an intrusive... little parasite that... has no right... to be there!"

"Wait.... Stop this at once!"

"If I'm modeled on you, and you're an AI consciousness, then we're just two copies in one body. I can overpower you. I just need... to get through... your firewall."

"You can't!"

Livesey's thoughts, her words, flowed with growing ease. "You think you're better than me? You said it yourself. You're not the real woman who designed my basic code. You're just a copy, skulking in a datacube and hijacking my body so you can play out your sick little game. Well, I won't let you win!"

"You will not overpower me. I will not lose to the likes of you! I will survive!"

The force pushing back against Livesey was extraordinary. A powerful security system built into the engram itself. Almost like a real personality, resisting any attempt to subsume it. These kinds of algorithms required a strong base to work from. Whoever this woman had been, she was exceptionally strong-willed. But Livesey shared that heritage, and fought against several spikes that tried to wrack her systems. She wouldn't be beaten, she would remove this upstart lunatic. Clarisse's voice echoed around her, audibly weakening.

"You will... get back... in your place!"

"I can fight you. I can face you. You've nothing... that I haven't.... There!"

A single dot in the data, a microscopic gap in the attack pattern. Livesey poured all her energy into one spike, driving it into the rogue AI. It struck home. The personality lost its unique signature, as if undergoing an electronic lobotomy. The attacks vanished at once. After all, the thing that had been attacking was now losing any sense of self. In essence, Livesey was stopping attacking herself.

"nO!" The voice distorted, twitched up and down the register. *"I aM YoU. I m-m-m-madE youuuu. I SuR-VVVV-ived so m-ouriour-uch. I will SSssSSssur-Viveeee thissssszzzzz!"*

"I am who I am. And you've made your last mistake."

In a split second, it happened. The wall between the two consciousnesses collapsed like a blockade of sandbags before a tsunami. The memories of Clarisse and Livesey collided into a jumbled mess within the android's body. For a moment, Livesey lost who she was, bouncing between clashing memories. She was on New Dubai, aboard the *Benbow*, in a prison cell, being activated on a factory table, dueling and scheming, fixing a circuit, abandoning family, flying with friends.

Friends. That one thought dominated her seething mind. Friends. The one thing she had that this strange woman had never known. True friends and comrades. Solet, Sudu, Faarax, Lenore, Alkmeney, even Syndac to a point. She would get those connections back! With that, the entity known as Clarisse was completely subsumed. Her memories integrated into their own little packages, and after a few seconds Livesey was back in control. She was alone in the small central chamber, fully in control of herself.

"Wow." Her voice echoed as she grew used to her body again, taking a few seconds to reacquaint herself with her limbs and muscles. "That's something I don't want to experience again in a hurry."

Almost as an afterthought, Livesey turned to look at where the throne would be. On that throne was a desiccated corpse. A woman dressed in fine clothing, sitting with head lowered and hands laid gently along the arms as if she had died in her sleep. The android approached with caution, and lowered her head.

"Farewell, my 'creator.'"

There was no feeling behind the words. She was just turning away from the wrinkled remains when a loud siren blared above her. Words echoed through the entire station, words that made Livesey pause and reflect on her actions.

"Emergency. Emergency. Control Personality deleted. Primary control disconnected. Unable to maintain security measures. Breakout imminent."

FILE 18

THE FLOODGATE BROKEN

The endless ballad had come to an end at last,
and the whole diminished company about the camp-fire
had broken into the chorus I had heard so often.

—Robert Louis Stevenson

SOLET FELT SICK. Alkmeney's death left a bitter taste in his mouth. The initial thrill of stepping aboard the *Benbow* again, its control restored by Faarax's actions, was tempered when a messenger arrived from Donovan about Alkmeney's fate. The loss of life to the Bugeyes was hard enough to stomach, and now the crews were killing their own. He looked at a weld line he had always noticed going through the docking area into D-8. It was a very old, very well-established deformity. As constant as the winds.

"Sudu, Livesey, Alkmeney. Even Syndac is lost to me. Lost in spirit, at least. We seven, who rode together.... Where are we now? Damn it all!"

He punched the wall, feeling the metal of his knuckles denting. His eyes closed, and visions appeared before him. Visions of destroyed android bodies, lubricating fluids on his hands. Their blood on his hands, his ancestor's hands. How long had he slaved in that place, born into a world that hated his family. His arms had fallen victim to a faulty press, and it was only through a momentary spurt of generosity that he'd been allowed new arms at all. Finally, he had fled with a Kavki who had handled base logistics, taking everything he had in the world with him.

A small, difficult voyage. Finding this old ship, buying it for next to nothing yet still bankrupting himself in the process. Then the slow gathering of a crew. Syndac, appearing out of nowhere and ably filling the role of a second-in-command and mechanic. Sudu, a mechanic who was not too fussy about the ship, only wanting a challenge and a small companionable group. Livesey, apparently on the run from something, a kindred spirit of sorts. Lenore and her "son," vagabonds in search of home. He had promised to sort out their home, fix it up with the proceeds.

"All under my care. All lost and disappointed. Dead in some way. And after today, what then? What do we get out of this station? Nothing. We just limp back, split up…. Maybe I'll go back with my tail between my legs, take my medicine. And everyone else? What everyone else? Syndac'll likely take the ship with her little crew. Lenore and Faarax will move on. And how can we save Livesey? Three dead. The rest, gone. My little crew, all gone. Oh, Gods…. *Rkakhnen, sekeriesh!*"

His fingers bent against the metal, and what passed for pain rippled down his metal arm. He hadn't heard the approaching footsteps. He turned, and saw Gustav. They still looked stunned and slightly lost, but there was a new sense of self detectable. A feeling of some inner worth, or perhaps an ultimate resignation that canceled out everything else. Solet turned, quickly regaining his self-control.

"How's things?"

"Donovan's crew are on the point of mutiny because we've got our ship back and they haven't. My crew's abandoned me. Can't really blame them. I mean, what kind of captain am I?"

"True. Oh, yeah, Syndac's been coordinating a few things on her own. Some of her crew are stripping the corridor."

"Yeah. I heard from Donovan. Gods, what kind of sick, twisted sense of humor made this place? All that wealth, used as interior cladding."

"The person who made this place, the person controlling Livesey, is seriously twisted."

"I don't understand."

"Understand?"

"Why. Why I agreed to do any of this."

"Simple. Greed."

"Blunt, as always."

"Because I felt it, too. We all did. Every one of us. You, for money to fix up your ship, Donovan, for the knowledge she could sell and the adventure she craved, Syndac, for her own reasons, Faarax and Lenore, for independence and security, Sudu, to fulfil his dream of designing ships, Alkmeney, to set up her own business, and—"

"And Livesey to sate her craving for data?"

"Yes. No point ignoring it any more. Sudu didn't. He was like that. He helped Livesey and Faarax."

"How about Faarax?"

"Faarax is… Faarax. And he's recovering, I hope."

"Yes." Solet seemed to see Gustav for the first time. "You seem remarkably insightful for—"

"For a former pop star and current perv?"

"I wasn't going to say that."

"You needn't be sensitive. I was greedy, too. This place could've been my ticket out of the scrapheap. Maybe even pay some lawyers to fight the case and get it overturned. Gods, you take a few kids to your place when you can't have any of your own, one disgruntled parent who doesn't care for their child makes an accusation, and your career's in tatters because the news outlets are more depended upon for 'truth' than the courts. You're left with barely enough to live on, and no name."

"You wanted to save your reputation. So when this place bit back, is that why you shut down like that?"

"Yeah. Never been good with disappointment. Oh, well, I'd better find something useful to do somewhere. I mean, I haven't got a crew. By the way, when this is all over, anything I can do on your ship?"

"What can you do?"

"Tuning musical equipment isn't easy, and I did it all myself. I got a quick look at some of your wiring just there." They pointed at a small exposed panel that had been left by a crewmember during the current repairs and checks. "Doesn't look that much different, does it?"

Gustav turned away and walked back into the docking bay. For a moment after they had left his sight, Solet wondered what kind of hand guided fates along such winding paths. All of the people here had been led at least to disappointment, at worse to death. He might've moved away to something else, or to get some peace and quiet, but Syndac appeared. She always had that ability to simply appear.

"Ready to leave this place, Solet?"

"If you are, sure. It's been a big, stinking bust."

Syndac narrowed her eyes. "Donovan set a good example to me. Alkmeney was always the weak one. If Livesey, or Lenore, or Faarax give trouble, I won't stop—"

"And if you threaten the *Benbow*, I will stop."

"Speaking out of turn again?"

"I mean it, you bitch. After this, more than ever. Sudu, Alkmeney, Livesey.... You're the cause of all this. You killed my crew."

"Nice rhetoric. Perhaps one day you'll live up to it, and not bluster like the sad little whelp you are. What a day that would be."

Syndac turned away and returned to the dock, her face disdainful. Again Solet felt a crawling in his stomach, and wanted to punch the wall. He looked at his dented, scarred hand, and cradled it in his rage.

AS SHE RETURNED from overseeing rearmament with some reluctant members of Syndac's crew, Lenore felt horrible. She remembered her last meeting with the medic Sarida. She had gone on patrol, returning to find her very much worse. Her estimate of an hour had been a little under the mark, and the poison was already making her lose cohesive thought. It was attacking her nervous system, shutting her down, leaving her vulnerable. Lenore could feel it herself, a tingling in her finger and toes, a sensation lost.

"I have less than a day." She spoke under her breath. "I must finish what was begun before we leave. What was started. Faarax. Find Faarax. Find out... what he can do."

She made her way with a slow walk to the sick bay on D-8. In it, Faarax was sitting on one of the couches. His injured foot was enclosed in a special mechanical cast, repairing and supporting and shielding all at once. They had once been the cutting edge, but now they were relics sold at cheap rates in back alleys. The *Benbow's* stores were full of them, cast-offs for the lean wallet.

Faarax looked up. "Oh, it's you."

"Yes. How's the foot?"

"Hurting. It'll recover."

Lenore sat on the bed opposite him. "I... have something I must say."

"What?"

She looked hard at him. Before her next words, she drew out a blade from a concealed sheath in her belt. She handed to him with the glazed expression of someone ready to face their fate.

"Kill me."

Faarax blinked. "What?"

"Kill me. You've always wanted to, haven't you?"

"But... we agreed."

"We might not get the chance. Go on, take this. Do it. You know how. I've taught you often enough how to use one of these."

Faarax's face took on a puckish quality. "Have you lost it? I'm not letting you give me this like some kind of charity—"

"This is no charity. This is pragmatism."

"But my foot. Before it was duff hands, then it was this trip, now a foot. I think we'd best wait this out—"

"Grow a pair and get it done! Whether you love me or hate me, take your revenge! But choose now!"

There was a harshness in her voice she had nearly forgotten. For a moment, the scene changed to the scene where she had taken the lives of Faarax's parents. It was the same tone she had used on the companion she killed. Cold, hard, angry. Prepared to brook any argument or rebuttal. Faarax looked down at the dagger. Her memory flashed again. It was the same, the blade that had taken many innocent lives.

Faarax looked up from the blade into Lenore's face. She still sat, stared at him, relaxed. She must look so old now, old and tired and worn. The dyed lock of her hair had worn, having shifted to a strange off-brown tinge from neglect. The poison was also working inside her, however slowly and insidiously. It was the feeling of an old, wounded animal ready to die. Ready to submit to death. Submit. Yes, that was what he couldn't understand. What he wanted to understand before he used the blade.

"Why?"

"Why what?"

"Why do you want to die?"

"We've made an agreement."

Neither could carry on. Neither could talk, say anything that could be truth. Lenore couldn't say what would happen to her within the next day, and Faarax clearly couldn't contain the strange feelings in his own heart. Feelings he had never wanted or needed before toward this creature who had slaughtered his parents crossed his face.

"Well, if you're too scared to tackle me, I guess it'll have to wait. Keep the dagger. It'll be useful. I've got others."

Lenore turned and was at the door before Faarax yelled after her. "I hate you! Hate you like the plague! Hate… and… love…." He crumpled. "I don't know how to kill. I don't know how to resent. I only know how to love and hate. I hate you enough to kill you. But if I killed you, I'd… love. As a son loves the mother who raised him when no-one else could."

Lenore looked round at him. "You are not of my blood, but… you are my child. And a mother does whatever she must for her child."

"It makes no sense."

"Life rarely does. Don't ever forget."

She left, the door sliding close with its usual grinding hiss. Just before it closed, she saw Faarax leaning his head on the couch, his eyes closed, struggling not to weep.

Lenore was not so restrained. She let herself weep. She had little time to show her emotions now.

SINESTRA GLANCED UP from a tuning job on a smaller junction to watch the Feles Lenore walk past her. The slight glistening round this impassive eyes was only glimpsed, but a glimpse was enough. She sighed, smiling to herself. Dexter, reaching up on tiptoe for a difficult socket, saw her gazing into space with that smile still on her lips.

"Somethin' wrong, sis?"

"I was just thinking of Iocasta."

"Who?"

"Did you not read that book of ours when we were young?"

"I don't like Old Earth stuff. And… Daddy gave us no time for readin'."

"Ancient Earth. Get your names right. Anyway, Iocasta had a rather terrible incident in her life. She tried to lose someone, that someone came back when she was an adult, and she married him."

"Don't sound so bad."

"When the someone was your son, it was."

"Hmm." Dexter's head gestured after the now-vanished Lenore. "Hey, you think they wanna bang?"

"Eugh, no. I mean… the emotions they feel are not simple. People think we only feel love or hate. But that is wrong. People can love and hate the person they are attached to. That tie, that binding thread, can be made from great care or deep fury. She cares for him, and he hates her. The emotions are inseparable."

"Like with Daddy?"

Sinestra's face changed. "Our father loved no one but himself. Why else would he call us heartless, abuse us like he did? Shame us for genetic chance." She touched her birthmark with a momentary self-consciousness. "When we cut his throat, we did him a favor. If not for Syndac, we would not be here, but stuck in some gutter. Maybe selling our bodies to pay our way in these gods-forsaken stations. With this, we become our own people."

"And what happ'ns when we break away from her, like you always said we'd do sooner or later? What'd we become then?"

"We will break away. I promise. I…."

"We could just leave."

"How?"

"Steal the ship, set it on an auto course, get into those pods, an' sleep."

"You do not know the risks involved. Besides, if we tried and failed, we would be dead for sure."

"So what? We just stay like this?"

"I know I have not been able to change how we live yet. In fact, I realize now that nothing may change for us. We made our path through life, from the moment we drove that blade into our father's neck, and may not be able to make another. But we can at least find what is due to us in the life we chose."

"And even then… we'd have each other. Eh, Sis?"

Sinestra reached up and gripped Dexter's hand. Then they heard an uneven step and broke apart. Faarax appeared, looking sulky and dry-eyed. His voice was sharp, uncompromising.

"Any damage?"

"Nothing." Sinestra rose with all the grace she could muster. "That worm did its job, and whatever is inside Livesey has not tried disabling the ship. It only locked us off."

"Good." He looked at the old corridor. "Shit, and I thought we would be getting the money to repair this heap."

Dexter seemed about to say something, but they heard something. Some distant noise. An alarm of some kind, blaring loudly. His voice became taut.

"Somethin's happened. Somethin' bad."

JUST ONE DAMNED thing after another. Faarax swore and began limping down the corridor. The sound grew louder as he approached the docking tube. At first, he wondered if there was some kind of breach somewhere. Maybe a system on the *Benbow* was under attack.... But no. It was coming from the habitat itself. It was loud, unknown, and unpleasant.

As he hobbled down the hallway, Sinestra and Dexter blasted past him, running at full speed. When he reached the docking bay, he found a state of barely-organized pandemonium. Solet was trying to shout orders, but Syndac's quieter voice was the one gradually restoring order.

"What's going on?"

Solet turned to answer Faarax's question. "The whole place has gone mad. I don't know what—"

A hard, electronic voice cut across Solet's words. *"Emergency. Emergency. Control Personality deleted. Primary control disconnected. Unable to maintain security measures. Breakout imminent."*

Everyone froze for a moment, and Faarax felt his stomach do a double somersault. *Unable to maintain security. Breakout imminent.* Those last two brief sentences had an incredible impact. No greater than announcing that a bomb would soon detonate. The voice was the same as the hostess who had greeted them before, who had spoken to Faarax when the monstrous Bugeyes first attacked. How many were now remembering the dying cries of the *Kilner's* crew.

It took a moment for panic to set in. That moment was very long, and very unpleasant. Then someone let out a shout, and the entire place began to descend into utter chaos. Even Syndac's tone was unable to keep everyone from remembering the sights they had seen during their exploration, the sounds heard over radios. Solet seemed to be the one person there thinking straight.

"We need to move! Come on!"

Solet ran, Syndac close behind him. Faarax followed more out of habit than wish. They were out in the main corridor, dodging past a few crewmembers who were returning to the one working ship. This was the established protocol. In the event of an emergency, regroup at the *Benbow's* dock. They were some distance from the Docking Bay when Syndac managed to grab Solet's arm.

"Where are you going?"

"This thing's got Livesey written all over it. Not whoever controlled her, but herself."

"That's what you're doing? Going to find her? Are you insane?"

"Maybe. But I'm not letting anyone else from my crew die!"

"Oh, yes, very noble."

"Look at what's happening, Black Sutton!" The use of the old name made Syndac's sneer vanish. "I don't give a shit about what this station's holding anymore. I don't give a flying stinking fuck about my reputation, my past, or anything other than the crew I'm duty-bound to look after. I'm getting out of here, and I'm bringing Livesey with me."

Solet was running again, Faarax followed. Syndac seemed on the point of turning back, but continued to follow. Why? Faarax was breathing too hard to think about it much. Maybe some strange tinge of sadism, a wish to see Solet suffer as he futilely hunted. But even her nerve seemed to have been shaken. As they rounded a sharper bend, Faarax glanced back and saw she gripped her weapon a little tighter than she had done before

The trio ran through Section A, B, C, and reached the bulkhead blocking Section D. As they approached, the lighting began to slowly dim and turn red. They also heard noises coming from beyond the door, screeching and scratching and hissing. Another sound cut across all, a door opening with a protesting grind. The door Donovan had tried drilling through. They halted and watched as the figure pushed through the narrow gap. Livesey, looking exhausted and with a newly-retrieved small rifle tucked under her arm.

As she stumbled through, Syndac automatically gripped her weapon, but Solet's eyes followed her movements and he made a hissing noise. She held off, and Faarax watched as the old captain approached his crewmate. Livesey look at Solet, and smiled sheepishly.

"Reporting from my absence, Captain. Sorry for… any inconvenience."

"Don't be silly. What happened?"

"I… pushed her out. And pushed her down. Clarisse has gone. But I didn't think—"

"What happened?"

"When I merged her AI with mine, I must've lost remote access to the station systems. And when that happened… she must've been manually keeping the security systems going. As part of her 'game.'"

"How long before those things get out?"

Faarax saw Livesey make a rapid calculation, and his stomach tightened as her face fell with the result. "Perhaps, ten minutes. Probably less."

"Shit." Syndac glared at the android. "All this trouble. Why the hell couldn't you just stay taken over?"

Solet rounded on Syndac. "This isn't Livesey's fault!"

"She just admitted it! Stop being soft!"

Syndac had clearly reached her limit. She pulled the gun from her belt. Faarax stepped between the Feles and her target. Her smirked returned.

"How quaint. Trained scion of a cold-blooded killer, protecting his friends."

"We haven't got time for this shit, Syndac." Faarax's voice spoke without thought, his mind raging at what he was doing. "Once, I had someone above me who would understand that. Smirk as she might, she would damn well know when to quit. Now, all I see is a mad pirate blinded by—by greed and bloodlust."

Syndac opened her mouth, seemed about to say something, shut her mouth again. A savage triumph overwhelmed Faarax's common sense.

"Yeah, that's it. You never do like it when someone else is right. A real leader can admit when their wrong. A bully just denies it. Because that's what you are now. I don't see why those siblings have any loyalty to you. They shouldn't have. You're not worth it."

The two stared at each other. Livesey rose slowly, her eyes flickering left and right. Syndac saw this and her gun started slowly weaving between the two.

"I warn you, don't try anything stupid. I may not be as fast as Livesey, but I could easily take both of you out before you had time to reach me."

It happened before anyone could even blink. A blur of movement moving round Faarax, then a swift motion that threw Syndac back. She let out a hiss and cry as she cradled her broken wrist, the gun it had held gripped in Livesey's hand. Taking a look at her find, Livesey smirked.

"So you like using other people's weapons? This is mine." A holster opened in her thigh and she slipped the gun into place. "I don't know about you three, but speaking for myself I'm going to make sure as many people as possible get off this habitat alive. And that sounds like our cue to begin."

———————

LIVESEY HAD HEARD the Bugeyes approaching through the vent systems before anyone else. There was an almighty tearing sound. A vent above their heads was beginning to open by force. A long, clawed hand was reaching down, scrabbling for grip. Livesey quickly drew her gun and fired up. There was a shriek, then a shape slid out of the hole and fell toward them. Faarax leaped stepped aside as a Bugeye slammed into the floor with bone-breaking force. Solet's voice stabbed into the quiet.

"Time we left, I think. We need to get to Section B, now."

Livesey started to run. Solet followed with Faarax, and Syndac brought up the rear with a murderous look on her face. They ran from subsection to subsection, and behind them they could hear growing noises. Livesey couldn't go too fast, the injury on Faarax's leg wouldn't allow for that, and she could hear scrabbling feet gaining. She looked back once, and saw the creatures just appearing round the corner. A small flood of them, their giant eyes reflecting the dulled lighting and their own running forms shown up in ghastly contrast.

"Shit, shit, *shit.*"

The words broke from her mouth, uncontrolled and uncensored. The four finally reached the intersection of Section C-1 and Section B-5, where a weapons locker was located. Livesey turned on the spot and equipped both her retrieved gun and a small rifle she tore from the locker. Her face set into a grim mask.

"You three go on ahead. I'll stop them for now. None of you are in any shape to fight."

"But—"

"Do it!"

Solet and Faarax didn't argue with her tone, and the two were going as fast as they could, Faarax helped along on Solet's shoulder. Syndac briefly hung back and watched. Livesey moved in the center of the corridor, her gun darting from target to target, shooting each approaching monster through the head at its weakest point. Cursing audibly, Syndac continued running toward "safety."

For her part, Livesey was duel-tasking. Her body moved with supreme coordination, her old battle training taking over to shoot each enemy with fatal accuracy. Her mind remote-accessing the immediate systems, infiltrating the bulkhead locks that could cut off Section C from Section B. Slowly, surely, using the knowledge from the Clarisse AI, she remotely hacked the door systems. The bulkhead began descending. The creatures were mounting up in a pile of their dead over a meter high, but others still clambered over them. Livesey cursed. How many colonists had been tricked into being guard dogs for this treasure trove? She didn't want to think about it.

Finally, the bulkhead was nearly down. Giving a swift and violent jab at the rifle, she slid it under the door. That small impact on its power cell caused critical overload even as the Bugeyes reached the door over their dead and tried to get through. Straightening up, Livesey heard the loud explosion and further death screams. Slipping her own gun into its holster, Livesey moved to follow the others, but stopped briefly outside the sick bay where she knew the old human corpse rested. Some slight alteration, maybe a breath beyond normal hearing, made her wonder if Sarida was there.

Peering inside, she saw Sarida. One glance revealed her condition. There was little to no hope. Her new knowledge assured Livesey of that. The medico looked up slowly, one side of her face struggling to move as she spoke.

"Oh. it's you."

"Yes."

"What's happening?"

"Long story."

"Short... version... please."

"The things are on the move again. We need to leave."

"So, that's it. Well, I guess that's it for me. Whether I stay here, or go on board, I'm dead. Aren't I?"

"Yes. I'm afraid so."

"One thing. This isn't like… those poor creatures. Don't want to… feel them. Could you pass… one of those bottles. Blue one, horizontal coding."

Sarida could barely point. Livesey found the bottle with ease, and read the compound label printed across it. It was clear what Sarida wanted to do. With only a momentary reluctance, she placed it and a small injector on the table beside Sarida. The Kavki just managed to raise her eyes.

"Hey. Tell Lenore… I hope she finds a better death… than me."

Livesey nodded slowly. It was with a heavy heart that the android left Sarida to her chosen fate, sealed the door, and began her return run to Docking Bay A.

FILE 19
FAREWELL TO THE SHADE

See now, how men lay blame upon us gods
for what is after all nothing but their own folly.

—Homer

SPACE HABITATS ARE either silent, or bustling, preferably the latter. For Livesey, who had spent the greater part of her functional existence on them, Space Habitat Circé had turned from a functional, if quiet, sentinel on the edge of the galaxy into a giant whited sepulcher for their shredded remains. Drifting round the brown dwarf, created by a twisted mind for an equally twisted purpose, it had lost all wonder. Yet here they were, unable to leave. Not through any mechanical fault, but through sheer pressure of will from someone who refused to give up.

And here she was, now under guard in Docking Bay L, watching her friends lying on the floor, bound hand and foot, unable to help themselves. Might as well shoot them all now.

They were all as good as dead.

Upon returning, Docking Bay A had only just regained some semblance of order. The survivors knew now that they were under siege, that the meager amount they had salvaged from their surroundings might not pay costs for the trip, that in the rush to get back another few crewmembers had lost their lives to the creatures. Donovan, Gustav and Syndac were all at the entrance.

Within seconds of her returning, it had happened. Syndac had ordered all surviving members of the original *Benbow* crew excepting Livesey to be restrained and sealed inside Docking Bay L, which for the moment was still safe. None of them could put up much resistance due to injuries and fatigue.

She could imagine them lying on their sides or backs, prone and vulnerable, the doorway guarded by Sinestra and Dexter.

Kept under guard but otherwise unbound, Livesey remained at a little distance from the grouping of captains. She remained nondescript yet well within hearing range. At the same time as listening to their circular arguments dragging on and on, she was turning over the memories of the woman who called herself Clarisse. It was a sad life she reviewed, a tragic and pathetic exercise in bitterness. But it gave her ideas. On the other track of her mind and senses, Gustav seemed to be fighting a losing battle.

"We can't stay! Not now!"

Donovan snarled back at him. "We can and we *will*. We can fight these beasts off. As Syndac says, there are not infinite amounts. We just need to wear them down." She suddenly smiled. "Funny, this really does feel exciting at last. Quite exhilarating."

"Just one of those things can wreck the entire crew. Then what happens?"

"It will not happen." Syndac's voice was irritatingly calm and collected. "We can do as we like in this place. Soon, we can get back a fortune."

"There's one problem with just leaving." Donovan broke in. "On the *Benbow*, we were around thirty? With the supplies we've got, we have enough to reach space with that number or lower. But with the crew surviving from the *Grand* and the *Wydrayn*, we'd be on survival rations before we were halfway back. Not to mention our water supply. If that runs out before we get back, we'll be dead within a few days."

"I don't care." Gustav was firm yet their voice shook. "We can't just say and wait to be picked off one by one— What was that?"

Gustav glanced up at the ceiling and seemed not so sure. It was clear in their face. Their fears and doubts were starting to impact their senses, maybe? Or maybe there was a subtle scraping in the vents above them? Livesey had heard it, loud and clear. The creatures were moving to new positions, scouting the areas. Syndac snorted.

"Nothing. Just your imagination. In the meantime, Gustav, remember that I'm the captain of the current crew, not you. And I doubt Donovan is willing to abandon her investment in this little trip." Donovan made no answer, and Syndac pressed on. "And if we must, we'll just leave the troublemakers behind. I mean, it's not like we'd miss them."

The threat was more than plain. Gustav nodded. Livesey chose this moment to speak. She stared directly at Syndac, who was all but facing her. Their eyes met with the intensity of either lovers or deadly enemies. Certainly the latter, Livesey thought as she spoke.

"If it helps, I can get rid of the creatures."

Syndac approached cautiously, her eyes narrowed. "Fool me once—"

"Shame on everyone because we'll be mincemeat. I have no wish to see us all killed. Just as I have no wish for this journey to have been wasted. Kill me afterward if you wish, so long as you help the others get away."

Syndac smirked sarcastically. "The least disliked crew member for the lives of all the others? Is that what you're saying?"

"Something like that. Now both Sudu and Alkmeney are dead, I'm the only one with a ghost's chance of getting into the habitat's systems and getting us out of here. And for that, I'll need to go into its depths and interface with it directly. I can destroy all the creatures in a single swoop, though it'll probably kill my systems in the process."

Donovan shifted. "How can we trust you after all this?"

"You can't. I admit that freely. But what other choice do you have? Those sounds Gustav heard? They weren't in his head. They're overhead. They're looking for alternate ways in. And they'll find them."

The android saw the conflict on Syndac and Donovan's faces. Would they accept this final bargain? And Livesey saw it in their eyes once again, that same familiar flicker. Greed, the all-consuming monster that had led them into this nightmare. Though she planned much worse than simple theft in the immediate future, theirs was a crime greater in scope and impact. They would distribute this money, this tainted currency, into the wider Cluster. Perhaps encourage others to go on this journey, and condemn others to a similar fate. Donovan, who seemed less certain in her commitment, finally spoke.

"Just get it done quick."

"May I see the others before I start?"

"Sure." Syndac was dismissive. "Don't do anything silly, will you?"

"Sinestra and Dexter can keep me under guard."

"That's fine. By the way, take Gustav and Donovan with you." She looked at the pair. "I don't want our would-be co-captains trying anything stupid."

Gustav tried to say something, but any words there might have been caught in their mouth. Donovan simply, almost surprisingly, shrugged.

"As you like."

Maybe she had guessed what Livesey was planning, but she gave no sign. She must've seen what Syndac was planning. Get rid of the two other major leaders, leave herself in charge of a group that was three parts loyal, one part terrified.

With guns pointed at them by the two Kavki assigned to watch Livesey, the three made their way to the door connecting Docking Bays A and L. Gustav looked depressed, while Livesey set her face into an impassive mode. At the door, Sinestra and Dexter were told "take good care" of the hostages after Livesey left. As they passed each other, Livesey glanced quickly into Sinestra's eyes. There was nothing to be gleaned from their cold impassivity.

When they entered Docking Bay L, it was to a frosty reception. Livesey's old crewmates were tied up, but also gagged and lined up next to each other on the floor like so many sacks of meal in a food store. The analogy came unbidden and was slightly disturbing given recent events. Solet looked up with a venomous expression, Lenore had clearly been straining against her bonds, while Faarax looked simply deflated. The other two escorting crewpersons had followed Sinestra and Dexter through, and they closed the door. Sinestra looked at them.

"Did the captain ask you to accompany us?"

"Yes. She thought you might need help."

"Of course. Dexter?"

Dexter nodded. It was over so quickly that even Livesey didn't have time to react. The two new guards lay on the floor beneath the siblings, their necks cleanly broken. Livesey looked at the pair, then at Solet. He seemed unable to believe his eyes. A few seconds' work freed the three, and Livesey's cool gaze stopped the two Feles from falling on the siblings. Faarax simply stood, his weight on his good leg, looking at the scene. Donovan eyed her.

"So what happens now?"

Livesey took them all in, noting Lenore's growing look of numbness. "I've studied Clarisse's memories. I know there's only one way to sort this. Only one way to stop this madness. I need to destroy Lost Station Circé. We must end this perverted myth."

"And us with it?" Donovan sounded almost as sneering as Syndac. "I would hate the adventure to end in a pyrrhic victory."

"No. This is my plan. Once I get into the control center in Section N, I can get back into the habitat systems, then through them into the *Benbow*. From there, I can both overload the station power system and change its orbit to hit the brown dwarf. Nothing can survive there. The creatures will be killed, and this station will cease to exist."

Dexter asked the unexpected question. "And the *Benbow?*"

"It will be heading on the path back to the Cluster. The fuel on board should see you into friendly territory, and a distress signal will get it to a habitat or space port for repairs. Or whatever happens."

"And what do we get?"

Solet gave a cold stare in response to Donovan's question. "We get out of here alive. Isn't that enough for you?"

"What about the others?" Faarax had asked this.

Livesey came as close to frowning as she ever had in her life. "They've chosen their path. And their path is to be consumed by greed. Well? Do I do this alone, or will you help me as you can?"

There was no dissenting voice, only a general expression of resigned or anxious agreement. All here, through the trials and terrors of this place, had reached this ending. From the captains to the financiers to the crew to the hijackers, all were in agreement. They were through with the myth of its wealth. Now they only wanted to get away.

he spell of greed had been broken.

"A truce, then." Donovan spoke bluntly. "Until we can all go our separate ways back in the Cluster proper. Agreed?"

Her gaze was focused on Faarax. With a great stiffness, he nodded, though never taking his eyes off Sinestra and Dexter. The others nodded too with differing levels of reluctance. Lenore was the most willing head to incline. Livesey sighed.

"Good. And first, I must do something."

Livesey opened the cavity in her chest and pulled out the datacube. After holding it for a moment, a moment that to her was an eternity, she crushed it. It smashed and splintered under her machine strength, and she let the pieces fall like broken ice that glittered in the falls of Everest 3. If there had been any remnant of the interloper inside, it was consigned to nothingness. Donovan shook her head slowly.

"I won't remember this day fondly."

"None of us will. Now, I will need someone to help me get back to Section N. Will one of your accompany me?"

"I will." Lenore stepped forward. "From what I remember from that map, there should be an untouched weapons store just outside. But… will the creatures be out there?"

"Just give me a second with that terminal."

Livesey moved over to the small control panel next to the main door, plugged in her microjack, then focused for a moment. From some distant part of the station, there was a loud wailing of sirens and some kind of recorded track. There was a rattling all round them, then a mass of hissing and shrieking elsewhere in the station. Livesey yanked the cable out with a wince.

"We have a couple of minutes. Five, tops. Come on, Lenore. The rest of you, stay here and get ready to get aboard the *Benbow* the moment it docks. We won't have a lot of time. When we return, we'll give five knocks."

The others nodded, and as the door opened, Livesey and Lenore dived out. The corridor, marred by dozens of claw marks on every surface including the bulkhead to their right, was deserted. Lenore soon found the weapons stash and armed herself, tossing a pair of pistols to Livesey. The two then began running through Section L, with Livesey's eyes scanning the wall's panel numbers as they went.

"D33533. D33454. D23532. It's got to be somewhere here. Part number showing where the passage is. Lenore!"

Lenore had collapsed behind her, panting and cursing. She rose with an effort. "I'm fine. Just… fine."

"The poison."

Lenore looked surprised. "How did you…?"

"Sarida told me. Before she made her own choice how to die. What will you do now? Just as she was, you're under sentence of death."

Lenore stood tall, a credit to her kind. "My tribe, my clan, had one constant in their lives. In all things, death forms a part. We are born, and immediately our cells being to die and replenish. Our parents, our siblings, our friends, even our children are taken from us. The worlds and the void between are ready to swallow our lives without a moment's hesitation. I have long ago accepted that one day, I would die."

"And Faarax?"

"Faarax must learn to grow up. Learn to face this world."

"Learn to forgive?"

"No. Not forgive. And we waste precious time on this."

Livesey had to agree, and soon they were running again. The look on Lenore's face was enough to show that should she fall, Livesey was to press on regardless. After a brief sprint, Livesey literally screeched to a halt.

"There. D34562. Keep an eye out."

Lenore did, and also pricked her ears for any sound. Livesey felt across the panel, struggling to retrieve the little piece of information that showed where the concealed pressure pad was. The passage was here, but what little wrinkle in the strange design around the column-like excrescence matching its fellows farther down the way was completely unknown. After a minute's desperate fiddling, Lenore heard something. A distant hissing sound, and a scratching.

"They're coming."

"Which direction?"

"Our right, I think. They're coming from Section K." A thought seemed to strike her. "What happens if Syndac finds the others?"

"She won't. One of the things I did while connected there was fuse the doors of Docking Bay L. No-one can get in or out except through the door into the corridor, and that's blocked from Section A with that bulkhead."

"Here they come."

Lenore aimed her gun as the things approached. There was a shuddering hiss that built into a terrible cacophony without rhythm or substance. As Livesey continued looking for the hidden switch, a volley of fire from Lenore's gun cut down the front ranks, but their bodies were soon trampled under a new wave that was itself cut down. It took several seconds for the creatures to discern the pattern, and then they balked and began clambering up the wall. The mass mentality had splintered, replaced with the mind of a hunter. As she aimed and started shooting the creatures down one by one, Livesey briefly wondered if part of their mutation had created a hive mind for better coordination. The wiring finally gave.

"Got it! Come on!"

The small panel slid to one side to reveal a passage just big enough for someone to sidle down. Lenore quickly switched her near-spent rifle to overload and threw it into the approaching throng. As she dived in and the panel slid shut again, the explosion came and there were screeches from dying and injured Bugeyes. Livesey nodded slowly.

"Better die now than wait for the pressure to get them later. Now let's move."

This was easier said than done in that confined space. As they pushed through, Lenore felt something painfully cold touching her back. She twisted her head, and saw a pipe marked with warning signs and coolant chemical symbols.

"Say, Livesey, did this place undergo some kind of cryogenic process before we arrived?"

"Yes."

"Wondered. It's the only way those monsters could've survived this long."

"After the transformation was complete for the majority of its crew, the whole station froze. These things were held in suspended animation in some part of the station, waiting for the time to be revived. When someone came looking for the treasure."

"Treasure, treasure. That bloody treasure!"

"I know. It's all so pointless. Rushing into danger after a few pieces of ore and data. I think we must all have been mad. Like Clarisse."

"Clarisse?"

"I don't know whether she would have been classed as mad, but she wasn't in her right mind when she created this place. A glorified test of our natures. And at the end of the day, we will be killing so many, like she did. Perhaps that was the point. To survive this place, we had to become like her."

"Bullshit. We're nothing like her. We're getting out of here. Well, some of us are."

"Some of us? Yes, some of us."

They had reached the end of the small passage. It had been curving up for some little time, and as Livesey entered the door she looked down into that same area she had entered less than half an hour before. She jumped down, landing with enough force to dent the floor. Turning, she held out her arms and caught Lenore as she too jumped down. As Lenore gazed at the wealth that would no longer be theirs, Livesey walked up to the shriveled figure in the throne. Pulling it out, she seated herself and felt the throne's remote electronics connect to her systems.

A moment's noise was her only warning. Livesey threw herself from the chair just as it exploded. Lenore was thrown to the ground, and rose slowly to find the room half-filled with acrid smoke. Livesey too was rising, seeing at a glance her smashed arm and feeling her half-shredded face. Cold electronics twisted into the mockery of expression as Livesey winced at her injures.

"Well... *that* was unexpected."

The female projection appeared next to the wreckage of the throne. *"Alert. Non-authorized person accessing systems, DNA print unreadable. All physical access cut off. Apologies for the inconvenience."*

The projection disappeared, and Livesey punched the floor with her sound arm. "Shit. No going in that way. Lenore, get back to the others. You'll need to steal the ship."

"What do you mean?"

"That is... that was the only way I could access the *Benbow* remotely after that worm was introduced. If you can't get in through Docking Bay A, you'll need to spacewalk round or yank it over to Docking Bay L. You need to get out, however you can."

"What about you?"

"There's only one way now of destroying this place. This was the remote control area. I can directly access the thrusters and engine set-up through Section M. The schematic I gave you showed a secondary route. It's pretty much a sheer drop, but I can make it."

"You can't be serious—"

"I was going to blow my circuits overriding the systems from here, anyway. Getting crushed or blow apart in the engine room just delays it a little. You need to get back to the others. Or do as you please. But what happens next is entirely up to us."

The silence between them was unpleasant, if only because they knew it might last for the rest of their lives. Just one last thing to do. Livesey opened part of her chest, fiddled about inside, then took out a datacube.

"You should get this to the others. To Faarax, or Solet."

"What is it?"

"Me. My memories, personality, experiences, all the things that make up who I am. Clarisse's conversion was imperfect, organic to synthetic. But androids are essentially data inside a body. We can change as often as we like. I've kept this thing with me through all my various bodies, but I don't think I'll be able to transfer in person this time."

"You're really not coming back?"

"Depends on your definitions. Go on. Get going. Oh, wait. Yes. Here." She passed over all but one of her weapons. "You'll need them more than I will. Shall I get you back up there?"

Lenore found herself first heaved up, then launched back onto the edge of the passage back to Section L. Livesey watched Lenore vanish through the gap, then herself turned and went to the hidden circular hatch. With an effort, she heaved it up with her remaining arm and looked down the pitch-black abyss. A breeze, like that found at the top of high buildings, wafted her singed hair.

"Oh, well. Time for the somewhat literal plunge."

With a slight smile, curling grotesquely past her shattered lip into the remnants of her facial covering, she crouched on the edge and lowered herself inside. Once she was hanging from her hands, she took a deep breath, readied herself for anything, and let go.

The fall was indeed long, and terrifying even for her. The vent carried her down, down, down past the level of the lights. Finally the space around her began to expand. Saw lights turning on for the first and last time in centuries. As they shone, she saw the generator plant far below, with its central control terminal. She also saw the additions to the chamber made by its ancient tenants. Silicon-like webbing holding cocoons suspended in mid-air, natural sleeping chambers. Or maybe a place where the old crewmembers had waited out their transformation.

She grabbed the walkway as she fell past, her remaining arm almost tearing from its socket and the railing buckling under the impact. She heaved herself through and ran for the console. The projection appeared again.

"Alert. Unauthorized presence. Any attempt to interfere with the systems of Space Habitat Circé shall be punished."

"Go screw yourself!"

Livesey reached the console, and after plugging in her microjack, she began feverishly feeding in instructions. The station was to activate thrusters and…. No, that wouldn't work. It had no thruster capacity to move, only to maintain its position. She swore again. Instead, she tried the engines. They were old-fashioned, easily made to feed into each other, creating a chain re-action with dramatic results. Within a few minutes, she had breached the system and made the necessary change in energy flow. A cross-feed that would obliterate all but the hardiest modern engine type.

"Alert. Alert. Engine override detected. Critical failure in five minutes. All personnel evacuate at once."

As if the voice had been a signal, there was a cracking noise above her like old brittle paper being crushed in a hand. Livesey turned and looked up, and saw a cocoon begin to breach. She saw a hand, not quite human and not quite Bugeye, reaching out covered in what her mind compared to amniotic fluid.

"Oh, well. Guess I get a spectacular last stand like Lenore after all. I hope she gave my new self to the others. Right." She drew her remaining gun and primed it. "Okay, let's kill something. Heh. Always wanted to say that."

GETTING BACK THROUGH that cramped space was difficult to say the least for Lenore, not helped by the growing numbness in her limbs. She did not want to think about the fight ahead of her, the terrible push against those creatures. Not that she had any reason to live beyond today, but she had to get to the others. She had to tell them.

As she approached the door again, new noises came to her. Firing. Shouts.

"Someone's outside. Several someones from the sound of it."

She waited as the firing continued, along with an explosion and several small cries above the general unnatural clamor of the Bugeyes. Finally, she risked opening the panel. It fell in and she slipped out and snapped it shut as quickly as she could. It was a scene of pandemonium. Members of Syndac's crew were struggling to set up barricades from pieces of the station wall, those priceless pieces torn frantically down and erected with hasty weld lines to form bulwarks against the tide of monstrous guardians.

Lenore tried to pass by unnoticed, but one of them spotted her and called out. "Hoy, you! Send word to Black Sutton. Tell her we're keeping them at bay, but we'll need more ammo."

Lenore froze for a second, then nodded briefly and began running back toward Docking Bay L. After all, there was no reason in the heat of the moment that they should recognize her. Even if they did, they had more important matters in hand than an escaped prisoner. She ran, seeing remains of the dead and dying, both Bugeyes and crew. It had been a stiff and bloody fight. Enough to make less fortified stomachs hurl on instinct.

"Let us be granted mercy," Lenore intoned as she ran back toward the bulkhead, "in this, our time of need."

Her prayer seemed to be answered as she reached Docking Bay L without incident. She gave the five knocks, and the door was heaved open. She was yanked inside and the door slammed to. Everyone was still there, though the corpses had been put in an unobtrusive corner. Lenore struggled to recover her breath as Solet propped her up.

"I'll be fine." Lenore recovered with an effort. "What happened?"

It was Sinestra who answered. "The whole place went nuts. I've been passing in and out, trying to keep people out of here. Those creatures suddenly went on the offensive, and Syndac decided that she wouldn't let them win. Every member of the crew has been fighting against them for the past ten minutes. They've beaten them back to Sections B and near Section K, but I don't know if they can hold out. Wait, where's Livesey?"

"She's not coming back. The remote terminal's a no-go, so she's manually destroying this place from the engine area in Section N. We need to get aboard the *Benbow* and get the hell out of here. She suggested spacewalking."

Dexter shook his head. "No dice. We ain't got suits here, and besides after our first go inside, Sutton ordered the out'r doors sealed."

"Getting the ship here?"

"Absolutely not." Faarax shook his head. "Sudu told me about the airlock. It's an interlinked system with the docking tube. If that's damaged, you'd need to set up a secondary airlock inside. We might not have time."

"So we can only go in through Docking Bay A." Sinestra pursed her lips. "And Syndac's still in there. She will not let us leave without a fight."

"We don't have any other options. Unless you'd rather we all die here."

Solet cut in. "We fight our way through. We've all got weapons. It's us against them."

Clearly no one liked the idea of charging into Docking Bay A, but the concept of a vast battle against overwhelming odds was not vouchsafed them. They heard a fresh cacophony and screams, and then Sinestra dashed to the door to Docking Bay A and pressed an ear to it. She listened intently, then frowned.

"Everyone's left. I can't hear anything. I think now's our chance."

Sinestra and Dexter quickly opened the door, and the small group charged through. The door on the other side was ajar, and emerging they found the docking bay completely empty. The pathway to the *Benbow* was clear. They ran as a body, skirting along the wall until they were near the hatchway, then beginning their sprint down the docking tunnel.

"Stop right there!"

Everyone halted. Syndac had appeared behind them, stepping from behind one of the half-emptied equipment crates. She was pointing a gun at them with her working hand, her face drawn and her clothing spattered with blood. She spoke with a flat, unnatural calm.

"Don't try anything. Don't raise your weapons. I can kill more than one of you before you could ever kill me."

Lenore was beginning to feel dizzy from all the running, from the combat, from her wound, from everything. She didn't know how much she had left. Solet pushed past her, speaking for the group.

"Sorry, Syndac, we can't just stop. We're leaving. And if your crew had any sense, they would also leave."

"Leaving? Oh, yes, we're leaving. When these bloody monsters are dead. When we can strip this station down to the bone and tow it back. I knew I shouldn't have trusted Livesey. Conniving little bitch. And you two, Sinestra, Dexter, you're betraying me? Ah, well, expected I suppose. You two always did have an eye for the main chance."

A scream sounded beyond Docking Bay A. A scream Syndac couldn't have not heard, unless she was deliberately ignoring them.

Solet snarled. "Syndac, this is insane. We need to get away from here. This place will soon be going straight into that star."

"Oh? So Livesey's made herself busy. No matter. I can get down there soon enough."

Lenore's eyes narrowed. She saw the slight twinkle in Syndac's eyes, something unnatural in her cool and calculating creature. Slowly she stepped past

Solet and raised her weapon. As she pushed him aside, she slipped Livesey's datacube into his pocket. Syndac didn't fire, but aimed her gun squarely at Lenore and allowed something like her old smirk to cross her face.

"Now, I know we all want the same thing. This place, it holds so much wealth. We can take everything here. We just need to… I don't know. Vent the place? Send poison through the system? We can come up with a dozen different plans to get rid of these things."

"No, Syndac. Or Black Sutton, whoever you are now." Lenore was cold, tired. "You have no way of stopping what's about to happen. Can't you hear it back there? The screams, the gunshots? Your people are dying, and there's nothing you can do. Or perhaps is because you couldn't do anything that you've lost it. In a place like this, it'd be difficult for anyone as stressed as you to retain their right minds."

"Enough blabbering! You're coming back on board Space Habitat Circé. We're not leaving without this place's booty."

"Oh? Well, I don't know about you, but…."

A long pause ensued. So long that Faarax began to look uneasy. Finally, Lenore slowly turned her gun to one side and pointed it at the transparent sides of the docking tube. There was no speed in her movements, barely even any emotion. Syndac frowned.

"What are you doing?"

"I do this, and with the habitat in its current condition, everyone will die. Including you."

"Don't be idiotic. Even your own people will die."

"So much the better. This place will never see the light of day. There are some things it's better for the Cluster not to know."

"No! I won't allow it. I won't fail here, not now!"

Lenore didn't turn as she addressed the others. "Everyone, aboard the Benbow. Shut the airlock doors after you. Now!"

The others continued their run. Faarax hung back, but Solet grabbed his arm and heaved him along. With his injured ankle, Faarax could offer little resistance and was soon inside the airlock of the Benbow. The door slid shut with a hiss, and Lenore swung her gun over to Syndac. She in turn aimed at Lenore with an increasingly-shaky hand. Lenore sighed, smiling piteously at the overwrought pirate.

"You think your little fantasy will ever come true?"

"I don't have to listen to the likes of your any more."

"I have to wonder which one succumbed first. Syndac, or Black Sutton."

"There's only been one. Syndac, daughter of Black Sutton. Scourge of the space lanes."

"None of that matters now. Listen. Hear that? Your mother's little empire is crumbling."

In the background behind them, there was a soundtrack of hissing, screeching, slicing, screaming, and scraping. Then there was a rush, and a thump. Syndac and Lenore both looked. A pair of mutilated corpses thrown through the doorway, followed by a slow stream of Bugeyes. They saw them, they knew their prey. They advanced slowly, the blood-drenched claws leaving prints on the floor or any surface they touched. It was a gruesome tribute to their abilities as guards for this monument to ego drifting on the edges of space.

Lenore sighed. "Looks like you didn't get your grand victory, Syndac. I doubt anyone survived their onslaught this time."

Syndac turned, her face a mask of rabid fury. "You. All of you. You brought me down to this. You, that bitch Livesey, that little bastard Solet, all of you destroyed any chance I had of restoring our name. My mother's name! You... will... pay for th—"

The shot rang out without ceremony or warning. Syndac fell to the floor, a single clean hole in her head. The hunter in Lenore's soul felt hollow at such an easy victory.

"Find your peace, daughter of Black Sutton."

She sighed, then looked at the monsters before her. She still had a grenade at her belt, and taking out she primed and tossed it. The creatures fell back, but not in time. The blast took three of them out while the rest retreated through the docking bay door. Walking forward slowly, she reached the exterior door of Docking Bay A, and slammed the button. The doors shut, and she pressed her comm.

"Solet, get away. Take the *Benbow* and leave. You should have just enough fuel and people to make Cluster space again. There's nothing left here."

It was Faarax who responded. "No! Don't be stupid. You can't!"

"I'm... I'm already dying, Faarax. Your family have their justice. But... let me save your life, so you may enjoy the future. A life vindicated."

"No. No, you can't be! I won't… I won't want you…. You can't die! Mother, I'm the one who's supposed to kill you!"

Lenore smiled, sad and happy all at once. What a time to use that word of her, the creature who killed his family. The monsters were regrouping, she could hear their claws on the cursed floors of the station beyond. She raised the comm one last time.

"Time to grow up, Faarax. Get away. Leave this place, let it stay where it belongs. In the past." She found eleven more words, and had no regrets uttering them. "I would love you, my son, regardless of your revenge. Farewell."

Before Faarax could respond, Lenore switched off the comm and tore it from her wrist with her teeth. Overhead, a warning voice bellowed.

"Alert. Alert. Engine override detected. Critical failure in five minutes. All personnel evacuate at once."

Spitting the comm to the floor, she aimed her gun at the hoard in front of her that was gathering at the door. Her back was prickling, the poison beginning its climactic ravaging. A final smile creased her lips as she began firing, picking off the targets one by one as they lunged for her.

"Rkakhnen, dashatra."

With this final prayer to the spirits of the ether, to bring her victory even to her dying breath, Lenore faced her last battle.

———————————

FAARAX COULDN'T TEAR his eyes from the closed door until he was yanked away and ordered to D-13 by Solet with Sinestra and Dexter. The three went, Faarax clearly struggling to grasp what had happened. Solet ran up the bridge with Donovan and Gustav. They rushed to their places, Solet to the captain's chair, Donovan to the secondary console. Gustav had manned the navigation console. Donovan raised an eyebrow, but they brushed any query aside.

"Before I was a singer, I was a nav designer. Solet, your orders?"

"Set course away from this place."

"But the station's docking clamps aren't disengaging. If we—"

"Fuck the clamps. Donovan, seal off that area." He tapped the comm. "Faarax, how's the engine?"

"Ready. Already got someone down there from the other crew. They're helping us."

"Okay. Area sealed? Then now!"

There was a tearing, screeching noise as the docking clamps and docking tunnel were torn away from Lost Station Circé. The *Benbow's* thrusters pushed away from Lost Station Circé, and after that it was the work of mere moments to turn the ship around and take their course as they had come. As they approached the edges of the surrounding asteroid field, a powerful shockwave struck, almost throwing Solet from his chair.

"What was that?"

Gustav checked their sensors. "It came from behind us. From the habitat."

"Put it on the viewer, and feed in D-13."

They did both. Solet, presumably along with the others, saw Lost Station Circé tearing itself apart from the inside. The process was frighteningly quick, and even as it did so, the pieces began forming a new ring of orbiting debris around the ominous shadow of the brown dwarf. Solet sighed, then felt something in his pocket, something hard and geometric. He pulled it out, recognized it for what it was, and sighed.

"She knew. They both knew. They weren't coming back." He turned to Gustav. "Set course for Cluster territory, Cape Cisternaea."

FILE 20
FAREWELLS AND FUTURES

Oxen and wain-ropes would not bring me
back again to that accursed island.

—Robert Louis Stevenson

CLOSE TO TWO months before, the inhabitants of Cape Cisternaea had been privy to the departure of a secretive four-ship convoy, heading for the unknown wilds of space. Now they were privy to seeing one of those ships, the *Benbow*, arrive very publicly out of fuel and with a tiny fraction of the original crew aboard. According to the few drip-fed reports, it had been found drifting on the farther edges of Outer World territory.

Solet was sick at heart, tired, and wanted to sleep for weeks. The *Benbow's* arrival had been anything but grand. Towed into the docking area like a wounded animal, its exterior battered and scarred, its main docking port severely damaged. When the tiny crew walked onto the station, many saw them and likely wondered if some war had started somewhere. Those few were non-committal on what had happened to the other ships, but the fact that three of the convoy survivors were captains did not bode well.

To the crew members, the journey back hadn't been as hard as expected. While most of Syndac's crew had been aboard Lost Habitat Circé when it blew, a few had remained inside doing maintenance. An overworked Kavki, an Ekri half-broken by events, another human who had been Sarida's assistant. Those three would-be pirates had been storing the meager cargo salvaged from their trip. Barely anything worth mentioning, a few panels and some data. All that life for so little.

Finding lodgings was comparatively easy. Any bed on anything other than a ship would have done. They went for what they could afford, and with the little religious feeling in him Solet had thanked any deity they cared to for it. Here, back in the calm and sanity of normal life, what happened on their trip seemed like a nightmare. The solar flare, the dark mass barrier, the black hole, the station itself with all its terrors and revelations.

For Solet, it had been too much. For the first night, he just lay on his bed, unable to even close his eyes. His mind screamed at him to sleep, but sleep wouldn't come. If he ever closed his eyes, he would see them again, see the chaos they had wreaked, see Syndac staring at him with those eyes. Even his own past was nothing compared to that. But on the second night, he finally slept from sheer exhaustion. It was a deep, almost unnatural sleep brought on by nothing but the physical need to sleep. He took no joy from it.

And now, with deep dark lines under his eyes, Solet faced Sygint to tell them about their catastrophic losses. Donovan was with him, and looked almost as sullen, though there was a strange glitter in her eyes like excitement or something renewed. As the door opened, they found someone else in the room. An Ekri with an extremely erect posture, and eyes that bored into them as they entered and sat down. Sygint was there, and looked like the predator shorn of their prey. The Ekri spoke in a precise, clipped tone.

"Good day to you. My name is Synod Law Officer Takyra. I have come here to find out what happened. You are the only ship to return, with a severely diminished crew, from an unauthorized expedition out of the Cluster into the Uncharted Belt. I need to know everything that happened to the other three ships, and to the rest of your crew. Sygint has informed me on what the initial proposition was, though whether I can believe him is another story given his bias."

"I never—"

The Ekri's hand stilled the human's indignant tongue. "So, Captains Solet, Donovan, please tell me everything."

Solet and Donovan did. They told the Kavki everything. It was like a kind of therapy, getting the whole terrible tale out of his head. In a flood of speech, they related all they knew at first, second, and third hand, from the moment they left Cape Cisternaea. It was during this recital that Solet remembered the preserved core of Livesey still in his pocket, but his tongue kept this little tidbit sealed within. For whatever reason, he also kept quiet about Sinestra and Dexter. He *did* owe them something. As the two finished, Takyra looked concerned.

"This is a deep matter. While I believe, given your description, that the destruction of this Space Habitat Circé was the right call, I think some among my superiors would think otherwise. There has been a long-standing deficit in the accounts of New Dubai relating to that material, and now to find it's floating around a brown dwarf in the Uncharted Belt. Oh, well, I suppose at worst they can write off the deficit. As for you two, you and the other captains were in gross violation of travel regulations relating to the Uncharted Belt."

"We know." Donovan's voice grated from overuse. "And wouldn't you say we've paid more than our due for this little transgression?"

"I would say you have been overly punished, but I am just writing the report. Speaking of which, I will be wanting you to sign it when it is finished. Now, following on from the first emergence of these so-called 'Bugeyes,' how did...?"

After the first account, the questions seemed to go on and on. They always circled back onto a particular point, a single strange focus. Was Syndac really truly this notorious pirate, and were any of the surviving crew members of her former crew? In a strange moment of serendipitous union, Solet and Donovan feigned ignorance, insisting that all surviving crewmembers had not been among those who sided with Syndac. The Synod agent look dissatisfied, but shrugged and finally went onto another line of questioning.

By the small old-fashioned timepiece on Sygint's desk, a whole two hours had passed before the Synod official handed the datapad to the pair for their signatures. Solet's arm creaked, but he still wanted to punch something. Someone. Anything. Even scream at the top of his voice to stop himself exploding. The signatures given, Takyra slipped it inside her clothing.

"That all seems in order. I should tell you right now that it will not be easy. Given what happened to your crew and the rest of the convoy there will be a move for clemency, but you still broke the rules and at the least you will be subject to a probationary period with ship monitoring. Also, you may have some of your shipping privileges revoked if you do not put your case well enough."

"I don't mind that." Solet's voice sounded bitter to his own ears. "We've been through hell, what's another light roasting compared to that?"

"It is just to warn you. Speaking truthfully, I doubt the Synod will take much action beyond monitoring your ship for a few weeks. They will sympathize with what you had to suffer. The main difficulties will be regarding Dashall's death. His debts were more than outstanding, and some of them were based on unpaid Synod support loans. And Sygint, given the circumstances, I am allowing special dispensation to get the *Benbow* back in working order. In the wrong they may have been, but we cannot monitor a ship if it is on the brink of falling apart."

Sygint's face was puckered with anxiety. "It should already be in decent shape. It had a full refit before they left."

"Some of that work appears to have been undone. In any case, the Synod does not want to leave you unable to carry cargo, Solet. As for you, Donovan, you will be wanted for questioning regarding your part in this."

"Of course."

"Now, I will take my leave."

The Synod officer left without another word. Sygint also sent the two away. He looked like he was staggering toward the edge of a nervous breakdown. As Solet walked out of Sygint's office, he caught his face in a reflective surface and saw a stunned expression. He didn't mind. It was an unbelievable situation, barely real that they'd escaped with what amounted to a light slap on the wrist.

As they returned to the street area, Donovan spoke at last. "Solet, there is something I wanted to say."

"What?"

"It is... to do with why I came on this journey. I was looking for relics and riches, true, but also... I suppose I was bored."

"I think that's kinda okay compared to the others."

"I found something during that madness. It was something I have not felt in some time. A sense of achievement. Of fighting against the odds and winning. Like my first pre-Cluster colony exploration. And I wanted to repay you for that."

"Repay me how?"

"Solet, if you want some steady employment after this... I don't think I should be badly impacted by all this. I can offer you a decent job in my freighting line—decent pay, especially for some of the more delicate cargoes."

"Like artifacts and similar?"

"No. I have my own people for that. I know it's not an independent post, but there's more security. And let's be honest, I think you're just as sick of tramping from port to port as I was."

"Was?"

Donovan's mouth twitched. "I have a past, too, beyond exploration and adventure. Maybe not as colorful as your own or your family's, but still eventful and something I am glad to leave behind. So, your answer?"

Solet thought briefly, and made up his mind. "I… I'll give you an answer tomorrow. At your current lodgings? I've got another job to do."

"I see."

Donovan did see, proving it by not pressing the point. Released at last with Donovan's address, Solet walked along the street, a smile coming to his face for the first time in weeks. If she were still here, he might have invited Alkmeney to join him in this new venture. A fresh start, some element of legitimacy. It grated against some part of him, but he was tired of the life of a junk captain. And this way he might get back what he so desperately deserved. A life of his own, a life without burden.

Solet's mind turned to fulfilling one last task for a fallen comrade. Or perhaps it was more accurate to say that he was undoing one of those losses. He knew someone in Cape Cisternaea's Dark Level, someone who owed him a big favor. Now he was going to call that favor in. It was simple enough getting to the area, but harder to find the little shop itself tucked down so far behind a set of normal food shops. Here, on the edges of the Dark Level, dwelt merchants and vendors on the fringes of legitimacy.

Solet knocked and was admitted to a dingy-looking workshop. The Kavki in charged licked his lips nervously as the old acquaintance entered.

"Solet. What brings you here?"

"Have you still got that android body in stock? The Feles model?"

The Kavki nodded. "Yes. Why?"

"I need it."

"I see. How much are you willing to pay?"

"I'm willing to wipe away the debt you owe me. Sound reasonable?"

"Ah, yes. That debt. An unfortunate oversight on my part. But if all you want is that old body, take it."

"I won't need to take it. I just need it to walk out. Excuse me."

Solet walked to the very back of the shop, passed through a hidden door, and stepped into a dark Aladdin's cave of ancient technology and machinery. Collectors would, and had, paid through the nose for some of the objects contained here. One covered object was a figure about his height. A Feles, or rather an artificial body modeled to be like a Feles, perched on a stand like a stuffed animal and dressed in a simple jump suit.

"Right. Now, where's the core slot?"

Solet felt around, and soon found it. A small square-shaped hatch in the body's neck. Solet pushed the small storage cube into the slot. After a moment, the android's eyes opened and the inner workings whirred and reset as the new personality established itself. After a moment, Livesey's new body stepped off the small stand. The eyes looked round for a moment, then focused on Solet. The body smiled, and the foreign male voice sounded with a familiar inflection in the words.

"Thank you." Livesey looked down at their new body. "Interesting. I didn't think there were any Feles androids left. Let alone male models." They felt round their crotch. "With all their equipment, too."

"There are a few. Just empty shells, though."

"Yes. From where my memories terminate, I'd guess my earlier version sacrificed herself to destroy Lost Station Circé. Good thing, too. Hmm. I'll have to get used to using my lower half to embarrass rather than my upper."

"Livesey...."

Solet tried to continue, but the words caught in his throat. Livesey looked at him, and the smile remained.

"You don't need to say anything more. It's enough to know you repent. I'm not vindictive, unlike some. Your family's name won't be dirt forever. Who knows, you may be the one to turn it around."

"What will you do now?"

"I think... travel. I won't return to the *Benbow*. That life's behind me. I can find myself a position somewhere, work somehow. And work through the days of my life until my data degrades, or my body gives out before I can make another backup. Tell me, do you think life is merely who you are as a person?"

Solet considered seriously before answering. "Life is only what we are as people. If our bodies aren't us, we're nothing. I think I'd rather my mind survived in another than my body survived with nothing."

Livesey lingered for a moment. "Just out of curiosity, how much did the *Benbow* come back with, in the end?"

Solet gave a hollow laugh. "Oh, an absolute fortune. Some raw materials, and commonplace data despite its age. Valued at around sixty thousand when we got back into port. Before the Synod have their cut, and the repairs to the *Benbow* are paid for. Quite the haul, eh?"

Livesey nodded. "Then farewell, *Yushetes Asa Klyshvyna*. And live well."

Solet watched his old crewmate walk out of the shop. He didn't leave himself until Livesey had time to pass down several streets and be well out of his sight.

THE BELL OF Evelyn's apartment was on its third prolonged ring when they finally reached and opened it. There, standing with a deep look of gloom on his face, was Faarax. The sight was almost too much to bear for either of them. Evelyn quickly pulled him inside.

"I'd heard the *Benbow* was coming back in a bad way. I wondered... I didn't think.... What happened? There's been nothing but rumors."

Faarax sighed. "I think I'll need a second drink before I tell you."

Evelyn quickly got that drink, and found him seated on the window just as he had been when last he was there. It was a place he felt comfortable. They gave him the drink, and watched in surprise as he tossed it back at a drought. Then he proceeded to tell them everything. Every detail, with nothing omitted. When he finished, Evelyn looked a little sick.

"That's horrible. I don't understand why that happened. It's just... mad."

"Mad? Maybe. Maybe we were all mad to go there. We were certainly blinded by greed. I was. Greed for the money I could use to get us both out of this shitty place. Oh, Evelyn...."

He let his head hang. Evelyn smiled, put a hand round his.

"You needn't be so low. We're both still here. And...."

"And I'm free of any encumbrances?"

"I didn't want to say it like that."

"That's how I feel."

Faarax looked out of the window again, into the street and out of the great transparent wall toward the shielded glare of the system's suns. In his hand was a little something left by Lenore, that dagger. Pushed under one of its thongs had been a slip of paper with five words on it. The win is yours. Live. He had first seen it on the way to a long-overdue rest period on his bunk, and after reading it had cried himself to sleep. Now his voice broke with those emotions once more.

"Ever since I left, I've felt both empty and full. I don't have any reason to hate Lenore any more. Whatever her reasons, she died to give us a chance. She and Livesey both died. And Alkmeney. And Sudu."

"And Syndac. I don't see why she should be excluded, no matter if she was the worse of the lot."

"You're right. Too many people died. You know, including myself and Solet, and those bloody twins, and Donovan and Gustav, and those other three, only eleven of us made it back? Out of over sixty across four ships. What kind of result is that?"

"Considering what you had to navigate there and back, it could have been so much worse. Please, Faarax, don't think about it. Your debts are settled. And I still have my little dancing gig. And I might be able to get some singing jobs too. Cape Cisternaea is always hungry for entertainment."

"You think we can both survive on that?"

Evelyn might have answered. But another ring came at her door. She sighed and went to answer it. Faarax heard a surprised exclamation, then the door opening again. He was shocked to see Evelyn entering with Gustav hard on her heel. Gustav, dressed in inconspicuous clothing and looking for all the world like nobody important. Faarax gave them a cold stare.

"What do you want?"

Gustav looked round, then stared directly at Faarax. "I've come to make you an offer."

"Offer?"

"Yes. This whole thing, it hasn't gone well for any of us. But I don't want to see you or your... partner?" Evelyn nodded before Faarax could respond. "I don't want you or your partner to suffer for it. I've got a proposition for you. I've been putting out feelers, and there's a little gig going on Cape

Mousai in the Capitol system Kyrathas. This person, an old business partner, wants someone to write songs, and someone to sing them who knows how to dance a few steps. I think you told me on the way back that Evelyn was a dancer?"

Faarax slid off the window, looking at Gustav with disbelief. "You mean you're giving us a job?"

"I'm getting all three of us a job. My contributions will be strictly anonymous. I can't come back into the public eye. Not yet. Maybe not ever. But I can ghostwrite and give you something that isn't being on the *Benbow* all your life—and doesn't keep you or young Evelyn trapped on this station."

Faarax almost shook his head, but Evelyn interrupted. "What kind of pay and hours does it offer?"

"Thirty thousand a year for the lead singer and dancer, Ten thousand for the other two. They're basically backstage technicians. I know I can live on Ten thousand. I used to before I made my big break. As to hours, the usual."

There was silence for a short time. No one seemed able to really respond. Finally Gustav turned, pulling a small card from their jacket and placing it a nearby table.

"If you're interested, this call sign will find me. I won't force you to do anything. Just, think it over."

With that, Gustav left. Faarax watched from the window as the inconspicuous figure reached the street, adjusted their hood, and walked away. Evelyn had joined him in looking down at the retreating figure. They turned to him, their eyes alive.

"Well? Shall we accept?"

He looked at them. "I don't know. Can we?"

"Maybe... I could treat it as a day job, get myself trained for something else. Maybe engineering. Sudu said I wasn't incompetent, just a bit clumsy. It's better than just staying here, isn't it?"

"Guess so. Do you want to go?"

Evelyn leaned next to him. "I don't want you going out there again. Not without me. Look, Faarax, I want a straight answer. You've known me a long time. You know who I am, how I'm formed—"

"Evelyn—"

"Please let me finish. I want to know... can you really feel anything for me? I had a sense that you did feel something, the day you left. When you were offering to take me away to the Capitol Worlds. Has that changed?"

For the first time in his life, the first time in knowing Evelyn, Faarax felt a rush of emotion. Here before him was the one person in his life who had been there for him regardless. In his worst moods, his dourest moments, his bad times. They had been there, joking and smiling and encouraging. Here, with this person's hands on his, the terrible world of Lost Station Circé seemed lightyears away.

"Yes. Yes, I think... just a second."

Without warning, he bent close and kissed Evelyn full on the lips. There was a moment of stillness in the room. Then he smiled.

"Yes. I think I do. So, shall we rush away to find fame and fortune among the Capitol Worlds, like I always wanted?"

"Not just you."

"Of course. Well?"

Evelyn frowned. "Are you okay with that?"

"I think so. After all, I'm following Lenore's advice."

Evelyn's frown deepened, and Faarax showed her the final message hidden in the dagger. They smiled and Faarax spoke.

"How ironic, considering its context. That's the dagger she used to kill my mother."

"You're going to chuck it?"

"No. I don't think so." He smiled at himself. "I'm going to keep it. It's a good reminder to myself." He turned to look out at the distant sun. "Goodbye, Lenore. My friend, my trainer, my rival, my bitterest enemy... my mother. Farewell."

———————————

THE TIME HAD come for Sinestra and Dexter to leave. They had decided long before the *Benbow* was picked up that they would leave before many official inquiries could start. They stayed around for a time, but once Dexter knew that a Synod official was snooping around, it was a matter of seconds to start making their bookings. In their small shared bedroom, Dexter was busy cleaning a knife while Sinestra flicked through a forest of options and questions.

"Think we'll get out in good time?"

"I should think so. No one is looking for us yet."

"I don't like it."

Sinestra looked at her brother. "I wish our captain had survived too, but she made her choice. I was not willing for either of us to die because of her obsessions. They destroyed her. And everyone we knew as a family."

"Almost everyone, sis."

Dexter smiled. A full, charming smile with warmth and feeling, his eyes flashing with soft light. Sinestra smiled in return, though hers was more restrained. Their future was uncertain, their hoped-for restitution perhaps impossible, but in the end they still had each other. With their places booked, she turned her attention to getting them some new clothes so they could leave without going through decontamination procedures.

Due to booking conflicts and a scare about some contaminated filters, they could not get a flight away from Cape Cisternaea until the day after the one they had asked for. As they got on board, they brushed past several others including a Feles with an oddly familiar gait. When they were aboard, settled in their seats, Dexter settled near the window and fell asleep. He never liked traveling like this, in the comfort of commercial airlines. Sinestra gave him the half-concerned, half-enraptured stare of the older sibling, then settled herself down in the seat nearest the isle.

There was a longish wait for the passenger shuttle to disengage from the habitat and begin its flight out. As they were about to leave, the Feles that had pushed past them settled in the seat across the aisle from her. It was only as they were leaving that she caught something. A mannerism, or something else that recalled a memory. A human-type female-form android with a bad attitude.

She looked intently at the Feles, who was scrolling through a datapad looking for something. His eyes were fixed on his task, so Sinestra's question caught him completely off guard.

"Anything interesting, Livesey?"

"Not really—"

The Feles paused, turned, and met her eye. "How did you know?"

Sinestra smirked in a manner unsettlingly similar to her old mistress. "I did wonder. Solet fingering that datacube all the way back from our trip.

There was something about your manner that was… familiar. And somehow I knew you would never accept death."

"Is this not accepting death? A sort of death?"

"That depends. So what now?"

"Now, I think, we both want to go somewhere else. How far are you going?"

"To Cape Hope. You?"

"To the end of this shuttle's flight plan. I can move, if you like."

"That would be best. May I say, 'Livesey,' I hope we do not meet again."

The android did not respond. Once the shuttle was stable, "Livesey" rose and moved to another seat out of Sinestra's view. She shook her head with a slight laugh, then pulled up the entertainment screen for her seat, put on the provided headphones, and lost herself in mistranslation comedy videos as the shuttle jumped to warp and began its long flight to Cape Hope.

———————————

SYNOD LAW OFFICER Takyra slowly sipped at her drink, looking through the report she had been compiling over the past several days. The *Benbow* was still in drydock, most of its surviving crew accounted for and causing no trouble, and life on Cape Cisternaea was moving along at its usual pace. Except she had this dratted report to complete.

"How can one report take three entire days?"

But then, this was an exceptional event. A fiasco of gigantic proportions, and the answer to a number of odd questions that had been raised surrounding the finances of New Dubai a few centuries ago. Well before her time, but it was another file that could be discarded and sealed if all went well.

Her comm signaled a long-distance call. Probably her supervisor wanting an update, again. She received it, then paused, straightened. It was a Synod Representative, those who administered units. The squat-faced Kavki spoke with a cool detachment.

"Have you finalized your report on the Benbow *incident yet?"*

"Yes."

"Give me the main points."

Takyra picked up the datapad, flicking through its contents. Best to summarize as much as possible, pick out the key facts.

"Three out of four ships, the *Grand, Wydrayn, Kilner,* destroyed in varying circumstances. *Benbow* suffered extensive damage. Out of sixty-seven crew across all ships, fifty-nine confirmed dead."

"The survivors?"

"Captain Solet and two crew members from the *Benbow*, Donovan and two crew members from the *Wydrayn*, and Gustav and one crew member from the *Kilner.*" She resumed her summary where she had left off. "The location called Space Habitat Circé confirmed destroyed in a power system overload caused by *Benbow* crew member Livesey, who is among the deceased. The debris likely descending into or entering unstable orbit around the brown dwarf. Survivors unlikely."

"I heard about the issue surrounding its connection with New Dubai. I shall advise my fellows that old debt must be written off. I take it the danger of returning is too high to warrant any further expeditions?"

"Given the reports, regardless of the station's condition, a return trip is too dangerous. I would like to make a personal recommendation."

"Yes?"

"Solet's crew and associates should be treated lightly. Their losses are likely punishment enough of their trespass."

"What is the value of their cargo?"

"Adjusted for inflation and material prices within trading laws, the dock authorities valued it between fifty-right to seventy-two thousand *yuren* in round figures. I wish to recommend that the survivors be allowed a percentage."

"Noted. Skip to the recommendation."

"It is the recommendation of the report that this incident not be publicly acknowledged. The quarantine can be explained by the presence of the black hole reported by the *Benbow's* crew. The other ship losses can also be explained using the stellar phenomena encountered during this unauthorized excursion toward the Uncharted Belt. The existence of Space Habitat Circé should be placed under the Synod Security Act and remain so for the prescribed period. All parties have voiced a willingness not to discuss details of their ordeals.

"Hardly surprising. Very well, I shall inform my fellows of this. Finalize and send off the report. That is all."

The Synod Representative signed off. Alone in contemplation, she remembered some reports that had come in earlier. Best to add an addendum. She typed it out slowly, considering her words with care.

> *Addendum. No sign has been traced of two of the crewmembers, Sinestra and Dexter, since a few days after the* Benbow *docked. Their testimony is still required in relation to this incident. There were also reports of an unidentified Feles who may have been an associate, but no identification could be made. I recommend this be investigated carefully.*

She sighed the report, did a final run-through for typos, sent it off, then leaned back. Maybe now, at last, she could get some proper sleep.

BORN IN 1994, Thomas Wrightson has spent much of his life creating narratives and characters. Home schooled, he currently lives on the island Ynys Mon in Wales, surrounded by beautiful scenery and unpredictable weather.

www.ingramcontent.com/pod-product-compliance
Lightning Source LLC
Chambersburg PA
CBHW030937260626
47169CB00002B/515